Dover Thrift Study Edition

Adventures of Huckleberry Finn

MARK TWAIN

DOVER PUBLICATIONS, INC.
Mineola, New York

Copyright

Copyright © 2009 by Dover Publications, Inc.
Pages 221–323 copyright © 1994 by Research & Education Association, Inc.
All rights reserved.

Bibliographical Note

This Dover edition, first published in 2009, is an unabridged, slightly corrected republication of the text of the first American edition of *Adventures of Huckleberry Finn,* originally published by Charles L. Webster and Company, New York, 1885, plus literary analysis and perspectives from *MAXnotes® for Huckleberry Finn*, first published by Research & Education Association, Inc., Piscataway, New Jersey in 1994.

Library of Congress Cataloging-in-Publication Data

Twain, Mark, 1835–1910.
　　Adventures of Huckleberry Finn / Mark Twain. — Thrift study ed.
　　　　p. cm. — (Dover thrift study edition)
　　"This Dover edition, first published in 2009, is an unabridged, slightly corrected republication of the text of the first American edition of Adventures of Huckleberry Finn, originally published by Charles L. Webster and Company, New York, 1885, plus literary analysis and perspectives from MAXnotes for Huckleberry Finn, first published by Research & Education Association, Inc., Piscataway, New Jersey in 1994"—T.p. verso.
　　ISBN-13: 978-0-486-47584-4
　　ISBN-10: 0-486-47584-0
　　1. Finn, Huckleberry (Fictitious character)—Fiction. 2. Runaway children—Fiction. 3. Boys—Fiction. 4. Mississippi River—Fiction. 5. Male friendship—Fiction. 6. Fugitive slaves—Fiction. 7. Missouri—Fiction. 8. Twain, Mark, 1835–1910. Adventures of Huckleberry Finn—Examinations—Study guides. I. Title.

PS1305.A1 2009b
813'.4—dc22

2009026177

Manufactured in the United States by Courier Corporation
47584005
www.doverpublications.com

Publisher's Note

Combining the complete text of a classic novel or drama with a comprehensive study guide, Dover Thrift Study Editions are the most effective way to gain a thorough understanding of the major works of world literature.

The study guide features up-to-date and expert analysis of every chapter or section from the source work. Questions and fully explained answers follow, allowing readers to analyze the material critically. Character lists, author bios, and discussions of the work's historical context are also provided.

Each Dover Thrift Study Edition includes everything a student needs to prepare for homework, discussions, reports, and exams.

Contents

Adventures of Huckleberry Finn

MARK TWAIN

Contents

SCENE: The Mississippi Valley.
TIME: Forty to Fifty Years Ago.

Notice

PERSONS attempting to find a motive in this narrative will be prosecuted; persons attempting to find a moral in it will be banished; persons attempting to find a plot in it will be shot.

BY ORDER OF THE AUTHOR
PER G. G., CHIEF OF ORDNANCE.

Explanatory

IN this book a number of dialects are used, to wit: the Missouri negro dialect; the extremest form of the backwoods South-Western dialect; the ordinary "Pike-County" dialect; and four modified varieties of this last. The shadings have not been done in a hap-hazard fashion, or by guess-work; but pains-takingly, and with the trustworthy guidance and support of personal familiarity with these several forms of speech.

I make this explanation for the reason that without it many readers would suppose that all these characters were trying to talk alike and not succeeding.

THE AUTHOR.

Chapter I

You don't know about me, without you have read a book by the name of "The Adventures of Tom Sawyer," but that ain't no matter. That book was made by Mr. Mark Twain, and he told the truth, mainly. There was things which he stretched, but mainly he told the truth. That is nothing. I never seen anybody but lied, one time or another, without it was Aunt Polly, or the widow, or maybe Mary. Aunt Polly — Tom's Aunt Polly, she is — and Mary, and the Widow Douglas, is all told about in that book — which is mostly a true book; with some stretchers, as I said before.

Now the way that the book winds up, is this: Tom and me found the money that the robbers hid in the cave, and it made us rich. We got six thousand dollars apiece — all gold. It was an awful sight of money when it was piled up. Well, Judge Thatcher, he took it and put it out at interest, and it fetched us a dollar a day apiece, all the year round — more than a body could tell what to do with. The Widow Douglas, she took me for her son, and allowed she would sivilize me; but it was rough living in the house all the time, considering how dismal regular and decent the widow was in all her ways; and so when I couldn't stand it no longer, I lit out. I got into my old rags, and my sugar-hogshead again, and was free and satisfied. But Tom Sawyer, he hunted me up and said he was going to start a band of robbers, and I might join if I would go back to the widow and be respectable. So I went back.

The widow she cried over me, and called me a poor lost lamb, and she called me a lot of other names, too, but she never meant no harm by it. She put me in them new clothes again, and I couldn't do nothing but sweat and sweat, and feel all cramped up. Well, then, the old thing commenced again. The widow rung a bell for supper, and you had to come to time. When you got to the table you couldn't go right to eating, but you had to wait for the widow to tuck down her head and grumble a little over the victuals, though there warn't really anything the matter

1

with them. That is, nothing only everything was cooked by itself. In a barrel of odds and ends it is different; things get mixed up, and the juice kind of swaps around, and the things go better.

After supper she got out her book and learned me about Moses and the Bulrushers; and I was in a sweat to find out all about him; but by-and-by she let it out that Moses had been dead a considerable long time; so then I didn't care no more about him; because I don't take no stock in dead people.

Pretty soon I wanted to smoke, and asked the widow to let me. But she wouldn't. She said it was a mean practice and wasn't clean, and I must try to not do it any more. That is just the way with some people. They get down on a thing when they don't know nothing about it. Here she was a bothering about Moses, which was no kin to her, and no use to anybody, being gone, you see, yet finding a power of fault with me for doing a thing that had some good in it. And she took snuff too; of course that was all right, because she done it herself.

Her sister, Miss Watson, a tolerable slim old maid, with goggles on, had just come to live with her, and took a set at me now, with a spelling-book. She worked me middling hard for about an hour, and then the widow made her ease up. I couldn't stood it much longer. Then for an hour it was deadly dull, and I was fidgety. Miss Watson would say, "Don't put your feet up there, Huckleberry;" and "don't scrunch up like that, Huckleberry — set up straight;" and pretty soon she would say, "Don't gap and stretch like that, Huckleberry — why don't you try to behave?" Then she told me all about the bad place, and I said I wished I was there. She got mad, then, but I didn't mean no harm. All I wanted was to go somewheres; all I wanted was a change, I warn't particular. She said it was wicked to say what I said; said she wouldn't say it for the whole world; *she* was going to live so as to go to the good place. Well, I couldn't see no advantage in going where she was going, so I made up my mind I wouldn't try for it. But I never said so, because it would only make trouble, and wouldn't do no good.

Now she had got a start, and she went on and told me all about the good place. She said all a body would have to do there was to go around all day long with a harp and sing, forever and ever. So I didn't think much of it. But I never said so. I asked her if she reckoned Tom Sawyer would go there, and, she said, not by a considerable sight. I was glad about that, because I wanted him and me to be together.

Miss Watson she kept pecking at me, and it got tiresome and lonesome. By-and-by they fetched the niggers in and had prayers, and then everybody was off to bed. I went up to my room with a piece of candle and put it on the table. Then I set down in a chair by the window and tried to think of something cheerful, but it warn't no use. I felt so lonesome I most wished I was dead. The stars was shining, and the leaves rustled in the woods ever so mournful; and I heard an owl, away off, who-whooing about somebody that was dead, and a whippowill and a dog crying about somebody that was going to die; and the wind was trying to whisper something to me and I couldn't make out what it was, and so it made the cold shivers run over me. Then away out in the woods I heard that kind of a sound that a ghost makes when it wants to tell about something that's on its mind and can't make itself understood, and so can't rest easy in its grave and has to go about that way every night grieving. I got so down-hearted and scared, I did wish I had some company. Pretty soon a spider went crawling up my shoulder, and I flipped it off and it lit in the candle; and before I could budge it was all shriveled up. I didn't need anybody to tell me that that was an awful bad sign and would fetch me some bad luck, so I was scared and most shook the clothes off of me. I got up and turned around in my tracks three times and crossed my breast every time; and then I tied up a little lock of my hair with a thread to keep witches away. But I hadn't no confidence. You do that when you've lost a horse-shoe that you've found, instead of nailing it up over the door, but I hadn't ever heard anybody say it was any way to keep off bad luck when you'd killed a spider.

I set down again, a shaking all over, and got out my pipe for a smoke; for the house was all as still as death, now, and so the widow wouldn't know. Well, after a long time I heard the clock away off in the town go boom — boom — boom — twelve licks — and all still again — stiller than ever. Pretty soon I heard a twig snap, down in the dark amongst the trees — something was a stirring. I set still and listened. Directly I could just barely hear a "*me-yow! me-yow!*" down there. That was good! Says I, "*me-yow! me-yow!*" as soft as I could, and then I put out the light and scrambled out of the window onto the shed. Then I slipped down to the ground and crawled in amongst the trees, and sure enough there was Tom Sawyer waiting for me.

Chapter II

We went tip-toeing along a path amongst the trees back towards the end of the widow's garden, stooping down so as the branches wouldn't scrape our heads. When we was passing by the kitchen I fell over a root and made a noise. We scrouched down and laid still. Miss Watson's big nigger, named Jim, was setting in the kitchen door; we could see him pretty clear, because there was a light behind him. He got up and stretched his neck out about a minute, listening. Then he says,

"Who dah?"

He listened some more; then he come tip-toeing down and stood right between us; we could a touched him, nearly. Well, likely it was minutes and minutes that there warn't a sound, and we all there so close together. There was a place on my ankle that got to itching; but I dasn't scratch it; and then my ear begun to itch; and next my back, right between my shoulders. Seemed like I'd die if I couldn't scratch. Well, I've noticed that thing plenty of times since. If you are with the quality, or at a funeral, or trying to go to sleep when you ain't sleepy — if you are anywheres where it won't do for you to scratch, why you will itch all over in upwards of a thousand places. Pretty soon Jim says:

"Say — who is you? Whar is you? Dog my cats ef I didn' hear sumf'n. Well, I knows what I's gwyne to do. I's gwyne to set down here and listen tell I hears it agin."

So he set down on the ground betwixt me and Tom. He leaned his back up against a tree, and stretched his legs out till one of them most touched one of mine. My nose begun to itch. It itched till the tears come into my eyes. But I dasn't scratch. Then it begun to itch on the inside. Next I got to itching underneath. I didn't know how I was going to set still. This miserableness went on as much as six or seven minutes; but it seemed a sight longer than that. I was itching in eleven different places now. I reckoned I couldn't stand it more'n a minute longer, but I set my teeth hard and got ready to try. Just then Jim begun to breathe heavy; next he begun to snore — and then I was pretty soon comfortable again.

Tom he made a sign to me — kind of a little noise with his mouth — and we went creeping away on our hands and knees. When we was ten foot off, Tom whispered to me and wanted to tie Jim to the tree for fun; but I said no; he might wake and make a disturbance, and then they'd find out I warn't in. Then Tom said he hadn't got candles enough, and he would slip in the kitchen and get some more. I didn't want him to try. I said Jim might wake up and come. But Tom wanted to resk it; so we slid in there and got three candles, and Tom laid five cents on the table for pay. Then we got out, and I was in a sweat to get away; but nothing would do Tom but he must crawl to where Jim was, on his hands and knees, and play something on him. I waited, and it seemed a good while, everything was so still and lonesome.

As soon as Tom was back, we cut along the path, around the garden fence, and by-and-by fetched up on the steep top of the hill the other side of the house. Tom said he slipped Jim's hat off of his head and hung it on a limb right over him, and Jim stirred a little, but he didn't wake.

Afterwards Jim said the witches bewitched him and put him in a trance, and rode him all over the State, and then set him under the trees again and hung his hat on a limb to show who done it. And next time Jim told it he said they rode him down to New Orleans; and after that, every time he told it he spread it more and more, till by-and-by he said they rode him all over the world, and tired him most to death, and his back was all over saddle-boils. Jim was monstrous proud about it, and he got so he wouldn't hardly notice the other niggers. Niggers would come miles to hear Jim tell about it, and he was more looked up to than any nigger in that country. Strange niggers would stand with their mouths open and look him all over, same as if he was a wonder. Niggers is always talking about witches in the dark by the kitchen fire; but whenever one was talking and letting on to know all about such things, Jim would happen in and say, "Hm! What you know 'bout witches?" and that nigger was corked up and had to take a back seat. Jim always kept that five-center piece around his neck with a string and said it was a charm the devil give to him with his own hands and told him he could cure anybody with it and fetch witches whenever he wanted to, just by saying something to it; but he never told what it was he said to it. Niggers would come from all around there and give Jim anything they had, just for a sight of that five-center piece; but they wouldn't touch it, because the devil had had his hands on it. Jim was most ruined, for a servant, because he got so stuck up on account of having seen the devil and been rode by witches.

Well, when Tom and me got to the edge of the hill-top, we looked away down into the village and could see three or four lights twinkling, where there was sick folks, may be; and the stars over us was sparkling ever so fine; and down by the village was the river, a whole mile broad, and awful still and grand. We went down the hill and found Jo Harper, and Ben Rogers, and two or three more of the boys, hid in the old tanyard. So we unhitched a skiff and pulled down the river two mile and a half, to the big scar on the hillside, and went ashore.

We went to a clump of bushes, and Tom made everybody swear to keep the secret, and then showed them a hole in the hill, right in the thickest part of the bushes. Then we lit the candles and crawled in on our hands and knees. We went about two hundred yards, and then the cave opened up. Tom poked about amongst the passages and pretty soon ducked under a wall where you wouldn't a noticed that there was a hole. We went along a narrow place and got into a kind of room, all damp and sweaty and cold, and there we stopped. Tom says:

"Now we'll start this band of robbers and call it Tom Sawyer's Gang. Everybody that wants to join has got to take an oath, and write his name in blood."

Everybody was willing. So Tom got out a sheet of paper that he had wrote the oath on, and read it. It swore every boy to stick to the band, and never tell any of the secrets; and if anybody done anything to any boy in the band, whichever boy was ordered to kill that person and his family must do it, and he mustn't eat and he mustn't sleep till he had killed them and hacked a cross in their breasts, which was the sign of the band. And nobody that didn't belong to the band could use that mark, and if he did he must be sued; and if he done it again he must be killed. And if anybody that belonged to the band told the secrets, he must have his throat cut, and then have his carcass burnt up and the ashes scattered all around, and his name blotted off of the list with blood and never mentioned again by the gang, but have a curse put on it and be forgot, forever.

Everybody said it was a real beautiful oath, and asked Tom if he got it out of his own head. He said, some of it, but the rest was out of pirate books, and robber books, and every gang that was high-toned had it.

Some thought it would be good to kill the *families* of boys that told the secrets. Tom said it was a good idea, so he took a pencil and wrote it in. Then Ben Rogers says:

"Here's Huck Finn, he hain't got no family — what you going to do 'bout him?"

"Well, hain't he got a father?" says Tom Sawyer.

"Yes, he's got a father, but you can't never find him, these days. He used to lay drunk with the hogs in the tanyard, but he hain't been seen in these parts for a year or more."

They talked it over, and they was going to rule me out, because they said every boy must have a family or somebody to kill, or else it wouldn't be fair and square for the others. Well, nobody could think of anything to do — everybody was stumped, and set still. I was most ready to cry; but all at once I thought of a way, and so I offered them Miss Watson — they could kill her. Everybody said:

"Oh, she'll do, she'll do. That's all right. Huck can come in."

Then they all stuck a pin in their fingers to get blood to sign with, and I made my mark on the paper.

"Now," says Ben Rogers, "what's the line of business of this Gang?"

"Nothing only robbery and murder," Tom said.

"But who are we going to rob? houses — or cattle — or ——"

"Stuff! stealing cattle and such things ain't robbery, it's burglary," says Tom Sawyer. "We ain't burglars. That ain't no sort of style. We are highwaymen. We stop stages and carriages on the road, with masks on, and kill the people and take their watches and money."

"Must we always kill the people?"

"Oh, certainly. It's best. Some authorities think different, but mostly it's considered best to kill them. Except some that you bring to the cave here and keep them till they're ransomed."

"Ransomed? What's that?"

"I don't know. But that's what they do. I've seen it in books; and so of course that's what we've got to do."

"But how can we do it if we don't know what it is?"

"Why blame it all, we've *got* to do it. Don't I tell you it's in the books? Do you want to go to doing different from what's in the books, and get things all muddled up?"

"Oh, that's all very fine to *say*, Tom Sawyer, but how in the nation are these fellows going to be ransomed if we don't know how to do it to them? that's the thing I want to get at. Now what do you *reckon* it is?"

"Well I don't know. But per'aps if we keep them till they're ransomed, it means that we keep them till they're dead."

"Now, that's something *like*. That'll answer. Why couldn't you said that before? We'll keep them till they're ransomed to death — and a bothersome lot they'll be, too, eating up everything and always trying to get loose."

"How you talk, Ben Rogers. How can they get loose when there's a guard over them, ready to shoot them down if they move a peg?"

"A guard. Well, that *is* good. So somebody's got to set up all night and never get any sleep, just so as to watch them. I think that's foolishness. Why can't a body take a club and ransom them as soon as they get here?"

"Because it ain't in the books so — that's why. Now Ben Rogers, do you want to do things regular, or don't you? — that's the idea. Don't you reckon that the people that made the books knows what's the correct thing to do? Do you reckon *you* can learn 'em anything? Not by a good deal. No, sir, we'll just go on and ransom them in the regular way."

"All right. I don't mind; but I say it's a fool way, anyhow. Say — do we kill the women, too?"

"Well, Ben Rogers, if I was as ignorant as you I wouldn't let on. Kill the women? No — nobody ever saw anything in the books like that. You fetch them to the cave, and you're always as polite as pie to them; and by-and-by they fall in love with you and never want to go home any more."

"Well, if that's the way, I'm agreed, but I don't take no stock in it. Mighty soon we'll have the cave so cluttered up with women, and fellows waiting to be ransomed, that there won't be no place for the robbers. But go ahead, I ain't got nothing to say."

Little Tommy Barnes was asleep, now, and when they waked him up he was scared, and cried, and said he wanted to go home to his ma, and didn't want to be a robber any more.

So they all made fun of him, and called him cry-baby, and that made him mad, and he said he would go straight and tell all the secrets. But Tom give him five cents to keep quiet, and said we would all go home and meet next week and rob somebody and kill some people.

Ben Rogers said he couldn't get out much, only Sundays, and so he wanted to begin next Sunday; but all the boys said it would be wicked to do it on Sunday, and that settled the thing. They agreed to get together and fix a day as soon as they could, and then we elected Tom Sawyer first captain and Jo Harper second captain of the Gang, and so started home.

I clumb up the shed and crept into my window just before day was breaking. My new clothes was all greased up and clayey, and I was dog-tired.

Chapter III

Well, I got a good going-over in the morning, from old Miss Watson, on account of my clothes; but the widow she didn't scold, but only cleaned off the grease and clay and looked so sorry that I thought I would behave a while if I could. Then Miss Watson she took me in the closet and prayed, but nothing come of it. She told me to pray every day, and whatever I asked for I would get it. But it warn't so. I tried it. Once I got a fish-line, but no hooks. It warn't any good to me without hooks. I tried for the hooks three or four times, but somehow I couldn't make it work. By-and-by, one day, I asked Miss Watson to try for me, but she said I was a fool. She never told me why, and I couldn't make it out no way.

I set down, one time, back in the woods, and had a long think about it. I says to myself, if a body can get anything they pray for, why don't Deacon Winn get back the money he lost on pork? Why can't the widow get back her silver snuff-box that was stole? Why can't Miss Watson fat up? No, says I to myself, there ain't nothing in it. I went and told the widow about it, and she said the thing a body could get by praying for it was "spiritual gifts." This was too many for me, but she told me what she meant — I must help other people, and do everything I could for other people, and look out for them all the time, and never think about myself. This was including Miss Watson, as I took it. I went out in the woods and turned it over in my mind a long time, but I couldn't see no advantage about it — except for the other people — so at last I reckoned I wouldn't worry about it any more, but just let it go. Sometimes the widow would take me one side and talk about Providence in a way to make a body's mouth water; but maybe next day Miss Watson would take hold and knock it all down again. I judged I could see that there was two

Providences, and a poor chap would stand considerable show with the widow's Providence, but if Miss Watson's got him there warn't no help for him any more. I thought it all out, and reckoned I would belong to the widow's, if he wanted me, though I couldn't make out how he was agoing to be any better off then than what he was before, seeing I was so ignorant and so kind of low-down and ornery.

Pap he hadn't been seen for more than a year, and that was comfortable for me; I didn't want to see him no more. He used to always whale me when he was sober and could get his hands on me; though I used to take to the woods most of the time when he was around. Well, about this time he was found in the river drowned, about twelve mile above town, so people said. They judged it was him, anyway; said this drowned man was just his size, and was ragged, and had uncommon long hair — which was all like pap — but they couldn't make nothing out of the face, because it had been in the water so long it warn't much like a face at all. They said he was floating on his back in the water. They took him and buried him on the bank. But I warn't comfortable long, because I happened to think of something. I knowed mighty well that a drownded man don't float on his back, but on his face. So I knowed, then, that this warn't pap, but a woman dressed up in a man's clothes. So I was uncomfortable again. I judged the old man would turn up again by-and-by, though I wished he wouldn't.

We played robber now and then about a month, and then I resigned. All the boys did. We hadn't robbed nobody, we hadn't killed any people, but only just pretended. We used to hop out of the woods and go charging down on hog-drovers and women in carts taking garden stuff to market, but we never hived any of them. Tom Sawyer called the hogs "ingots," and he called the turnips and stuff "julery" and we would go to the cave and pow-wow over what we had done and how many people we had killed and marked. But I couldn't see no profit in it. One time Tom sent a boy to run about town with a blazing stick, which he called a slogan (which was the sign for the Gang to get together), and then he said he had got secret news by his spies that next day a whole parcel of Spanish merchants and rich A-rabs was going to camp in Cave Hollow with two hundred elephants, and six hundred camels, and over a thousand "sumter" mules, all loaded down with di'monds, and they didn't have only a guard of four hundred soldiers, and so we would lay in ambuscade, as he called it, and kill the lot and scoop the things. He said we must slick up our swords and guns, and get ready. He never could go after even a turnip-cart but he must have the swords and guns all scoured up for it; though they was only lath and broom-sticks, and you might scour at them till you rotted and then they warn't worth a mouthful of ashes more than what they was before. I didn't believe we could lick such a crowd of Spaniards and A-rabs, but I wanted to see the camels and elephants, so I was on hand next day, Saturday, in the ambuscade; and when we got the word, we rushed out of the woods and down the hill. But there warn't no Spaniards and A-rabs, and there warn't no camels nor no elephants. It warn't anything but a Sunday-school picnic, and only a primer-class at that. We busted it up, and chased the children up the hollow; but we never got anything but some doughnuts and jam, though Ben Rogers got a rag doll, and Jo Harper got a hymn-book and a tract; and then the teacher charged in and made us drop everything and cut. I didn't see no di'monds, and I told Tom Sawyer so. He said there was loads of them there, anyway; and he said there was A-rabs there, too, and elephants and things. I said, why couldn't we see them, then? He said if I warn't so ignorant, but had read a book called "Don Quixote," I would know without asking. He said it was all done by enchantment. He said there was hundreds of soldiers there, and elephants and treasure, and so on, but we had enemies which he called magicians, and they had turned the whole thing into an infant Sunday school, just out of spite. I said, all right, then the thing for us to do was to go for the magicians. Tom Sawyer said I was a numskull.

"Why," says he, "a magician could call up a lot of genies, and they would hash you up like nothing before you could say Jack Robinson. They are as tall as a tree and as big around as a church."

"Well," I says, "s'pose we got some genies to help *us* — can't we lick the other crowd then?"

"How you going to get them?"

"I don't know. How do *they* get them?"

"Why they rub an old tin lamp or an iron ring, and then the genies come tearing in, with the thunder and lightning a-ripping around and the smoke a-rolling, and everything they're told to do they up and do it. They don't think nothing of pulling a shot tower up by the roots, and belting a Sunday-school superintendent over the head with it — or any other man."

"Who makes them tear around so?"

"Why, whoever rubs the lamp or the ring. They belong to whoever rubs the lamp or the ring, and they've got to do whatever he says. If he tells them to build a palace forty miles long, out of di'monds, and fill it full of chewing gum, or whatever you want, and fetch an emperor's daughter from China for you to marry, they've got to do it — and they've got to do it before sun-up next morning, too. And more — they've got to waltz that palace around over the country wherever you want it, you understand."

"Well," says I, "I think they are a pack of flatheads for not keeping the palace themselves 'stead of fooling them away like that. And what's more — if I was one of them I would see a man in Jericho before I would drop my business and come to him for the rubbing of an old tin lamp."

"How you talk, Huck Finn. Why, you'd *have* to come when he rubbed it, whether you wanted to or not."

"What, and I as high as a tree and as big as a church? All right, then; I *would* come; but I lay I'd make that man climb the highest tree there was in the country."

"Shucks, it ain't no use to talk to you, Huck Finn. You don't seem to know anything, somehow — perfect sap-head."

I thought all this over for two or three days, and then I reckoned I would see if there was anything in it. I got an old tin lamp and an iron ring and went out in the woods and rubbed and rubbed till I sweat like an Injun, calculating to build a palace and sell it; but it warn't no use, none of the genies come. So then I judged that all that stuff was only just one of Tom Sawyer's lies. I reckoned he believed in the A-rabs and the elephants, but as for me I think different. It had all the marks of a Sunday school.

Chapter IV

Well, three or four months run along, and it was well into the winter, now. I had been to school most all the time, and could spell, and read, and write just a little, and could say the multiplication table up to six times seven is thirty-five, and I don't reckon I could ever get any further than that if I was to live forever. I don't take no stock in mathematics, anyway.

At first I hated the school, but by and-by I got so I could stand it. Whenever I got uncommon tired I played hookey, and the hiding I got next day done me good and cheered me up. So the longer I went to school the easier it got to be. I was getting sort of used to the widow's ways, too, and they warn't so raspy on me. Living in a house, and sleeping in a bed, pulled on me pretty tight, mostly, but before the cold weather I used to slide out and sleep in the woods, sometimes, and so that was a rest to me. I liked the old ways best, but I was getting so I liked the new ones, too, a little bit. The widow said I was coming along slow but sure, and doing very satisfactory. She said she warn't ashamed of me.

One morning I happened to turn over the salt-cellar at breakfast. I reached for some of it as quick as I could, to throw over my left shoulder and keep off the bad luck, but Miss Watson was in ahead of me, and crossed me off. She says, "Take your hands away, Huckleberry — what a mess you are always making." The widow put in a good word for me, but that warn't going to keep off the bad luck, I knowed that well enough. I started out, after breakfast, feeling worried and shaky, and wondering where it was going to fall on me, and what it was going to be. There is ways to keep off some kinds of bad luck, but this wasn't one of them kind; so I never tried to do anything, but just poked along low-spirited and on the watch-out.

I went down the front garden and clumb over the stile, where you go through the high board fence. There was an inch of new snow on the ground, and I seen somebody's tracks. They had come up from the quarry and stood around the stile a while, and then went on around the garden fence. It was funny they hadn't come in, after standing around so. I couldn't make it out. It was very curious, somehow. I was going to follow around, but I stooped down to look at the tracks first. I didn't notice anything at first, but next I did. There was a cross in the left boot-heel made with big nails, to keep off the devil.

I was up in a second and shinning down the hill. I looked over my shoulder every now and then, but I didn't see nobody. I was at Judge Thatcher's as quick as I could get there. He said:

"Why, my boy, you are all out of breath. Did you come for your interest?"

"No sir," I says; "is there some for me?"

"Oh, yes, a half-yearly is in, last night. Over a hundred and fifty dollars. Quite a fortune for you. You better let me invest it along with your six thousand, because if you take it you'll spend it."

"No sir," I says, "I don't want to spend it. I don't want it at all — nor the six thousand, nuther. I want you to take it; I want to give it to you — the six thousand and all."

He looked surprised. He couldn't seem to make it out. He says:

"Why, what can you mean, my boy?"

I says, "Don't you ask me no questions about it, please. You'll take it — won't you?"

He says:

"Well I'm puzzled. Is something the matter?"

"Please take it," says I, "and don't ask me nothing — then I won't have to tell no lies."

He studied a while, and then he says:

"Oho-o. I think I see. You want to *sell* all your property to me — not give it. That's the correct idea."

Then he wrote something on a paper and read it over, and says:

"There — you see it says 'for a consideration.' That means I have bought it of you and paid you for it. Here's a dollar for you. Now, you sign it."

So I signed it, and left.

Miss Watson's nigger, Jim, had a hair-ball as big as your fist, which had been took out of the fourth stomach of an ox, and he used to do magic with it. He said there was a spirit inside of it, and it knowed everything. So I went to him that night and told him pap was here again, for I found his tracks in the snow. What I wanted to know, was, what he was going to do, and was he going to stay? Jim got out his hair-ball, and said something over it, and then he held it up and dropped it on the floor. It fell pretty solid, and only rolled about an inch. Jim tried it again, and then another time, and it acted just the same. Jim got down on his knees and put his ear against it and listened. But it warn't no use; he said it wouldn't talk. He said sometimes it wouldn't talk without money. I told him I had an old slick counterfeit quarter that warn't no good because the brass showed through the silver a little, and it wouldn't pass nohow, even if the brass didn't show, because it was so slick it felt greasy, and so that would tell on it every time. (I reckoned I wouldn't say nothing about the dollar I got from the judge.) I said it was pretty bad money, but maybe the hair-ball would take it, because maybe it wouldn't know the difference. Jim smelt it, and bit it, and rubbed it, and said he would manage so the hair-ball would think it was good. He said he would split open a raw Irish potato and stick the quarter in between and keep it there all night, and next morning you couldn't see no brass, and it wouldn't feel greasy no more, and so anybody in town would take it in a minute, let alone a hair-ball. Well, I knowed a potato would do that, before, but I had forgot it.

Jim put the quarter under the hair-ball and got down and listened again. This time he said the hair-ball was all right. He said it would tell my whole fortune if I wanted it to. I says, go on. So the hair-ball talked to Jim, and Jim told it to me. He says:

"Yo' ole father doan' know, yit, what he's a-gwyne to do. Sometimes he spec he'll go 'way, en den agin he spec he'll stay. De bes' way is to res' easy en let de ole man take his own way. Dey's two angels hoverin' roun' 'bout him. One uv 'em is white en shiny, en 'tother one is black. De white one gits him to go right, a little while, den de black one sail in en bust it all up. A body can't tell, yit, which one gwyne to fetch him at de las'. But you is all right. You gwyne to have considable trouble in yo' life, en considable joy. Sometimes you gwyne to git hurt, en sometimes you gwyne to git sick; but every time you's gwyne to git well agin. Dey's two gals flyin' 'bout you in yo' life. One uv 'em's light en 'tother one is dark.

One is rich en 'tother is po'. You's gwyne to marry de po' one fust en de rich one by-en-by. You wants to keep 'way fum de water as much as you kin, en don't run no resk, 'kase it's down in de bills dat you's gwyne to git hung."

When I lit my candle and went up to my room that night, there set pap, his own self!

Chapter V

I had shut the door to. Then I turned around, and there he was. I used to be scared of him all the time, he tanned me so much. I reckoned I was scared now, too; but in a minute I see I was mistaken. That is, after the first jolt, as you may say, when my breath sort of hitched — he being so unexpected; but right away after, I see I warn't scared of him worth bothering about.

He was most fifty, and he looked it. His hair was long and tangled and greasy, and hung down, and you could see his eyes shining through like he was behind vines. It was all black, no gray; so was his long, mixed-up whiskers. There warn't no color in his face, where his face showed; it was white; not like another man's white, but a white to make a body sick, a white to make a body's flesh crawl — a tree-toad white, a fish-belly white. As for his clothes — just rags, that was all. He had one ankle resting on 'tother knee; the boot on that foot was busted, and two of his toes stuck through, and he worked them now and then. His hat was laying on the floor; an old black slouch with the top caved in, like a lid.

I stood a-looking at him; he set there a-looking at me, with his chair tilted back a little. I set the candle down. I noticed the window was up; so he had clumb in by the shed. He kept a-looking me all over. By-and-by he says:

"Starchy clothes — very. You think you're a good deal of a big-bug, *don't* you?"

"Maybe I am, maybe I ain't," I says.

"Don't you give me none o' your lip," says he. "You've put on considerable many frills since I been away. I'll take you down a peg before I get done with you. You're educated, too, they say; can read and write. You think you're better'n your father, now, don't you, because he can't? *I'll* take it out of you. Who told you you might meddle with such hifalut'n foolishness, hey? — who told you you could?"

"The widow. She told me."

"The widow, hey? — and who told the widow she could put in her shovel about a thing that ain't none of her business?"

"Nobody never told her."

"Well, I'll learn her how to meddle. And looky here — you drop that school, you hear? I'll learn people to bring up a boy to put on airs over his own father and let on to be better'n what *he* is. You lemme catch you fooling around that school again, you hear? Your mother couldn't read, and she couldn't write, nuther, before she died. None of the family couldn't, before *they* died. *I* can't; and here you're a-swelling yourself up like this. I ain't the man to stand it — you hear? Say — lemme hear you read."

I took up a book and begun something about General Washington and the wars. When I'd read about a half a minute, he fetched the book a whack with his hand and knocked it across the house. He says:

"It's so. You can do it. I had my doubts when you told me. Now looky here; you stop that putting on frills. I won't have it. I'll lay for you, my smarty; and if I catch you about that school I'll tan you good. First you know you'll get religion, too. I never see such a son."

He took up a little blue and yaller picture of some cows and a boy, and says:

"What's this?"

"It's something they give me for learning my lessons good."

He tore it up, and says —

"I'll give you something better — I'll give you a cowhide."

He set there a-mumbling and a-growling a minute, and then he says —

"*Ain't* you a sweet-scented dandy, though? A bed; and bedclothes; and a look'n-glass; and a piece of carpet on the floor — and your own father got to sleep with the hogs in the tanyard. I never see such a son. I bet I'll take some o' these frills out o' you before I'm done with you. Why there ain't no end to your airs — they say you're rich. Hey? — how's that?"

"They lie — that's how."

"Looky here — mind how you talk to me; I'm a-standing about all I can stand, now — so don't gimme no sass. I've been in town two days, and I hain't heard nothing but about you bein' rich. I heard about it away down the river, too. That's why I come. You git me that money to-morrow — I want it."

"I hain't got no money."

"It's a lie. Judge Thatcher's got it. You git it. I want it."

"I hain't got no money, I tell you. You ask Judge Thatcher; he'll tell you the same."

"All right. I'll ask him; and I'll make him pungle, too, or I'll know the reason why. Say — how much you got in your pocket? I want it."

"I hain't got only a dollar, and I want that to ——"

"It don't make no difference what you want it for — you just shell it out."

He took it and bit it to see if it was good, and then he said he was going down town to get some whisky; said he hadn't had a drink all day. When he had got out on the shed, he put his head in again, and cussed me for putting on frills and trying to be better than him; and when I reckoned he was gone, he come back and put his head in again, and told me to mind about that school, because he was going to lay for me and lick me if I didn't drop that.

Next day he was drunk, and he went to Judge Thatcher's and bully-ragged him and tried to make him give up the money, but he couldn't, and then he swore he'd make the law force him.

The judge and the widow went to law to get the court to take me away from him and let one of them be my guardian; but it was a new judge that had just come, and he didn't know the old man; so he said courts mustn't interfere and separate families if they could help it; said he'd druther not take a child away from its father. So Judge Thatcher and the widow had to quit on the business.

That pleased the old man till he couldn't rest. He said he'd cowhide me till I was black and blue if I didn't raise some money for him. I borrowed three dollars from Judge Thatcher, and pap took it and got drunk and went a-blowing around and cussing and whooping and carrying on; and he kept it up all over town, with a tin pan, till most midnight; then they jailed him, and next day they had him before court, and jailed him again for a week. But he said *he* was satisfied; said he was boss of his son, and he'd make it warm for *him*.

When he got out the new judge said he was going to make a man of him. So he took him to his own house, and dressed him up clean and nice, and had him to breakfast and dinner and supper with the family, and was just old pie to him, so to speak. And after supper he talked to him about temperance and such things till the old man cried, and said he'd been a fool, and fooled away his life; but now he was agoing to turn over a new leaf and be a man nobody wouldn't be ashamed of, and he hoped the judge would help him and not look down on him. The judge said he could hug him for them words; so *he* cried, and his wife she cried again; pap said he'd been a man that had always been misunderstood before, and the judge said he believed it. The old man said that what a man wanted that was down, was sympathy; and the judge said it

was so; so they cried again. And when it was bedtime, the old man rose
up and held out his hand, and says:

"Look at it gentlemen, and ladies all; take ahold of it; shake it. There's
a hand that was the hand of a hog; but it ain't so no more; it's the hand of
a man that's started in on a new life, and 'll die before he'll go back. You
mark them words — don't forget I said them. It's a clean hand now; shake
it — don't be afeard."

So they shook it, one after the other, all around, and cried. The
judge's wife she kissed it. Then the old man he signed a pledge — made
his mark. The judge said it was the holiest time on record, or something
like that. Then they tucked the old man into a beautiful room, which
was the spare room, and in the night sometime he got powerful thirsty
and clumb out onto the porch-roof and slid down a stanchion and
traded his new coat for a jug of forty-rod, and clumb back again and had
a good old time; and towards daylight he crawled out again, drunk as a
fiddler, and rolled off the porch and broke his left arm in two places and
was most froze to death when somebody found him after sun-up. And
when they come to look at that spare room, they had to take soundings
before they could navigate it.

The judge he felt kind of sore. He said he reckoned a body could
reform the ole man with a shot-gun, maybe, but he didn't know no other
way.

Chapter VI

Well, pretty soon the old man was up and around again, and then he
went for Judge Thatcher in the courts to make him give up that money,
and he went for me, too, for not stopping school. He catched me a
couple of times and thrashed me, but I went to school just the same, and
dodged him or out-run him most of the time. I didn't want to go to
school much, before, but I reckoned I'd go now to spite pap. That law
trial was a slow business; appeared like they warn't ever going to get
started on it; so every now and then I'd borrow two or three dollars off of
the judge for him, to keep from getting a cowhiding. Every time he got
money he got drunk; and every time he got drunk he raised Cain around
town; and every time he raised Cain he got jailed. He was just suited —
this kind of thing was right in his line.

He got to hanging around the widow's too much, and so she told him
at last, that if he didn't quit using around there she would make trouble

for him. Well, *wasn't* he mad? He said he would show who was Huck Finn's boss. So he watched out for me one day in the spring, and catched me, and took me up the river about three mile, in a skiff, and crossed over to the Illinois shore where it was woody and there warn't no houses but an old log hut in a place where the timber was so thick you couldn't find it if you didn't know where it was.

He kept me with him all the time, and I never got a chance to run off. We lived in that old cabin, and he always locked the door and put the key under his head, nights. He had a gun which he had stole, I reckon, and we fished and hunted, and that was what we lived on. Every little while he locked me in and went down to the store, three miles, to the ferry, and traded fish and game for whisky and fetched it home and got drunk and had a good time, and licked me. The widow she found out where I was, by-and-by, and she sent a man over to try to get hold of me, but pap drove him off with the gun, and it warn't long after that till I was used to being where I was, and liked it, all but the cowhide part.

It was kind of lazy and jolly, laying off comfortable all day, smoking and fishing, and no books nor study. Two months or more run along, and my clothes got to be all rags and dirt, and I didn't see how I'd ever got to like it so well at the widow's, where you had to wash, and eat on a plate, and comb up, and go to bed and get up regular, and be forever bothering over a book and have old Miss Watson pecking at you all the time. I didn't want to go back no more. I had stopped cussing, because the widow didn't like it; but now I took to it again because pap hadn't no objections. It was pretty good times up in the woods there, take it all around.

But by-and-by pap got too handy with his hick'ry, and I couldn't stand it. I was all over welts. He got to going away so much, too, and locking me in. Once he locked me in and was gone three days. It was dreadful lonesome. I judged he had got drowned and I wasn't ever going to get out any more. I was scared. I made up my mind I would fix up some way to leave there. I had tried to get out of that cabin many a time, but I couldn't find no way. There warn't a window to it big enought for a dog to get through. I couldn't get up the chimbly, it was too narrow. The door was thick solid oak slabs. Pap was pretty careful not to leave a knife or anything in the cabin when he was away; I reckon I had hunted the place over as much as a hundred times; well, I was 'most all the time at it, because it was about the only way to put in the time. But this time I found something at last; I found an old rusty wood-saw without any handle; it was laid in between a rafter and the clapboards of the roof. I greased it up and went to work. There was an old horse-blanket nailed against the logs at the far end of the cabin behind the table, to keep the wind from blowing through the chinks and putting the candle out. I got under the table and raised the blanket and went to work to saw a section of the big bottom log out, big enough to let me through. Well, it was a good long job, but I was getting towards the end of it when I heard pap's gun in the woods. I got rid of the signs of my work, and dropped the blanket and hid my saw, and pretty soon pap come in.

Pap warn't in a good humor — so he was his natural self. He said he was down to town, and everything was going wrong. His lawyer said he reckoned he would win his lawsuit and get the money, if they ever got started on the trial; but then there was ways to put it off a long time, and Judge Thatcher knowed how to do it. And he said people allowed there'd be another trial to get me away from him and give me to the widow for my guardian, and they guessed it would win, this time. This shook me up considerable, because I didn't want to go back to the widow's any more and be so cramped up and sivilized, as they called it. Then the old man got to cussing, and cussed everything and everybody he could think of, and then cussed them all over again to make sure he hadn't skipped any, and after that he polished off with a kind of a general cuss all round, including a considerable parcel of people which he didn't know the names of, and so called them what's-his-name, when he got to them, and went right along with his cussing.

He said he would like to see the widow get me. He said he would watch out, and if they tried to come any such game on him he knowed of a place six or seven mile off, to stow me in, where they might hunt till they dropped and they couldn't find me. That made me pretty uneasy again, but only for a minute; I reckoned I wouldn't stay on hand till he got that chance.

The old man made me go to the skiff and fetch the things he had got. There was a fifty-pound sack of corn meal, and a side of bacon, ammunition, and a four-gallon jug of whisky, and an old book and two newspapers for wadding, besides some tow. I toted up a load, and went back and set down on the bow of the skiff to rest. I thought it all over, and I reckoned I would walk off with the gun and some lines, and take to the woods when I run away. I guessed I wouldn't stay in one place, but just tramp right across the country, mostly night times, and hunt and fish to keep alive, and so get so far away that the old man nor the widow couldn't ever find me any more. I judged I would saw out and leave that night if pap got drunk enough, and I reckoned he would. I got so full of it I didn't notice how long I was staying, till the old man hollered and asked me whether I was asleep or drownded.

I got the things all up to the cabin, and then it was about dark. While I was cooking supper the old man took a swig or two and got sort of warmed up, and went to ripping again. He had been drunk over in town, and laid in the gutter all night, and he was a sight to look at. A body would a thought he was Adam, he was just all mud. Whenever his liquor begun to work, he most always went for the govment. This time he says:

"Call this a govment! why, just look at it and see what it's like. Here's the law a-standing ready to take a man's son away from him — a man's own son, which he has had all the trouble and all the anxiety and all the expense of raising. Yes, just as that man has got that son raised at last, and ready to go to work and begin to do suthin' for *him* and give him a rest, the law up and goes for him. And they call *that* govment! That ain't all, nuther. The law backs that old Judge Thatcher up and helps him to keep me out o' my property. Here's what the law does. The law takes a man worth six thousand dollars and upards, and jams him into an old trap of a cabin like this, and lets him go round in clothes that ain't fitten for a hog. They call that govment! A man can't get his rights in a govment like this. Sometimes I've a mighty notion to just leave the country for good and all. Yes, and I *told* 'em so; I told old Thatcher so to his face. Lots of 'em heard me, and can tell what I said. Says I, for two cents I'd leave the blamed country and never come anear it agin. Them's the very words. I says, look at my hat — if you call it a hat — but the lid raises up and the rest of it goes down till it's below my chin, and then it ain't rightly a hat at all, but more like my head was shoved up through a jint o' stove-pipe. Look at it, says I — such a hat for me to wear — one of the wealthiest men in this town, if I could git my rights.

"Oh, yes, this is a wonderful govment, wonderful. Why, looky here. There was a free nigger there, from Ohio; a mulatter, most as white as a white man. He had the whitest shirt on you ever see, too, and the shiniest hat; and there ain't a man in that town that's got as fine clothes as what he had; and he had a gold watch and chain, and a silver-headed cane — the awfulest old gray-headed nabob in the State. And what do you think? they said he was a p'fessor in a college, and could talk all kinds of languages, and knowed everything. And that ain't the wust. They said he could *vote*, when he was at home. Well, that let me out. Thinks I, what is the country a-coming to? It was 'lection day, and I was just about to go and vote, myself, if I warn't too drunk to get there; but when they told me there was a State in this country where they'd let that nigger vote, I drawed out. I says I'll never vote agin. Them's the very words I said; they all heard me; and the country may rot for all me — I'll never vote agin as long as I live. And to see the cool way of that nigger — why, he wouldn't a give me the road if I hadn't shoved him out o' the way. I says to the people, why ain't this nigger put up at auction and sold? — that's what I want to know. And what do you reckon they said?

Why, they said he couldn't be sold till he'd been in the State six months, and he hadn't been there that long yet. There, now — that's a specimen. They call that a govment that can't sell a free nigger till he's been in the State six months. Here's a govment that calls itself a govment, and lets on to be a govment, and thinks it is a govment, and yet's got to set stock-still for six whole months before it can take ahold of a prowling, thieving, infernal, white-shirted free nigger, and ——"

Pap was agoing on so, he never noticed where his old limber legs was taking him to, so he went head over heels over the tub of salt pork, and barked both shins, and the rest of his speech was all the hottest kind of language — mostly hove at the nigger and the govment, though he give the tub some, too, all along, here and there. He hopped around the cabin considerable, first on one leg and then on the other, holding first one shin and then the other one, and at last he let out with his left foot all of a sudden and fetched the tub a rattling kick. But it warn't good judgment, because that was the boot that had a couple of his toes leaking out of the front end of it; so now he raised a howl that fairly made a body's hair raise, and down he went in the dirt, and rolled there, and held his toes; and the cussing he done then laid over anything he had ever done previous. He said so his own self, afterwards. He had heard old Sowberry Hagan in his best days, and he said it laid over him, too; but I reckon that was sort of piling it on, maybe.

After supper pap took the jug, and said he had enough whisky there for two drunks and one delirium tremens. That was always his word. I judged he would be blind drunk in about an hour, and then I would steal the key, or saw myself out, one or 'tother. He drank, and drank, and tumbled down on his blankets, by-and-by; but luck didn't run my way. He didn't go sound asleep, but was uneasy. He groaned, and moaned, and thrashed around this way and that, for a long time. At last I got so sleepy I couldn't keep my eyes open, all I could do, and so before I knowed what I was about I was sound asleep, and the candle burning.

I don't know how long I was asleep, but all of a sudden there was an awful scream and I was up. There was pap, looking wild and skipping around every which way and yelling about snakes. He said they was crawling up his legs; and then he would give a jump and scream, and say one had bit him on the cheek — but I couldn't see no snakes. He started and run round and round the cabin, hollering "take him off! take him off! he's biting me on the neck!" I never see a man look so wild in the eyes. Pretty soon he was all fagged out, and fell down panting; then he rolled over and over, wonderful fast, kicking things every which way, and striking and grabbing at the air with his hands, and screaming, and saying there was devils ahold of him. He wore out, by-and-by, and laid still a while, moaning. Then he laid stiller, and didn't make a sound. I could hear the owls and the wolves, away off in the woods, and it seemed terrible still. He was laying over by the corner. By-and-by he raised up, part way, and listened, with his head to one side. He says very low:

"Tramp — tramp — tramp; that's the dead; tramp — tramp — tramp; they're coming after me; but I won't go — Oh, they're here! don't touch me — don't! hands off — they're cold; let go — Oh, let a poor devil alone!"

Then he went down on all fours and crawled off begging them to let him alone, and he rolled himself up in his blanket and wallowed in under the old pine table, still a-begging; and then he went to crying. I could hear him through the blanket.

By-and-by he rolled out and jumped up on his feet looking wild, and he see me and went for me. He chased me round and round the place, with a clasp-knife, calling me the Angel of Death and saying he would kill me and then I couldn't come for him no more. I begged, and told him I was only Huck, but he laughed *such* a screechy laugh, and roared and cussed, and kept on chasing me up. Once when I turned short and dodged under his arm he made a grab and got me by the jacket between my shoulders, and I thought I was gone; but I slid out of the jacket quick as lightning, and saved myself. Pretty soon he was all tired out, and dropped down with his back against the door, and said he would rest a minute and then kill me. He put his knife under him, and said he would sleep and get strong, and then he would see who was who.

So he dozed off, pretty soon. By-and-by I got the old split-bottom chair and clumb up, as easy as I could, not to make any noise, and got down the gun. I slipped the ramrod down it to make sure it was loaded, and then I laid it across the turnip barrel, pointing towards pap, and set down behind it to wait for him to stir. And how slow and still the time did drag along.

Chapter VII

"Git up! what you 'bout!"

I opened my eyes and looked around, trying to make out where I was. It was after sun-up, and I had been sound asleep. Pap was standing over me, looking sour — and sick, too. He says —

"What you doin' with this gun?"

I judged he didn't know nothing about what he had been doing, so I says:

"Somebody tried to get in, so I was laying for him."

"Why didn't you roust me out?"

"Well I tried to, but I couldn't; I couldn't budge you."

"Well, all right. Don't stand there palavering all day, but out with you and see if there's a fish on the lines for breakfast. I'll be along in a minute."

He unlocked the door and I cleared out, up the river bank. I noticed some pieces of limbs and such things floating down, and a sprinkling of bark; so I knowed the river had begun to rise. I reckoned I would have great times, now, if I was over at the town. The June rise used to be always luck for me; because as soon as that rise begins, here comes cordwood floating down, and pieces of log rafts—sometimes a dozen logs together; so all you have to do is to catch them and sell them to the wood yards and the sawmill.

I went along up the bank with one eye out for pap and 'tother one out for what the rise might fetch along. Well, all at once, here comes a canoe; just a beauty, too, about thirteen or fourteen foot long, riding high like a duck. I shot head first off of the bank, like a frog, clothes and all on, and struck out for the canoe. I just expected there'd be somebody laying down in it, because people often done that to fool folks, and when a chap had pulled a skiff out most to it they'd raise up and laugh at him. But it warn't so this time. It was a drift-canoe, sure enough, and I clumb in and paddled her ashore. Thinks I, the old man will be glad when he sees this—she's worth ten dollars. But when I got to shore pap wasn't in sight yet, and as I was running her into a little creek like a gully, all hung over with vines and willows, I struck another idea; I judged I'd hide her good, and then, stead of taking to the woods when I run off, I'd go down the river about fifty mile and camp in one place for good, and not have such a rough time tramping on foot.

It was pretty close to the shanty, and I thought I heard the old man coming, all the time; but I got her hid; and then I out and looked around a bunch of willows, and there was the old man down the path apiece just drawing a bead on a bird with his gun. So he hadn't seen anything.

When he got along, I was hard at it taking up a "trot" line. He abused me a little for being so slow, but I told him I fell in the river and that was what made me so long. I knowed he would see I was wet, and then he would be asking questions. We got five cat-fish off of the lines and went home.

While we laid off, after breakfast, to sleep up, both of us being about wore out, I got to thinking that if I could fix up some way to keep pap and the widow from trying to follow me, it would be a certainer thing than trusting to luck to get far enough off before they missed me; you see, all kinds of things might happen. Well, I didn't see no way for a while, but by-and-by pap raised up a minute, to drink another barrel of water, and he says:

"Another time a man comes a-prowling round here, you roust me out, you hear? That man warn't here for no good. I'd a shot him. Next time, you roust me out, you hear?"

Then he dropped down and went to sleep again—but what he had been saying give me the very idea I wanted. I says to myself, I can fix it now so nobody won't think of following me.

About twelve o'clock we turned out and went along up the bank. The river was coming up pretty fast, and lots of drift-wood going by on the rise. By-and-by, along comes part of a log raft—nine logs fast together. We went out with the skiff and towed it ashore. Then we had dinner. Anybody but pap would a waited and seen the day through, so as to catch more stuff; but that warn't pap's style. Nine logs was enough for one time; he must shove right over to town and sell. So he locked me in and took the skiff and started off towing the raft about half-past three. I judged he wouldn't come back that night. I waited till I reckoned he had got a good start, then I out with my saw and went to work on that log again. Before he was 'tother side of the river I was out of the hole; him and his raft was just a speck on the water away off yonder.

I took the sack of corn meal and took it to where the canoe was hid, and shoved the vines and branches apart and put it in; then I done the same with the side of bacon; then the whisky jug; I took all the coffee and sugar there was, and all the ammunition; I took the wadding; I took the bucket and gourd, I took a dipper and a tin cup, and my old saw and two blankets, and the skillet and the coffee-pot. I took fish-lines and matches and other things—everything that was worth a cent. I cleaned out the place. I wanted an axe, but there wasn't any, only the one out at the wood pile, and I knowed why I was going to leave that. I fetched out the gun, and now I was done.

I had wore the ground a good deal, crawling out of the hole and dragging out so many things. So I fixed that as good as I could from the outside by scattering dust on the place, which covered up the smoothness and the sawdust. Then I fixed the piece of log back into its place, and put two rocks under it and one against it to hold it there,—for it was bent up at that place, and didn't quite touch ground. If you stood four or five foot away and didn't know it was sawed, you wouldn't ever notice it; and besides, this was the back of the cabin and it warn't likely anybody would go fooling around there.

It was all grass clear to the canoe; so I hadn't left a track. I followed around to see. I stood on the bank and looked out over the river. All safe.

So I took the gun and went up a piece into the woods and was hunting around for some birds, when I see a wild pig; hogs soon went wild in them bottoms after they had got away from the prairie farms. I shot this fellow and took him into camp.

I took the axe and smashed in the door — I beat it and hacked it considerable, a-doing it. I fetched the pig in and took him back nearly to the table and hacked into his throat with the ax, and laid him down on the ground to bleed — I say ground, because it *was* ground — hard packed, and no boards. Well, next I took an old sack and put a lot of big rocks in it, — all I could drag — and I started it from the pig and dragged it to the door and through the woods down to the river and dumped it in, and down it sunk, out of sight. You could easy see that something had been dragged over the ground. I did wish Tom Sawyer was there, I knowed he would take an interest in this kind of business, and throw in the fancy touches. Nobody could spread himself like Tom Sawyer in such a thing as that.

Well, last I pulled out some of my hair, and bloodied the ax good, and stuck it on the back side, and slung the ax in the corner. Then I took up the pig and held him to my breast with my jacket (so he couldn't drip) till I got a good piece below the house and then dumped him into the river. Now I thought of something else. So I went and got the bag of meal and my old saw out of the canoe and fetched them to the house. I took the bag to where it used to stand, and ripped a hole in the bottom of it with the saw, for there warn't no knives and forks on the place — pap done everything with his clasp-knife, about the cooking. Then I carried the sack about a hundred yards across the grass and through the willows east of the house, to a shallow lake that was five mile wide and full of rushes — and ducks too, you might say, in the season. There was a slough or a creek leading out of it on the other side, that went miles away, I don't know where, but it didn't go to the river. The meal sifted out and made a little track all the way to the lake. I dropped pap's whetstone there too, so as to look like it had been done by accident. Then I tied up the rip in the meal sack with a string, so it wouldn't leak no more, and took it and my saw to the canoe again.

It was about dark, now; so I dropped the canoe down the river under some willows that hung over the bank, and waited for the moon to rise. I made fast to a willow; then I took a bite to eat, and by-and-by laid down in the canoe to smoke a pipe and lay out a plan. I says to myself, they'll follow the track of that sackful of rocks to the shore and then drag the river for me. And they'll follow that meal track to the lake and go browsing down the creek that leads out of it to find the robbers that killed me and took the things. They won't ever hunt the river for anything but my dead carcass. They'll soon get tired of that, and won't bother no more about me. All right; I can stop anywhere I want to. Jackson's Island is good enough for me; I know that island pretty well, and nobody ever comes there. And then I can paddle over to town, nights, and slink around and pick up things I want. Jackson's Island's the place.

I was pretty tired, and the first thing I knowed, I was asleep. When I woke up I didn't know where I was, for a minute. I set up and looked around, a little scared. Then I remembered. The river looked miles and miles across. The moon was so bright I could a counted the drift logs that went a slipping along, black and still, hundred of yards out from shore. Everything was dead quiet, and it looked late, and *smelt* late. You know what I mean — I don't know the words to put it in.

I took a good gap and a stretch, and was just going to unhitch and start, when I heard a sound away over the water. I listened. Pretty soon I made it out. It was that dull kind of a regular sound that comes from oars working in rowlocks when it's a still night. I peeped out through the willow branches, and there it was — a skiff, away across the water. I couldn't tell how many was in it. It kept a-coming, and when it was abreast of me I see there warn't but one man in it. Thinks I, maybe it's pap, though I warn't expecting him. He dropped below me, with the current, and by-and-by he come a-swinging up shore in the easy water, and he went by so close I could a reached out the gun and touched him. Well, it *was* pap, sure enough — and sober, too, by the way he laid to his oars.

I didn't lose no time. The next minute I was a-spinning down stream soft but quick in the shade of the bank. I made two mile and a half, and then struck out a quarter of a mile or more towards the middle of the river, because pretty soon I would be passing the ferry landing and people might see me and hail me. I got out amongst the drift-wood and then laid down in the bottom of the canoe and let her float. I laid there and had a good rest and a smoke out of my pipe, looking away into the sky, not a cloud in it. The sky looks ever so deep when you lay down on your back in the moonshine; I never knowed it before. And how far a body can hear on the water such nights! I heard people talking at the ferry landing. I heard what they said, too, every word of it. One man said it was getting towards the long days and the short nights, now. 'Tother one said *this* warn't one of the short ones, he reckoned — and then they laughed, and he said it over again and they laughed again; then they waked up another fellow and told him, and laughed, but he didn't laugh; he ripped out something brisk and said let him alone. The first fellow said he 'lowed to tell it to his old woman — she would think it was pretty good; but he said that warn't nothing to some things he had said in his time. I heard one man say it was nearly three o'clock, and he hoped daylight wouldn't wait more than about a week longer. After that, the talk got further and further away, and I couldn't make out the words any more, but I could hear the mumble; and now and then a laugh, too, but it seemed a long ways off.

I was away below the ferry now. I rose up and there was Jackson's Island, about two mile and a half down stream, heavy-timbered and standing up out of the middle of the river, big and dark and solid, like a steamboat without any lights. There warn't any signs of the bar at the head — it was all under water, now.

It didn't take me long to get there. I shot past the head at a ripping rate, the current was so swift, and then I got into the dead water and landed on the side towards the Illinois shore. I run the canoe into a deep dent in the bank that I knowed about; I had to part the willow branches to get in; and when I made fast nobody could a seen the canoe from the outside.

I went up and set down on a log at the head of the island and looked out on the big river and the black driftwood, and away over to the town, three mile away, where there was three or four lights twinkling. A monstrous big lumber raft was about a mile up stream, coming along down, with a lantern in the middle of it. I watched it come creeping down, and when it was most abreast of where I stood I heard a man say, "Stern oars, there! heave her head to stabboard!" I heard that just as plain as if the man was by my side.

There was a little gray in the sky, now; so I stepped into the woods and laid down for a nap before breakfast.

Chapter VIII

The sun was up so high when I waked, that I judged it was after eight o'clock. I laid there in the grass and the cool shade, thinking about things and feeling rested and ruther comfortable and satisfied. I could see the sun out at one or two holes, but mostly it was big trees all about, and gloomy in there amongst them. There was freckled places on the ground where the light sifted down through the leaves, and the freckled places swapped about a little, showing there was a little breeze up there. A couple of squirrels set on a limb and jabbered at me very friendly.

I was powerful lazy and comfortable — didn't want to get up and cook breakfast. Well, I was dozing off again, when I thinks I hears a deep sound of "boom!" away up the river. I rouses up and rests on my elbow and listens; pretty soon I hears it again. I hopped up and went and looked out at a hole in the leaves, and I see a bunch of smoke laying on the water a long ways up — about abreast the ferry. And there was the ferry-boat full of people, floating along down. I knowed what was the matter, now. "Boom!" I see the white smoke squirt out of the ferry-boat's side. You see, they was firing cannon over the water, trying to make my carcass come to the top.

I was pretty hungry, but it warn't going to do for me to start a fire, because they might see the smoke. So I set there and watched the cannon-smoke and listened to the boom. The river was a mile wide, there, and it always looks pretty on a summer morning — so I was having a good enough time seeing them hunt for my remainders, if I only had a bite to eat. Well, then I happened to think how they always put quicksilver in loaves of bread and float them off because they always go right to the drownded carcass and stop there. So says I, I'll keep a lookout, and if any of them's floating around after me, I'll give them a show. I changed to the Illinois edge of the island to see what luck I could have, and I warn't disappointed. A big double loaf come along, and I most got it, with a long stick, but my foot slipped and she floated out further. Of course I was where the current set in the closest to the shore — I knowed enough for that. But by-and-by along comes another one, and this time I won. I took out the plug and shook out the little dab of quicksilver, and set my teeth in. It was "baker's bread" — what the quality eat — none of your low-down corn-pone.

I got a good place amongst the leaves, and set there on a log, munching the bread and watching the ferry-boat, and very well satisfied. And then something struck me. I says, now I reckon the widow or the parson or somebody prayed that this bread would find me, and here it has gone and done it. So there ain't no doubt but there is something in that thing. That is, there's something in it when a body like the widow or the parson prays, but it don't work for me, and I reckon it don't work for only just the right kind.

I lit a pipe and had a good long smoke and went on watching. The ferry-boat was floating with the current, and I allowed I'd have a chance to see who was aboard when she come along, because she would come in close, where the bread did. When she'd got pretty well along down towards me, I put out my pipe and went to where I fished out the bread, and laid down behind a log on the bank in a little open place. Where the log forked I could peep through.

By-and-by she come along, and she drifted in so close that they could a run out a plank and walked ashore. Most everybody was on the boat.

Pap, and Judge Thatcher, and Becky Thatcher, and Jo Harper, and Tom
Sawyer, and his old Aunt Polly, and Sid and Mary, and plenty more.
Everybody was talking about the murder, but the captain broke in and
says:

"Look sharp, now; the current sets in the closest here, and maybe he's
washed ashore and got tangled amongst the brush at the water's edge. I
hope so, anyway."

I didn't hope so. They all crowded up and leaned over the rails, nearly
in my face, and kept still, watching with all their might. I could see them
first-rate, but they couldn't see me. Then the captain sung out:

"Stand away!" and the cannon let off such a blast right before me that it
made me deef with the noise and pretty near blind with the smoke, and I
judged I was gone. If they'd a had some bullets in, I reckon they'd a got the
corpse they was after. Well, I see I warn't hurt, thanks to goodness. The
boat floated on and went out of sight around the shoulder of the island. I
could hear the booming, now and then, further and further off, and by-
and-by after an hour, I didn't hear it no more. The island was three mile
long. I judged they had got to the foot, and was giving it up. But they
didn't yet a while. They turned around the foot of the island and started
up the channel on the Missouri side, under steam, and booming once in
a while as they went. I crossed over to that side and watched them. When
they got abreast the head of the island they quit shooting and dropped
over to the Missouri shore and went home to the town.

I knowed I was all right now. Nobody else would come a-hunting after
me. I got my traps out of the canoe and made me a nice camp in the
thick woods. I made a kind of a tent out of my blankets to put my things
under so the rain couldn't get at them. I catched a cat-fish and haggled
him open with my saw, and towards sundown I started my camp fire and
had supper. Then I set out a line to catch some fish for breakfast.

When it was dark I set by my camp fire smoking, and feeling pretty
satisfied; but by-and-by it got sort of lonesome, and so I went and set on
the bank and listened to the currents washing along, and counted the
stars and drift-logs and rafts that come down, and then went to bed; there
ain't no better way to put in time when you are lonesome; you can't stay
so, you soon get over it.

And so for three days and nights. No difference — just the same thing.
But the next day I went exploring around down through the island. I was
boss of it; it all belonged to me, so to say, and I wanted to know all about
it; but mainly I wanted to put in the time. I found plenty strawberries,
ripe and prime; and green summer-grapes, and green razberries; and the
green blackberries was just beginning to show. They would all come
handy by-and-by, I judged.

Well, I went fooling along in the deep woods till I judged I warn't far from the foot of the island. I had my gun along, but I hadn't shot nothing; it was for protection; thought I would kill some game nigh home. About this time I mighty near stepped on a good sized snake, and it went sliding off through the grass and flowers, and I after it, trying to get a shot at it. I clipped along, and all of a sudden I bounded right on to the ashes of a camp fire that was still smoking.

My heart jumped up amongst my lungs. I never waited for to look further, but uncocked my gun and went sneaking back on my tip-toes as fast as ever I could. Every now and then I stopped a second, amongst the thick leaves, and listened; but my breath come so hard I couldn't hear nothing else. I slunk along another piece further, then listened again; and so on, and so on; if I see a stump, I took it for a man; if I trod on a stick and broke it, it made me feel like a person had cut one of my breaths in two and I only got half, and the short half, too.

When I got to camp I warn't feeling very brash, there warn't much sand in my craw; but I says, this ain't no time to be fooling around. So I got all my traps into my canoe again so as to have them out of sight, and I put out the fire and scattered the ashes around to look like an old last year's camp, and then clumb a tree.

I reckon I was up in the tree two hours; but I didn't see nothing, I didn't hear nothing — I only *thought* I heard and seen as much as a thousand things. Well, I couldn't stay up there forever; so at last I got down, but I kept in the thick woods and on the lookout all the time. All I could get to eat was berries and what was left over from breakfast.

By the time it was night I was pretty hungry. So when it was good and dark, I slid out from shore before moonrise and paddled over to the Illinois bank — about a quarter of a mile. I went out in the woods and cooked a supper, and I had about made up my mind I would stay there all night, when I hear a *plunkety-plunk, plunkety-plunk*, and says to myself, horses coming; and next I hear people's voices. I got everything into the canoe as quick as I could, and then went creeping through the woods to see what I could find out. I hadn't got far when I hear a man say:

"We better camp here, if we can find a good place; the horses is about beat out. Let's look around."

I didn't wait, but shoved out and paddled away easy. I tied up in the old place, and reckoned I would sleep in the canoe.

I didn't sleep much. I couldn't, somehow, for thinking. And every time I waked up I thought somebody had me by the neck. So the sleep didn't do me no good. By-and-by I says to myself, I can't live this way; I'm agoing to find out who it is that's here on the island with me; I'll find out or bust. Well, I felt better, right off.

So I took my paddle and slid out from shore just a step or two, and then let the canoe drop along down amongst the shadows. The moon was shining, and outside of the shadows it made it most as light as day. I poked along well onto an hour, everything still as rocks and sound asleep. Well by this time I was most down to the foot of the island. A little ripply, cool breeze begun to blow, and that was as good as saying the night was about done. I give her a turn with the paddle and brung her nose to shore; then I got my gun and slipped out and into the edge of the woods. I set down there on a log and looked out through the leaves. I see the moon go off watch and the darkness begin to blanket the river. But in a little while I see a pale streak over the tree-tops, and knowed the day was coming. So I took my gun and slipped off towards where I had run across that camp fire, stopping every minute or two to listen. But I hadn't no luck, somehow; I couldn't seem to find the place. But by-and-by, sure enough, I catched a glimpse of fire, away through the trees. I went for it, cautious and slow. By-and-by I was close enough to have a look, and there laid a man on the ground. It most give me the fan-tods. He had a blanket around his head, and his head was nearly in the fire. I set there behind a clump of bushes, in about six foot of him, and kept my eyes on him steady. It was getting gray daylight, now. Pretty soon he gapped, and stretched himself, and hove off the blanket, and it was Miss Watson's Jim! I bet I was glad to see him. I says:

"Hello, Jim!" and skipped out.

He bounced up and stared at me wild. Then he drops down on his knees, and puts his hands together and says:

"Doan' hurt me — don't! I hain't ever done no harm to a ghos'. I awluz liked dead people, en done all I could for 'em. You go en git in de river agin, whah you b'longs, en doan' do nuffn to Ole Jim, 'at 'uz awluz yo' fren'."

Well, I warn't long making him understand I warn't dead. I was ever so glad to see Jim. I warn't lonesome, now. I told him I warn't afraid of *him* telling the people where I was. I talked along, but he only set there and looked at me; never said nothing. Then I says:

"It's good daylight. Le's get breakfast. Make up your camp fire good."

"What's de use er makin' up de camp fire to cook strawbries en sich truck? But you got a gun, hain't you? Den we kin git sumfn better den strawbries."

"Strawberries and such truck," I says. "Is that what you live on?"

"I couldn' git nuffn else," he says.

"Why, how long you been on the island, Jim?"

"I come heah de night arter you's killed."

"What, all that time?"

"Yes-indeedy."

"And ain't you had nothing but that kind of rubbage to eat?"

"No, sah — nuffn else."

"Well, you must be most starved, ain't you?"

"I reck'n I could eat a hoss. I think I could. How long you ben on de islan'?"

"Since the night I got killed."

"No! W'y, what has you lived on? But you got a gun. Oh, yes, you got a gun. Dat's good. Now you kill sumfn en I'll make up de fire."

So we went over to where the canoe was, and while he built a fire in a grassy open place amongst the trees, I fetched meal and bacon and coffee, and coffee-pot and frying-pan, and sugar and tin cups, and the nigger was set back considerable, because he reckoned it was all done with witchcraft. I catched a good big cat-fish, too, and Jim cleaned him with his knife, and fried him.

When breakfast was ready, we lolled on the grass and eat it smoking hot. Jim laid it in with all his might, for he was most about starved. Then when we had got pretty well stuffed, we laid off and lazied.

By-and-by Jim says:

"But looky here, Huck, who wuz it dat 'uz killed in dat shanty, ef it warn't you?"

Then I told him the whole thing, and he said it was smart. He said Tom Sawyer couldn't get up no better plan than what I had. Then I says:

"How do you come to be here, Jim, and how'd you get here?"

He looked pretty uneasy, and didn't say nothing for a minute. Then he says:

"Maybe I better not tell."

"Why, Jim?"

"Well, dey's reasons. But you wouldn' tell on me ef I 'uz to tell you, would you, Huck?"

"Blamed if I would, Jim."

"Well, I b'lieve you, Huck. I — I *run off.*"

"Jim!"

"But mind, you said you wouldn't tell — you know you said you wouldn't tell, Huck."

"Well, I did. I said I wouldn't, and I'll stick to it. Honest *injun* I will. People would call me a low down Ablitionist and despise me for keeping mum — but that don't make no difference. I ain't agoing to tell, and I ain't agoing back there anyways. So now, le's know all about it."

"Well, you see, it 'uz dis way. Ole Missus — dat's Miss Watson — she pecks on me all de time, en treats me pooty rough, but she awluz said she wouldn' sell me down to Orleans. But I noticed dey wuz a nigger trader roun' de place considable, lately, en I begin to git oneasy. Well, one night I creeps to de do', pooty late, en de do' warn't quite shet, en I hear ole missus tell de widder she gwyne to sell me down to Orleans, but she didn' want to, but she could git eight hund'd dollars for me, en it 'uz sich a big stack o' money she couldn' resis'. De widder she try to git her to say she wouldn' do it, but I never waited to hear de res'. I lit out mighty quick, I tell you.

"I tuck out en shin down de hill en 'spec to steal a skift 'long de sho' som'ers 'bove de town, but dey wuz people a-stirrin' yit, so I hid in de ole tumble-down cooper shop on de bank to wait for everybody to go 'way. Well, I wuz dah all night. Dey wuz somebody roun' all de time. 'Long 'bout six in de mawnin', skifts begin to go by, en 'bout eight er nine every skift dat went 'long wuz talkin' 'bout how yo' pap come over to de town en say you's killed. Dese las' skifts wuz full o' ladies en genlmen agoin' over for to see de place. Sometimes dey'd pull up at de sho' en take a res' b'fo' dey started acrost, so by de talk I got to know all 'bout de killin'. I 'uz powerful sorry you's killed, Huck, but I ain't no mo', now.

"I laid dah under de shavins all day. I 'uz hungry, but I warn't afeared; bekase I knowed ole missus en de widder wuz goin' to start to de camp-meetn' right arter breakfas' en be gone all day, en dey knows I goes off wid de cattle 'bout daylight, so dey wouldn' 'spec to see me roun' de place, en so dey wouldn' miss me tell arter dark in de evenin'. De yuther servants wouldn' miss me, kase dey'd shin out en take holiday, soon as de ole folks 'uz out'n de way.

"Well, when it come dark I tuck out up de river road, en went 'bout two mile er more to whah dey warn't no houses. I'd made up my mine 'bout what I's agwyne to do. You see ef I kep' on tryin' to git away afoot, de dogs 'ud track me; ef I stole a skift to cross over, dey'd miss dat skift, you see, en dey'd know 'bout whah I'd lan' on de yuther side en whah to pick up my track. So I says, a raff is what I's arter; it doan' *make* no track.

"I see a light a-comin' roun' de p'int, bymeby, so I wade' in en shove' a log ahead o' me, en swum more'n half-way acrost de river, en got in 'mongst de drift-wood, en kep' my head down low, en kinder swum agin de current tell de raff come along. Den I swum to de stern uv it, en tuck aholt. It clouded up en 'uz pooty dark for a little while. So I clumb up en laid down on de planks. De men 'uz all 'way yonder in de middle, whah de lantern wuz. De river wuz arisin' en dey wuz a good current; so I reck'n'd 'at by fo' in de mawnin' I'd be twenty-five mile down de river, en den I'd slip in, jis' b'fo' daylight, en swim asho' en take to de woods on de Illinoi side.

"But I didn' have no luck. When we 'uz mos' down to de head er de islan', a man begin to come aft wid de lantern. I see it warn't no use fer to wait, so I slid overboad, en struck out fer de islan'. Well, I had a notion I could lan' mos' anywhers, but I couldn't — bank too bluff. I 'uz mos' to de foot er de islan' b'fo' I foun' a good place. I went into de woods en jedged I wouldn' fool wid raffs no mo', long as dey move de lantern roun' so. I had my pipe en a plug er dog-leg, en some matches in my cap, en dey warn't wet, so I 'uz all right."

"And so you ain't had no meat nor bread to eat all this time? Why didn't you get mud-turkles?"

"How you gwyne to git'm? You can't slip up on um en grab um; en how's a body gwyne to hit um wid a rock? How could a body do it in de night? en I warn't gwyne to show myself on de bank in de daytime."

"Well, that's so. You've had to keep in the woods all the time, of course. Did you hear 'em shooting the cannon?"

"Oh, yes. I knowed dey was arter you. I see um go by heah; watched um thoo de bushes."

Some young birds come along, flying a yard or two at a time and lighting. Jim said it was a sign it was going to rain. He said it was a sign when young chickens flew that way, and so he reckoned it was the same way when young birds done it. I was going to catch some of them, but Jim wouldn't let me. He said it was death. He said his father laid mighty sick once, and some of them catched a bird, and his old granny said his father would die, and he did.

And Jim said you musn't count the things you are going to cook for dinner, because that would bring bad luck. The same if you shook the table-cloth after sundown. And he said if a man owned a bee-hive, and that man died, the bees must be told about it before sun-up next morning, or else the bees would all weaken down and quit work and die. Jim said bees wouldn't sting idiots; but I didn't believe that, because I had tried them lots of times myself, and they wouldn't sting me.

I had heard about some of these things before, but not all of them. Jim knowed all kinds of signs. He said he knowed most everything. I said it looked to me like all the signs was about bad luck, and so I asked him if there warn't any good-luck signs. He says:

"Mighty few — an' *dey* ain' no use to a body. What you want to know when good luck's a-comin' for? want to keep it off?" And he said: "Ef you's got hairy arms en a hairy breas', it's a sign dat you's agwyne to be rich. Well, dey's some use in a sign like dat, 'kase it's so fur ahead. You see, maybe you's got to be po ' a long time fust, en so you might git discourage' en kill yo'sef 'f you didn' know by de sign dat you gwyne to be rich bymeby."

"Have you got hairy arms and a hairy breast, Jim?"

"What's de use to ax dat question? don' you see I has?"

"Well, are you rich?"

"No, but I ben rich wunst, and gwyne to be rich agin. Wunst I had foteen dollars, but I tuck to specalat'n', en got busted out."

"What did you speculate in, Jim?"

"Well, fust I tackled stock."

"What kind of stock?"

"Why, live stock. Cattle, you know. I put ten dollars in a cow. But I ain' gwyne to resk no mo' money in stock. De cow up 'n' died on my han's."

"So you lost the ten dollars."

"No, I didn' lose it all. I on'y los' 'bout nine of it. I sole de hide en taller for a dollar en ten cents."

"You had five dollars and ten cents left. Did you speculate any more?"

"Yes. You know dat one-laigged nigger dat b'longs to old Misto Bradish? well, he sot up a bank, en say anybody dat put in a dollar would git fo' dollars mo' at de en' er de year. Well, all de niggers went in, but dey didn' have much. I wuz de on'y one dat had much. So I stuck out for mo' dan fo' dollars, en I said 'f I didn' git it I'd start a bank mysef. Well o' course dat nigger want' to keep me out er de business, bekase he say dey warn't business 'nough for two banks, so he say I could put in my five dollars en he pay me thirty-five at de en' er de year.

"So I done it. Den I reck'n'd I'd inves' de thirty-five dollars right off en keep things a-movin'. Dey wuz a nigger name' Bob, dat had ketched a wood-flat, en his marster didn' know it; en I bought it off'n him en told him to take de thirty-five dollars when de en' er de year come; but somebody stole de wood-flat dat night, en nex' day de one-laigged nigger say de bank 's busted. So dey didn' none uv us git no money."

"What did you do with the ten cents, Jim?"

"Well, I 'uz gwyne to spen' it, but I had a dream, en de dream tole me to give it to a nigger name' Balum—Balum's Ass dey call him for short, he's one er dem chuckle-heads, you know. But he's lucky, dey say, en I see I warn't lucky. De dream say let Balum inves' de ten cents en he'd make a raise for me. Well, Balum he tuck de money, en when he wuz in church he hear de preacher say dat whoever give to de po' len' to de Lord, en boun' to git his money back a hund'd times. So Balum he tuck en give de ten cents to de po', en laid low to see what wuz gwyne to come of it."

"Well, what did come of it, Jim?"

"Nuffn' never come of it. I couldn' manage to k'leck dat money no way; en Balum he couldn'. I ain' gwyne to len' no mo' money 'dout I see de security. Boun' to git yo' money back a hund'd times, de preacher says! Ef I could git de ten *cents* back, I'd call it squah, en be glad er de chanst."

"Well, it's all right, anyway, Jim, long as you're going to be rich again some time or other."

"Yes — en I's rich now, come to look at it. I owns mysef, en I's wuth eight hund'd dollars. I wisht I had de money, I wouldn' want no mo'.'"

Chapter IX

I wanted to go and look at a place right about the middle of the island, that I'd found when I was exploring; so we started, and soon got to it, because the island was only three miles long and a quarter of a mile wide.

This place was a tolerable long steep hill or ridge, about forty foot high. We had a rough time getting to the top, the sides was so steep and the bushes so thick. We tramped and clumb around all over it, and by-and-by found a good big cavern in the rock, most up to the top on the side towards Illinois. The cavern was as big as two or three rooms bunched together, and Jim could stand up straight in it. It was cool in there. Jim was for putting our traps in there, right away, but I said we didn't want to be climbing up and down there all the time.

Jim said if we had the canoe hid in a good place, and had all the traps in the cavern, we could rush there if anybody was to come to the island, and they would never find us without dogs. And besides, he said them little birds had said it was going to rain, and did I want the things to get wet?

So we went back and got the canoe and paddled up abreast the cavern, and lugged all the traps up there. Then we hunted up a place close by to hide the canoe in, amongst the thick willows. We took some fish off of the lines and set them again, and begun to get ready for dinner.

The door of the cavern was big enough to roll a hogshead in, and on one side of the door the floor stuck out a little bit and was flat and a good place to build a fire on. So we built it there and cooked dinner.

We spread the blankets inside for a carpet, and eat our dinner in there. We put all the other things handy at the back of the cavern. Pretty soon it darkened up and begun to thunder and lighten; so the birds was right about it. Directly it begun to rain, and it rained like all fury, too, and I never see the wind blow so. It was one of these regular summer storms. It would get so dark that it looked all blue-black outside, and lovely; and the rain would thrash along by so thick that the trees off a little ways looked dim and spider-webby; and here would come a blast of wind that would bend the trees down and turn up the pale underside of the leaves; and then a perfect ripper of a gust would follow along and set the branches to tossing their arms as if they was just wild; and next, when it was just about the bluest and blackest — *fst!* it was as bright as glory and you'd have a little glimpse of tree-tops a-plunging about, away off yonder in the storm, hundreds of yards further than you could see before; dark as sin again in a second, and now you'd hear the thunder let go with an awful crash and then go rumbling, grumbling, tumbling down the sky towards the under side of the world, like rolling empty barrels down stairs, where it's long stairs and they bounce a good deal, you know.

"Jim, this is nice," I says. "I wouldn't want to be nowhere else but here. Pass me along another hunk of fish and some hot corn-bread."

"Well, you wouldn't a ben here, 'f it hadn't a ben for Jim. You'd a ben down dah in de woods widout any dinner, en gittn' mos' drownded, too, dat you would, honey. Chickens knows when its gwyne to rain, en so do de birds, chile."

The river went on raising and raising for ten or twelve days, till at last it was over the banks. The water was three or four foot deep on the island in the low places and on the Illinois bottom. On that side it was a good many miles wide; but on the Missouri side it was the same old distance across — a half a mile — because the Missouri shore was just a wall of high bluffs.

Daytimes we paddled all over the island in the canoe. It was mighty cool and shady in the deep woods even if the sun was blazing outside. We went winding in and out amongst the trees; and sometimes the vines hung so thick we had to back away and go some other way. Well, on every old broken-down tree, you could see rabbits, and snakes, and such things; and when the island had been overflowed a day or two, they got so tame, on account of being hungry, that you could paddle right up and put your hand on them if you wanted to; but not the snakes and turtles — they would slide off in the water. The ridge our cavern was in, was full of them. We could a had pets enough if we'd wanted them.

One night we catched a little section of a lumber raft — nice pine planks. It was twelve foot wide and about fifteen or sixteen foot long, and the top stood above water six or seven inches, a solid level floor. We could see saw-logs go by in the daylight, sometimes, but we let them go; we didn't show ourselves in daylight.

Another night, when we was up at the head of the island, just before daylight, here comes a frame house down, on the west side. She was a two-story, and tilted over, considerable. We paddled out and got aboard — clumb in at an up-stairs window. But it was too dark to see yet, so we made the canoe fast and set in her to wait for daylight.

The light begun to come before we got to the foot of the island. Then we looked in at the window. We could make out a bed, and a table, and two old chairs, and lots of things around about on the floor; and there was clothes hanging against the wall. There was something laying on the floor in the far corner that looked like a man. So Jim says:

"Hello, you!"

But it didn't budge. So I hollered again, and then Jim says:

"De man ain't asleep — he's dead. You hold still — I'll go en see."

He went and bent down and looked, and says:

"It's a dead man. Yes, indeedy; naked, too. He's ben shot in de back. I reck'n he's ben dead two er three days. Come in, Huck, but doan' look at his face — it's too gashly."

I didn't look at him at all. Jim throwed some old rags over him, but he needn't done it; I didn't want to see him. There was heaps of old greasy cards scattered around over the floor, and old whisky bottles, and a couple of masks made out of black cloth; and all over the walls was the ignorantest kind of words and pictures, made with charcoal. There was two old dirty calico dresses, and a sun-bonnet, and some women's under-clothes, hanging against the wall, and some men's clothing, too. We put the lot into the canoe; it might come good. There was a boy's old speckled straw hat on the floor; I took that too. And there was a bottle that had had milk in it, and it had a rag stopper for a baby to suck. We would a took the bottle, but it was broke. There was a seedy old chest, and an old hair trunk with the hinges broke. They stood open, but there warn't nothing left in them that was any account. The way things was scattered about, we reckoned the people left in a hurry and warn't fixed so as to carry off most of their stuff.

We got an old tin lantern, and a butcher knife without any handle, and a bran-new Barlow knife worth two bits in any store, and a lot of tallow candles, and a tin candlestick, and a gourd, and a tin cup, and a ratty old bed-quilt off the bed, and a reticule with needles and pins and beeswax and buttons and thread and all such truck in it, and a hatchet and some nails, and a fish-line as thick as my little finger, with some monstrous hooks on it, and a roll of buckskin, and a leather dog-collar, and a horse-shoe, and some vials of medicine that didn't have no label on them; and just as we was leaving I found a tolerable good curry-comb, and Jim he found a ratty old fiddle-bow, and a wooden leg. The straps was broke off of it, but barring that, it was a good enough leg, though it was too long for me and not long enough for Jim, and we couldn't find the other one, though we hunted all around.

And so, take it all around, we made a good haul. When we was ready to shove off, we was a quarter of a mile below the island, and it was pretty broad day; so I made Jim lay down in the canoe and cover up with the quilt, because if he set up, people could tell he was a nigger a good ways off. I paddled over to the Illinois shore, and drifted down most a half a mile doing it. I crept up the dead water under the bank, and hadn't no accidents and didn't see nobody. We got home all safe.

Chapter X

After breakfast I wanted to talk about the dead man and guess out how he come to be killed, but Jim didn't want to. He said it would fetch bad luck; and besides, he said, he might come and ha'nt us; he said a man that warn't buried was more likely to go a-ha'nting around than one that was planted and comfortable. That sounded pretty reasonable, so I didn't say no more; but I couldn't keep from studying over it and wishing I knowed who shot the man, and what they done it for.

We rummaged the clothes we'd got, and found eight dollars in silver sewed up in the lining of an old blanket overcoat. Jim said he reckoned the people in that house stole the coat, because if they'd a knowed the money was there they wouldn't a left it. I said I reckoned they killed him, too; but Jim didn't want to talk about that. I says:

"Now you think it's bad luck; but what did you say when I fetched in the snake-skin that I found on the top of the ridge day before yesterday? You said it was the worst bad luck in the world to touch a snake-skin with my hands. Well, here's your bad luck! We've raked in all this truck and eight dollars besides. I wish we could have some bad luck like this every day, Jim."

"Never you mind, honey, never you mind. Don't you git too peart. It's a-comin'. Mind I tell you, it's a-comin'."

It did come, too. It was a Tuesday that we had that talk. Well, after dinner Friday, we was laying around in the grass at the upper end of the ridge, and got out of tobacco. I went to the cavern to get some, and found a rattlesnake in there. I killed him, and curled him up on the foot of Jim's blanket, ever so natural, thinking there'd be some fun when Jim found him there. Well, by night I forgot all about the snake, and when Jim flung himself down on the blanket while I struck a light, the snake's mate was there, and bit him.

He jumped up yelling, and the first thing the light showed was the varmint curled up and ready for another spring. I laid him out in a second with a stick, and Jim grabbed pap's whisky jug and begun to pour it down.

He was barefooted, and the snake bit him right on the heel. That all comes of my being such a fool as to not remember that wherever you leave a dead snake its mate always comes there and curls around it. Jim told me to chop off the snake's head and throw it away, and then skin the body and roast a piece of it. I done it, and he eat it and said it would help cure him. He made me take off the rattles and tie them around his wrist, too. He said that that would help. Then I slid out quiet and throwed the snakes clear away amongst the bushes; for I warn't going to let Jim find out it was all my fault, not if I could help it.

Jim sucked and sucked at the jug, and now and then he got out of his head and pitched around and yelled; but every time he come to himself he went to sucking at the jug again. His foot swelled up pretty big, and so did his leg; but by-and-by the drunk begun to come, and so I judged he was all right; but I'd druther been bit with a snake than pap's whisky.

Jim was laid up for four days and nights. Then the swelling was all gone and he was around again. I made up my mind I wouldn't ever take aholt of a snake-skin again with my hands, now that I see what had come of it. Jim said he reckoned I would believe him next time. And he said that handling a snake-skin was such awful bad luck that maybe we hadn't got to the end of it yet. He said he druther see the new moon over his left shoulder as much as a thousand times than take up a snake-skin in his hand. Well, I was getting to feel that way myself, though I've always reckoned that looking at the new moon over your left shoulder is one of the carelessest and foolishest things a body can do. Old Hank Bunker done it once, and bragged about it; and in less than two years he got drunk and fell off of the shot tower and spread himself out so that he was just a kind of a layer, as you may say; and they slid him edgeways between two barn doors for a coffin, and buried him so, so they say, but I didn't see it. Pap told me. But anyway, it all come of looking at the moon that way, like a fool.

Well, the days went along, and the river went down between its banks again; and about the first thing we done was to bait one of the big hooks with a skinned rabbit and set it and catch a cat-fish that was as big as a man, being six foot two inches long, and weighed over two hundred pounds. We couldn't handle him, of course; he would a flung us into Illinois. We just set there and watched him rip and tear around till he drownded. We found a brass button in his stomach, and a round ball, and lots of rubbage. We split the ball open with the hatchet, and there was a spool in it. Jim said he'd had it there a long time, to coat it over so and make a ball of it. It was as big a fish as was ever catched in the

Mississippi, I reckon. Jim said he hadn't ever seen a bigger one. He would a been worth a good deal over at the village. They peddle out such a fish as that by the pound in the market house there; everybody buys some of him; his meat's as white as snow and makes a good fry.

Next morning I said it was getting slow and dull, and I wanted to get a stirring up, some way. I said I reckoned I would slip over the river and find out what was going on. Jim liked that notion; but he said I must go in the dark and look sharp. Then he studied it over and said, couldn't I put on some of them old things and dress up like a girl? That was a good notion, too. So we shortened up one of the calico gowns and I turned up my trowser-legs to my knees and got into it. Jim hitched it behind with the hooks, and it was a fair fit. I put on the sun-bonnet and tied it under my chin, and then for a body to look in and see my face was like looking down a joint of stove-pipe. Jim said nobody would know me, even in the daytime, hardly. I practiced around all day to get the hang of the things, and by-and-by I could do pretty well in them, only Jim said I didn't walk like a girl; and he said I must quit pulling up my gown to get at my britches pocket. I took notice, and done better.

I started up the Illinois shore in the canoe just after dark.

I started across to the town from a little below the ferry landing, and the drift of the current fetched me in at the bottom of the town. I tied up and started along the bank. There was a light burning in a little shanty that hadn't been lived in for a long time, and I wondered who had took up quarters there. I slipped up and peeped in at the window. There was a woman about forty year old in there, knitting by a candle that was on a pine table. I didn't know her face; she was a stranger, for you couldn't start a face in that town that I didn't know. Now this was lucky, because I was weakening; I was getting afraid I had come; people might know my voice and find me out. But if this woman had been in such a little town two days she could tell me all I wanted to know; so I knocked at the door, and made up my mind I wouldn't forget I was a girl.

Chapter XI

"Come in," says the woman, and I did. She says:

"Take a cheer."

I done it. She looked me all over with her little shiny eyes, and says:

"What might your name be?"

"Sarah Williams."

"Where 'bouts do you live? In this neighborhood?"

"No'm. In Hookerville, seven mile below. I've walked all the way and I'm all tired out."

"Hungry, too, I reckon. I'll find you something."

"No'm, I ain't hungry. I was so hungry I had to stop two mile below here at a farm; so I ain't hungry no more. It's what makes me so late. My mother's down sick, and out of money and everything, and I come to tell my uncle Abner Moore. He lives at the upper end of the town, she says. I hain't ever been here before. Do you know him?"

"No; but I don't know everybody yet. I haven't lived here quite two weeks. It's a considerable ways to the upper end of the town. You better stay here all night. Take off your bonnet."

"No," I says, "I'll rest a while, I reckon, and go on. I ain't afeard of the dark."

She said she wouldn't let me go by myself, but her husband would be in by-and-by, maybe in a hour and a half, and she'd send him along with me. Then she got to talking about her husband, and about her relations up the river, and her relations down the river, and about how much better off they used to was, and how they didn't know but they'd made a mistake coming to our town, instead of letting well alone — and so on and so on, till I was afeard I had made a mistake coming to her to find out what was going on in the town; but by-and-by she dropped onto pap and the murder, and then I was pretty willing to let her clatter right along. She told about me and Tom Sawyer finding the six thousand dollars (only she got it ten) and all about pap and what a hard lot he was, and what a hard lot I was, and at last she got down to where I was murdered. I says:

"Who done it? We've heard considerable about these goings on, down in Hookerville, but we don't know who 'twas that killed Huck Finn."

"Well, I reckon there's a right smart chance of people *here* that 'd like to know who killed him. Some thinks old Finn done it himself."

"No — is that so?"

"Most everybody thought it at first. He'll never know how nigh he come to getting lynched. But before night they changed around and judged it was done by a runaway nigger named Jim."

"Why *he* ——"

I stopped. I reckoned I better keep still. She run on, and never noticed I had put in at all.

"The nigger run off the very night Huck Finn was killed. So there's a reward out for him — three hundred dollars. And there's a reward out for old Finn too — two hundred dollars. You see, he come to town the morning after the murder, and told about it, and was out with 'em on the ferry-boat hunt, and right away after he up and left. Before night they wanted to lynch him, but he was gone, you see. Well, next day they found out the nigger was gone; they found out he hadn't ben seen sence ten o'clock the night the murder was done. So then they put it on him, you see, and while they was full of it, next day back comes old Finn and went boo-hooing to Judge Thatcher to get money to hunt for the nigger all over Illinois with. The judge give him some, and that evening he got drunk and was around till after midnight with a couple of mighty hard looking strangers, and then went off with them. Well, he hain't come back sence, and they ain't looking for him back till this thing blows over a little, for people thinks now that he killed his boy and fixed things so folks would think robbers done it, and then he'd get Huck's money without having to bother a long time with a lawsuit. People do say he warn't any too good to do it. Oh, he's sly, I reckon. If he don't come back for a year, he'll be all right. You can't prove anything on him, you know; everything will be quieted down then, and he'll walk into Huck's money as easy as nothing."

"Yes, I reckon so, 'm. I don't see nothing in the way of it. Has everybody quit thinking the nigger done it?"

"Oh, no, not everybody. A good many thinks he done it. But they'll get the nigger pretty soon, now, and maybe they can scare it out of him."

"Why, are they after him yet?"

"Well, you're innocent, ain't you! Does three hundred dollars lay round every day for people to pick up? Some folks thinks the nigger ain't far from here. I'm one of them — but I hain't talked it around. A few days ago I was talking with an old couple that lives next door in the log shanty, and they happened to say hardly anybody ever goes to that island over yonder that they call Jackson's Island. Don't anybody live there? says I. No, nobody, says they. I didn't say any more, but I done some thinking. I was pretty near certain I'd seen smoke over there, about the head of the island, a day or two before that, so I says to myself, like as not that nigger's hiding over there; anyway, says I, it's worth the trouble to give the place a hunt. I hain't seen any smoke sence, so I reckon maybe he's gone, if it was him; but husband's going over to see — him and another man. He was gone up the river; but he got back to-day and I told him as soon as he got here two hours ago."

I had got so uneasy I couldn't set still. I had to do something with my hands; so I took up a needle off of the table and went to threading it. My hands shook, and I was making a bad job of it. When the woman stopped talking, I looked up, and she was looking at me pretty curious, and smiling a little. I put down the needle and thread and let on to be interested — and I was, too — and says:

"Three hundred dollars is a power of money. I wish my mother could get it. Is your husband going over there to-night?"

"Oh, yes. He went up town with the man I was telling you of, to get a boat and see if they could borrow another gun. They'll go over after midnight."

"Couldn't they see better if they was to wait till daytime?"

"Yes. And couldn't the nigger see better, too? After midnight he'll likely be asleep, and they can slip around through the woods and hunt up his camp fire all the better for the dark, if he's got one."

"I didn't think of that."

The woman kept looking at me pretty curious, and I didn't feel a bit comfortable. Pretty soon she says:

"What did you say your name was, honey?"

"M — Mary Williams."

Somehow it didn't seem to me that I said it was Mary before, so I didn't look up; seemed to me I said it was Sarah; so I felt sort of cornered, and was afeared maybe I was looking it, too. I wished the woman would say something more; the longer she set still, the uneasier I was. But now she says:

"Honey, I thought you said it was Sarah when you first come in?"

"Oh, yes'm, I did. Sarah Mary Williams. Sarah's my first name. Some calls me Sarah, some calls me Mary."

"Oh, that's the way of it?"

"Yes'm."

I was feeling better, then, but I wished I was out of there, anyway. I couldn't look up yet.

Well, the woman fell to talking about how hard times was, and how poor they had to live, and how the rats was as free as if they owned the place, and so forth and so on, and then I got easy again. She was right about the rats. You'd see one stick his nose out of a hole in the corner every little while. She said she had to have things handy to throw at them when she was alone, or they wouldn't give her no peace. She showed me a bar of lead, twisted up into a knot, and said she was a good shot with it generly, but she'd wrenched her arm a day or two ago, and didn't know whether she could throw true, now. But she watched for a chance, and directly she banged away at a rat, but she missed him wide, and said "Ouch!" it hurt her arm so. Then she told me to try for the next one. I wanted to be getting away before the old man got back, but of course I didn't let on. I got the thing, and the first rat that showed his nose I let drive, and if he'd a stayed where he was he'd a been a tolerable sick rat. She said that that was first-rate, and she reckoned I would hive the next one. She went and got the lump of lead and fetched it back and brought along a hank of yarn, which she wanted me to help her with. I held up my two hands and she put the hank over them and went on talking about her and her husband's matters. But she broke off to say:

"Keep your eye on the rats. You better have the lead in your lap, handy."

So she dropped the lump into my, lap, just at that moment, and I clapped my legs together on it and she went on talking. But only about a minute. Then she took off the hank and looked me straight in the face, but very pleasant, and says:

"Come, now — what's your real name?"

"Wh-what, mum?"

"What's your real name? Is it Bill, or Tom, or Bob? — or what is it?"

I reckon I shook like a leaf, and I didn't know hardly what to do. But I says:

"Please to don't poke fun at a poor girl like me, mum. If I'm in the way, here, I'll ——"

"No, you won't. Set down and stay where you are. I ain't going to hurt you, and I ain't going to tell on you, nuther. You just tell me your secret, and trust me. I'll keep it; and what's more, I'll help you. So'll my old man, if you want him to. You see, you're a runaway 'prentice — that's all. It ain't anything. There ain't any harm in it. You've been treated bad, and you made up your mind to cut. Bless you, child, I wouldn't tell on you. Tell me all about it, now — that's a good boy."

So I said it wouldn't be no use to try to play it any longer, and I would just make a clean breast and tell her everything, but she mustn't go back on her promise. Then I told her my father and mother was dead, and the law had bound me out to a mean old farmer in the country thirty mile back from the river, and he treated me so bad I couldn't stand it no longer; he went away to be gone a couple of days, and so I took my chance and stole some of his daughter's old clothes, and cleared out, and I had been three nights coming the thirty miles; I traveled nights, and hid day-times and slept, and the bag of bread and meat I carried from home lasted me all the way and I had a plenty. I said I believed my uncle Abner Moore would take care of me, and so that was why I struck out for this town of Goshen."

"Goshen, child? This ain't Goshen. This is St. Petersburg. Goshen's ten mile further up the river. Who told you this was Goshen?"

"Why, a man I met at day-break this morning, just as I was going to turn into the woods for my regular sleep. He told me when the roads forked I must take the right hand, and five mile would fetch me to Goshen."

"He was drunk I reckon. He told you just exactly wrong."

"Well, he did act like he was drunk, but it ain't no matter now. I got to be moving along. I'll fetch Goshen before day-light."

"Hold on a minute. I'll put you up a snack to eat. You might want it."

So she put me up a snack, and says:

"Say — when a cow's laying down, which end of her gets up first? Answer up prompt, now — don't stop to study over it. Which end gets up first?"

"The hind end, mum."

"Well, then, a horse?"

"The for'rard end, mum."

"Which side of a tree does the most moss grow on?"

"North side."

"If fifteen cows is browsing on a hillside, how many of them eats with their heads pointed the same direction?"

"The whole fifteen, mum."

"Well, I reckon you *have* lived in the country. I thought maybe you was trying to hocus me again. What's your real name, now?"

"George Peters, mum."

"Well, try to remember it, George. Don't forget and tell me it's Elexander before you go, and then get out by saying it's George-Elexander when I catch you. And don't go about women in that old calico. You do a girl tolerable poor, but you might fool men, maybe. Bless you, child, when you set out to thread a needle, don't hold the thread still and fetch the needle up to it; hold the needle still and poke the thread at it — that's the way a woman most always does; but a man always does 'tother way. And when you throw at a rat or anything, hitch yourself up a tip-toe, and fetch your hand up over your head as awkard as you can, and miss your rat about six or seven foot. Throw stiff-armed from the shoulder, like there was a pivot there for it to turn on — like a girl; not from the wrist and elbow, with your arm out to one side, like a boy. And mind you, when a girl tries to catch anything in her lap, she throws her knees apart; she don't clap them together, the way you did when you catched the lump of lead. Why, I spotted you for a boy when you was threading the needle; and I contrived the other things just to make certain. Now trot along to your uncle, Sarah Mary Williams George Elexander Peters, and if you get into trouble you send word to Mrs. Judith Loftus, which is me, and I'll do what I can to get you out of it. Keep the river road, all the way, and next time you tramp, take shoes and socks with you. The river road's a rocky one, and your feet 'll be in a condition when you get to Goshen, I reckon."

I went up the bank about fifty yards, and then I doubled on my tracks and slipped back to where my canoe was, a good piece below the house. I jumped in and was off in a hurry. I went up stream far enough to make the head of the island, and then started across. I took off the sun-bonnet, for I didn't want no blinders on, then. When I was about the middle, I hear the clock begin to strike; so I stops and listens; the sound come faint over the water, but clear — eleven. When I struck the head of the island I never waited to blow, though I was most winded, but I shoved right into the timber where my old camp used to be, and started a good fire there on a high-and-dry spot.

Then I jumped in the canoe and dug out for our place a mile and a half below, as hard as I could go. I landed, and slopped through the timber and up the ridge and into the cavern. There Jim laid, sound asleep on the ground. I roused him out and says:

"Git up and hump yourself, Jim! There ain't a minute to lose. They're after us!"

Jim never asked no questions, he never said a word; but the way he worked for the next half an hour showed about how he was scared. By that time everything we had in the world was on our raft and she was ready to be shoved out from the willow cove where she was hid. We put out the camp fire at the cavern the first thing, and didn't show a candle outside after that.

I took the canoe out from shore a little piece and took a look, but if there was a boat around I couldn't see it, for stars and shadows ain't good to see by. Then we got out the raft and slipped along down in the shade, past the foot of the island dead still, never saying a word.

Chapter XII

It must a been close onto one o'clock when we got below the island at last, and the raft did seem to go mighty slow. If a boat was to come along, we was going to take to the canoe and break for the Illinois shore; and it was well a boat didn't come, for we hadn't ever thought to put the gun into the canoe, or a fishing-line or anything to eat. We was in ruther too much of a sweat to think of so many things. It warn't good judgment to put *everything* on the raft.

If the men went to the island, I just expect they found the camp fire I built, and watched it all night for Jim to come. Anyways, they stayed away from us, and if my building the fire never fooled them it warn't no fault of mine. I played it as low-down on them as I could.

When the first streak of day begun to show, we tied up to a tow-head in a big bend on the Illinois side, and hacked off cotton-wood branches with the hatchet and covered up the raft with them so she looked like there had been a cave-in in the bank there. A tow-head is a sand-bar that has cotton-woods on it as thick as harrow-teeth.

We had mountains on the Missouri shore and heavy timber on the Illinois side, and the channel was down the Missouri shore at that place, so we warn't afraid of anybody running across us. We laid there all day and watched the rafts and steamboats spin down the Missouri shore, and up-bound steamboats fight the big river in the middle. I told Jim all about the time I had jabbering with that woman; and Jim said she was a smart one, and if she was to start after us herself *she* wouldn't set down and watch a camp fire — no, sir, she'd fetch a dog. Well, then, I said, why couldn't she tell her husband to fetch a dog? Jim said he bet she did think of it by the time the men was ready to start, and he believed they must a gone up town to get a dog and so they lost all that time, or else we wouldn't be here on a tow-head sixteen or seventeen mile below the village — no, indeedy, we would be in that same old town again. So I said I didn't care what was the reason they didn't get us, as long as they didn't.

When it was beginning to come on dark, we poked our heads out of the cottonwood thicket and looked up, and down, and across; nothing in sight; so Jim took up some of the top planks of the raft and built a snug wigwam to get under in blazing weather and rainy, and to keep the things dry. Jim made a floor for the wigwam, and raised it a foot or more above the level of the raft, so now the blankets and all the traps was out of the reach of steamboat waves. Right in the middle of the wigwam we made a layer of dirt about five or six inches deep with a frame around it for to hold it to its place; this was to build a fire on in sloppy weather or chilly; the wigwam would keep it from being seen. We made an extra steering oar, too, because one of the others might get broke, on a snag or something. We fixed up a short forked stick to hang the old lantern on; because we must always light the lantern whenever we see a steamboat coming down stream, to keep from getting run over; but we wouldn't have to light it for up-stream boats unless we see we was in what they call a "crossing;" for the river was pretty high yet, very low banks being still a little under water; so up-bound boats didn't always run the channel, but hunted easy water.

This second night we run between seven and eight hours, with a current that was making over four mile an hour. We catched fish, and talked, and we took a swim now and then to keep off sleepiness. It was kind of solemn, drifting down the big still river, laying on our backs looking up at the stars, and we didn't ever feel like talking loud, and it warn't often that we laughed, only a little kind of a low chuckle. We had mighty good weather, as a general thing, and nothing ever happened to us at all, that night, nor the next, nor the next.

Every night we passed towns, some of them away up on black hill-sides, nothing but just a shiny bed of lights, not a house could you see. The fifth night we passed St. Louis, and it was like the whole world lit up. In St. Petersburg they used to say there was twenty or thirty thousand people in St. Louis, but I never believed it till I see that wonderful spread of lights at two o'clock that still night. There warn't a sound there; everybody was asleep.

Every night, now, I used to slip ashore, towards ten o'clock, at some little village, and buy ten or fifteen cents' worth of meal or bacon or other stuff to eat; and sometimes I lifted a chicken that warn't roosting comfortable, and took him along. Pap always said, take a chicken when you get a chance, because if you don't want him yourself you can easy find somebody that does, and a good deed ain't ever forgot. I never see pap when he didn't want the chicken himself, but that is what he used to say, anyway.

Mornings, before daylight, I slipped into corn fields and borrowed a watermelon, or a mushmelon, or a punkin, or some new corn, or things of that kind. Pap always said it warn't no harm to borrow things, if you was meaning to pay them back, sometime; but the widow said it warn't anything but a soft name for stealing, and no decent body would do it. Jim said he reckoned the widow was partly right and pap was partly right; so the best way would be for us to pick out two or three things from the list and say we wouldn't borrow them anymore — then he reckoned it wouldn't be no harm to borrow the others. So we talked it over all one night, drifting along down the river, trying to make up our minds whether to drop the watermelons, or the cantelopes, or the mush-melons, or what. But towards daylight we got it all settled satisfactory, and concluded to drop crabapples and p'simmons. We warn't feeling just right, before that, but it was all comfortable now. I was glad the way it come out, too, because crabapples ain't ever good, and the p'simmons wouldn't be ripe for two or three months yet.

We shot a water-fowl, now and then, that got up too early in the morning or didn't go to bed early enough in the evening. Take it all around, we lived pretty high.

The fifth night below St. Louis we had a big storm after midnight, with a power of thunder and lightning, and the rain poured down in a solid sheet. We stayed in the wigwam and let the raft take care of itself. When the lightning glared out we could see a big straight river ahead, and high rocky bluffs on both sides. By-and-by says I, "Hel-*lo*, Jim, looky yonder!" It was a steamboat that had killed herself on a rock. We was drifting straight down for her. The lightning showed her very distinct. She was leaning over, with part of her upper deck above water, and you could see every little chimbly-guy clean and clear, and a chair by the big bell, with an old slouch hat hanging on the back of it when the flashes come.

Well, it being away in the night, and stormy, and all so mysterious-like, I felt just the way any other boy would a felt when I see that wreck laying there so mournful and lonesome in the middle of the river. I wanted to get aboard of her and slink around a little, and see what there was there. So I says:

"Le's land on her, Jim."

But Jim was dead against it, at first. He says:

"I doan' want to go fool'n 'long er no wrack. We's doin' blame' well, en we better let blame' well alone, as de good book says. Like as not dey's a watchman on dat wrack."

"Watchman your grandmother," I says; "there ain't nothing to watch but the texas and the pilot-house; and do you reckon anybody's going to resk his life for a texas and a pilot-house such a night as this, when it's likely to break up and wash off down the river any minute?" Jim couldn't say nothing to that, so he didn't try. "And besides," I says, "we might borrow something worth having, out of the captain's stateroom. Seegars, I bet you — and cost five cents apiece, solid cash. Steamboat captains is always rich, and get sixty dollars a month, and *they* don't care a cent what a thing costs, you know, long as they want it. Stick a candle in your pocket; I can't rest, Jim, till we give her a rummaging. Do you reckon Tom Sawyer would ever go by this thing? Not for pie, he wouldn't. He'd call it an adventure — that's what he'd call it; and he'd land on that wreck if it was his last act. And wouldn't he throw style into it? — wouldn't he spread himself, nor nothing? Why, you'd think it was Christopher C'lumbus discovering Kingdom-Come. I wish Tom Sawyer *was* here."

Jim he grumbled a little, but give in. He said we mustn't talk any more than we could help, and then talk mighty low. The lightning showed us the wreck again, just in time, and we fetched the starboard derrick, and made fast there.

The deck was high out, here. We went sneaking down the slope of it to labboard, in the dark, towards the texas, feeling our way slow with our feet, and spreading our hands out to fend off the guys, for it was so dark we couldn't see no sign of them. Pretty soon we struck the forward end of the skylight, and clumb onto it; and the next step fetched us in front of the captain's door, which was open, and by Jimminy, away down through the texas-hall we see a light! and all in the same second we seem to hear low voices in yonder!

Jim whispered and said he was feeling powerful sick, and told me to come along. I says, all right; and was going to start for the raft; but just then I heard a voice wail out and say:

"Oh, please don't, boys; I swear I won't ever tell!"

Another voice said, pretty loud:

"It's a lie, Jim Turner. You've acted this way before. You always want more'n your share of the truck, and you've always got it, too, because you've swore 't if you didn't you'd tell. But this time you've said it jest one time too many. You're the meanest, treacherousest hound in this country."

By this time Jim was gone for the raft. I was just a-biling with curiosity; and I says to myself, Tom Sawyer wouldn't back out now, and so I won't either; I'm agoing to see what's going on here. So I dropped on my hands and knees, in the little passage, and crept aft in the dark, till there warn't but about one stateroom betwixt me and the cross-hall of the texas. Then, in there I see a man stretched on the floor and tied hand and foot, and two men standing over him, and one of them had a dim lantern in his hand, and the other one had a pistol. This one kept pointing the pistol at the man's head on the floor and saying —

"I'd *like* to! And I orter, too, a mean skunk!"

The man on the floor would shrivel up, and say: "Oh, please don't, Bill — I hain't ever goin' to tell."

And every time he said that, the man with the lantern would laugh, and say:

" 'Deed you *ain't!* You never said no truer thing 'n that, you bet you." And once he said: "Hear him beg! and yit if we hadn't got the best of him and tied him, he'd a killed us both. And what *for?* Jist for noth'n. Jist because we stood on our *rights* — that's what for. But I lay you ain't agoin' to threaten nobody any more, Jim Turner. Put *up* that pistol, Bill."

Bill says:

"I don't want to, Jake Packard. I'm for killin' him — and didn't he kill old Hatfield jist the same way — and don't he deserve it?"

"But I don't *want* him killed, and I've got my reasons for it."

"Bless yo' heart for them words, Jake Packard! I'll never forget you, long's I live!" says the man on the floor, sort of blubbering.

Packard didn't take no notice of that, but hung up his lantern on a nail, and started towards where I was, there in the dark, and motioned Bill to come. I crawfished as fast as I could, about two yards, but the boat slanted so that I couldn't make very good time; so to keep from getting run over and catched I crawled into a stateroom on the upper side. The men come a-pawing along in the dark, and when Packard got to my stateroom, he says:

"Here — come in here."

And in he come, and Bill after him. But before they got in, I was up in the upper berth, cornered, and sorry I come. Then they stood there, with their hands on the ledge of the berth, and talked. I couldn't see them, but I could tell where they was, by the whisky they'd been having. I was glad I didn't drink whisky; but it wouldn't made much difference, anyway, because most of the time they couldn't a treed me because I didn't breathe. I was too scared. And besides, a body *couldn't* breathe, and hear such talk. They talked low and earnest. Bill wanted to kill Turner. He says:

"He's said he'll tell, and he will. If we was to give both our shares to him *now*, it wouldn't make no difference after the row, and the way we've served him. Shore's you're born, he'll turn State's evidence; now you hear *me*. I'm for putting him out of his troubles."

"So'm I," says Packard, very quiet.

"Blame it, I'd sorter begun to think you wasn't. Well, then, that's all right. Les' go and do it."

"Hold on a minute; I hain't had my say yit. You listen to me. Shooting's good, but there's quieter ways if the thing's *got* to be done. But what I say, is this; it ain't good sense to go court'n around after a halter, if you can git at what you're up to in some way that's jist as good and at the same time don't bring you into no resks. Ain't that so?"

"You bet it is. But how you goin' to manage it this time?"

"Well, my idea is this: we'll rustle around and gether up whatever pickins we've overlooked in the staterooms, and shove for shore and hide the truck. Then we'll wait. Now I say it ain't agoin' to be more 'n two hours befo' this wrack breaks up and washes off down the river. See? He'll be drownded, and won't have nobody to blame for it but his own self. I reckon that's a considerable sight better'n killin' of him. I'm unfavorable to killin' a man as long as you can git around it; it ain't good sense, it ain't good morals. Ain't I right?"

"Yes — I reck'n you are. But s'pose she *don't* break up and wash off?"

"Well, we can wait the two hours, anyway, and see, can't we?"

"All right, then; come along."

So they started, and I lit out, all in a cold sweat, and scrambled forward. It was dark as pitch there; but I said in a kind of a coarse whisper, "Jim!" and he answered up, right at my elbow, with a sort of a moan, and I says:

"Quick, Jim, it ain't no time for fooling around and moaning; there's a gang of murderers in yonder, and if we don't hunt up their boat and set her drifting down the river so these fellows can't get away from the wreck, there's one of 'em going to be in a bad fix. But if we find their boat we can put *all* of 'em in a bad fix — for the Sheriff 'll get 'em. Quick — hurry! I'll hunt the labboard side, you hunt the stabboard. You start at the raft, and ——"

"Oh, my lordy, lordy! *Raf*'? Dey ain' no raf' no mo', she done broke loose en gone! — 'en here we is!"

Chapter XIII

Well, I catched my breath and most fainted. Shut up on a wreck with such a gang as that! But it warn't no time to be sentimentering. We'd *got* to find that boat, now — had to have it for ourselves. So we went a-quaking and shaking down the stabboard side, and slow work it was, too — seemed a week before we got to the stern. No sign of a boat. Jim said he didn't believe he could go any further — so scared he hadn't hardly any strength left, he said. But I said come on, if we get left on this wreck, we are in a fix, sure. So on we prowled, again. We struck for the stern of the texas, and found it, and then scrabbled along forwards on the skylight, hanging on from shutter to shutter, for the edge of the skylight was in the water. When we got pretty close to the cross-hall door, there was the skiff, sure enough! I could just barely see her. I felt ever so thankful. In another second I would a been aboard of her; but just then the door opened. One of the men stuck his head out, only about a couple of foot from me, and I thought I was gone; but he jerked it in again, and says:

"Heave that blame lantern out o' sight, Bill!"

He flung a bag of something into the boat, and then got in himself, and set down. It was Packard. Then Bill *he* come out and got in. Packard says, in a low voice:

"All ready — shove off!"

I couldn't hardly hang onto the shutters, I was so weak. But Bill says:

"Hold on — 'd you go through him?"

"No. Didn't you?"

"No. So he's got his share o' the cash, yet."

"Well, then, come along — no use to take truck and leave money."

"Say — won't he suspicion what we're up to?"

"Maybe he won't. But we got to have it anyway. Come along."

So they got out and went in.

The door slammed to, because it was on the careened side; and in a half second I was in the boat, and Jim come a tumbling after me. I out with my knife and cut the rope, and away we went!

We didn't touch an oar, and we didn' speak nor whisper, nor hardly even breathe. We went gliding swift along, dead silent, past the tip of the paddle-box, and past the stern; then in a second or two more we was a hundred yards below the wreck, and the darkness soaked her up, every last sign of her, and we was safe, and knowed it.

When we was three or four hundred yards down stream, we see the lantern show like a little spark at the texas door, for a second, and we knowed by that that the rascals had missed their boat, and was beginning to understand that they was in just as much trouble, now, as Jim Turner was.

Then Jim manned the oars, and we took out after our raft. Now was the first time that I begun to worry about the men — I reckon I hadn't had time to before. I begun to think how dreadful it was, even for murderers, to be in such a fix. I says to myself, there ain't no telling but I might come to be a murderer myself, yet, and then how would *I* like it? So says I to Jim:

"The first light we see, we'll land a hundred yards below it or above it, in a place where it's a good hiding-place for you and the skiff, and then I'll go and fix up some kind of a yarn, and get somebody to go for that gang and get them out of their scrape, so they can be hung when their time comes."

But that idea was a failure; for pretty soon it begun to storm again, and this time worse than ever. The rain poured down, and never a light showed; everybody in bed, I reckon. We boomed along down the river, watching for lights and watching for our raft. After a long time the rain let up, but the clouds staid, and the lightning kept whimpering, and by-and-by a flash showed us a black thing ahead, floating, and we made for it.

It was the raft, and mighty glad was we to get aboard of it again. We seen a light, now, away down to the right, on shore. So I said I would go for it. The skiff was half full of plunder which that gang had stole, there on the wreck. We hustled it onto the raft in a pile, and I told Jim to float along down, and show a light when he judged he had gone about two mile, and keep it burning till I come; then I manned my oars and shoved for the light. As I got down towards it, three or four more showed — up on a hillside. It was a village. I closed in above the shore-light, and laid on my oars and floated. As I went by, I see it was a lantern hanging on the jackstaff of a double-hull ferry-boat. I skimmed around for the watchman, a-wondering whereabouts he slept; and by-and-by I found him roosting on the bitts, forward, with his head down between his knees. I give his shoulder two or three little shoves, and begun to cry.

He stirred up, in a kind of a startlish way; but when he see it was only me, he took a good gap and stretch, and then he says:

"Hello, what's up? Don't cry, bub. What's the trouble?"

I says:

"Pap, and mam, and sis, and ——"

Then I broke down. He says:

"Oh, dang it, now, *don't* take on so, we all has to have our troubles and this'n 'll come out all right. What's the matter with 'em?"

"They're — they're — are you the watchman of the boat?"

"Yes," he says, kind of pretty-well-satisfied like. "I'm the captain and the owner, and the mate, and the pilot, and watchman, and head deck-hand; and sometimes I'm the freight and passengers. I ain't as rich as old Jim Hornback, and I can't be so blame' generous and good to Tom, Dick and Harry as what he is, and slam around money the way he does; but I've told him a many a time 't I wouldn't trade places with him; for, says I, a sailor's life's the life for me, and I'm derned if I'*d* live two mile out o' town, where there ain't nothing ever goin' on, not for all his spondulicks and as much more on top of it. Says I ——"

I broke in and says:

"They're in an awful peck of trouble, and ——"

"*Who* is?"

"Why, pap, and mam, and sis, and Miss Hooker; and if you'd take your ferry-boat and go up there ——"

"Up where? Where are they?"

"On the wreck."

"What wreck?"

"Why, there ain't but one."

"What, you don't mean the *Walter Scott?*"

"Yes."

"Good land! what are they doin' *there*, for gracious sakes?"

"Well, they didn't go there a-purpose."

"I bet they didn't! Why, great goodness, there ain't no chance for 'em if they don't git off mighty quick! Why, how in the nation did they ever git into such a scrape?"

"Easy enough. Miss Hooker was a-visiting, up there to the town ——"

"Yes, Booth's Landing — go on."

"She was a-visiting, there at Booth's Landing, and just in the edge of the evening she started over with her nigger woman in the horse-ferry, to stay all night at her friend's house, Miss What-you-may-call-her, I disremember her name, and they lost their steering-oar, and swung around and went a-floating down, stern-first, about two mile, and saddle-baggsed on the wreck, and the ferry man and the nigger woman and the horses was all lost, but Miss Hooker she made a grab and got aboard the wreck. Well, about an hour after dark, we come along down in our trading-scow, and it was so dark we didn't notice the wreck till we was right on it; and so *we* saddle-baggsed; but all of us was saved but Bill Whipple — and oh, he *was* the best cretur! — I most wish't it had been me, I do."

"My George! It's the beatenest thing I ever struck. And *then* what did you all do?"

"Well, we hollered and took on, but it's so wide there, we couldn't make nobody hear. So pap said somebody got to get ashore and get help somehow. I was the only one that could swim, so I made a dash for it, and Miss Hooker she said if I didn't strike help sooner, come here and hunt up her uncle, and he'd fix the thing. I made the land about a mile below, and been fooling along ever since, trying to get people to do something, but they said, 'What, in such a night and such a current? there ain't no sense in it; go for the steam-ferry.' Now if you'll go, and ——"

"By Jackson, I'd *like* to, and blame it I don't know but I will; but who in the dingnation's agoin' to *pay* for it? Do you reckon your pap ——"

"Why *that's* all right. Miss Hooker she told me, *particular*, that her uncle Hornback ——"

"Great guns! is *he* her uncle? Looky here, you break for that light over yonder-way, and turn out west when you git there, and about a quarter of a mile out you'll come to the tavern; tell 'em to dart you out to Jim Hornback's and he'll foot the bill. And don't you fool around any, because he'll want to know the news. Tell him I'll have his niece all safe before he can get to town. Hump yourself, now; I'm agoing up around the corner here, to roust out my engineer."

I struck for the light, but as soon as he turned the corner I went back and got into my skiff and bailed her out and then pulled up shore in the easy water about six hundred yards, and tucked myself in among some woodboats; for I couldn't rest easy till I could see the ferry-boat start. But take it all around, I was feeling ruther comfortable on accounts of taking all this trouble for that gang, for not many would a done it. I wished the widow knowed about it. I judged she would be proud of me for helping these rapscallions, because rapscallions and dead beats is the kind the widow and good people takes the most interest in.

Well, before long, here comes the wreck, dim and dusky, sliding along down! A kind of cold shiver went through me, and then I struck out for her. She was very deep, and I see in a minute there warn't much chance for anybody being alive in her. I pulled all around her and hollered a little, but there wasn't any answer; all dead still. I felt a little bit heavy-hearted about the gang, but not much, for I reckoned if they could stand it, I could.

Then here comes the ferry-boat; so I shoved for the middle of the river on a long down-stream slant; and when I judged I was out of eye-reach, I laid on my oars, and looked back and see her go and smell around the wreck for Miss Hooker's remainders, because the captain would know her uncle Hornback would want them; and then pretty soon the ferry-boat give it up and went for shore, and I laid into my work and went a-booming down the river.

It did seem a powerful long time before Jim's light showed up; and when it did show, it looked like it was a thousand mile off. By the time I got there the sky was beginning to get a little gray in the east; so we struck for an island, and hid the raft, and sunk the skiff, and turned in and slept like dead people.

Chapter XIV

By-and-by, when we got up, we turned over the truck the gang had stole off of the wreck, and found boots, and blankets, and clothes, and all sorts of other things, and a lot of books, and a spyglass, and three boxes of seegars. We hadn't ever been this rich before, in neither of our lives. The seegars was prime. We laid off all the afternoon in the woods talking, and me reading the books, and having a general good time. I told Jim all about what happened inside the wreck, and at the ferry-boat; and I said these kinds of things was adventures; but he said he didn't want no more adventures. He said that when I went in the texas and he crawled back to get on the raft and found her gone, he nearly died; because he judged it was all up with *him*, anyway it could be fixed; for if he didn't get saved he would get drownded; and if he did get saved, whoever saved him would send him back home so as to get the reward, and then Miss Watson would sell him South, sure. Well, he was right; he was most always right; he had an uncommon level head, for a nigger.

I read considerable to Jim about kings, and dukes, and earls, and such, and how gaudy they dressed, and how much style they put on, and called each other your majesty, and your grace, and your lordship, and so on, 'stead of mister; and Jim's eyes bugged out, and he was interested. He says:

"I didn' know dey was so many un um. I hain't hearn 'bout none un um, skasely, but ole King Sollermun, onless you counts dem kings dat's in a pack er k'yards. How much do a king git?"

"Get?" I says; "why, they get a thousand dollars a month if they want it; they can have just as much as they want; everything belongs to them."

"*Ain*' dat gay? En what dey got to do, Huck?"

"*They* don't do nothing! Why how you talk. They just set around."

"No — is dat so?"

"Of course it is. They just set around. Except maybe when there's a war; then they go to the war. But other times they just lazy around; or go hawking — just hawking and sp — Sh! — d' you hear a noise?"

We skipped out and looked; but it warn't nothing but the flutter of a steamboat's wheel, away down coming around the point; so we come back.

"Yes," says I, "and other times, when things is dull, they fuss with the parlyment; and if everybody don't go just so he whacks their heads off. But mostly they hang round the harem."

"Roun' de which?"

"Harem."

"What's de harem?"

"The place where he keep his wives. Don't you know about the harem? Solomon had one; he had about a million wives."

"Why, yes, dat's so; I — I'd done forgot it. A harem's a bo'd'n-house, I reck'n. Mos' likely dey has rackety times in de nussery. En I reck'n de wives quarrels considable; en dat 'crease de racket. Yit dey say Sollermun de wises' man dat ever live'. I doan' take no stock in dat. Bekase why: would a wise man want to live in de mids' er sich a blimblammin' all de time? No — 'deed he wouldn't. A wise man 'ud take en buil' a biler-factry; en den he could shet *down* de biler-factry when he want to res'."

"Well, but he *was* the wisest man, anyway; because the widow she told me so, her own self."

"I doan k'yer what de widder say, he *warn't* no wise man, nuther. He had some er de dad-fetchedes' ways I ever see. Does you know 'bout dat chile dat he 'uz gwyne to chop in two?"

"Yes, the widow told me all about it."

"*Well*, den! Warn' dat de beatenes' notion in de worl'? You jes' take en look at it a minute. Dah's de stump, dah — dat's one er de women; heah's you — dat's de yuther one; I's Sollermun; en dish-yer dollar bill's de chile. Bofe un you claims it. What does I do? Does I shin aroun' mongs' de neighbors en fine out which un you de bill *do* b'long to, en han' it over to de right one, all safe en soun', de way dat anybody dat had any gumption would? No — I take en whack de bill in *two*, en give half un it to you, en de yuther half to de yuther woman. Dat's de way Sollermun was gwyne to do wid de chile. Now I want to ast you: what's de use er dat half a bill? — can't buy noth'n wid it. En what use is a half a chile? I would'n give a dern for a million un um."

"But hang it, Jim, you've clean missed the point — blame it, you've missed it a thousand mile."

"Who? Me? Go 'long. Doan' talk to *me* 'bout yo' pints. I reck'n I knows sense when I sees it; en dey ain' no sense in sich doin's as dat. De 'spute warn't 'bout a half a chile, de 'spute was 'bout a whole chile; en de man dat think he kin settle a 'spute 'bout a whole chile wid a half a chile, doan' know enough to come in out'n de rain. Doan' talk to me 'bout Sollermun, Huck, I knows him by de back."

"But I tell you you don't get the point."

"Blame de pint! I reck'n I knows what I knows. En mine you, de *real* pint is down furder — it's down deeper. It lays in de way Sollermun was raised. You take a man dat's got on'y one er two chillen; is dat man gwyne to be waseful o' chillen? No, he ain't; he can't 'ford it. *He* know how to value 'em. But you take a man dat's got 'bout five million chillen runnin' roun' de house, en it's diffunt. *He* as soon chop a chile in two as a cat. Dey's plenty mo'. A chile er two, mo' er less, warn't no consekens to Sollermun, dad fetch him!"

I never see such a nigger. If he got a notion in his head once, there warn't no getting it out again. He was the most down on Solomon of any nigger I ever see. So I went to talking about other kings, and let Solomon slide. I told about Louis Sixteenth that got his head cut off in France long time ago; and about his little boy the dolphin, that would a been a king, but they took and shut him up in jail, and some say he died there.

"Po' little chap."

"But some says he got out and got away, and come to America."

"Dat's good! But he'll be pooty lonesome — dey ain' no kings here, is dey, Huck?"

"No."

"Den he cain't git no situation. What he gwyne to do?"

"Well, I don't know. Some of them gets on the police, and some of them learns people how to talk French."

"Why, Huck, doan' de French people talk de same way we does?"

"No, Jim; you couldn't understand a word they said — not a single word."

"Well, now, I be ding-busted! How do dat come?"

"*I* don't know; but it's so. I got some of their jabber out of a book. Spose a man was to come to you and say *Polly-voo-franzy* — what would you think?"

"I wouldn' think nuff'n; I'd take en bust him over de head. Dat is, if he warn't white. I wouldn't 'low no nigger to call me dat."

"Shucks, it ain't calling you anything. It's only saying do you know how to talk French."

"Well, den, why couldn't he *say* it?"

"Why, he *is* a-saying it. That's a Frenchman's *way* of saying it."

"Well, it's a blame' ridicklous way, en I doan' want to hear no mo' 'bout it. Dey ain' no sense in it."

"Looky here, Jim; does a cat talk like we do?"

"No, a cat don't."

"Well, does a cow?"

"No, a cow don't, nuther."

"Does a cat talk like a cow, or a cow talk like a cat?"

"No, dey don't."

"It's natural and right for 'em to talk different from each other, ain't it?"

" 'Course."

"And ain't it natural and right for a cat and a cow to talk different from *us*?"

"Why, mos' sholy it is."

"Well, then, why ain't it natural and right for a *Frenchman* to talk different from us? You answer me that."

"Is a cat a man, Huck?"

"No."

"Well, den, dey ain't no sense in a cat talkin' like a man. Is a cow a man? — er is a cow a cat?"

"No, she ain't either of them."

"Well, den, she ain' got no business to talk like either one er the yuther of 'em. Is a Frenchman a man?"

"Yes."

"*Well*, den! Dad blame it, why doan' he *talk* like a man? You answer me *dat!*"

I see it warn't no use wasting words — you can't learn a nigger to argue. So I quit.

Chapter XV

We judged that three nights more would fetch us to Cairo, at the bottom of Illinois, where the Ohio River comes in, and that was what we was after. We would sell the raft and get on a steamboat and go way up the Ohio amongst the free States, and then be out of trouble.

Well, the second night a fog begun to come on, and we made for a tow-head to tie to, for it wouldn't do to try to run in fog; but when I paddled ahead in the canoe, with the line, to make fast, there warn't anything but little saplings to tie to. I passed the line around one of them right on the edge of the cut bank, but there was a stiff current, and the raft come booming down so lively she tore it out by the roots and away she went. I see the fog closing down, and it made me so sick and scared I couldn't budge for most a half a minute it seemed to me — and then there warn't no raft in sight; you couldn't see twenty yards. I jumped into the canoe and run back to the stern and grabbed the paddle and set her back a stroke. But she didn't come. I was in such a hurry I hadn't untied her. I got up and tried to untie her, but I was so excited my hands shook so I couldn't hardly do anything with them.

As soon as I got started I took out after the raft, hot and heavy, right down the tow-head. That was all right as far as it went, but the tow-head warn't sixty yards long, and the minute I flew by the foot of it I shot out into the solid white fog, and hadn't no more idea which way I was going than a dead man.

Thinks I, it won't do to paddle; first I know I'll run into the bank or a tow-head or something; I got to set still and float, and yet it's mighty fidgety business to have to hold your hands still at such a time. I whooped and listened. Away down there, somewheres, I hears a small whoop, and up comes my spirits. I went tearing after it, listening sharp to hear it again. The next time it come, I see I warn't heading for it but heading away to the right of it. And the next time, I was heading away to the left of it — and not gaining on it much, either, for I was flying around, this way and that and 'tother, but it was going straight ahead all the time.

I did wish the fool would think to beat a tin pan, and beat it all the time, but he never did, and it was the still places between the whoops that was making the trouble for me. Well, I fought along, and directly I hears the whoop *behind* me. I was tangled good, now. That was somebody else's whoop, or else I was turned around.

I throwed the paddle down. I heard the whoop again; it was behind me yet, but in a different place; it kept coming, and kept changing its place, and I kept answering, till by-and-by it was in front of me again and I knowed the current had swung the canoe's head down stream and I was all right, if that was Jim and not some other raftsman hollering. I couldn't tell nothing about voices in a fog, for nothing don't look natural nor sound natural in a fog.

The whooping went on, and in about a minute I come a booming down on a cut bank with smoky ghosts of big trees on it, and the current threw me off to the left and shot by, amongst a lot of snags that fairly roared, the current was tearing by them so swift.

In another second or two it was solid white and still again. I set perfectly still, then, listening to my heart thump, and I reckon I didn't draw a breath while it thumped a hundred.

I just give up, then: I knowed what the matter was. That cut bank was an island, and Jim had gone down 'tother side of it. It warn't no tow-head, that you could float by in ten minutes. It had the big timber of a regular island; it might be five or six mile long and more than a half a mile wide.

I kept quiet, with my ears cocked, about fifteen minutes, I reckon. I was floating along, of course, four or five mile an hour; but you don't ever think of that. No, you *feel* like you are laying dead still on the water; and if a little glimpse of a snag slips by, you don't think to yourself how fast *you're* going, but you catch your breath and think, my! how that snag's tearing along. If you think it ain't dismal and lonesome out in a fog that way, by yourself, in the night, you try it once — you'll see.

Next, for about a half an hour, I whoops now and then; at last I hears the answer a long ways off, and tries to follow it, but I couldn't do it, and directly I judged I'd got into a nest of tow-heads, for I had little dim glimpses of them on both sides of me, sometimes just a narrow channel between; and some that I couldn't see, I knowed was there, because I'd hear the wash of the current against the old dead brush and trash that hung over the banks. Well, I warn't long losing the whoops, down amongst the tow-heads; and I only tried to chase them a little while, anyway, because it was worse than chasing a Jack-o-lantern. You never knowed a sound dodge around so, and swap places so quick and so much.

I had to claw away from the bank pretty lively, four or five times, to keep from knocking the islands out of the river; and so I judged the raft must be butting into the bank every now and then, or else it would get further ahead and clear out of hearing — it was floating a little faster than what I was.

Well, I seemed to be in the open river again, by-and-by, but I couldn't hear no sign of a whoop nowheres. I reckoned Jim had fetched up on a snag, maybe, and it was all up with him. I was good and tired, so I laid down in the canoe and said I wouldn't bother no more. I didn't want to go to sleep, of course; but I was so sleepy I couldn't help it; so I thought I would take just one little cat-nap.

But I reckon it was more than a cat-nap, for when I waked up the stars was shining bright, the fog was all gone, and I was spinning down a big bend stern first. First I didn't know where I was; I thought I was dreaming; and when things begun to come back to me, they seemed to come up dim out of last week.

It was a monstrous big river here, with the tallest and the thickest kind of timber on both banks; just a solid wall, as well as I could see, by the stars. I looked away down stream, and seen a black speck on the water. I took out after it; but when I got to it it warn't nothing but a couple of saw-logs made fast together. Then I see another speck, and chased that; then another, and this time I was right. It was the raft.

When I got to it Jim was setting there with his head down between his knees, asleep, with his right arm hanging over the steering oar. The other oar was smashed off, and the raft was littered up with leaves and branches and dirt. So she'd had a rough time.

I made fast and laid down under Jim's nose on the raft, and begun to gap, and stretch my fists out against Jim, and says:

"Hello, Jim, have I been asleep? Why didn't you stir me up?"

"Goodness gracious, is dat you, Huck? En you ain' dead — you ain' drownded — you's back agin? It's too good for true, honey, it's too good for true. Lemme look at you, chile, lemme feel o' you. No, you ain' dead! you's back agin, live en soun', jis de same ole Huck — de same ole Huck, thanks to goodness!"

"What's the matter with you, Jim? You been a drinking?"

"Drinkin'? Has I ben a drinkin'? Has I had a chance to be a drinkin'?"

"Well, then, what makes you talk so wild?"

"How does I talk wild?"

"*How?* why, hain't you been talking about my coming back, and all that stuff, as if I'd been gone away?"

"Huck — Huck Finn, you look me in de eye; look me in de eye. *Hain't* you ben gone away?"

"Gone away? Why, what in the nation do you mean? *I* hain't been gone anywheres. Where would I go to?"

"Well, looky here, boss, dey's sumf'n wrong, dey is. Is I *me*, or who *is* I? Is I heah, or whah *is* I? Now dat's what I wants to know?"

"Well, I think you're here, plain enough, but I think you're a tangle-headed old fool, Jim."

"I is, is I? Well you answer me dis. Didn't you tote out de line in de canoe, fer to make fas' to de tow-head?"

"No, I didn't. What tow-head? I hain't seen no tow-head."

"You hain't seen no tow-head? Looky here — didn't de line pull loose en de raf' go a hummin' down de river, en leave you en de canoe behine in de fog?"

"What fog?"

"Why *de* fog. De fog dat's ben aroun' all night. En didn't you whoop, en didn't I whoop, tell we got mix' up in de islands en one un us got los' en 'tother one was jis' as good as los', 'kase he didn' know whah he wuz? En didn't I bust up agin a lot er dem islands en have a turrible time en mos' git drownded? Now ain' dat so, boss—ain't it so? You answer me dat."

"Well, this is too many for me, Jim. I hain't seen no fog, nor no islands, nor no troubles, nor nothing. I been setting here talking with you all night till you went to sleep about ten minutes ago, and I reckon I done the same. You couldn't a got drunk in that time, so of course you've been dreaming."

"Dad fetch it, how is I gwyne to dream all dat in ten minutes?"

"Well, hang it all, you did dream it, because there didn't any of it happen."

"But Huck, it's all jis' as plain to me as——"

"It don't make no difference how plain it is, there ain't nothing in it. I know, because I've been here all the time."

Jim didn't say nothing for about five minutes, but set there studying over it. Then he says:

"Well, den, I reck'n I did dream it, Huck; but dog my cats ef it ain't de powerfullest dream I ever see. En I hain't ever had no dream b'fo' dat's tired me like dis one."

"Oh, well, that's all right, because a dream does tire a body like everything, sometimes. But this one was a staving dream—tell me all about it, Jim."

So Jim went to work and told me the whole thing right through, just as it happened, only he painted it up considerable. Then he said he must start in and " 'terpret" it, because it was sent for a warning. He said the first tow-head stood for a man that would try to do us some good, but the current was another man that would get us away from him. The whoops was warnings that would come to us every now and then, and if we didn't try hard to make out to understand them they'd just take us into bad luck, 'stead of keeping us out of it. The lot of tow-heads was troubles we was going to get into with quarrelsome people and all kinds of mean folks, but if we minded our business and didn't talk back and aggravate them, we would pull through and get out of the fog and into the big clear river, which was the free States, and wouldn't have no more trouble.

It had clouded up pretty dark just after I got onto the raft, but it was clearing up again, now.

"Oh, well, that's all interpreted well enough, as far as it goes, Jim," I says; "but what does *these* things stand for?"

It was the leaves and rubbish on the raft, and the smashed oar. You could see them first rate, now.

Jim looked at the trash, and then looked at me, and back at the trash again. He had got the dream fixed so strong in his head that he couldn't seem to shake it loose and get the facts back into its place again, right away. But when he did get the thing straightened around, he looked at me steady, without ever smiling, and says:

"What do dey stan' for? I's gwyne to tell you. When I got all wore out wid work, en wid de callin' for you, en went to sleep, my heart wuz mos' broke bekase you wuz los', en I didn' k'yer no mo' what become er me en de raf'. En when I wake up en fine you back agin', all safe en soun', de tears come en I could a got down on my knees en kiss' yo' foot I's so thankful. En all you wuz thinkin 'bout wuz how you could make a fool uv ole Jim wid a lie. Dat truck dah is *trash*; en trash is what people is dat puts dirt on de head er dey fren's en makes 'em ashamed."

Then he got up slow, and walked to the wigwam, and went in there, without saying anything but that. But that was enough. It made me feel so mean I could almost kissed *his* foot to get him to take it back.

It was fifteen minutes before I could work myself up to go and humble myself to a nigger — but I done it, and I warn't ever sorry for it afterwards, neither. I didn't do him no more mean tricks, and I wouldn't done that one if I'd a knowed it would make him feel that way.

Chapter XVI

We slept most all day, and started out at night, a little ways behind a monstrous long raft that was as long going by as a procession. She had four long sweeps at each end, so we judged she carried as many as thirty men, likely. She had five big wigwams aboard, wide apart, and an open camp fire in the middle, and a tall flag-pole at each end. There was a power of style about her. It *amounted* to something being a raftsman on such a craft as that.

We went drifting down into a big bend, and the night clouded up and got hot. The river was very wide, and was walled with solid timber on both sides; you couldn't see a break in it hardly ever, or a light. We talked about Cairo, and wondered whether we would know it when we got to it. I said likely we wouldn't, because I had heard say there warn't but about a dozen houses there, and if they didn't happen to have them lit up, how was we going to know we was passing a town? Jim said if the two big rivers joined together there, that would show. But I said maybe we might think we was passing the foot of an island and coming into the same old river again. That disturbed Jim — and me too. So the question was, what to do? I said, paddle ashore the first time a light showed, and tell them pap was behind, coming along with a trading-scow, and was a green hand at the business, and wanted to know how far it was to Cairo. Jim thought it was a good idea, so we took a smoke on it and waited.

There warn't nothing to do, now, but to look out sharp for the town, and not pass it without seeing it. He said he'd be mighty sure to see it, because he'd be a free man the minute he seen it, but if he missed it he'd be in the slave country again and no more show for freedom. Every little while he jumps up and says:

"Dah she is!"

But it warn't. It was Jack-o-lanterns, or lightning-bugs; so he set down again, and went to watching, same as before. Jim said it made him all over trembly and feverish to be so close to freedom. Well, I can tell you it made me all over trembly and feverish, too, to hear him, because I begun to get it through my head that he *was* most free — and who was to blame for it? Why, *me*. I couldn't get that out of my conscience, no how nor no way. It got to troubling me so I couldn't rest; I couldn't stay still in one place. It hadn't ever come home to me before, what this thing was that I was doing. But now it did; and it staid with me, and scorched me more and more. I tried to make out to myself that *I* warn't to blame, because *I* didn't run Jim off from his rightful owner; but it warn't no use, conscience up and says, every time, "But you knowed he was running for his freedom, and you could a paddled ashore and told somebody." That was so — I couldn't get around that, noway. That was where it pinched. Conscience says to me, "What had poor Miss Watson done to you, that you could see her nigger go off right under your eyes and never say one single word? What did that poor old woman do to you, that you could treat her so mean? Why, she tried to learn you your book, she tried to learn you your manners, she tried to be good to you every way she knowed how. *That's* what she done."

I got to feeling so mean and so miserable I most wished I was dead. I fidgeted up and down the raft, abusing myself to myself, and Jim was fidgeting up and down past me. We neither of us could keep still. Every time he danced around and says, "Dah's Cairo!" it went through me like a shot, and I thought if it *was* Cairo I reckoned I would die of miserableness.

Jim talked out loud all the time while I was talking to myself. He was saying how the first thing he would do when he got to a free State he would go to saving up money and never spend a single cent, and when he got enough he would buy his wife, which was owned on a farm close to where Miss Watson lived; and then they would both work to buy the two children, and if their master wouldn't sell them, they'd get an Ab'litionist to go and steal them.

It most froze me to hear such talk. He wouldn't ever dared to talk such talk in his life before. Just see what a difference it made in him the minute he judged he was about free. It was according to the old saying, "give a nigger an inch and he'll take an ell." Thinks I, this is what comes of my not thinking. Here was this nigger which I had as good as helped to run away, coming right out flat-footed and saying he would steal his children — children that belonged to a man I didn't even know; a man that hadn't ever done me no harm.

I was sorry to hear Jim say that, it was such a lowering of him. My conscience got to stirring me up hotter than ever, until at last I says to it, "Let up on me — it ain't too late, yet — I'll paddle ashore at the first light, and tell." I felt easy, and happy, and light as a feather, right off. All my troubles was gone. I went to looking out sharp for a light, and sort of singing to myself. By-and-by one showed. Jim sings out:

"We's safe, Huck, we's safe! Jump up and crack yo' heels, dat's de good ole Cairo at las', I jis knows it!"

I says:

"I'll take the canoe and go see, Jim. It mightn't be, you know."

He jumped and got the canoe ready, and put his old coat in the bottom for me to set on, and give me the paddle; and as I shoved off, he says:

"Pooty soon I'll be a-shout'n for joy, en I'll say, it's all on accounts o' Huck; I's a free man, en I couldn't ever ben free ef it hadn' ben for Huck; Huck done it. Jim won't ever forgit you, Huck; you's de bes' fren' Jim's ever had; en you's de *only* fren' ole Jim's got now."

I was paddling off, all in a sweat to tell on him; but when he says this, it seemed to kind of take the tuck all out of me. I went along slow then, and I warn't right down certain whether I was glad I started or whether I warn't. When I was fifty yards off, Jim says:

"Dah you goes, de ole true Huck; de on'y white genlman dat ever kep' his promise to ole Jim."

Well, I just felt sick. But I says, I *got* to do it — I can't get *out* of it. Right then, along comes a skiff with two men in it, with guns, and they stopped and I stopped. One of them says:

"What's that, yonder?"

"A piece of a raft," I says.

"Do you belong on it?"

"Yes, sir."

"Any men on it?"

"Only one, sir."

"Well, there's five niggers run off to-night, up yonder above the head of the bend. Is your man white or black?"

I didn't answer up prompt. I tried to, but the words wouldn't come. I tried, for a second or two, to brace up and out with it, but I warn't man enough — hadn't the spunk of a rabbit. I see I was weakening; so I just give up trying, and up and says —

"He's white."

"I reckon we'll go and see for ourselves."

"I wish you would," says I, "because it's pap that's there, and maybe you'd help me tow the raft ashore where the light is. He's sick — and so is mam and Mary Ann."

"Oh, the devil! we're in a hurry, boy. But I s'pose we've got to. Come — buckle to your paddle, and let's get along."

I buckled to my paddle and they laid to their oars. When we had made a stroke or two, I says:

"Pap'll be mighty much obleeged to you, I can tell you. Everybody goes away when I want them to help me tow the raft ashore, and I can't do it by myself."

"Well, that's infernal mean. Odd, too. Say, boy, what's the matter with your father?"

"It's the — a — the — well, it ain't anything, much."

They stopped pulling. It warn't but a mighty little ways to the raft, now. One says:

"Boy, that's a lie. What *is* the matter with your pap? Answer up square, now, and it'll be the better for you."

"I will, sir, I will, honest — but don't leave us, please. It's the — the — gentlemen, if you'll only pull ahead, and let me heave you the head-line, you won't have to come a-near the raft — please do."

"Set her back, John, set her back!" says one. They backed water. "Keep away, boy — keep to looard. Confound it, I just expect the wind has blowed it to us. Your pap's got the small-pox, and you know it precious well. Why didn't you come out and say so? Do you want to spread it all over?"

"Well," says I, a-blubbering, "I've told everybody before, and then they just went away and left us."

"Poor devil, there's something in that. We are right down sorry for you, but we — well, hang it, we don't want the small-pox, you see. Look here, I'll tell you what to do. Don't you try to land by yourself, or you'll smash everything to pieces. You float along down about twenty miles and you'll come to a town on the left-hand side of the river. It will be long after sun-up, then, and when you ask for help, you tell them your folks are all down with chills and fever. Don't be a fool again, and let people guess what is the matter. Now we're trying to do you a kindness; so you just put twenty miles between us, that's a good boy. It wouldn't do any good to land yonder where the light is—it's only a wood-yard. Say—I reckon your father's poor, and I'm bound to say he's in pretty hard luck. Here— I'll put a twenty dollar gold piece on this board, and you get it when it floats by. I feel mighty mean to leave you, but my kingdom! it won't do to fool with small-pox, don't you see?"

"Hold on, Parker," says the other man, "here's a twenty to put on the board for me. Good-bye, boy, you do as Mr. Parker told you, and you'll be all right."

"That's so, my boy—good-bye, good-bye. If you see any runaway niggers, you get help and nab them, and you can make some money by it."

"Good-bye, sir," says I, "I won't let no runaway niggers get by me if I can help it."

They went off, and I got aboard the raft, feeling bad and low, because I knowed very well I had done wrong, and I see it warn't no use for me to try to learn to do right; a body that don't get *started* right when he's little, ain't got no show—when the pinch comes there ain't nothing to back him up and keep him to his work, and so he gets beat. Then I thought a minute, and says to myself, hold on,—s'pose you'd a done right and give Jim up; would you felt better than what you do now? No, says I, I'd feel bad—I'd feel just the same way I do now. Well, then, says I, what's the use you learning to do right, when it's troublesome to do right and ain't no trouble to do wrong, and the wages is just the same? I was stuck. I couldn't answer that. So I reckoned I wouldn't bother no more about it, but after this always do whichever come handiest at the time.

I went into the wigwam; Jim warn't there. I looked all around; he warn't anywhere. I says:

"Jim!"

"Here I is, Huck. Is dey out o' sight yit? Don't talk loud."

He was in the river, under the stern oar, with just his nose out. I told him they was out of sight, so he come aboard. He says:

"I was a-listenin' to all de talk, en I slips into de river en was gwyne to shove for sho' if dey come aboard. Den I was gwyne to swim to de raf' agin when dey was gone. But lawsy, how you did fool 'em, Huck! Dat *wuz* de smartes' dodge! I tell you, chile, I 'speck it save' ole Jim—ole Jim ain't gwyne to forgit you for dat, honey."

Then we talked about the money. It was a pretty good raise, twenty dollars apiece. Jim said we could take deck passage on a steamboat now, and the money would last us as far as we wanted to go in the free States. He said twenty mile more warn't far for the raft to go, but he wished we was already there.

Towards daybreak we tied up, and Jim was mighty particular about hiding the raft good. Then he worked all day fixing things in bundles, and getting all ready to quit rafting.

That night about ten we hove in sight of the lights of a town away down in a left-hand bend.

I went off in the canoe, to ask about it. Pretty soon I found a man out in the river with a skiff, setting a trot-line. I ranged up and says:

"Mister, is that town Cairo?"

"Cairo? no. You must be a blame' fool."

"What town is it, mister?"

"If you want to know, go and find out. If you stay here botherin' around me for about a half a minute longer, you'll get something you won't want."

I paddled to the raft. Jim was awful disappointed, but I said never mind, Cairo would be the next place, I reckoned.

We passed another town before daylight, and I was going out again; but it was high ground, so I didn't go. No high ground about Cairo, Jim said. I had forgot it. We laid up for the day, on a tow-head tolerable close to the left-hand bank. I begun to suspicion something. So did Jim. I says:

"Maybe we went by Cairo in the fog that night."

He says:

"Doan' less' talk about it, Huck. Po' niggers can't have no luck. I awluz 'spected dat rattle-snake skin warn't done wid it's work."

"I wish I'd never seen that snake-skin, Jim — I do wish I'd never laid eyes on it."

"It ain't yo' fault, Huck; you didn' know. Don't you blame yo'self 'bout it."

When it was daylight, here was the clear Ohio water in shore, sure enough, and outside was the old regular Muddy! So it was all up with Cairo.

We talked it all over. It wouldn't do to take to the shore; we couldn't take the raft up the stream, of course. There warn't no way but to wait for dark, and start back in the canoe and take the chances. So we slept all day amongst the cotton-wood thicket, so as to be fresh for the work, and when we went back to the raft about dark the canoe was gone!

We didn't say a word for a good while. There warn't anything to say. We both knowed well enough it was some more work of the rattle-snake skin; so what was the use to talk about it? It would only look like we was finding fault, and that would be bound to fetch more bad luck — and keep on fetching it, too, till we knowed enough to keep still.

By-and-by we talked about what we better do, and found there warn't no way but just to go along down with the raft till we got a

chance to buy a canoe to go back in. We warn't going to borrow it
when there warn't anybody around, the way pap would do, for that
might set people after us.

So we shoved out, after dark, on the raft.

Anybody that don't believe yet, that it's foolishness to handle a snake-
skin, after all that that snake-skin done for us, will believe it now, if they
read on and see what more it done for us.

The place to buy canoes is off of rafts laying up at shore. But we didn't
see no rafts laying up; so we went along during three hours and more.
Well, the night got gray, and ruther thick, which is the next meanest
thing to fog. You can't tell the shape of the river, and you can't see no
distance. It got to be very late and still, and then along comes a steamboat up the river. We lit the lantern, and judged she would see it. Upstream boats didn't generly come close to us; they go out and follow the
bars and hunt for easy water under the reefs; but nights like this they bull
right up the channel against the whole river.

We could hear her pounding along, but we didn't see her good till she
was close. She aimed right for us. Often they do that and try to see how
close they can come without touching; sometimes the wheel bites off a
sweep, and then the pilot sticks his head out and laughs, and thinks he's
mighty smart. Well, here she comes, and we said she was going to try to
shave us; but she didn't seem to be sheering off a bit. She was a big one,
and she was coming in a hurry, too, looking like a black cloud with rows
of glow-worms around it; but all of a sudden she bulged out, big and
scary, with a long row of wide-open furnace doors shining like red-hot
teeth, and her monstrous bows and guards hanging right over us. There
was a yell at us, and a jingling of bells to stop the engines, a pow-wow of
cussing, and whistling of steam — and as Jim went overboard on one side
and I on the other, she come smashing straight through the raft.

I dived — and I aimed to find the bottom, too, for a thirty-foot wheel
had got to go over me, and I wanted it to have plenty of room. I could
always stay under water a minute; this time I reckon I staid under
water a minute and a half. Then I bounced for the top in a hurry, for I
was nearly busting. I popped out to my arm-pits and blowed the water
out of my nose, and puffed a bit. Of course there was a booming
current; and of course that boat started her engines again ten seconds
after she stopped them, for they never cared much for raftsmen; so now
she was churning along up the river, out of sight in the thick weather,
though I could hear her.

I sung out for Jim about a dozen times, but I didn't get any answer; so I
grabbed a plank that touched me while I was "treading water," and
struck out for shore, shoving it ahead of me. But I made out to see that

the drift of the current was towards the left-hand shore, which meant that I was in a crossing; so I changed off and went that way.

It was one of these long, slanting, two-mile crossings; so I was a good long time in getting over. I made a safe landing, and clum up the bank. I couldn't see but a little ways, but I went poking along over rough ground for a quarter of a mile or more, and then I run across a big old-fashioned double log house before I noticed it. I was going to rush by and get away, but a lot of dogs jumped out and went to howling and barking at me, and I knowed better than to move another peg.

Chapter XVII

In about half a minute somebody spoke out of a window, without putting his head out, and says:

"Be done, boys! Who's there?"

I says:

"It's me."

"Who's me?"

"George Jackson, sir."

"What do you want?"

"I don't want nothing, sir. I only want to go along by, but the dogs won't let me."

"What are you prowling around here this time of night, for — hey?"

"I warn't prowling around, sir; I fell overboard off of the steamboat."

"Oh, you did, did you? Strike a light there, somebody. What did you say your name was?"

"George Jackson, sir. I'm only a boy."

"Look here; if you're telling the truth, you needn't be afraid — nobody'll hurt you. But don't try to budge; stand right where you are. Rouse out Bob and Tom, some of you, and fetch the guns. George Jackson, is there anybody with you?"

"No, sir, nobody."

I heard the people stirring around in the house, now, and see a light. The man sung out:

"Snatch that light away, Betsy, you old fool — ain't you got any sense? Put it on the floor behind the front door. Bob, if you and Tom are ready, take your places."

"All ready."

"Now, George Jackson, do you know the Shepherdsons?"

"No, sir — I never heard of them."

"Well, that may be so, and it mayn't. Now, all ready. Step forward, George Jackson. And mind, don't you hurry — come mighty slow. If there's anybody with you, let him keep back — if he shows himself he'll be shot. Come along, now. Come slow; push the door open, yourself — just enough to squeeze in, d' you hear?"

I didn't hurry, I couldn't if I'd a wanted to. I took one slow step at a time, and there warn't a sound, only I thought I could hear my heart. The dogs were as still as the humans, but they followed a little behind me. When I got to the three log door-steps, I heard them unlocking and unbarring and unbolting. I put my hand on the door and pushed it a little and a little more, till somebody said, "There, that's enough — put your head in." I done it, but I judged they would take it off.

The candle was on the floor, and there they all was, looking at me, and me at them, for about a quarter of a minute. Three big men with guns pointed at me, which made me wince, I tell you; the oldest, gray and about sixty, the other two thirty or more — all of them fine and handsome — and the sweetest old gray-headed lady, and back of her two young women which I couldn't see right well. The old gentleman says:

"There — I reckon it's all right. Come in."

As soon as I was in, the old gentleman he locked the door and barred it and bolted it, and told the young men to come in with their guns, and they all went in a big parlor that had a new rag carpet on the floor, and got together in a corner that was out of range of the front windows — there warn't none on the side. They held the candle, and took a good look at me, and all said, "Why *he* ain't a Shepherdson — no, there ain't any Shepherdson about him." Then the old man said he hoped I wouldn't mind being searched for arms, because he didn't mean no harm by it — it was only to make sure. So he didn't pry into my pockets, but only felt outside with his hands, and said it was all right. He told me to make myself easy and at home, and tell all about myself; but the old lady says:

"Why bless you, Saul, the poor thing's as wet as he can be; and don't you reckon it may be he's hungry?"

"True for you, Rachel — I forgot."

So the old lady says:

"Betsy" (this was a nigger woman), "you fly around and get him something to eat, as quick as you can, poor thing; and one of you girls go and wake up Buck and tell him — Oh, here he is himself. Buck, take this little stranger and get the wet clothes off from him and dress him up in some of yours that's dry."

Buck looked about as old as me — thirteen or fourteen or along there, though he was a little bigger than me. He hadn't on anything but a shirt,

and he was very frowsy-headed. He come in gaping and digging one fist
into his eyes, and he was dragging a gun along with the other one. He
says:

"Ain't they no Shepherdsons around?"

They said, no, 'twas a false alarm.

"Well," he says, "if they'd a ben some, I reckon I'd a got one."

They all laughed, and Bob says:

"Why, Buck, they might have scalped us all, you've been so slow in
coming."

"Well, nobody come after me, and it ain't right. I'm always kep' down;
I don't get no show."

"Never mind, Buck, my boy," says the old man, "you'll have show
enough, all in good time, don't you fret about that. Go 'long with you
now, and do as your mother told you."

When we got up stairs to his room, he got me a coarse shirt and a
roundabout and pants of his, and I put them on. While I was at it he
asked me what my name was, but before I could tell him, he started to
telling me about a blue jay and a young rabbit he had catched in the
woods day before yesterday, and he asked me where Moses was when
the candle went out. I said I didn't know; I hadn't heard about it before,
no way.

"Well, guess," he says.

"How'm I going to guess," says I, "when I never heard tell about it
before?"

"But you can guess, can't you? It's just as easy."

"*Which* candle?" I says.

"Why, any candle," he says.

"I don't know where he was," says I; "where was he?"

"Why he was in the *dark*! That's where he was!"

"Well, if you knowed where he was, what did you ask me for?"

"Why, blame it, it's a riddle, don't you see? Say, how long are you
going to stay here? You got to stay always. We can just have booming
times — they don't have no school now. Do you own a dog? I've got a
dog — and he'll go in the river and bring out chips that you throw in. Do
you like to comb up, Sundays, and all that kind of foolishness? You bet I
don't, but ma she makes me. Confound these ole britches, I reckon I'd
better put 'em on, but I'd ruther not, it's so warm. Are you all ready? All
right — come along, old hoss."

Cold corn-pone, cold corn-beef, butter and butter-milk — that is what
they had for me down there, and there ain't nothing better that ever I've
come across yet. Buck and his ma and all of them smoked cob pipes,
except the nigger woman, which was gone, and the two young women.

They all smoked and talked, and I eat and talked. The young women
had quilts around them, and their hair down their backs. They all asked
me questions, and I told them how pap and me and all the family was
living on a little farm down at the bottom of Arkansaw, and my sister
Mary Ann run off and got married and never was heard of no more,
and Bill went to hunt them and he warn't heard of no more, and Tom
and Mort died, and then there warn't nobody but just me and pap
left, and he was just trimmed down to nothing, on account of his
troubles; so when he died I took what there was left, because the farm
didn't belong to us, and started up the river, deck passage, and fell
overboard; and that was how I come to be here. So they said I could have
a home there as long as I wanted it. Then it was most daylight, and
everybody went to bed, and I went to bed with Buck, and when I waked
up in the morning, drat it all, I had forgot what my name was. So I laid
there about an hour trying to think, and when Buck waked up, I says:

"Can you spell, Buck?"

"Yes," he says.

"I bet you can't spell my name," says I.

"I bet you what you dare I can," says he.

"All right," says I, "go ahead."

"G-o-r-g-e J-a-x-o-n — there now," he says.

"Well," says I, "you done it, but I didn't think you could. It ain't no
slouch of a name to spell — right off without studying."

I set it down, private, because somebody might want *me* to spell it,
next, and so I wanted to be handy with it and rattle it off like I was used
to it.

It was a mighty nice family, and a mighty nice house, too. I hadn't
seen no house out in the country before that was so nice and had so
much style. It didn't have an iron latch on the front door, nor a wooden
one with a buckskin string, but a brass knob to turn, the same as houses
in a town. There warn't no bed in the parlor, not a sign of a bed; but
heaps of parlors in towns has beds in them. There was a big fireplace that
was bricked on the bottom, and the bricks was kept clean and red by
pouring water on them and scrubbing them with another brick; sometimes they washed them over with red water-paint that they call Spanish-
brown, same as they do in town. They had big brass dog-irons that could
hold up a saw-log. There was a clock on the middle of the mantel-piece,
with a picture of a town painted on the bottom half of the glass front, and
a round place in the middle of it for the sun, and you could see the
pendulum swing behind it. It was beautiful to hear that clock tick; and
sometimes when one of these peddlers had been along and scoured her
up and got her in good shape, she would start in and strike a hundred

and fifty before she got tuckered out. They wouldn't took any money for her.

Well, there was a big outlandish parrot on each side of the clock, made out of something like chalk, and painted up gaudy. By one of the parrots was a cat made of crockery, and a crockery dog by the other; and when you pressed down on them they squeaked, but didn't open their mouths nor look different nor interested. They squeaked through underneath. There was a couple of big wild-turkey-wing fans spread out behind those things. On a table in the middle of the room was a kind of a lovely crockery basket that had apples and oranges and peaches and grapes piled up in it which was much redder and yellower and prettier than real ones is, but they warn't real because you could see where pieces had got chipped off and showed the white chalk or whatever it was, underneath.

This table had a cover made out of beautiful oil-cloth, with a red and blue spread-eagle painted on it, and a painted border all around. It come all the way from Philadelphia, they said. There was some books too, piled up perfectly exact, on each corner of the table. One was a big family Bible, full of pictures. One was "Pilgrim's Progress," about a man that left his family it didn't say why. I read considerable in it now and then. The statements was interesting, but tough. Another was "Friendship's Offering," full of beautiful stuff and poetry; but I didn't read the poetry. Another was Henry Clay's Speeches, and another was Dr. Gunn's Family Medicine, which told you all about what to do if a body was sick or dead. There was a Hymn Book, and a lot of other books. And there was nice split-bottom chairs, and perfectly sound, too — not bagged down in the middle and busted, like an old basket.

They had pictures hung on the walls — mainly Washingtons and Lafayettes, and battles, and Highland Marys, and one called "Signing the Declaration." There was some that they called crayons, which one of the daughters which was dead made her own self when she was only fifteen years old. They was different from any pictures I ever see before; blacker, mostly, than is common. One was a woman in a slim black dress, belted small under the arm-pits, with bulges like a cabbage in the middle of the sleeves, and a large black scoop-shovel bonnet with a black veil, and white slim ankles crossed about with black tape, and very wee black slippers, like a chisel, and she was leaning pensive on a tombstone on her right elbow, under a weeping willow, and her other hand hanging down her side holding a white handkerchief and a reticule, and underneath the picture it said "Shall I Never See Thee More Alas." Another one was a young lady with her hair all combed up straight to the top of her head, and knotted there in front of a comb like a chair-back, and she was crying into a handkerchief and had a dead bird laying on its back in her other hand with its heels up, and underneath the picture it said "I Shall Never Hear Thy Sweet Chirrup More Alas." There was one where a young lady was at a window looking up at the moon, and tears running down her cheeks; and she had an open letter in one hand with black sealing-wax showing on one edge of it, and she was mashing a locket with a chain to it against her mouth, and underneath the picture it said "And Art Thou Gone Yes Thou Art Gone Alas." These was all nice pictures, I reckon, but I didn't somehow seem to take to them, because if ever I was down a little, they always give me the fan-tods. Everybody was sorry she died, because she had laid out a lot more of these pictures to do, and a body could see by what she had done what they had lost. But I reckoned, that with her disposition, she was having a better time in the graveyard. She was at work on what they said was her greatest picture when she took sick, and every day and every night it was her prayer to be allowed to live till she got it done, but she never got the chance. It was a picture of a young woman in a long white gown, standing on the rail of a bridge all ready to jump off, with her hair all down her back, and looking up to the moon, with the tears running down her face, and she had two arms folded across her breast, and two arms stretched out in front, and two more reaching up towards the moon—and the idea was, to see which pair would look best and then scratch out all the other arms; but, as I was saying, she died before she got her mind made up, and now they kept this picture over the head of the bed in her room, and every time her birthday come they hung flowers on it. Other times it was hid with a little curtain. The young woman in the picture had a kind of a nice sweet face, but there was so many arms it made her look too spidery, seemed to me.

This young girl kept a scrap-book when she was alive, and used to paste obituaries and accidents and cases of patient suffering in it out of the *Presbyterian Observer*, and write poetry after them out of her own head. It was very good poetry. This is what she wrote about a boy by the name of Stephen Dowling Bots that fell down a well and was drownded:

ODE TO STEPHEN DOWLING BOTS, DEC'D.

And did young Stephen sicken,
    And did young Stephen die?
And did the sad hearts thicken,
    And did the mourners cry?

No; such was not the fate of
    Young Stephen Dowling Bots;

> Though sad hearts round him thickened,
>   'Twas not from sickness' shots.
>
> No whooping-cough did rack his frame,
>   Nor measles drear, with spots;
> Not these impaired the sacred name
>   Of Stephen Dowling Bots.
>
> Despised love struck not with woe
>   That head of curly knots,
> Nor stomach troubles laid him low,
>   Young Stephen Dowling Bots.
>
> O no. Then list with tearful eye,
>   Whilst I his fate do tell.
> His soul did from this cold world fly,
>   By falling down a well.
>
> They got him out and emptied him;
>   Alas it was too late;
> His spirit was gone for to sport aloft
>   In the realms of the good and great.

If Emmeline Grangerford could make poetry like that before she was fourteen, there ain't no telling what she could a done by-and-by. Buck said she could rattle off poetry like nothing. She didn't ever have to stop to think. He said she would slap down a line, and if she couldn't find anything to rhyme with it she would just scratch it out and slap down another one, and go ahead. She warn't particular, she could write about anything you choose to give her to write about, just so it was sadful. Every time a man died, or a woman died, or a child died, she would be on hand with her "tribute" before he was cold. She called them tributes. The neighbors said it was the doctor first, then Emmeline, then the undertaker — the undertaker never got in ahead of Emmeline but once, and then she hung fire on a rhyme for the dead person's name, which was Whistler. She warn't ever the same, after that; she never complained, but she kind of pined away and did not live long. Poor thing, many's the time I made myself go up to the little room that used to be hers and get out her poor old scrap-book and read in it when her pictures had been aggravating me and I had soured on her a little. I liked all that family, dead ones and all, and warn't going to let anything come between us. Poor Emmeline made poetry about all the dead people when she was alive, and it didn't seem right that there warn't nobody to make some about her, now she was gone; so I tried to sweat out a verse or two myself, but I couldn't seem to make it go, somehow. They kept Emmeline's room trim and nice and all the things fixed in it just the way she liked to have them when she was alive, and nobody ever slept there. The old lady took care of the room herself, though there was plenty of niggers, and she sewed there a good deal and read her Bible there, mostly.

Well, as I was saying about the parlor, there was beautiful curtains on the windows: white, with pictures painted on them, of castles with vines all down the walls, and cattle coming down to drink. There was a little old piano, too, that had tin pans in it, I reckon, and nothing was ever so lovely as to hear the young ladies sing, "The Last Link is Broken" and play "The Battle of Prague" on it. The walls of all the rooms was plastered, and most had carpets on the floors, and the whole house was whitewashed on the outside.

It was a double house, and the big open place betwixt them was roofed and floored, and sometimes the table was set there in the middle of the day, and it was a cool, comfortable place. Nothing couldn't be better. And warn't the cooking good, and just bushels of it too!

Chapter XVIII

Col. Grangerford was a gentleman, you see. He was a gentleman all over; and so was his family. He was well born, as the saying is, and that's worth as much in a man as it is in a horse, so the Widow Douglas said, and nobody ever denied that she was of the first aristocracy in our town; and pap he always said it, too, though he warn't no more quality than a mud-cat, himself. Col. Grangerford was very tall and very slim, and had a darkish-paly complexion, not a sign of red in it anywheres; he was clean-shaved every morning, all over his thin face, and he had the thinnest kind of lips, and the thinnest kind of nostrils, and a high nose, and heavy eyebrows, and the blackest kind of eyes, sunk so deep back that they seemed like they was looking out of caverns at you, as you may say. His forehead was high, and his hair was black and straight, and hung to his shoulders. His hands was long and thin, and every day of his life he put on a clean shirt and a full suit from head to foot made out of linen so white it hurt your eyes to look at it; and on Sundays he wore a blue tail-coat with brass buttons on it. He carried a mahogany cane with a silver head to it. There warn't no frivolishness about him, not a bit, and he warn't ever loud. He was as kind as he could be — you could feel that, you know, and so you had confidence. Sometimes he smiled, and it was good to see; but when he straightened himself up like a liberty-pole, and the lightning begun to flicker out from under his eyebrows you wanted to climb a tree first, and find out what the matter was afterwards. He didn't ever have to tell anybody to mind their manners — everybody was always good mannered where he was. Everybody loved to have him around, too; he was sunshine most always — I mean he made it seem like good weather. When he turned into a cloud-bank it was awful dark for a half a minute and that was enough; there wouldn't nothing go wrong again for a week.

When him and the old lady come down in the morning, all the family got up out of their chairs and give them good-day, and didn't set down again till they had set down. Then Tom and Bob went to the sideboard where the decanters was, and mixed a glass of bitters and handed it to him, and he held it in his hand and waited till Tom's and Bob's was mixed, and then they bowed and said "Our duty to you, sir, and madam;" and *they* bowed the least bit in the world and said thank you, and so they drank, all three, and Bob and Tom poured a spoonful of water on the sugar and the mite of whisky or apple brandy in the bottom of their tumblers, and give it to me and Buck, and we drank to the old people too.

Bob was the oldest, and Tom next. Tall, beautiful men with very broad shoulders and brown faces, and long black hair and black eyes. They dressed in white linen from head to foot, like the old gentleman, and wore broad Panama hats.

Then there was Miss Charlotte, she was twenty-five, and tall and proud and grand, but as good as she could be, when she warn't stirred up; but when she was, she had a look that would make you wilt in your tracks, like her father. She was beautiful.

So was her sister, Miss Sophia, but it was a different kind. She was gentle and sweet, like a dove, and she was only twenty.

Each person had their own nigger to wait on them — Buck, too. My nigger had a monstrous easy time, because I warn't used to having anybody do anything for me, but Buck's was on the jump most of the time.

This was all there was of the family, now; but there used to be more — three sons; they got killed; and Emmeline that died.

The old gentleman owned a lot of farms, and over a hundred niggers. Sometimes a stack of people would come there, horseback, from ten or fifteen mile around, and stay five or six days, and have such junketings round about and on the river, and dances and picnics in the woods, day-times, and balls at the house, nights. These people was mostly kin-folks of the family. The men brought their guns with them. It was a handsome lot of quality, I tell you.

There was another clan of aristocracy around there — five or six families — mostly of the name of Shepherdson. They was as high-toned, and well born, and rich and grand, as the tribe of Grangerfords. The Shepherdsons and the Grangerfords used the same steamboat landing, which was about two mile above our house; so sometimes when I went up there with a lot of our folks I used to see a lot of the Shepherdsons there, on their fine horses.

One day Buck and me was away out in the woods, hunting, and heard a horse coming. We was crossing the road. Buck says:

"Quick! Jump for the woods!"

We done it, and then peeped down the woods through the leaves. Pretty soon a splendid young man come galloping down the road, setting his horse easy and looking like a soldier. He had his gun across his pommel. I had seen him before. It was young Harney Shepherdson. I heard Buck's gun go off at my ear, and Harney's hat tumbled off from his head. He grabbed his gun and rode straight to the place where we was hid. But we didn't wait. We started through the woods on a run. The woods warn't thick, so I looked over my shoulder, to dodge the bullet, and twice I seen Harney cover Buck with his gun; and then he rode away the way he come — to get his hat, I reckon, but I couldn't see. We never stopped running till we got home. The old gentleman's eyes blazed a minute — 'twas pleasure, mainly, I judged — then his face sort of smoothed down, and he says, kind of gentle:

"I don't like that shooting from behind a bush. Why didn't you step into the road, my boy?"

"The Shepherdsons don't, father. They always take advantage."

Miss Charlotte she held her head up like a queen while Buck was telling his tale, and her nostrils spread and her eyes snapped. The two young men looked dark, but never said nothing. Miss Sophia she turned pale, but the color come back when she found the man warn't hurt.

Soon as I could get Buck down by the corn-cribs under the trees by ourselves, I says:

"Did you want to kill him, Buck?"

"Well, I bet I did."

"What did he do to you?"

"Him? He never done nothing to me."

"Well, then, what did you want to kill him for?"

"Why nothing — only it's on account of the feud."

"What's a feud?"

"Why, where was you raised? Don't you know what a feud is?"

"Never heard of it before — tell me about it."

"Well," says Buck, "a feud is this way. A man has a quarrel with another man, and kills him; then that other man's brother kills *him*; then the other brothers, on both sides, goes for one another; then the _cousins_ chip in — and by-and-by everybody's killed off, and there ain't no more feud. But it's kind of slow, and takes a long time."

"Has this one been going on long, Buck?"

"Well I should _reckon!_ it started thirty year ago, or som'ers along there. There was trouble 'bout something and then a lawsuit to settle it; and the suit went agin one of the men, and so he up and shot the man that won the suit — which he would naturally do, of course. Anybody would."

"What was the trouble about, Buck? — land?"

"I reckon maybe — I don't know."

"Well, who done the shooting? — was it a Grangerford or a Shepherdson?"

"Laws, how do _I_ know? it was so long ago."

"Don't anybody know?"

"Oh, yes, pa knows, I reckon, and some of the other old folks; but they don't know, now, what the row was about in the first place."

"Has there been many killed, Buck?"

"Yes — right smart chance of funerals. But they don't always kill. Pa's got a few buck-shot in him; but he don't mind it 'cuz he don't weigh much anyway. Bob's been carved up some with a bowie, and Tom's been hurt once or twice."

"Has anybody been killed this year, Buck?"

"Yes, we got one and they got one. 'Bout three months ago, my cousin Bud, fourteen year old, was riding through the woods, on t'other side of the river, and didn't have no weapon with him, which was blame' foolishness, and in a lonesome place he hears a horse a-coming behind him, and sees old Baldy Shepherdson a-linkin' after him with his gun in his hand and his white hair a-flying in the wind; and 'stead of jumping off and taking to the brush, Bud 'lowed he could outrun him; so they had it, nip and tuck, for five mile or more, the old man a-gaining all the time; so at last Bud seen it warn't any use, so he stopped and faced around so as to have the bullet holes in front, you know, and the old man he rode up and shot him down. But he didn't git much chance to enjoy his luck, for inside of a week our folks laid _him_ out."

"I reckon that old man was a coward, Buck."

"I reckon he _warn't_ a coward. Not by a blame' sight. There ain't a coward amongst them Shepherdsons — not a one. And there ain't no cowards amongst the Grangerfords, either. Why, that old man kep' up his end in a fight one day, for a half an hour, against three Grangerfords, and come out winner. They was all a-horseback; he lit off of his horse and got behind a little wood-pile, and kep' his horse before him to stop the bullets; but the Grangerfords staid on their horses and capered around the old man, and peppered away at him, and he peppered away at them. Him and his horse both went home pretty leaky and crippled, but the Grangerfords had to be *fetched* home — and one of 'em was dead, and another died the next day. No, sir, if a body's out hunting for cowards, he don't want to fool away any time amongst them Shepherdsons, becuz they don't breed any of that *kind*."

Next Sunday we all went to church, about three mile, everybody a-horseback. The men took their guns along, so did Buck, and kept them between their knees or stood them handy against the wall. The Shepherdsons done the same. It was pretty ornery preaching — all about brotherly love, and such-like tiresomeness; but everybody said it was a good sermon, and they all talked it over going home, and had such a powerful lot to say about faith, and good works, and free grace, and preforeordestination, and I don't know what all, that it did seem to me to be one of the roughest Sundays I had run across yet.

About an hour after dinner everybody was dozing around, some in their chairs and some in their rooms, and it got to be pretty dull. Buck and a dog was stretched out on the grass in the sun, sound asleep. I went up to our room, and judged I would take a nap myself. I found that sweet Miss Sophia standing in her door, which was next to ours, and she took me in her room and shut the door very soft, and asked me if I liked her, and I said I did; and she asked me if I would do something for her and not tell anybody, and I said I would. Then she said she'd forgot her Testament, and left it in the seat at church, between two other books and would I slip out quiet and go there and fetch it to her, and not say nothing to nobody. I said I would. So I slid out and slipped off up the road, and there warn't anybody at the church, except maybe a hog or two, for there warn't any lock on the door, and hogs likes a puncheon floor in summer-time because it's cool. If you notice, most folks don't go to church only when they've got to; but a hog is different.

Says I to myself something's up — it ain't natural for a girl to be in such a sweat about a Testament; so I give it a shake, and out drops a little piece of paper with *"Half-past two"* wrote on it with a pencil. I ransacked it, but couldn't find anything else. I couldn't make anything out of that, so I put the paper in the book again, and when I got home and up stairs, there was Miss Sophia in her door waiting for me. She pulled me in and shut the door; then she looked in the Testament till she found the paper, and as soon as she read it she looked glad; and before a body could think, she grabbed me and give me a squeeze, and said I was the best boy in the world, and not to tell anybody. She was mighty red in the face, for a minute, and her eyes lighted up and it made her powerful pretty. I was a good deal astonished, but when I got my breath I asked her what the paper was about, and she asked me if I had read it, and I said no, and she asked me if I could read writing, and I told her "no, only coarse-hand," and then she said the paper warn't anything but a book-mark to keep her place, and I might go and play now.

I went off down to the river, studying over this thing, and pretty soon I noticed that my nigger was following along behind. When we was out of sight of the house, he looked back and around a second, and then comes a-running, and says:

"Mars Jawge, if you'll come down into de swamp, I'll show you a whole stack o' water-moccasins."

Thinks I, that's mighty curious; he said that yesterday. He oughter know a body don't love water-moccasins enough to go around hunting for them. What is he up to anyway? So I says—

"All right, trot ahead."

I followed a half a mile, then he struck out over the swamp and waded ankle deep as much as another half mile. We come to a little flat piece of land which was dry and very thick with trees and bushes and vines, and he says—

"You shove right in dah, jist a few steps, Mars Jawge, dah's whah dey is. I's seed 'm befo', I don't k'yer to see 'em no mo'."

Then he slopped right along and went away, and pretty soon the trees hid him. I poked into the place a-ways, and come to a little open patch as big as a bedroom, all hung around with vines, and found a man laying there asleep—and by jings it was my old Jim!

I waked him up, and I reckoned it was going to be a grand surprise to him to see me again, but it warn't. He nearly cried, he was so glad, but he warn't surprised. Said he swum along behind me, that night, and heard me yell every time, but dasn't answer, because he didn't want nobody to pick *him* up, and take him into slavery again. Says he—

"I got hurt a little, en couldn't swim fas', so I wuz a considable ways behine you, towards de las'; when you landed I reck'ned I could ketch up wid you on de lan' 'dout havin' to shout at you, but when I see dat house I begin to go slow. I 'uz off too fur to hear what dey say to you—I wuz 'fraid o' de dogs—but when it uz all quiet agin, I knowed you's in de house, so I struck out for de woods to wait for day. Early in de mawnin' some er de niggers come along, gwyne to de fields, en dey tuck me en showed me dis place, whah de dogs can't track me on accounts o' de water, en dey brings me truck to eat every night, en tells me how you's a gitt'n along."

"Why didn't you tell my Jack to fetch me here sooner, Jim?"

"Well, 'twarn't no use to 'sturb you, Huck, tell we could do sumfn—

but we's all right, now. I ben a-buyin' pots en pans en vittles, as I got a chanst, en a patchin' up de raf', nights, when——"

"*What* raft, Jim?"

"Our ole raf'."

"You mean to say our old raft warn't smashed all to flinders?"

"No, she warn't. She was tore up a good deal — one en' of her was — but dey warn't no great harm done, on'y our traps was mos' all los'. Ef we hadn' dive' so deep en swum so fur under water, en de night hadn' ben so dark, en we warn't so sk'yerd, en ben sich punkin-heads, as de sayin' is, we'd a seed de raf'. But it's jis' as well we didn't, 'kase now she's all fixed up agin mos' as good as new, en we's got a new lot o' stuff, too, in de place o' what 'uz los'."

"Why, how did you get hold of the raft again, Jim — did you catch her?"

"How I gwyne to ketch her, en I out in de woods? No, some er de niggers foun' her ketched on a snag, along heah in de ben', en dey hid her in a crick, 'mongst de willows, en dey wuz so much jawin' 'bout which un 'um she b'long to de mos', dat I come to heah 'bout it pooty soon, so I ups en settles de trouble by tellin' 'um she don't b'long to none uv um, but to you en me; en I ast 'm if dey gwyne to grab a young white genlman's propaty, en git a hid'n for it? Den I gin 'm ten cents apiece, en dey 'uz mighty well satisfied, en wisht some mo' raf's 'ud come along en make 'm rich agin. Dey's mighty good to me, dese niggers is, en whatever I wants 'm to do fur me, I doan' have to ast 'm twice, honey. Dat Jack's a good nigger, en pooty smart."

"Yes, he is. He ain't ever told me you was here; told me to come, and he'd show me a lot of water-moccasins. If anything happens, *he* ain't mixed up in it. He can say he never seen us together, and it'll be the truth."

I don't want to talk much about the next day. I reckon I'll cut it pretty short. I waked up about dawn, and was agoing to turn over and go to sleep again, when I noticed how still it was — didn't seem to be anybody stirring. That warn't usual. Next I noticed that Buck was up and gone. Well, I gets up, a-wondering, and goes down stairs — nobody around; everything as still as a mouse. Just the same outside; thinks I, what does it mean? Down by the wood-pile I comes across my Jack, and says:

"What's it all about?"

Says he:

"Don't you know, Mars Jawge?"

"No," says I, "I don't."

"Well, den, Miss Sophia's run off! 'deed she has. She run off in de night, sometime — nobody don't know jis' when — run off to git married to dat young Harney Shepherdson, you know — leastways, so dey 'spec. De fambly foun' it out, 'bout half an hour ago — maybe a little mo' — en' I *tell* you dey warn't no time los'. Sich another hurryin' up guns en hosses *you* never see! De women folks has gone for to stir up de relations, en ole Mars Saul en de boys tuck dey guns en rode up de river road for to try to ketch dat young man en kill him 'fo' he kin git acrost de river wid Miss Sophia. I reck'n dey's gwyne to be mighty rough times."

"Buck went off 'thout waking me up."

"Well I reck'n he *did!* Dey warn't gwyne to mix you up in it. Mars Buck he loaded up his gun en 'lowed he's gwyne to fetch home a Shepherdson or bust. Well, dey'll be plenty un 'm dah, I reck'n, en you bet you he'll fetch one ef he gits a chanst."

I took up the river road as hard as I could put. By-and-by I begin to hear guns a good ways off. When I come in sight of the log store and the wood-pile where the steamboats lands, I worked along under the trees and brush till I got to a good place, and then I clumb up into the forks of a cotton-wood that was out of reach, and watched. There was a wood-rank four foot high, a little ways in front of the tree, and first I was going to hide behind that; but maybe it was luckier I didn't.

There was four or five men cavorting around on their horses in the open place before the log store, cussing and yelling, and trying to get at a couple of young chaps that was behind the wood-rank alongside of the steamboat landing — but they couldn't come in. Every time one of them showed himself on the river side of the wood-pile he got shot at. The two boys was squatting back to back behind the pile, so they could watch both ways.

By-and-by the men stopped cavorting around and yelling. They started riding towards the store; then up gets one of the boys, draws a steady bead over the wood-rank, and drops one of them out of his saddle. All the men jumped off of their horses and grabbed the hurt one and started to carry him to the store; and that minute the two boys started on the run. They got half-way to the tree I was in before the men noticed. Then the men see them, and jumped on their horses and took out after them. They gained on the boys, but it didn't do no good, the boys had too good a start; they got to the wood-pile that was in front of my tree, and slipped in behind it, and so they had the bulge on the men again. One of the boys was Buck, and the other was a slim young chap about nineteen years old.

The men ripped around awhile, and then rode away. As soon as they was out of sight, I sung out to Buck and told him. He didn't know what to make of my voice coming out of the tree, at first. He was awful surprised.

He told me to watch out sharp and let him know when the men come in sight again; said they was up to some devilment or other — wouldn't be gone long. I wished I was out of that tree, but I dasn't come down. Buck begun to cry and rip, and 'lowed that him and his cousin Joe (that was the other young chap) would make up for this day, yet. He said his father and his two brothers was killed, and two or three of the enemy. Said the Shepherdsons laid for them, in ambush. Buck said his father and brothers ought to waited for their relations — the Shepherdsons was too strong for them. I asked him what was become of young Harney and Miss Sophia. He said they'd got across the river and was safe. I was glad of that; but the way Buck did take on because he didn't manage to kill Harney that day he shot at him — I hain't ever heard anything like it.

All of a sudden, bang! bang! bang! goes three or four guns — the men had slipped around through the woods and come in from behind without their horses! The boys jumped for the river — both of them hurt — and as they swum down the current the men run along the bank shooting at them and singing out, "Kill them, kill them!" It made me so sick I most fell out of the tree. I ain't agoing to tell *all* that happened — it would make me sick again if I was to do that. I wished I hadn't ever come ashore that night, to see such things. I ain't ever going to get shut of them — lots of times I dream about them.

I staid in the tree till it begun to get dark, afraid to come down. Sometimes I heard guns away off in the woods; and twice I seen little gangs of men gallop past the log store with guns; so I reckoned the trouble was still agoing on. I was mighty down-hearted; so I made up my mind I wouldn't ever go anear that house again, because I reckoned I was to blame, somehow. I judged that that piece of paper meant that Miss Sophia was to meet Harney somewheres at half-past two and run off; and I judged I ought to told her father about that paper and the curious way she acted, and then maybe he would a locked her up and this awful mess wouldn't ever happened.

When I got down out of the tree, I crept along down the river bank a piece, and found the two bodies laying in the edge of the water, and tugged at them till I got them ashore; then I covered up their faces, and got away as quick as I could. I cried a little when I was covering up Buck's face, for he was mighty good to me.

It was just dark, now. I never went near the house, but struck through the woods and made for the swamp. Jim warn't on his island, so I tramped off in a hurry for the crick, and crowded through the willows, red-hot to jump aboard and get out of that awful country — the raft was gone! My souls, but I was scared! I couldn't get my breath for most a minute. Then I raised a yell. A voice not twenty-five foot from me, says —

"Good lan'! is dat you, honey? Doan' make no noise."

It was Jim's voice — nothing ever sounded so good before. I run along the bank a piece and got aboard, and Jim he grabbed me and hugged me, he was so glad to see me. He says —

"Laws bless you, chile, I 'uz right down sho' you's dead agin. Jack's been heah, he say he reck'n you's ben shot, kase you didn' come home no mo'; so I's jes' dis minute a startin' de raf' down towards de mouf er de crick, so's to be all ready for to shove out en leave soon as Jack comes agin en tells me for certain you *is* dead. Lawsy, I's mighty glad to git you back agin, honey."

I says —

"All right — that's mighty good; they won't find me, and they'll think I've been killed, and floated down the river — there's something up there that'll help them to think so — so don't you lose no time, Jim, but just shove off for the big water as fast as ever you can."

I never felt easy till the raft was two mile below there and out in the middle of the Mississippi. Then we hung up our signal lantern, and judged that we was free and safe once more. I hadn't had a bite to eat since yesterday; so Jim he got out some corn-dodgers and buttermilk, and pork and cabbage, and greens — there ain't nothing in the world so good, when it's cooked right — and whilst I eat my supper we talked, and had a good time. I was powerful glad to get away from the feuds, and so was Jim to get away from the swamp. We said there warn't no home like a raft, after all. Other places do seem so cramped up and smothery, but a raft don't. You feel mighty free and easy and comfortable on a raft.

Chapter XIX

Two or three days and nights went by; I reckon I might say they swum by, they slid along so quiet and smooth and lovely. Here is the way we put in the time. It was a monstrous big river down there — sometimes a mile and a half wide; we run nights, and laid up and hid day-times; soon as night was most gone, we stopped navigating and tied up — nearly always in the dead water under a tow-head; and then cut young cotton-woods and willows and hid the raft with them. Then we set out the lines. Next we slid into the river and had a swim, so as to freshen up and cool off; then we set down on the sandy bottom where the water was about knee deep, and watched the daylight come. Not a sound, anywheres — perfectly still — just like the whole world was asleep, only sometimes the bull-frogs a-cluttering, maybe. The first thing to see, looking away over the water, was a kind of dull line — that was the woods on t'other side — you couldn't make nothing else out; then a pale place in the sky; then more paleness, spreading around; then the river softened up, away off, and warn't black any more, but gray; you could see little dark spots drifting along, ever so far away — trading scows, and such things; and long black streaks — rafts; sometimes you could hear a sweep screaking; or jumbled up voices, it was so still, and sounds come so far; and by-and-by you could see a streak on the water which you know by the look of the streak that there's a snag there in a swift current which breaks on it and makes that streak look that way; and you see the mist curl up off of the water, and the east reddens up, and the river, and you make out a log cabin in the edge of the woods, away on the bank on t'other side of the river, being a wood-yard, likely, and piled by them cheats so you can throw a dog through it anywheres; then the nice breeze springs up, and comes fanning you from over there, so cool and fresh, and sweet to smell, on account of the woods and the flowers; but sometimes not that way, because they've left dead fish laying around, gars, and such, and they do get pretty rank; and next you've got the full day, and everything smiling in the sun, and the song-birds just going it!

A little smoke couldn't be noticed, now, so we would take some fish off of the lines, and cook up a hot breakfast. And afterwards we would watch the lonesomeness of the river, and kind of lazy along, and by-and-by lazy off to sleep. Wake up, by-and-by, and look to see what done it, and maybe see a steamboat, coughing along up stream, so far off towards the other side you couldn't tell nothing about her only whether she was stern-wheel or side-wheel; then for about an hour there wouldn't be nothing to hear nor nothing to see — just solid lonesomeness. Next you'd see a raft sliding by, away off yonder, and maybe a galoot on it chopping, because they're most always doing it on a raft; you'd see the ax flash, and come down — you don't hear nothing; you see that ax go up again, and by the time it's above the man's head, then you hear the *k'chunk!* — it had took all that time to come over the water. So we would put in the day, lazying around, listening to the stillness. Once there was a thick fog, and the rafts and things that went by was beating tin pans so the steamboats wouldn't run over them. A scow or a raft went by so close we could hear them talking and cussing and laughing — heard them plain; but we couldn't see no sign of them; it made you feel crawly, it was like spirits carrying on that way in the air. Jim said he believed it was spirits; but I says:

"No, spirits wouldn't say, 'dern the dern fog.'"

Soon as it was night, out we shoved; when we got her out to about the middle, we let her alone, and let her float wherever the current wanted her to; then we lit the pipes, and dangled our legs in the water and talked about all kinds of things — we was always naked, day and night, whenever the mosquitoes would let us — the new clothes Buck's folks made for me was too good to be comfortable, and besides I didn't go much on clothes, nohow.

Sometimes we'd have that whole river all to ourselves for the longest time. Yonder was the banks and the islands, across the water; and maybe a spark — which was a candle in a cabin window — and sometimes on the water you could see a spark or two — on a raft or a scow, you know; and maybe you could hear a fiddle or a song coming over from one of them crafts. It's lovely to live on a raft. We had the sky, up there, all speckled with stars, and we used to lay on our backs and look up at them, and discuss about whether they was made, or only just happened — Jim he allowed they was made, but I allowed they happened; I judged it would have took too long to *make* so many. Jim said the moon could a *laid* them; well, that looked kind of reasonable, so I didn't say nothing against it, because I've seen a frog lay most as many, so of course it could be done. We used to watch the stars that fell, too, and see them streak down. Jim allowed they'd got spoiled and was hove out of the nest.

Once or twice of a night we would see a steamboat slipping along in the dark, and now and then she would belch a whole world of sparks up out of her chimbleys, and they would rain down in the river and look awful pretty; then she would turn a corner and her lights would wink out and her pow-wow shut off and leave the river still again; and by-and-by her waves would get to us, a long time after she was gone, and joggle the raft a bit, and after that you wouldn't hear nothing for you couldn't tell how long, except maybe frogs or something.

After midnight the people on shore went to bed, and then for two or three hours the shores was black — no more sparks in the cabin windows. These sparks was our clock — the first one that showed again meant morning was coming, so we hunted a place to hide and tie up, right away.

One morning about day-break, I found a canoe and crossed over a chute to the main shore — it was only two hundred yards — and paddled about a mile up a crick amongst the cypress woods, to see if I couldn't get some berries. Just as I was passing a place where a kind of a cow-path crossed the crick, here comes a couple of men tearing up the path as tight as they could foot it. I thought I was a goner, for whenever anybody was after anybody I judged it was *me* — or maybe Jim. I was about to dig out from there in a hurry, but they was pretty close to me then, and sung out and begged me to save their lives — said they hadn't been doing nothing, and was being chased for it — said there was men and dogs a-coming. They wanted to jump right in, but I says —

"Don't you do it. I don't hear the dogs and horses yet; you've got time to crowd through the brush and get up the crick a little ways; then you take to the water and wade down to me and get in — that'll throw the dogs off the scent."

They done it, and soon as they was aboard I lit out for our tow-head, and in about five or ten minutes we heard the dogs and the men away off, shouting. We heard them come along towards the crick, but couldn't see them; they seemed to stop and fool around a while; then, as we got further and further away all the time, we couldn't hardly hear them at all; by the time we had left a mile of woods behind us and struck the river, everything was quiet, and we paddled over to the tow-head and hid in the cotton-woods and was safe.

One of these fellows was about seventy, or upwards, and had a bald head and very gray whiskers. He had an old battered-up slouch hat on, and a greasy blue woolen shirt, and ragged old blue jeans britches stuffed into his boot tops, and home-knit galluses — no, he only had one. He had an old long-tailed blue jeans coat with slick brass buttons, flung over his arm, and both of them had big fat ratty-looking carpet-bags.

The other fellow was about thirty and dressed about as ornery. After breakfast we all laid off and talked, and the first thing that come out was that these chaps didn't know one another.

"What got you into trouble?" says the baldhead to t'other chap.

"Well, I'd been selling an article to take the tartar off the teeth — and it does take it off, too, and generly the enamel along with it — but I staid about one night longer than I ought to, and was just in the act of sliding out when I ran across you on the trail this side of town, and you told me they were coming, and begged me to help you to get off. So I told you I was expecting trouble myself and would scatter out *with* you. That's the whole yarn — what's yourn?"

"Well, I'd ben a-runnin' a little temperance revival thar, 'bout a week, and was the pet of the women-folks, big and little, for I was makin' it mighty warm for the rummies, I *tell* you, and takin' as much as five or six dollars a night — ten cents a head, children and niggers free — and business a growin' all the time; when somehow or another a little report got around, last night, that I had a way of puttin' in my time with a private jug, on the sly. A nigger rousted me out this mornin', and told me the people was getherin' on the quiet, with their dogs and horses, and they'd be along pretty soon and give me 'bout half an hour's start, and then run me down, if they could; and if they got me they'd tar and feather me and ride me on a rail, sure. I didn't wait for no breakfast — I warn't hungry."

"Old man," says the young one, "I reckon we might double-team it together; what do you think?"

"I ain't undisposed. What's your line — mainly?"

"Jour printer, by trade; do a little in patent medicines; theatre-actor — tragedy, you know; take a turn at mesmerism and phrenology when there's a chance; teach singing-geography school for a change; sling a lecture, sometimes — oh, I do lots of things — most anything that comes handy, so it ain't work. What's your lay?"

"I've done considerble in the doctoring way in my time. Layin' on o' hands is my best holt — for cancer, and paralysis, and sich things; and I k'n tell a fortune pretty good, when I've got somebody along to find out the facts for me. Preachin's my line, too; and workin' camp-meetin's; and missionaryin around."

Nobody never said anything for a while; then the young man hove a sigh and says —

"Alas!"

"What're you alassin' about?" says the baldhead.

"To think I should have lived to be leading such a life, and be degraded down into such company." And he begun to wipe the corner of his eye with a rag.

"Dern your skin, ain't the company good enough for you?" says the baldhead, pretty pert and uppish.

"Yes, it *is* good enough for me; it's as good as I deserve; for who fetched me so low, when I was so high? *I* did myself. I don't blame *you*, gentlemen — far from it; I don't blame anybody. I deserve it all. Let the cold world do its worst; one thing I know — there's a grave somewhere for me. The world may go on just as it's always done, and take everything from me — loved ones, property, everything — but it can't take that. Some day I'll lie down in it and forget it all, and my poor broken heart will be at rest." He went on a-wiping.

"Drot your pore broken heart," says the baldhead; "what are you heaving your pore broken heart at *us* f'r? *We* hain't done nothing."

"No, I know you haven't. I ain't blaming you, gentlemen. I brought myself down — yes, I did it myself. It's right I should suffer — perfectly right — I don't make any moan."

"Brought you down from whar? Whar was you brought down from?"

"Ah, you would not believe me; the world never believes — let it pass — 'tis no matter. The secret of my birth——"

"The secret of your birth? Do you mean to say ——"

"Gentlemen," says the young man, very solemn, "I will reveal it to you, for I feel I may have confidence in you. By rights I am a duke!"

Jim's eyes bugged out when he heard that; and I reckon mine did, too. Then the baldhead says: "No! you can't mean it?"

"Yes. My great-grandfather, eldest son of the Duke of Bridgewater, fled to this country about the end of the last century, to breathe the pure air of freedom; married here, and died, leaving a son, his own father dying about the same time. The second son of the late duke seized the title and estates — the infant real duke was ignored. I am the lineal descendant of that infant — I am the rightful Duke of Bridgewater; and here am I, forlorn, torn from my high estate, hunted of men, despised by the cold world, ragged, worn, heart-broken, and degraded to the companionship of felons on a raft!"

Jim pitied him ever so much, and so did I. We tried to comfort him, but he said it warn't much use, he couldn't be much comforted; said if we was a mind to acknowledge him, that would do him more good than most anything else; so we said we would, if he would tell us how. He said we ought to bow, when we spoke to him, and say "Your Grace," or "My Lord," or "Your Lordship" — and he wouldn't mind it if we called him plain "Bridgewater," which he said was a title, anyway, and not a name; and one of us ought to wait on him at dinner, and do any little thing for him he wanted done.

Well, that was all easy, so we done it. All through dinner Jim stood around and waited on him, and says, "Will yo' Grace have some o' dis, or some o' dat?" and so on, and a body could see it was mighty pleasing to him.

But the old man got pretty silent, by-and-by — didn't have much to say, and didn't look pretty comfortable over all that petting that was going on around that duke. He seemed to have something on his mind. So, along in the afternoon, he says:

"Looky here, Bilgewater," he says, "I'm nation sorry for you, but you ain't the only person that's had troubles like that."

"No?"

"No, you ain't. You ain't the only person that's ben snaked down wrongfully out'n a high place."

"Alas!"

"No, you ain't the only person that's had a secret of his birth." And by jings, *he* begins to cry.

"Hold! What do you mean?"

"Bilgewater, kin I trust you?" says the old man, still sort of sobbing.

"To the bitter death!" He took the old man by the hand and squeezed it, and says, "The secret of your being: speak!"

"Bilgewater, I am the late Dauphin!"

You bet you Jim and me stared, this time. Then the duke says:

"You are what?"

"Yes, my friend, it is too true — your eyes is lookin' at this very moment on the pore disappeared Dauphin, Looy the Seventeen, son of Looy the Sixteen and Marry Antonette."

"You! At your age! No! You mean you're the late Charlemagne; you must be six or seven hundred years old, at the very least."

"Trouble has done it, Bilgewater, trouble has done it; trouble has brung these gray hairs and this premature balditude. Yes, gentlemen, you see before you, in blue jeans and misery, the wanderin', exiled, trampled-on and sufferin' rightful King of France."

Well, he cried and took on so, that me and Jim didn't know hardly what to do, we was so sorry — and so glad and proud we'd got him with us, too. So we set in, like we done before with the duke, and tried to comfort *him*. But he said it warn't no use, nothing but to be dead and done with it all could do him any good; though he said it often made him feel easier and better for a while if people treated him according to his rights, and got down on one knee to speak to him, and always called him "Your Majesty," and waited on him first at meals, and didn't set down in his presence till he asked them. So Jim and me set to majestying him, and doing this and that and t'other for him, and standing up till he told us we might set down. This done him heaps of good, and so he got cheerful and comfortable. But the duke kind of soured on him, and didn't look a bit satisfied with the way things was going; still, the king acted real friendly towards him, and said the duke's great-grandfather and all the other Dukes of Bilgewater was a good deal thought of by *his* father and was allowed to come to the palace considerable; but the duke staid huffy a good while, till by-and-by the king says:

"Like as not we got to be together a blamed long time, on this h-yer raft, Bilgewater, and so what's the use o' your bein' sour? It'll only make things oncomfortable. It ain't my fault I warn't born a duke, it ain't your fault you warn't born a king — so what's the use to worry? Make the best o' things the way you find 'em, says I — that's my motto. This ain't no bad thing that we've struck here — plenty grub and an easy life — come, give us your hand, Duke, and less all be friends."

The duke done it, and Jim and me was pretty glad to see it. It took away all the uncomfortableness, and we felt mighty good over it, because it would a been a miserable business to have any unfriendliness on the raft; for what you want, above all things, on a raft, is for everybody to be satisfied, and feel right and kind towards the others.

It didn't take me long to make up my mind that these liars warn't no kings nor dukes, at all, but just low-down humbugs and frauds. But I never said nothing, never let on; kept it to myself; it's the best way; then you don't have no quarrels, and don't get into no trouble. If they wanted us to call them kings and dukes, I hadn't no objections, 'long as it would keep peace in the family; and it warn't no use to tell Jim, so I didn't tell him. If I never learnt nothing else out of pap, I learnt that the best way to get along with his kind of people is to let them have their own way.

Chapter XX

They asked us considerable many questions; wanted to know what we covered up the raft that way for, and laid by in the day-time instead of running — was Jim a runaway nigger? Says I —

"Goodness sakes, would a runaway nigger run *south?*"

No, they allowed he wouldn't. I had to account for things some way, so I says:

"My folks was living in Pike County, in Missouri, where I was born, and they all died off but me and pa and my brother Ike. Pa, he 'lowed he'd break up and go down and live with Uncle Ben, who's got a little one-horse place on the river, forty-four mile below Orleans. Pa was pretty poor, and had some debts; so when he'd squared up there warn't nothing left but sixteen dollars and our nigger, Jim. That warn't enough to take us fourteen hundred mile, deck passage nor no other way. Well, when the river rose, pa had a streak of luck one day; he ketched this piece of a raft; so we reckoned we'd go down to Orleans on it. Pa's luck didn't hold out; a steamboat run over the forrard corner of the raft, one night, and we all went overboard and dove under the wheel; Jim and me come up, all right, but pa was drunk, and Ike was only four years old, so they never come up no more. Well, for the next day or two we had considerable trouble, because people was always coming out in skiffs and trying to take Jim away from me, saying they believed he was a runaway nigger. We don't run day-times no more, now; nights they don't bother us."

The duke says —

"Leave me alone to cipher out a way so we can run in the day-time if we want to. I'll think the thing over — I'll invent a plan that'll fix it. We'll let it alone for to-day, because of course we don't want to go by that town yonder in daylight — it mightn't be healthy."

Towards night it begun to darken up and look like rain; the heat lightning was squirting around, low down in the sky, and the leaves was beginning to shiver — it was going to be pretty ugly, it was easy to see that. So the duke and the king went to overhauling our wigwam, to see what the beds was like. My bed was a straw tick — better than Jim's, which was a corn-shuck tick; there's always cobs around about in a shuck tick, and they poke into you and hurt; and when you roll over, the dry shucks sound like you was rolling over in a pile of dead leaves; it makes such a rustling that you wake up. Well, the duke allowed he would take my bed; but the king allowed he wouldn't. He says —

"I should a reckoned the difference in rank would a sejested to you that a corn-shuck bed warn't just fitten for me to sleep on. Your Grace'll take the shuck bed yourself."

Jim and me was in a sweat again, for a minute, being afraid there was going to be some more trouble amongst them; so we was pretty glad when the duke says —

" 'Tis my fate to be always ground into the mire under the iron heel of oppression. Misfortune has broken my once haughty spirit; I yield, I submit; 'tis my fate. I am alone in the world — let me suffer; I can bear it."

We got away as soon as it was good and dark. The king told us to stand well out towards the middle of the river, and not show a light till we got a long ways below the town. We come in sight of the little bunch of lights by-and-by — that was the town, you know — and slid by, about a half mile out, all right. When we was three-quarters of a mile below, we hoisted up our signal lantern; and about ten o'clock it come on to rain and blow and thunder and lighten like everything; so the king told us to both stay on watch till the weather got better; then him and the duke crawled into the wigwam and turned in for the night. It was my watch below, till twelve, but I wouldn't a turned in, anyway, if I'd had a bed; because a body don't see such a storm as that every day in the week, not by a long sight. My souls, how the wind did scream along! And every second or two there'd come a glare that lit up the white-caps for a half a mile around, and you'd see the islands looking dusty through the rain, and the trees thrashing around in the wind; then comes a *h-wack!* — bum! bum! bumble-umble-um-bum-bum-bum-bum — and the thunder would go rumbling and grumbling away, and quit — and then *rip* comes another flash and another sockdolager. The waves most washed me off the raft, sometimes, but I hadn't any clothes on, and didn't mind. We didn't have to trouble about snags; the lightning was glaring and flittering around so constant that we could see them plenty soon enough to throw her head this way or that and miss them.

I had the middle watch, you know, but I was pretty sleepy by that time, so Jim he said he would stand the first half of it for me; he was always mighty good, that way, Jim was. I crawled into the wigwam, but the king and the duke had their legs sprawled around so there warn't no show for me; so I laid outside — I didn't mind the rain, because it was warm, and the waves warn't running so high, now. About two they come up again, though, and Jim was going to call me, but he changed his mind because he reckoned they warn't high enough yet to do any harm; but he was mistaken about that, for pretty soon all of a sudden along comes a regular ripper, and washed me overboard. It most killed Jim a-laughing. He was the easiest nigger to laugh that ever was, anyway.

I took the watch, and Jim he laid down and snored away; and by-and-by the storm let up for good and all; and the first cabin-light that showed, I rousted him out and we slid the raft into hiding-quarters for the day.

The king got out an old ratty deck of cards, after breakfast, and him and the duke played seven-up a while, five cents a game. Then they got tired of it, and allowed they would "lay out a campaign," as they called it. The duke went down into his carpet-bag and fetched up a lot of little printed bills, and read them out loud. One bill said "The celebrated Dr. Armand de Montalban of Paris," would "lecture on the Science of Phrenology" at such and such a place, on the blank day of blank, at ten cents admission, and "furnish charts of character at twenty-five cents apiece." The duke said that was *him*. In another bill he was the "world renowned Shaksperean tragedian, Garrick the Younger, of Drury Lane, London." In other bills he had a lot of other names and done other wonderful things, like finding water and gold with a "divining rod," "dissipating witch-spells," and so on. By-and-by he says —

"But the histrionic muse is the darling. Have you ever trod the boards, Royalty?"

"No," says the king.

"You shall, then, before you're three days older, Fallen Grandeur," says the duke. "The first good town we come to, we'll hire a hall and do the sword-fight in Richard III. and the balcony scene in Romeo and Juliet. How does that strike you?"

"I'm in, up to the hub, for anything that will pay, Bilgewater, but you see I don't know nothing about play-actn', and hain't ever seen much of it. I was too small when pap used to have 'em at the palace. Do you reckon you can learn me?"

"Easy!"

"All right. I'm jist a-freezn' for something fresh, anyway. Less commence, right away."

So the duke he told him all about who Romeo was, and who Juliet was, and said he was used to being Romeo, so the king could be Juliet.

"But if Juliet's such a young gal, Duke, my peeled head and my white whiskers is goin' to look oncommon odd on her, maybe."

"No, don't you worry — these country jakes won't ever think of that. Besides, you know, you'll be in costume, and that makes all the difference in the world; Juliet's in a balcony, enjoying the moonlight before she goes to bed, and she's got on her night-gown and her ruffled nightcap. Here are the costumes for the parts."

He got out two or three curtain-calico suits, which he said was meedyevil armor for Richard III. and t'other chap, and a long white cotton night-shirt and a ruffled night-cap to match. The king was satisfied; so the duke got out his book and read the parts over in the most splendid spread-eagle way, prancing around and acting at the same time, to show how it had got to be done; then he give the book to the king and told him to get his part by heart.

There was a little one-horse town about three mile down the bend, and after dinner the duke said he had ciphered out his idea about how to run in daylight without it being dangersome for Jim; so he allowed he would go down to the town and fix that thing. The king allowed he would go too, and see if he couldn't strike something. We was out of coffee, so Jim said I better go along with them in the canoe and get some.

When we got there, there warn't nobody stirring; streets empty, and perfectly dead and still, like Sunday. We found a sick nigger sunning himself in a back yard, and he said everybody that warn't too young or too sick or too old, was gone to camp-meeting, about two mile back in the woods. The king got the directions, and allowed he'd go and work that camp-meeting for all it was worth, and I might go, too.

The duke said what he was after was a printing office. We found it; a little bit of a concern, up over a carpenter shop — carpenters and printers all gone to the meeting, and no doors locked. It was a dirty, littered-up place, and had ink marks, and handbills with pictures of horses and runaway niggers on them, all over the walls. The duke shed his coat and said he was all right, now. So me and the king lit out for the camp-meeting.

We got there in about a half an hour, fairly dripping, for it was a most awful hot day. There was as much as a thousand people there, from twenty mile around. The woods was full of teams and wagons, hitched everywheres, feeding out of the wagon troughs and stomping to keep off the flies. There was sheds made out of poles and roofed over with branches, where they had lemonade and gingerbread to sell, and piles of watermelons and green corn and such-like truck.

The preaching was going on under the same kinds of sheds, only they was bigger and held crowds of people. The benches was made out of outside slabs of logs, with holes bored in the round side to drive sticks into for legs. They didn't have no backs. The preachers had high platforms to stand on, at one end of the sheds. The women had on sun-bonnets; and some had linsey-woolsey frocks, some gingham ones, and a few of the young ones had on calico. Some of the young men was barefooted, and some of the children didn't have on any clothes but just a tow-linen shirt. Some of the old women was knitting, and some of the young folks was courting on the sly.

The first shed we come to, the preacher was lining out a hymn. He lined out two lines, everybody sung it, and it was kind of grand to hear it, there was so many of them and they done it in such a rousing way; then he lined out two more for them to sing — and so on. The people woke up more and more, and sung louder and louder; and towards the end, some begun to groan, and some begun to shout. Then the preacher begun to preach; and begun in earnest, too; and went weaving first to one side of the platform and then the other, and then a leaning down over the front of it, with his arms and his body going all the time, and shouting his words out with all his might; and every now and then he would hold up his Bible and spread it open, and kind of pass it around this way and that, shouting, "It's the brazen serpent in the wilderness! Look upon it and live!" And people would shout out, "Glory! — A-a-*men!*" And so he went on, and the people groaning and crying and saying amen:

"Oh, come to the mourners' bench! come, black with sin! (*amen!*) come, sick and sore! (*amen!*) come, lame and halt, and blind! (*amen!*) come, pore and needy, sunk in shame! (*a-a-men!*) come all that's worn, and soiled, and suffering! — come with a broken spirit! come with a contrite heart! come in your rags and sin and dirt! the waters that cleanse is free, the door of heaven stands open — oh, enter in and be at rest!" (*a-a-men! glory, glory hallelujah!*)

And so on. You couldn't make out what the preacher said, any more, on account of the shouting and crying. Folks got up, everywheres in the crowd, and worked their way, just by main strength, to the mourners' bench, with the tears running down their faces; and when all the mourners had got up there to the front benches in a crowd, they sung, and shouted, and flung themselves down on the straw, just crazy and wild.

Well, the first I knowed, the king got agoing; and you could hear him over everybody; and next he went a-charging up on to the platform and the preacher he begged him to speak to the people, and he done it. He told them he was a pirate — been a pirate for thirty years, out in the Indian Ocean, and his crew was thinned out considerable, last spring, in a fight, and he was home now, to take out some fresh men, and thanks to goodness he'd been robbed last night, and put ashore off a steamboat without a cent, and he was glad of it, it was the blessedest thing that ever happened to him, because he was a changed man now, and happy for the first time in his life; and poor as he was, he was going to start right off and work his way back to the Indian Ocean and put in the rest of his life trying to turn the pirates into the true path; for he could do it better than anybody else, being acquainted with all the pirate crews in that ocean; and though it would take him a long time to get there, without money, he would get there anyway, and every time he convinced a pirate he would say to him, "Don't you thank me, don't you give me no credit, it all belongs to them dear people in Pokeville camp-meeting, natural brothers and benefactors of the race — and that dear preacher there, the truest friend a pirate ever had!"

And then he busted into tears, and so did everybody. Then somebody sings out, "Take up a collection for him, take up a collection!" Well, a half a dozen made a jump to do it, but somebody sings out, "Let *him* pass the hat around!" Then everybody said it, the preacher too.

So the king went all through the crowd with his hat, swabbing his eyes, and blessing the people and praising them and thanking them for being so good to the poor pirates away off there; and every little while the prettiest kind of girls, with the tears running down their cheeks, would up and ask him would he let them kiss him, for to remember him by; and he always done it; and some of them he hugged and kissed as many as five or six times — and he was invited to stay a week; and everybody wanted him to live in their houses, and said they'd think it was an honor; but he said as this was the last day of the camp-meeting he couldn't do no good, and besides he was in a sweat to get to the Indian Ocean right off and go to work on the pirates.

When we got back to the raft and he come to count up, he found he had collected eighty-seven dollars and seventy-five cents. And then he had fetched away a three-gallon jug of whisky, too, that he found under a wagon when we was starting home through the woods. The king said, take it all around, it laid over any day he'd ever put in in the missionary-ing line. He said it warn't no use talking, heathens don't amount to shucks, alongside of pirates, to work a camp-meeting with.

The duke was thinking *he'd* been doing pretty well, till the king come to show up, but after that he didn't think so so much. He had set up and printed off two little jobs for farmers, in that printing office — horse bills — and took the money, four dollars. And he had got in ten dollars worth of advertisements for the paper, which he said he would put in for four dollars if they would pay in advance — so they done it. The price of the paper was two dollars a year, but he took in three subscriptions for half a dollar apiece on condition of them paying him in advance; they were going to pay in cord-wood and onions, as usual, but he said he had just bought the concern and knocked down the price as low as he could afford it, and was going to run it for cash. He set up a little piece of poetry, which he made, himself, out of his own head — three verses — kind of sweet and saddish — the name of it was, "Yes, crush, cold world, this breaking heart" — and he left that all set up and ready to print in the paper and didn't charge nothing for it. Well, he took in nine dollars and a half, and said he'd done a pretty square day's work for it.

Then he showed us another little job he'd printed and hadn't charged for, because it was for us. It had a picture of a runaway nigger, with a bundle on a stick, over his shoulder, and "$200 reward" under it. The reading was all about Jim, and just described him to a dot. It said he run away from St. Jacques' plantation, forty mile below New Orleans, last winter, and likely went north, and whoever would catch him and send him back, he could have the reward and expenses.

"Now," says the duke, "after to-night we can run in the daytime if we want to. Whenever we see anybody coming, we can tie Jim hand and foot with a rope, and lay him in the wigwam and show this handbill and say we captured him up the river, and were too poor to travel on a steamboat, so we got this little raft on credit from our friends and are going down to get the reward. Handcuffs and chains would look still better on Jim, but it wouldn't go well with the story of us being so poor. Too much like jewelry. Ropes are the correct thing — we must preserve the unities, as we say on the boards."

We all said the duke was pretty smart, and there couldn't be no trouble about running daytimes. We judged we could make miles enough that night to get out of the reach of the pow-wow we reckoned the duke's work in the printing office was going to make in that little town — then we could boom right along, if we wanted to.

We laid low and kept still, and never shoved out till nearly ten o'clock; then we slid by, pretty wide away from the town, and didn't hoist our lantern till we was clear out of sight of it.

When Jim called me to take the watch at four in the morning, he says —

"Huck, does you reck'n we gwyne to run acrost any mo' kings on dis trip?"

"No," I says, "I reckon not."

"Well," says he, "dat's all right, den. I doan' mine one er two kings, but dat's enough. Dis one's powerful drunk, en de duke ain' much better."

I found Jim had been trying to get him to talk French, so he could hear what it was like; but he said he had been in this country so long, and had so much trouble, he'd forgot it.

Chapter XXI

It was after sun-up, now, but we went right on, and didn't tie up. The king and the duke turned out, by-and-by, looking pretty rusty; but after they'd jumped overboard and took a swim, it chippered them up a good deal. After breakfast the king he took a seat on a corner of the raft, and pulled off his boots and rolled up his britches, and let his legs dangle in the water, so as to be comfortable, and lit his pipe, and went to getting his Romeo and Juliet by heart. When he had got it pretty good, him and the duke begun to practice it together. The duke had to learn him over and over again, how to say every speech; and he made him sigh, and put his hand on his heart, and after a while he said he done it pretty well; "only," he says, "you mustn't bellow out *Romeo!* that way, like a bull — you must say it soft, and sick, and languishy, so — R-o-o-meo! that is the idea; for Juliet's a dear sweet mere child of a girl, you know, and she don't bray like a jackass."

Well, next they got out a couple of long swords that the duke made out of oak laths, and begun to practice the sword-fight — the duke called himself Richard III.; and the way they laid on, and pranced around the raft was grand to see. But by-and-by the king tripped and fell overboard, and after that they took a rest, and had a talk about all kinds of adventures they'd had in other times along the river.

After dinner, the duke says:

"Well, Capet, we'll want to make this a first-class show, you know, so I guess we'll add a little more to it. We want a little something to answer encores with, anyway."

"What's onkores, Bilgewater?"

The duke told him, and then says:

"I'll answer by doing the Highland fling or the sailor's hornpipe; and you — well, let me see — oh, I've got it — you can do Hamlet's soliloquy."

"Hamlet's which?"

"Hamlet's soliloquy, you know; the most celebrated thing in Shakespeare. Ah, it's sublime, sublime! Always fetches the house. I haven't got it in the book — I've only got one volume — but I reckon I can piece it out from memory. I'll just walk up and down a minute, and see if I can call it back from recollection's vaults."

So he went to marching up and down, thinking, and frowning horrible every now and then; then he would hoist up his eye-brows; next he would squeeze his hand on his forehead and stagger back and kind of moan; next he would sigh, and next he'd let on to drop a tear. It was beautiful to

see him. By-and-by he got it. He told us to give attention. Then he strikes a
most noble attitude, with one leg shoved forwards, and his arms stretched
away up, and his head tilted back, looking up at the sky; and then he
begins to rip and rave and grit his teeth; and after that, all through his
speech he howled, and spread around, and swelled up his chest, and just
knocked the spots out of any acting ever *I* see before. This is the speech —
I learned it, easy enough, while he was learning it to the king:

> To be, or not to be; that is the bare bodkin
> That makes calamity of so long life;
> For who would fardels bear, till Birnam Wood do come to Dunsinane,
> But that the fear of something after death
> Murders the innocent sleep,
> Great nature's second course,
> And makes us rather sling the arrows of outrageous fortune
> Than fly to others that we know not of.
> There's the respect must give us pause:
> Wake Duncan with thy knocking! I would thou couldst;
> For who would bear the whips and scorns of time,
> The oppressor's wrong, the proud man's contumely,
> The law's delay, and the quietus which his pangs might take,
> In the dead waste and middle of the night, when churchyards yawn
> In customary suits of solemn black,
> But that the undiscovered country from whose bourne no traveler returns,
> Breathes forth contagion on the world,
> And thus the native hue of resolution, like the poor cat i' the adage,
> Is sicklied o'er with care,
> And all the clouds that lowered o'er our housetops,
> With this regard their currents turn awry,
> And lose the name of action.
> 'Tis a consummation devoutly to be wished. But soft you, the fair Ophelia:
> Ope not thy ponderous and marble jaws,
> But get thee to a nunnery — go!

Well, the old man he liked that speech, and he mighty soon got it so
he could do it first rate. It seemed like he was just born for it; and when
he had his hand in and was excited, it was perfectly lovely the way he
would rip and tear and rair up behind when he was getting it off.

The first chance we got, the duke he had some show bills printed; and
after that, for two or three days as we floated along, the raft was a most
uncommon lively place, for there warn't nothing but sword-fighting and
rehearsing — as the duke called it — going on all the time. One morning,
when we was pretty well down the State of Arkansaw, we come in sight of
a little one-horse town in a big bend; so we tied up about three-quarters

of a mile above it, in the mouth of a crick which was shut in like a tunnel by the cypress trees, and all of us but Jim took the canoe and went down there to see if there was any chance in that place for our show.

We struck it mighty lucky; there was going to be a circus there that afternoon, and the country people was already beginning to come in, in all kinds of old shackly wagons, and on horses. The circus would leave before night, so our show would have a pretty good chance. The duke he hired the court house, and we went around and stuck up our bills. They read like this:

Shaksperean Revival!!!
Wonderful Attraction!
For One Night Only!
The world renowned tragedians,
David Garrick the younger, of Drury Lane Theatre, London,
and
Edmund Kean the elder, of the Royal Haymarket Theatre, White-
chapel, Pudding Lane, Piccadilly, London, and the
Royal Continental Theatres, in their sublime
Shaksperean Spectacle entitled
The Balcony Scene
in
Romeo and Juliet!!!

Romeo .... Mr. Garrick.
Juliet .... Mr. Kean.
Assisted by the whole strength of the company!
New costumes, new scenery, new appointments!
Also:
The thrilling, masterly, and blood-curdling
Broad-sword conflict
In Richard III.!!!

Richard III .... Mr. Garrick.
Richmond .... Mr. Kean.
also:
(by special request,)
Hamlet's Immortal Soliloquy!!
By the Illustrious Kean!
Done by him 300 consecutive nights in Paris!
For One Night Only,
On account of imperative European engagements!
Admission 25 cents; children and servants, 10 cents.

Then we went loafing around the town. The stores and houses was most all old shackly dried-up frame concerns that hadn't ever been painted; they was set up three or four foot above ground on stilts, so as to be out of reach of the water when the river was overflowed. The houses had little gardens around them, but they didn't seem to raise hardly anything in them but jimpson weeds, and sunflowers, and ash-piles, and old curled-up boots and shoes, and pieces of bottles, and rags, and played-out tin-ware. The fences was made of different kinds of boards, nailed on at different times; and they leaned every which-way, and had gates that didn't generly have but one hinge — a leather one. Some of the fences had been whitewashed, some time or another, but the duke said it was in Clumbus's time, like enough. There was generly hogs in the garden, and people driving them out.

All the stores was along one street. They had white-domestic awnings in front, and the country people hitched their horses to the awning-posts. There was empty dry-goods boxes under the awnings, and loafers roosting on them all day long, whittling them with their Barlow knives; and chawing tobacco, and gaping and yawning and stretching — a mighty ornery lot. They generly had on yellow straw hats most as wide as an umbrella, but didn't wear no coats nor waistcoats; they called one another Bill, and Buck, and Hank, and Joe, and Andy, and talked lazy and drawly, and used considerable many cuss-words. There was as many as one loafer leaning up against every awning-post, and he most always had his hands in his britches pockets, except when he fetched them out to lend a chaw of tobacco or scratch. What a body was hearing amongst them, all the time was —

"Gimme a chaw 'v tobacker, Hank."

"Cain't — I hain't got but one chaw left. Ask Bill."

Maybe Bill he gives him a chaw; maybe he lies and says he ain't got none. Some of them kinds of loafers never has a cent in the world, nor a chaw of tobacco of their own. They get all their chawing by borrowing — they say to a fellow, "I wisht you'd len' me a chaw, Jack, I jist this minute give Ben Thompson the last chaw I had" — which is a lie, pretty much every time; it don't fool nobody but a stranger; but Jack ain't no stranger, so he says —

"*You* give him a chaw, did you? so did your sister's cat's grandmother. You pay me back the chaws you've awready borry'd off'n me, Lafe Buckner, then I'll loan you one or two ton of it, and won't charge you no back intrust, nuther."

"Well, I *did* pay you back some of it wunst."

"Yes, you did — 'bout six chaws. You borry'd store tobacker and paid back nigger-head."

Store tobacco is flat black plug, but these fellows mostly chaws the natural leaf twisted. When they borrow a chaw, they don't generly cut it off with a knife, but they set the plug in between their teeth, and gnaw with their teeth and tug at the plug with their hands till they get it in two—then sometimes the one that owns the tobacco looks mournful at it when it's handed back, and says, sarcastic—

"Here, gimme the *chaw*, and you take the *plug*."

All the streets and lanes was just mud, they warn't nothing else *but* mud—mud as black as tar, and high about a foot deep in some places; and two or three inches deep in *all* the places. The hogs loafed and grunted around, everywheres. You'd see a muddy sow and a litter of pigs come lazying along the street and whollop herself right down in the way, where folks had to walk around her, and she'd stretch out, and shut her eyes, and wave her ears, whilst the pigs was milking her, and look as happy as if she was on salary. And pretty soon you'd hear a loafer sing out, "Hi! *so* boy! sick him, Tige!" and away the sow would go, squealing most horrible, with a dog or two swinging to each ear, and three or four dozen more a-coming; and then you would see all the loafers get up and watch the thing out of sight, and laugh at the fun and look grateful for the noise. Then they'd settle back again till there was a dog-fight. There couldn't anything wake them up all over, and make them happy all over, like a dog-fight—unless it might be putting turpentine on a stray dog and setting fire to him, or tying a tin pan to his tail and see him run himself to death.

On the river front some of the houses was sticking out over the bank, and they was bowed and bent, and about ready to tumble in. The people had moved out of them. The bank was caved away under one corner of some others, and that corner was hanging over. People lived in them yet, but it was dangersome, because sometimes a strip of land as wide as a house caves in at a time. Sometimes a belt of land a quarter of a mile deep will start in and cave along and cave along till it all caves into the river in one summer. Such a town as that has to be always moving back, and back, and back, because the river's always gnawing at it.

The nearer it got to noon that day, the thicker and thicker was the wagons and horses in the streets, and more coming all the time. Families fetched their dinners with them, from the country, and eat them in the wagons. There was considerable whiskey drinking going on, and I seen three fights. By-and-by somebody sings out—

"Here comes old Boggs!—in from the country for his little old monthly drunk—here he comes, boys!"

All the loafers looked glad—I reckoned they was used to having fun out of Boggs. One of them says—

"Wonder who he's a gwyne to chaw up this time. If he'd a chawed up all the men he's ben a gwyne to chaw up in the last twenty year, he'd have considerble ruputation, now."

Another one says, "I wisht old Boggs 'd threaten me, 'cuz then I'd know I warn't gwyne to die for a thousan' year."

Boggs comes a-tearing along on his horse, whooping and yelling like an Injun, and singing out —

"Cler the track, thar. I'm on the waw-path, and the price uv coffins is a gwyne to raise."

He was drunk, and weaving about in his saddle; he was over fifty year old, and had a very red face. Everybody yelled at him, and laughed at him, and sassed him, and he sassed back, and said he'd attend to them and lay them out in their regular turns, but he couldn't wait now, because he'd come to town to kill old Colonel Sherburn, and his motto was, "meat first, and spoon vittles to top off on."

He see me, and rode up and says —

"Whar'd you come f'm, boy? You prepared to die?"

Then he rode on. I was scared; but a man says —

"He don't mean nothing; he's always a carryin' on like that, when he's drunk. He's the best-naturedest old fool in Arkansaw — never hurt no-body, drunk nor sober."

Boggs rode up before the biggest store in town and bent his head down so he could see under the curtain of the awning, and yells —

"Come out here, Sherburn! Come out and meet the man you've swindled. You're the houn' I'm after, and I'm a gwyne to have you, too!"

And so he went on, calling Sherburn everything he could lay his tongue to, and the whole street packed with people listening and laughing and going on. By-and-by a proud-looking man about fifty-five — and he was a heap the best dressed man in that town, too — steps out of the store, and the crowd drops back on each side to let him come. He says to Boggs, mighty ca'm and slow — he says:

"I'm tired of this; but I'll endure it till one o'clock. Till one o'clock, mind — no longer. If you open your mouth against me only once, after that time, you can't travel so far but I will find you."

Then he turns and goes in. The crowd looked mighty sober; nobody stirred, and there warn't no more laughing. Boggs rode off blackguarding Sherburn as loud as he could yell, all down the street; and pretty soon back he comes and stops before the store, still keeping it up. Some men crowded around him and tried to get him to shut up, but he wouldn't; they told him it would be one o'clock in about fifteen minutes, and so he *must* go home — he must go right away. But it didn't do no good. He cussed away, with all his might, and throwed his hat down in the mud and rode over it, and pretty soon away he went a-raging down the street again, with his gray hair a-flying. Everybody that could get a chance at him tried their best to coax him off of his horse so they could lock him up and get him sober; but it warn't no use — up the street he would tear again, and give Sherburn another cussing. By-and-by somebody says —

"Go for his daughter! — quick, go for his daughter; sometimes he'll listen to her. If anybody can persuade him, she can."

So somebody started on a run. I walked down street a ways, and stopped. In about five or ten minutes, here comes Boggs again — but not on his horse. He was a-reeling across the street towards me, bareheaded, with a friend on both sides of him aholt of his arms and hurrying him along. He was quiet, and looked uneasy; and he warn't hanging back any, but was doing some of the hurrying himself. Somebody sings out —

"Boggs!"

I looked over there to see who said it, and it was that Colonel Sherburn. He was standing perfectly still, in the street, and had a pistol raised in his right hand — not aiming it, but holding it out with the barrel tilted up towards the sky. The same second I see a young girl coming on the run, and two men with her. Boggs and the men turned round, to see who called him, and when they see the pistol the men jumped to one side, and the pistol barrel come down slow and steady to a level — both barrels cocked. Boggs throws up both of his hands, and says, "O Lord, don't shoot!" Bang! goes the first shot, and he staggers back clawing at the air — bang! goes the second one, and he tumbles backwards onto the ground, heavy and solid, with his arms spread out. That young girl screamed out, and comes rushing, and down she throws herself on her father, crying, and saying, "Oh, he's killed him, he's killed him!" The crowd closed up around them, and shouldered and jammed one another, with their necks stretched, trying to see, and people on the inside trying to shove them back, and shouting, "Back, back! give him air, give him air!"

Colonel Sherburn he tossed his pistol onto the ground, and turned around on his heels and walked off.

They took Boggs to a little drug store, the crowd pressing around, just the same, and the whole town following, and I rushed and got a good place at the window, where I was close to him and could see in. They laid him on the floor, and put one large Bible under his head, and opened another one and spread it on his breast — but they tore open his shirt first, and I seen where one of the bullets went in. He made about a dozen long gasps, his breast lifting the Bible up when he drawed in his breath, and letting it down again when he breathed it out — and after that he laid still; he was dead. Then they pulled his daughter away from him, screaming and crying, and took her off. She was about sixteen, and very sweet and gentle-looking, but awful pale and scared.

Well, pretty soon the whole town was there, squirming and scrouging and pushing and shoving to get at the window and have a look, but people that had the places wouldn't give them up, and folks behind them was saying all the time, "Say, now, you've looked enough, you fellows; 'taint right and 'taint fair, for you to stay thar all the time, and never give nobody a chance; other folks has their rights as well as you."

There was considerable jawing back, so I slid out, thinking maybe there was going to be trouble. The streets was full, and everybody was excited. Everybody that seen the shooting was telling how it happened, and there was a big crowd packed around each one of these fellows, stretching their necks and listening. One long lanky man, with long hair and a big white fur stove-pipe hat on the back of his head, and a crooked-handled cane, marked out the places on the ground where Boggs stood, and where Sherburn stood, and the people following him around from one place to t'other and watching everything he done, and bobbing their heads to show they understood, and stooping a little and resting their hands on their thighs to watch him mark the places on the ground with his cane; and then he stood up straight and stiff where Sherburn had stood, frowning and having his hat-brim down over his eyes, and sung out, "Boggs!" and then fetched his cane down slow to a level, and says "Bang!" staggered backwards, says "Bang!" again, and fell down flat on his back. The people that had seen the thing said he done it perfect; said it was just exactly the way it all happened. Then as much as a dozen people got out their bottles and treated him.

Well, by-and-by somebody said Sherburn ought to be lynched. In about a minute everybody was saying it; so away they went, mad and yelling, and snatching down every clothes-line they come to, to do the hanging with.

Chapter XXII

They swarmed up the street towards Sherburn's house, a-whooping and yelling and raging like Injuns, and everything had to clear the way or get run over and tromped to mush, and it was awful to see. Children was heeling it ahead of the mob, screaming and trying to get out of the way; and every window along the road was full of women's heads, and there was nigger boys in every tree, and bucks and wenches looking over every fence; and as soon as the mob would get nearly to them they would break and skaddle back out of reach. Lots of the women and girls was crying and taking on, scared most to death.

They swarmed up in front of Sherburn's palings as thick as they could jam together, and you couldn't hear yourself think for the noise. It was a little twenty-foot yard. Some sung out "Tear down the fence! tear down the fence!" Then there was a racket of ripping and tearing and smashing, and down she goes, and the front wall of the crowd begins to roll in like a wave.

Just then Sherburn steps out on to the roof of his little front porch, with a double-barrel gun in his hand, and takes his stand, perfectly ca'm and deliberate, not saying a word. The racket stopped, and the wave sucked back.

Sherburn never said a word — just stood there, looking down. The stillness was awful creepy and uncomfortable. Sherburn run his eye slow along the crowd; and wherever it struck, the people tried a little to outgaze him, but they couldn't; they dropped their eyes and looked sneaky. Then pretty soon Sherburn sort of laughed; not the pleasant kind, but the kind that makes you feel like when you are eating bread that's got sand in it.

Then he says, slow and scornful:

"The idea of *you* lynching anybody! It's amusing. The idea of you thinking you had pluck enough to lynch a *man!* Because you're brave enough to tar and feather poor friendless cast-out women that come along here, did that make you think you had grit enough to lay your hands on a *man?* Why, a *man's* safe in the hands of ten thousand of your kind — as long as it's day-time and you're not behind him.

"Do I know you? I know you clear through. I was born and raised in the South, and I've lived in the North; so I know the average all around. The average man's a coward. In the North he lets anybody walk over him that wants to, and goes home and prays for a humble spirit to bear it. In the South one man, all by himself, has stopped a stage full of men, in the day-time, and robbed the lot. Your newspapers call you a brave people so much that you think you *are* braver than any other people — whereas you're just *as* brave, and no braver. Why don't your juries hang murderers? Because they're afraid the man's friends will shoot them in the back, in the dark — and it's just what they *would* do.

"So they always acquit; and then a *man* goes in the night, with a hundred masked cowards at his back, and lynches the rascal. Your mistake is, that you didn't bring a man with you; that's one mistake, and the other is that you didn't come in the dark, and fetch your masks. You brought *part* of a man — Buck Harkness, there — and if you hadn't had him to start you, you'd a taken it out in blowing.

"You didn't want to come. The average man don't like trouble and danger. *You* don't like trouble and danger. But if only *half* a man — like Buck Harkness, there — shouts 'Lynch him, lynch him!' you're afraid to back down — afraid you'll be found out to be what you are — *cowards* — and so you raise a yell, and hang yourselves onto that half-a-man's coat tail, and come raging up here, swearing what big things you're going to do. The pitifulest thing out is a mob; that's what an army is — a mob; they don't fight with courage that's born in them, but with courage that's borrowed from their mass, and from their officers. But a mob without any *man* at the head of it, is *beneath* pitifulness. Now the thing for *you* to do, is to droop your tails and go home and crawl in a hole. If any real lynching's going to be done, it will be done in the dark, Southern fashion; and when they come they'll bring their masks, and fetch a *man* along. Now *leave* — and take your half-a-man with you" — tossing his gun up across his left arm and cocking it, when he says this.

The crowd washed back sudden, and then broke all apart and went tearing off every which way, and Buck Harkness he heeled it after them, looking tolerable cheap. I could a staid, if I'd a wanted to, but I didn't want to.

I went to the circus, and loafed around the back side till the watchman went by, and then dived in under the tent. I had my twenty-dollar gold piece and some other money, but I reckoned I better save it, because there ain't no telling how soon you are going to need it, away from home and amongst strangers, that way. You can't be too careful. I ain't opposed to spending money on circuses, when there ain't no other way, but there ain't no use in *wasting* it on them.

It was a real bully circus. It was the splendidest sight that ever was, when they all come riding in, two and two, a gentleman and lady, side by side, the men just in their drawers and under-shirts, and no shoes nor stirrups, and resting their hands on their thighs, easy and comfortable — there must a' been twenty of them — and every lady with a lovely complexion, and perfectly beautiful, and looking just like a gang of real sure-enough queens, and dressed in clothes that cost millions of dollars, and just littered with diamonds. It was a powerful fine sight; I never see anything so lovely. And then one by one they got up and stood, and went a-weaving around the ring so gentle and wavy and graceful, the men looking ever so tall and airy and straight, with their heads bobbing and skimming along, away up there under the tent-roof, and every lady's rose-leafy dress flapping soft and silky around her hips, and she looking like the most loveliest parasol.

And then faster and faster they went, all of them dancing, first one foot stuck out in the air and then the other, the horses leaning more and more, and the ring-master going round and round the centre-pole, cracking his whip and shouting "hi! — hi!" and the clown cracking jokes behind him; and by-and-by all hands dropped the reins, and every lady put her knuckles on her hips and every gentleman folded his arms, and then how the horses did lean over and hump themselves! And so, one after the other they all skipped off into the ring, and made the sweetest bow I ever see, and then scampered out, and everybody clapped their hands and went just about wild.

Well, all through the circus they done the most astonishing things; and all the time that clown carried on so it most killed the people. The ring-master couldn't ever say a word to him but he was back at him quick as a wink with the funniest things a body ever said; and how he ever *could* think of so many of them, and so sudden and so pat, was what I couldn't noway understand. Why, I couldn't a thought of them in a year. And by-and-by a drunk man tried to get into the ring — said he wanted to ride; said he could ride as well as anybody that ever was. They argued and tried to keep him out, but he wouldn't listen, and the whole show come to a standstill. Then the people begun to holler at him and make fun of him, and that made him mad, and he begun to rip and tear; so that stirred up the people, and a lot of men begun to pile down off of the benches and swarm towards the ring, saying, "Knock him down! throw him out!" and one or two women begun to scream. So, then, the ring-master he made a little speech, and said he hoped there wouldn't be no disturbance, and if the man would promise he wouldn't make no more trouble, he would let him ride, if he thought he could stay on the horse. So everybody laughed and said all right, and the man got on. The minute he was on, the horse begun to rip and tear and jump and cavort around, with two circus men hanging onto his bridle trying to hold him, and the drunk man hanging onto his neck, and his heels flying in the air every jump, and the whole crowd of people standing up shouting and laughing till the tears rolled down. And at last, sure enough, all the circus men could do, the horse broke loose, and away he went like the very nation, round and round the ring, with that sot laying down on him and hanging to his neck, with first one leg hanging most to the ground on one side, and then t'other one on t'other side, and the people just crazy. It warn't funny to me, though; I was all of a tremble to see his danger. But pretty soon he struggled up astraddle and grabbed the bridle, a-reeling this way and that; and the next minute he sprung up and dropped the bridle and stood! and the horse agoing like a house afire too. He just stood up there, a-sailing around as easy and comfortable as if he warn't ever drunk in his life — and then he begun to pull off his clothes and sling them. He shed them so thick they kind of clogged up the air, and altogether he shed seventeen suits. And then, there he was, slim and handsome, and dressed the gaudiest and prettiest you ever saw, and he lit into that horse with his whip and made him fairly hum — and finally skipped off, and made his bow and danced off to the dressing-room, and everybody just a-howling with pleasure and astonishment.

Then the ring-master he see how he had been fooled, and he *was* the sickest ring-master you ever see, I reckon. Why, it was one of his own men! He had got up that joke all out of his own head, and never let on to nobody. Well, I felt sheepish enough, to be took in so, but I wouldn't a been in that ring-master's place, not for a thousand dollars. I don't know; there may be bullier circuses than what that one was, but I never struck them yet. Anyways it was plenty good enough for *me*; and wherever I run across it, it can have all of *my* custom, every time.

Well, that night we had *our* show; but there warn't only about twelve people there; just enough to pay expenses. And they laughed all the time, and that made the duke mad; and everybody left, anyway, before the show was over, but one boy which was asleep. So the duke said these Arkansaw lunkheads couldn't come up to Shakspeare; what they wanted was low comedy — and maybe something ruther worse than low comedy, he reckoned. He said he could size their style. So next morning he got some big sheets of wrapping-paper and some black paint, and drawed off some handbills and stuck them up all over the village. The bills said:

AT THE COURT HOUSE!
FOR 3 NIGHTS ONLY!
The World-Renowned Tragedians
DAVID GARRICK THE YOUNGER!
AND
EDMUND KEAN THE ELDER!
*Of the London and Continental
Theatres,*
In their Thrilling Tragedy of
THE KING'S CAMELOPARD
OR
THE ROYAL NONESUCH!!!
Admission 50 cents.

Then at the bottom was the biggest line of all — which said:

LADIES AND CHILDREN NOT ADMITTED.

"There," says he, "if that line don't fetch them, I don't know Arkansaw!"

Chapter XXIII

Well, all day him and the king was hard at it, rigging up a stage, and a curtain, and a row of candles for footlights; and that night the house was jam full of men in no time. When the place couldn't hold no more, the duke he quit tending door and went around the back way and come onto the stage and stood up before the curtain, and made a little speech, and praised up this tragedy, and said it was the most thrillingest one that ever was; and so he went on a-bragging about the tragedy and about Edmund Kean the Elder, which was to play the main principal part in it; and at last when he'd got everybody's expectations up high enough, he rolled up the curtain, and the next minute the king come a-prancing out on all fours, naked; and he was painted all over, ring-streaked-and-striped, all sorts of colors, as splendid as a rainbow. And—but never mind the rest of his outfit, it was just wild, but it was awful funny. The people most killed themselves laughing; and when the king got done capering, and capered off behind the scenes, they roared and clapped and stormed and haw-hawed till he come back and done it over again; and after that, they made him do it another time. Well, it would a made a cow laugh to see the shines that old idiot cut.

Then the duke he lets the curtain down, and bows to the people, and says the great tragedy will be performed only two nights more, on accounts of pressing London engagements, where the seats is all sold aready for it in Drury Lane; and then he makes them another bow, and says if he has succeeded in pleasing them and instructing them, he will be deeply obleeged if they will mention it to their friends and get them to come and see it.

Twenty people sings out:

"What, is it over? Is that *all*?"

The duke says yes. Then there was a fine time. Everybody sings out "sold," and rose up mad, and was agoing for that stage and them tragedians. But a big fine-looking man jumps up on a bench, and shouts:

"Hold on! Just a word, gentlemen." They stopped to listen. "We are sold—mighty badly sold. But we don't want to be the laughing-stock of this whole town, I reckon, and never hear the last of this thing as long as we live. No. What we want, is to go out of here quiet, and talk this show up, and sell the *rest* of the town! Then we'll all be in the same boat. Ain't that sensible?" ("You bet it is!—the jedge is right!" everybody sings out.) "All right, then—not a word about any sell. Go along home, and advise everybody to come and see the tragedy."

Next day you couldn't hear nothing around that town but how splendid that show was. House was jammed again, that night, and we sold this crowd the same way. When me and the king and the duke got home to the raft, we all had a supper; and by-and-by, about midnight, they made Jim and me back her out and float her down the middle of the river and fetch her in and hide her about two mile below town.

The third night the house was crammed again — and they warn't new-comers, this time, but people that was at the show the other two nights. I stood by the duke at the door, and I see that every man that went in had his pockets bulging, or something muffled up under his coat — and I see it warn't no perfumery neither, not by a long sight. I smelt sickly eggs by the barrel, and rotten cabbages, and such things; and if I know the signs of a dead cat being around, and I bet I do, there was sixty-four of them went in. I shoved in there for a minute, but it was too various for me, I couldn't stand it. Well, when the place couldn't hold no more people, the duke he give a fellow a quarter and told him to tend door for him a minute, and then he started around for the stage door, I after him; but the minute we turned the corner and was in the dark, he says:

"Walk fast, now, till you get away from the houses, and then shin for the raft like the dickens was after you!"

I done it, and he done the same. We struck the raft at the same time, and in less than two seconds we was gliding down stream, all dark and still, and edging towards the middle of the river, nobody saying a word. I reckoned the poor king was in for a gaudy time of it with the audience; but nothing of the sort; pretty soon he crawls out from under the wigwam, and says:

"Well, how'd the old thing pan out this time, Duke?"

He hadn't been up town at all.

We never showed a light till we was about ten mile below that village. Then we lit up and had a supper, and the king and the duke fairly laughed their bones loose over the way they'd served them people. The duke says:

"Greenhorns, flatheads! *I* knew the first house would keep mum and let the rest of the town get roped in; and I knew they'd lay for us the third night, and consider it was *their* turn now. Well, it *is* their turn, and I'd give something to know how much they'd take for it. I *would* just like to know how they're putting in their opportunity. They can turn it into a picnic, if they want to — they brought plenty provisions."

Them rapscallions took in four hundred and sixty-five dollars in that three nights. I never see money hauled in by the wagon-load like that, before.

By-and-by, when they was asleep and snoring, Jim says:

"Don't it 'sprise you, de way dem kings carries on, Huck?"

"No," I says, "it don't."

"Why don't it, Huck?"

"Well, it don't, because it's in the breed. I reckon they're all alike."

"But, Huck, dese kings o' ourn is regular rapscallions; dat's jist what dey is; dey's reglar rapscallions."

"Well, that's what I'm a-saying; all kings is mostly rapscallions, as fur as I can make out."

"Is dat so?"

"You read about them once—you'll see. Look at Henry the Eight; this'n 's a Sunday-School Superintendent to *him.* And look at Charles Second, and Louis Fourteen, and Louis Fifteen, and James Second, and Edward Second, and Richard Third, and forty more; besides all them Saxon heptarchies that used to rip around so in old times and raise Cain. My, you ought to seen old Henry the Eight when he was in bloom. He *was* a blossom. He used to marry a new wife every day, and chop off her head next morning. And he would do it just as indifferent as if he was ordering up eggs. 'Fetch up Nell Gwynn,' he says. They fetch her up. Next morning, 'Chop off her head!' And they chop it off. 'Fetch up Jane Shore,' he says; and up she comes. Next morning 'Chop off her head'— and they chop it off. 'Ring up Fair Rosamun.' Fair Rosamun answers the bell. Next morning, 'Chop off her head.' And he made every one of them tell him a tale every night; and he kept that up till he had hogged a thousand and one tales that way, and then he put them all in a book, and called it Domesday Book—which was a good name and stated the case. You don't know kings, Jim, but I know them; and this old rip of ourn is one of the cleanest I've struck in history. Well, Henry he takes a notion he wants to get up some trouble with this country. How does he go at it—give notice?—give the country a show? No. All of a sudden he heaves all the tea in Boston Harbor overboard, and whacks out a declaration of independence, and dares them to come on. That was *his* style—he never give anybody a chance. He had suspicions of his father, the Duke of Wellington. Well, what did he do?—ask him to show up? No—drownded him in a butt of mamsey, like a cat. Spose people left money laying around where he was—what did he do? He collared it. Spose he contracted to do a thing; and you paid him, and didn't set down there and see that he done it—what did he do? He always done the other thing. Spose he opened his mouth—what then? If he didn't shut it up powerful quick, he'd lose a lie, every time. That's the kind of a bug Henry was; and if we'd a had him along 'stead of our kings, he'd a fooled that town a heap worse than ourn done. I don't say that ourn is lambs, because they ain't, when you come right down to the cold facts; but they ain't nothing to *that* old ram, anyway. All I say is, kings is kings, and you got to make allowances. Take them all around, they're a mighty ornery lot. It's the way they're raised."

"But dis one do *smell* so like de nation, Huck."

"Well, they all do, Jim. We can't help the way a king smells; history don't tell no way."

"Now de duke, he's a tolerble likely man, in some ways."

"Yes, a duke's different. But not very different. This one's a middling hard lot, for a duke. When he's drunk, there ain't no near-sighted man could tell him from a king."

"Well, anyways, I doan' hanker for no mo' un um, Huck. Dese is all I kin stan'."

"It's the way I feel, too, Jim. But we've got them on our hands, and we got to remember what they are, and make allowances. Sometimes I wish we could hear of a country that's out of kings."

What was the use to tell Jim these warn't real kings and dukes? It wouldn't a done no good; and besides, it was just as I said; you couldn't tell them from the real kind.

I went to sleep, and Jim didn't call me when it was my turn. He often done that. When I waked up, just at day-break, he was setting there with his head down betwixt his knees, moaning and mourning to himself. I didn't take notice, nor let on. I knowed what it was about. He was thinking about his wife and his children, away up yonder, and he was low and homesick; because he hadn't ever been away from home before in his life; and I do believe he cared just as much for his people as white folks does for their'n. It don't seem natural, but I reckon it's so. He was often moaning and mourning that way, nights, when he judged I was asleep, and saying, "Po' little 'Lizabeth! po' little Johnny! it's mighty hard; I spec' I ain't ever gwyne to see you no mo', no mo'!" He was a mighty good nigger, Jim was.

But this time I somehow got to talking to him about his wife and young ones; and by-and-by he says:

"What makes me feel so bad dis time, 'uz bekase I hear sumpn over yonder on de bank like a whack, er a slam, while ago, en it mine me er de time I treat my little 'Lizabeth so ornery. She warn't on'y 'bout fo' year ole, en she tuck de sk'yarlet-fever, en had a powful rough spell; but she got well, en one day she was a-stannin' aroun', en I says to her, I says:

" 'Shet de do'.'"

"She never done it; jis' stood dah, kiner smilin' up at me. It make me mad; en I says agin, mighty loud, I says:

" 'Doan' you hear me? — shet de do'!'"

"She jis' stood de same way, kiner smilin' up. I was a-bilin'! I says:

" 'I lay I *make* you mine!'"

"En wid dat I fetch' her a slap side de head dat sont her a-sprawlin'. Den I went into de yuther room, en 'uz gone 'bout ten minutes; en when I come back, dah was dat do' a-stannin' open *yit*, en dat chile stannin' mos' right in it, a-lookin' down and mournin', en de tears runnin' down. My, but I *wuz* mad, I was agwyne for de chile, but jis' den — it was a do' dat open innerds — jis' den, 'long come de wind en slam it to, behine de chile, ker-*blam!* — en my lan', de chile never move'! My breff mos' hop outer me; en I feel so — so — I doan' know *how* I feel. I crope out, all a-tremblin', en crope aroun' en open de do' easy en slow, en poke my head in behine de chile, sof' en still, en all uv a sudden, I says *pow!* jis' as loud as I could yell. *She never budge!* Oh, Huck, I bust out a-cryin' en grab her up in my arms, en say, 'Oh, de po' little thing! de Lord God Amighty fogive po' ole Jim, kaze he never gwyne to fogive hisself as long's he live!' Oh, she was plumb deef en dumb, Huck, plumb deef en dumb — en I'd ben a-treat'n her so!"

Chapter XXIV

Next day, towards night, we laid up under a little willow tow-head out in the middle, where there was a village on each side of the river, and the duke and the king begun to lay out a plan for working them towns. Jim he spoke to the duke, and said he hoped it wouldn't take but a few hours, because it got mighty heavy and tiresome to him when he had to lay all day in the wigwam tied with the rope. You see, when we left him all alone we had to tie him, because if anybody happened on him all by himself and not tied, it wouldn't look much like he was a runaway nigger, you know. So the duke said it *was* kind of hard to have to lay roped all day, and he'd cipher out some way to get around it.

He was uncommon bright, the duke was, and he soon struck it. He dressed Jim up in King Lear's outfit — it was a long curtain-calico gown, and a white horse-hair wig and whiskers; and then he took his theatre-paint and painted Jim's face and hands and ears and neck all over a dead dull solid blue, like a man that's been drownded nine days. Blamed if he warn't the horriblest looking outrage I ever see. Then the duke took and wrote out a sign on a shingle so —

Sick Arab — but harmless when not out of his head.

And he nailed that shingle to a lath, and stood the lath up four or five foot in front of the wigwam. Jim was satisfied. He said it was a sight better than laying tied a couple of years every day and trembling all over every time there was a sound. The duke told him to make himself free and easy, and if anybody ever come meddling around, he must hop out of the wigwam, and carry on a little, and fetch a howl or two like a wild beast, and he reckoned they would light out and leave him alone. Which was sound enough judgment; but you take the average man, and he wouldn't wait for him to howl. Why, he didn't only look like he was dead, he looked considerable more than that.

These rapscallions wanted to try the Nonesuch again, because there was so much money in it, but they judged it wouldn't be safe, because maybe the news might a worked along down by this time. They couldn't hit no project that suited, exactly; so at last the duke said he reckoned he'd lay off and work his brains an hour or two and see if he couldn't put up something on the Arkansaw village; and the king he allowed he would drop over to t'other village, without any plan, but just trust in Providence to lead him the profitable way — meaning the devil, I reckon. We had all bought store clothes where we stopped last; and now the king put his'n on, and he told me to put mine on. I done it, of course. The king's duds was all black, and he did look real swell and starchy. I never knowed how clothes could change a body before. Why, before, he looked like the orneriest old rip that ever was; but now, when he'd take off his new white beaver and make a bow and do a smile, he looked that grand and good and pious that you'd say he had walked right out of the ark, and maybe was old Leviticus himself. Jim cleaned up the canoe, and I got my paddle ready. There was a big steamboat laying at the shore away up under the point, about three mile above town — been there a couple of hours, taking on freight. Says the king:

"Seein' how I'm dressed, I reckon maybe I better arrive down from St. Louis or Cincinnati, or some other big place. Go for the steamboat, Huckleberry; we'll come down to the village on her."

I didn't have to be ordered twice, to go and take a steamboat ride. I fetched the shore a half a mile above the village, and then went scooting along the bluff bank in the easy water. Pretty soon we come to a nice innocent-looking young country jake setting on a log swabbing the sweat off of his face, for it was powerful warm weather; and he had a couple of big carpet-bags by him.

"Run her nose in shore," says the king. I done it. "Wher' you bound for, young man?"

"For the steamboat; going to Orleans."

"Git aboard," says the king. "Hold on a minute, my servant 'll he'p you with them bags. Jump out and he'p the gentleman, Adolphus" — meaning me, I see.

I done so, and then we all three started on again. The young chap was mighty thankful; said it was tough work toting his baggage such weather. He asked the king where he was going, and the king told him he'd come down the river and landed at the other village this morning, and now he was going up a few mile to see an old friend on a farm up there. The young fellow says:

"When I first see you, I says to myself, 'It's Mr. Wilks, sure, and he come mighty near getting here in time.' But then I says again, 'No, I reckon it ain't him, or else he wouldn't be paddling up the river.' You *ain't* him, are you?"

"No, my name's Blodgett— Elexander Blodgett— *Reverend* Elexander Blodgett, I spose I must say, as I'm one o' the Lord's poor servants. But still I'm jist as able to be sorry for Mr. Wilks for not arriving in time, all the same, if he's missed anything by it— which I hope he hasn't."

"Well, he don't miss any property by it, because he'll get that all right; but he's missed seeing his brother Peter die— which he mayn't mind, nobody can tell as to that— but his brother would a give anything in this world to see *him* before he died; never talked about nothing else all these three weeks; hadn't seen him since they was boys together— and hadn't ever seen his brother William at all— that's the deef and dumb one— William ain't more than thirty or thirty-five. Peter and George was the only ones that come out here; George was the married brother; him and his wife both died last year. Harvey and William's the only ones that's left now; and, as I was saying, they haven't got here in time."

"Did anybody send 'em word?"

"Oh, yes; a month or two ago, when Peter was first took; because Peter said then that he sorter felt like he warn't going to get well this time. You see, he was pretty old, and George's g'yirls was too young to be much company for him, except Mary Jane the red-headed one; and so he was kinder lonesome after George and his wife died, and didn't seem to care much to live. He most desperately wanted to see Harvey— and William too, for that matter— because he was one of them kind that can't bear to make a will. He left a letter behind for Harvey, and said he'd told in it where his money was hid, and how he wanted the rest of the property divided up so George's g'yirls would be all right— for George didn't leave nothing. And that letter was all they could get him to put a pen to."

"Why do you reckon Harvey don't come? Wher' does he live?"

"Oh, he lives in England— Sheffield— preaches there— hasn't ever been in this country. He hasn't had any too much time— and besides he mightn't a got the letter at all, you know."

"Too bad, too bad he couldn't a lived to see his brothers, poor soul. You going to Orleans, you say?"

"Yes, but that ain't only a part of it. I'm going in a ship, next Wednesday, for Ryo Janeero, where my uncle lives."

"It's a pretty long journey. But it'll be lovely; I wisht I was agoing. Is Mary Jane the oldest? How old is the others?"

"Mary Jane's nineteen, Susan's fifteen, and Joanna's about fourteen — that's the one that gives herself to good works and has a hare-lip."

"Poor things! to be left alone in the cold world so."

"Well, they could be worse off. Old Peter had friends, and they ain't going to let them come to no harm. There's Hobson, the Babtis' preacher; and Deacon Lot Hovey, and Ben Rucker, and Abner Shackleford, and Levi Bell, the lawyer; and Dr. Robinson, and their wives, and the widow Bartley, and — well, there's a lot of them; but these are the ones that Peter was thickest with, and used to write about sometimes, when he wrote home; so Harvey 'll know where to look for friends when he gets here."

Well, the old man he went on asking questions till he just fairly emptied that young fellow. Blamed if he didn't inquire about everybody and everything in that blessed town, and all about all the Wilkses; and about Peter's business — which was a tanner; and about George's — which was a carpenter; and about Harvey's — which was a dissentering minister; and so on, and so on. Then he says:

"What did you want to walk all the way up to the steamboat for?"

"Because she's a big Orleans boat, and I was afeard she mightn't stop there. When they're deep they won't stop for a hail. A Cincinnati boat will, but this is a St. Louis one."

"Was Peter Wilks well off?"

"Oh, yes, pretty well off. He had houses and land, and it's reckoned he left three or four thousand in cash hid up som'ers."

"When did you say he died?"

"I didn't say, but it was last night."

"Funeral to-morrow, likely?"

"Yes, 'bout the middle of the day."

"Well, it's all terrible sad; but we've all got to go, one time or another. So what we want to do is to be prepared; then we're all right."

"Yes, sir, it's the best way. Ma used to always say that."

When we struck the boat, she was about done loading, and pretty soon she got off. The king never said nothing about going aboard, so I lost my ride, after all. When the boat was gone, the king made me paddle up another mile to a lonesome place, and then he got ashore, and says:

"Now hustle back, right off, and fetch the duke up here, and the new carpet-bags. And if he's gone over to t'other side, go over there and git him. And tell him to git himself up regardless. Shove along, now."

I see what *he* was up to; but I never said nothing, of course. When I got back with the duke, we hid the canoe and then they set down on a log, and the king told him everything, just like the young fellow had said it—every last word of it. And all the time he was a doing it, he tried to talk like an Englishman; and he done it pretty well too, for a slouch. I can't imitate him, and so I ain't agoing to try to; but he really done it pretty good. Then he says:

"How are you on the deef and dumb, Bilgewater?"

The duke said, leave him alone for that; said he had played a deef and dumb person on the histrionic boards. So then they waited for a steam-boat.

About the middle of the afternoon a couple of little boats come along, but they didn't come from high enough up the river; but at last there was a big one, and they hailed her. She sent out her yawl, and we went aboard, and she was from Cincinnati; and when they found we only wanted to go four or five mile, they was booming mad, and give us a cussing, and said they wouldn't land us. But the king was ca'm. He says:

"If gentlemen kin afford to pay a dollar a mile apiece, to be took on and put off in a yawl, a steamboat kin afford to carry 'em, can't it?"

So they softened down and said it was all right; and when we got to the village, they yawled us ashore. About two dozen men flocked down, when they see the yawl a coming; and when the king says—

"Kin any of you gentlemen tell me wher' Mr. Peter Wilks lives?" they give a glance at one another, and nodded their heads, as much as to say, "What d' I tell you?" Then one of them says, kind of soft and gentle:

"I'm sorry, sir, but the best we can do is to tell you where he *did* live yesterday evening."

Sudden as winking, the ornery old cretur went all to smash, and fell up against the man, and put his chin on his shoulder, and cried down his back, and says:

"Alas, alas, our poor brother—gone, and we never got to see him; oh, it's too, *too* hard!"

Then he turns around, blubbering, and makes a lot of idiotic signs to the duke on his hands, and blamed if *he* didn't drop a carpet-bag and bust out a-crying. If they warn't the beatenest lot, them two frauds, that ever I struck.

Well, the men gethered around, and sympathized with them, and said all sorts of kind things to them, and carried their carpet-bags up the hill for them, and let them lean on them and cry, and told the king all about his brother's last moments, and the king he told it all over again on his hands to the duke, and both of them took on about that dead tanner like they'd lost the twelve disciples. Well, if ever I struck anything like it, I'm a nigger. It was enough to make a body ashamed of the human race.

Chapter XXV

The news was all over town in two minutes, and you could see the people tearing down on the run, from every which way, some of them putting on their coats as they come. Pretty soon we was in the middle of a crowd, and the noise of the tramping was like a soldier-march. The windows and door-yards was full; and every minute somebody would say, over a fence:

"Is it *them?*"

And somebody trotting along with the gang would answer back and say,

"You bet it is."

When we got to the house, the street in front of it was packed, and the three girls was standing in the door. Mary Jane *was* red-headed, but that don't make no difference, she was most awful beautiful, and her face and her eyes was all lit up like glory, she was so glad her uncles was come. The king he spread his arms, and Mary Jane she jumped for them, and the hare-lip jumped for the duke, and there they *had* it! Everybody most, leastways women, cried for joy to see them meet again at last and have such good times.

Then the king he hunched the duke, private — I see him do it — and then he looked around and see the coffin, over in the corner on two chairs; so then, him and the duke, with a hand across each other's shoulder, and t'other hand to their eyes, walked slow and solemn over there, everybody dropping back to give them room, and all the talk and noise stopping, people saying "Sh!" and all the men taking their hats off and drooping their heads, so you could a heard a pin fall. And when they got there, they bent over and looked in the coffin, and took one sight, and then they bust out a crying so you could a heard them to Orleans, most; and then they put their arms around each other's necks, and hung their chins over each other's shoulders; and then for three minutes, or maybe four, I never see two men leak the way they done. And mind you, everybody was doing the same; and the place was that damp I never see anything like it. Then one of them got on one side of the coffin, and t'other on t'other side, and they kneeled down and rested their foreheads on the coffin, and let on to pray all to theirselves. Well, when it come to that, it worked the crowd like you never see anything like it, and so everybody broke down and went to sobbing right out loud — the poor girls, too; and every woman, nearly, went up to the girls, without saying a word, and kissed them, solemn, on the forehead, and then put their hand on their head, and looked up towards the sky, with the tears running down, and then busted out and went off sobbing and swabbing, and give the next woman a show. I never see anything so disgusting.

Well, by-and-by the king he gets up and comes forward a little, and works himself up and slobbers out a speech, all full of tears and flap-doodle about its being a sore trial for him and his poor brother to lose the diseased, and to miss seeing diseased alive, after the long journey of four thousand mile, but it's a trial that's sweetened and sanctified to us by this dear sympathy and these holy tears, and so he thanks them out of his heart and out of his brother's heart, because out of their mouths they can't, words being too weak and cold, and all that kind of rot and slush, till it was just sickening; and then he blubbers out a pious goody-goody Amen, and turns himself loose and goes to crying fit to bust.

And the minute the words was out of his mouth somebody over in the crowd struck up the doxolojer, and everybody joined in with all their might, and it just warmed you up and made you feel as good as church letting out. Music *is* a good thing; and after all that soul-butter and hogwash, I never see it freshen up things so, and sound so honest and bully.

Then the king begins to work his jaw again, and says how him and his nieces would be glad if a few of the main principal friends of the family would take supper here with them this evening, and help set up with the ashes of the diseased; and says if his poor brother laying yonder could speak, he knows who he would name, for they was names that was very dear to him, and mentioned often in his letters; and so he will name the same, to-wit, as follows, vizz: — Rev. Mr. Hobson, and Deacon Lot Hovey, and Mr. Ben Rucker, and Abner Shackleford, and Levi Bell, and Dr. Robinson, and their wives, and the widow Bartley.

Rev. Hobson and Dr. Robinson was down to the end of the town, a-hunting together; that is, I mean the doctor was shipping a sick man to t'other world, and the preacher was pinting him right. Lawyer Bell was away up to Louisville on some business. But the rest was on hand, and so they all come and shook hands with the king and thanked him and talked to him; and then they shook hands with the duke, and didn't say nothing but just kept a-smiling and bobbing their heads like a passel of sapheads whilst he made all sorts of signs with his hands and said "Goo-goo — goo-goo-goo," all the time, like a baby that can't talk.

So the king he blatted along, and managed to inquire about pretty much everybody and dog in town, by his name, and mentioned all sorts of little things that happened one time or another in the town, or to George's family, or to Peter; and he always let on that Peter wrote him the things, but that was a lie, he got every blessed one of them out of that young flathead that we canoed up to the steamboat.

Then Mary Jane she fetched the letter her father left behind, and the king he read it out loud and cried over it. It give the dwelling-house and three thousand dollars, gold, to the girls; and it give the tanyard (which was doing a good business), along with some other houses and land (worth about seven thousand), and three thousand dollars in gold to Harvey and William, and told where the six thousand cash was hid, down cellar. So these two frauds said they'd go and fetch it up, and have everything square and above-board; and told me to come with a candle. We shut the cellar door behind us, and when they found the bag they spilt it out on the floor, and it was a lovely sight, all them yaller-boys. My, the way the king's eyes did shine! He slaps the duke on the shoulder and says:

"Oh, *this* ain't bully, nor noth'n! Oh, no, I reckon not! Why, Biljy, it beats the Nonesuch, *don't* it!"

The duke allowed it did. They pawed the yaller-boys, and sifted them through their fingers and let them jingle down on the floor; and the king says:

"It ain't no use talkin'; bein' brothers to a rich dead man, and representatives of furrin heirs that's got left, is the line for you and me, Bilge. Thish-yer comes of trust'n to Providence. It's the best way, in the long run. I've tried 'em all, and ther' ain't no better way."

Most everybody would a been satisfied with the pile, and took it on trust; but no, they must count it. So they counts it, and it comes out four hundred and fifteen dollars short. Says the king:

"Dern him, I wonder what he done with that four hunderd and fifteen dollars?"

They worried over that a while, and ransacked all around for it. Then the duke says:

"Well, he was a pretty sick man, and likely he made a mistake — I reckon that's the way of it. The best way's to let it go, and keep still about it. We can spare it."

"Oh, shucks, yes, we can *spare* it. I don't k'yer noth'n 'bout that — it's the *count* I'm thinkin' about. We want to be awful square and open and aboveboard, here, you know. We want to lug this h-yer money up stairs and count it before everybody — then ther' ain't noth'n suspicious. But when the dead man says ther's six thous'n dollars, you know, we don't want to ——"

"Hold on," says the duke. "Less make up the deffisit" — and he begun to haul out yaller-boys out of his pocket.

"It's a most amaz'n' good idea, duke — you *have* got a rattlin' clever head on you," says the king. "Blest if the old Nonesuch ain't a heppin' us out agin" — and *he* begun to haul out yaller-jackets and stack them up.

It most busted them, but they made up the six thousand clean and clear.

"Say," says the duke, "I got another idea. Le's go up stairs and count this money, and then take and *give it to the girls.*"

"Good land, duke, lemme hug you! It's the most dazzling idea 'at ever a man struck. You have cert'nly got the most astonishin' head I ever see. Oh, this is the boss dodge, ther' ain't no mistake 'bout it. Let 'em fetch along their suspicions now, if they want to — this'll lay 'em out."

When we got up stairs, everybody gethered around the table, and the king he counted it and stacked it up, three hundred dollars in a pile — twenty elegant little piles. Everybody looked hungry at it, and licked their chops. Then they raked it into the bag again, and I see the king begin to swell himself up for another speech. He says:

"Friends all, my poor brother that lays yonder, has done generous by them that's left behind in the vale of sorrers. He has done generous by these-yer poor little lambs that he loved and sheltered, and that's left fatherless and motherless. Yes, and we that knowed him, knows that he would a done *more* generous by 'em if he hadn't ben afeard o' woundin' his dear William and me. Now, *wouldn't* he? Ther' ain't no question 'bout it, in *my* mind. Well, then — what kind o' brothers would it be, that'd stand in his way at sech a time? And what kind o' uncles would it be that'd rob — yes, *rob* — sech poor sweet lambs as these 'at he loved so, at sech a time? If I know William — and I *think* I do — he — well, I'll jest ask him." He turns around and begins to make a lot of signs to the duke with his hands; and the duke he looks at him stupid and leather-headed a while, then all of a sudden he seems to catch his meaning, and jumps for the king, goo-gooing with all his might for joy, and hugs him about fifteen times before he lets up. Then the king says, "I knowed it; I reckon *that* 'll convince anybody the way *he* feels about it. Here, Mary Jane, Susan, Joanner, take the money — take it *all*. It's the gift of him that lays yonder, cold but joyful."

Mary Jane she went for him, Susan and the hare-lip went for the duke, and then such another hugging and kissing I never see yet. And

everybody crowded up with the tears in their eyes, and most shook the
hands off of them frauds, saying all the time:

"You *dear* good souls! — how *lovely!* — how *could* you!"

Well, then, pretty soon all hands got to talking about the diseased
again, and how good he was, and what a loss he was, and all that; and
before long a big iron-jawed man worked himself in there from outside,
and stood a listening and looking, and not saying anything; and nobody
saying anything to him either, because the king was talking and they was
all busy listening. The king was saying — in the middle of something
he'd started in on —

" — they bein' partickler friends o' the diseased. That's why they're
invited here this evenin'; but to-morrow we want *all* to come —
everybody; for he respected everybody, he liked everybody, and so it's
fitten that his funeral orgies sh'd be public."

And so he went a-mooning on and on, liking to hear himself talk, and
every little while he fetched in his funeral orgies again, till the duke he
couldn't stand it no more; so he writes on a little scrap of paper,
"*obsequies,* you old fool," and folds it up and goes to goo-gooing and
reaching it over people's heads to him. The king he reads it, and puts it
in his pocket, and says:

"Poor William, afflicted as he is, his *heart's* aluz right. Asks me to
invite everybody to come to the funeral — wants me to make 'em all
welcome. But he needn't a worried — it was jest what I was at."

Then he weaves along again, perfectly ca'm, and goes to dropping in
his funeral orgies again every now and then, just like he done before.
And when he done it the third time, he says:

"I say orgies, not because it's the common term, because it ain't —
obsequies bein' the common term — but because orgies is the right
term. Obsequies ain't used in England no more, now — it's gone out. We
say orgies now, in England. Orgies is better, because it means the thing
you're after, more exact. It's a word that's made up out'n the Greek *orgo,*
outside, open, abroad; and the Hebrew *jeesum,* to plant, cover up; hence
in*ter.* So, you see, funeral orgies is an open er public funeral."

He was the *worst* I ever struck. Well, the iron-jawed man he laughed
right in his face. Everybody was shocked. Everybody says, "Why *doctor!*"
and Abner Shackleford says:

"Why, Robinson, hain't you heard the news? This is Harvey Wilks."

The king he smiled eager, and shoved out his flapper, and says:

"*Is* it my poor brother's dear good friend and physician? I ——"

"Keep your hands off of me!" says the doctor. "*You* talk like an
Englishman — *don't* you? It's the worse imitation I ever heard. *You* Peter
Wilks's brother. You're a fraud, that's what you are!"

Well, how they all took on! They crowded around the doctor, and tried to quiet him down, and tried to explain to him, and tell him how Harvey'd showed in forty ways that he *was* Harvey, and knowed everybody by name, and the names of the very dogs, and begged and *begged* him not to hurt Harvey's feelings and the poor girls' feelings, and all that; but it warn't no use, he stormed right along, and said any man that pretended to be an Englishman and couldn't imitate the lingo no better than what he did, was a fraud and a liar. The poor girls was hanging to the king and crying; and all of a sudden the doctor ups and turns on *them*. He says:

"I was your father's friend, and I'm your friend; and I warn you *as* a friend, and an honest one, that wants to protect you and keep you out of harm and trouble, to turn your backs on that scoundrel, and have nothing to do with him, the ignorant tramp, with his idiotic Greek and Hebrew as he calls it. He is the thinnest kind of an impostor — has come here with a lot of empty names and facts which he has picked up somewheres, and you take them for *proofs*, and are helped to fool yourselves by these foolish friends here, who ought to know better. Mary Jane Wilks, you know me for your friend, and for your unselfish friend, too. Now listen to me; turn this pitiful rascal out — I *beg* you to do it. Will you?"

Mary Jane straightened herself up, and my, but she was handsome! She says:

"*Here* is my answer." She hove up the bag of money and put it in the king's hands, and says, "Take this six thousand dollars, and invest for me and my sisters any way you want to, and don't give us no receipt for it."

Then she put her arm around the king on one side, and Susan and the hare-lip done the same on the other. Everybody clapped their hands and stomped on the floor like a perfect storm, whilst the king held up his head and smiled proud. The doctor says:

"All right, I wash *my* hands of the matter. But I warn you all that a time's coming when you're going to feel sick whenever you think of this day" — and away he went.

"All right, doctor," says the king, kinder mocking him, "we'll try and get 'em to send for you" — which made them all laugh, and they said it was a prime good hit.

Chapter XXVI

Well, when they was all gone, the king he asks Mary Jane how they was off for spare rooms, and she said she had one spare room, which would do for Uncle William, and she'd give her own room to Uncle Harvey, which was a little bigger, and she would turn into the room with her sisters and sleep on a cot; and up garret was a little cubby, with a pallet in it. The king said the cubby would do for his valley — meaning me.

So Mary Jane took us up, and she showed them their rooms, which was plain but nice. She said she'd have her frocks and a lot of other traps took out of her room if they was in Uncle Harvey's way, but he said they warn't. The frocks was hung along the wall, and before them was a curtain made out of calico that hung down to the floor. There was an old hair trunk in one corner, and a guitar box in another, and all sorts of little knick-knacks and jimcracks around, like girls brisken up a room with. The king said it was all the more homely and more pleasanter for these fixings, and so don't disturb them. The duke's room was pretty small, but plenty good enough, and so was my cubby.

That night they had a big supper, and all them men and women was there, and I stood behind the king and the duke's chairs and waited on them, and the niggers waited on the rest. Mary Jane she set at the head of the table, with Susan along side of her, and said how bad the biscuits was, and how mean the preserves was, and how ornery and tough the fried chickens was — and all that kind of rot, the way women always do for to force out compliments; and the people all knowed everything was tip-top, and said so — said "How *do* you get biscuits to brown so nice?" and "Where, for the land's sake *did* you get these amaz'n pickles?" and all that kind of humbug talky-talk, just the way people always does at a supper, you know.

And when it was all done, me and the hare-lip had supper in the kitchen off of the leavings, whilst the others was helping the niggers clean up the things. The hare-lip she got to pumping me about England, and blest if I didn't think the ice was getting mighty thin, sometimes. She says:

"Did you ever see the king?"

"Who? William Fourth? Well, I bet I have — he goes to our church." I knowed he was dead years ago, but I never let on. So when I says he goes to our church, she says:

"What — regular?"

"Yes — regular. His pew's right over opposite ourn — on 'tother side the pulpit."

"I thought he lived in London?"

"Well, he does. Where *would* he live?"

"But I thought *you* lived in Sheffield?"

I see I was up a stump. I had to let on to get choked with a chicken bone, so as to get time to think how to get down again. Then I says:

"I mean he goes to our church regular when he's in Sheffield. That's only in the summer-time, when he comes there to take the sea baths."

"Why, how you talk — Sheffield ain't on the sea."

"Well, who said it was?"

"Why, you did."

"I *didn't*, nuther."

"You did!"

"I didn't."

"You did."

"I never said nothing of the kind."

"Well, what *did* you say, then?"

"Said he come to take the sea *baths* — that's what I said."

"Well, then! how's he going to take the sea baths if it ain't on the sea?"

"Looky here," I says; "did you ever see any Congress water?"

"Yes."

"Well, did you have to go to Congress to get it?"

"Why, no."

"Well, neither does William Fourth have to go to the sea to get a sea bath."

"How does he get it, then?"

"Gets it the way people down here gets Congress-water — in barrels. There in the palace at Sheffield they've got furnaces, and he wants his water hot. They can't bile that amount of water away off there at the sea. They haven't got no conveniences for it."

"Oh, I see, now. You might a said that in the first place and saved time."

When she said that, I see I was out of the woods again, and so I was comfortable and glad. Next, she says:

"Do you go to church, too?"

"Yes — regular."

"Where do you set?"

"Why, in our pew."

"*Whose* pew?"

"Why, *ourn* — your Uncle Harvey's."

"His'n? What does *he* want with a pew?"

"Wants it to set in. What did you *reckon* he wanted with it?"

"Why, I thought he'd be in the pulpit."

Rot him, I forgot he was a preacher. I see I was up a stump again, so I played another chicken bone and got another think. Then I says:

"Blame it, do you suppose there ain't but one preacher to a church?"

"Why, what do they want with more?"

"What! — to preach before a king? I never see such a girl as you. They don't have no less than seventeen."

"Seventeen! My land! Why, I wouldn't set out such a string as that, not if I *never* got to glory. It must take 'em a week."

"Shucks, they don't *all* of 'em preach the same day — only *one* of 'em."

"Well, then, what does the rest of 'em do?"

"Oh, nothing much. Loll around, pass the plate — and one thing or another. But mainly they don't do nothing."

"Well, then, what are they *for?*"

"Why, they're for *style*. Don't you know nothing?"

"Well, I don't *want* to know no such foolishness as that. How is servants treated in England? Do they treat 'em better 'n we treat our niggers?"

"*No!* A servant ain't nobody there. They treat them worse than dogs."

"Don't they give 'em holidays, the way we do, Christmas and New Year's week, and Fourth of July?"

"Oh, just listen! A body could tell *you* hain't ever been to England, by that. Why, Hare-l — why, Joanna, they never see a holiday from year's end to year's end; never go to the circus, nor theatre, nor nigger shows, nor nowheres."

"Nor church?"

"Nor church."

"But *you* always went to church."

Well, I was gone up again. I forgot I was the old man's servant. But next minute I whirled in on a kind of an explanation how a valley was different from a common servant, and *had* to go to church whether he wanted to or not, and set with the family, on account of it's being the law. But I didn't do it pretty good, and when I got done I see she warn't satisfied. She says:

"Honest injun, now, hain't you been telling me a lot of lies?"

"Honest injun," says I.

"None of it at all?"

"None of it at all. Not a lie in it," says I.

"Lay your hand on this book and say it."

I see it warn't nothing but a dictionary, so I laid my hand on it and said it. So then she looked a little better satisfied, and says:

"Well, then, I'll believe some of it; but I hope to gracious if I'll believe the rest."

"What is it you won't believe, Joe?" says Mary Jane, stepping in with Susan behind her. "It ain't right nor kind for you to talk so to him, and him a stranger and so far from his people. How would you like to be treated so?"

"That's always your way, Maim — always sailing in to help somebody before they're hurt. I hain't done nothing to him. He's told some stretchers, I reckon; and I said I wouldn't swallow it all; and that's every bit and grain I *did* say. I reckon he can stand a little thing like that, can't he?"

"I don't care whether 'twas little or whether 'twas big, he's here in our house and a stranger, and it wasn't good of you to say it. If you was in his place, it would make you feel ashamed; and so you oughtn't to say a thing to another person that will make *them* feel ashamed."

"Why, Maim, he said——"

"It don't make no difference what he *said* — that ain't the thing. The thing is for you to treat him *kind*, and not be saying things to make him remember he ain't in his own country and amongst his own folks."

I says to myself, *this* is a girl that I'm letting that old reptile rob her of her money!

Then Susan *she* waltzed in; and if you'll believe me, she did give Hare-lip hark from the tomb!

Says I to myself, And this is *another* one that I'm letting him rob her of her money!

Then Mary Jane she took another inning, and went in sweet and lovely again — which was her way — but when she got done there warn't hardly anything left o' poor Hare-lip. So she hollered.

"All right, then," says the other girls, "you just ask his pardon."

She done it, too. And she done it beautiful. She done it so beautiful it was good to hear; and I wished I could tell her a thousand lies, so she could do it again.

I says to myself, this is *another* one that I'm letting him rob her of her money. And when she got through, they all jest laid theirselves out to make me feel at home and know I was amongst friends. I felt so ornery and low down and mean, that I says to myself, My mind's made up; I'll hive that money for them or bust.

So then I lit out — for bed, I said, meaning some time or another. When I got by myself, I went to thinking the thing over. I says to myself, shall I go to that doctor, private, and blow on these frauds? No — that won't do. He might tell who told him; then the king and the duke would make it warm for me. Shall I go, private, and tell Mary Jane? No — I dasn't do it. Her face would give them a hint, sure; they've got the money, and they'd slide right out and get away with it. If she was to fetch in help, I'd get mixed up in the business, before it was done with, I judge. No, there ain't no good way but one. I got to steal that money, somehow; and I got to steal it some way that they won't suspicion that I done it. They've got a good thing, here; and they ain't agoing to leave till they've played this family and this town for all they're worth, so I'll find a chance time enough. I'll steal it, and hide it; and by-and-by, when I'm away down the river, I'll write a letter and tell Mary Jane where it's hid. But I better hive it to-night, if I can, because the doctor maybe hasn't let up as much as he lets on he has; he might scare them out of here, yet.

So, thinks I, I'll go and search them rooms. Up stairs the hall was dark, but I found the duke's room, and started to paw around it with my hands; but I recollected it wouldn't be much like the king to let anybody else take care of that money but his own self; so then I went to his room and begun to paw around there. But I see I couldn't do nothing without a candle, and I dasn't light one, of course. So I judged I'd got to do the other thing — lay for them, and eavesdrop. About that time, I hears their footsteps coming, and was going to skip under the bed; I reached for it, but it wasn't where I thought it would be; but I touched the curtain that hid Mary Jane's frocks, so I jumped in behind that and snuggled in amongst the gowns, and stood there perfectly still.

They come in and shut the door; and the first thing the duke done was to get down and look under the bed. Then I was glad I hadn't found the bed when I wanted it. And yet, you know, it's kind of natural to hide under the bed when you are up to anything private. They sets down, then, and the king says:

"Well, what is it? and cut it middlin' short, because it's better for us to be down there a whoopin'-up the mournin', than up here givin' 'em a chance to talk us over."

"Well, this is it, Capet. I ain't easy; I ain't comfortable. That doctor lays on my mind. I wanted to know your plans. I've got a notion, and I think it's a sound one."

"What is it, duke?"

"That we better glide out of this, before three in the morning, and clip it down the river with what we've got. Specially, seeing we got it so easy — *given* back to us, flung at our heads, as you may say, when of course we allowed to have to steal it back. I'm for knocking off and lighting out."

That made me feel pretty bad. About an hour or two ago, it would a been a little different, but now it made me feel bad and disappointed. The king rips out and says:

"What! And not sell out the rest o' the property? March off like a passel o' fools and leave eight or nine thous'n' dollars' worth o' property layin' around jest sufferin' to be scooped in? — and all good salable stuff, too."

The duke he grumbled; said the bag of gold was enough, and he didn't want to go no deeper — didn't want to rob a lot of orphans of *everything* they had.

"Why, how you talk!" says the king. "We shan't rob 'em of nothing at all but jest this money. The people that *buys* the property is the suff'rers; because as soon's it's found out 'at we didn't own it — which won't be long after we've slid — the sale won't be valid, and it'll all go back to the estate. These-yer orphans 'll git their house back agin, and that's enough for *them*; they're young and spry, and k'n easy earn a livin'. *They* ain't agoing to suffer. Why, jest think — there's thous'n's and thous'n's that ain't nigh so well off. Bless you, *they* ain't got noth'n to complain of."

Well, the king he talked him blind; so at last he give in, and said all right, but said he believed it was blame foolishness to stay, and that doctor hanging over them. But the king says:

"Cuss the doctor! What do we k'yer for *him*? Hain't we got all the fools in town on our side? and ain't that a big enough majority in any town?"

So they got ready to go down stairs again. The duke says:

"I don't think we put that money in a good place."

That cheered me up. I'd begun to think I warn't going to get a hint of no kind to help me. The king says:

"Why?"

"Because Mary Jane 'll be in mourning from this out; and first you know the nigger that does up the rooms will get an order to box these duds up and put 'em away; and do you reckon a nigger can run across money and not borrow some of it?"

"Your head's level, agin, duke," says the king; and he come a fumbling under the curtain two or three foot from where I was. I stuck tight to the wall, and kept mighty still, though quivery; and I wondered what them fellows would say to me if they catched me; and I tried to think what I'd better do if they did catch me. But the king he got the bag before I could think more than about a half a thought, and he never suspicioned I was around. They took and shoved the bag through a rip in the straw tick that was under the feather bed, and crammed it in a foot or two amongst the straw and said it was all right, now, because a nigger only makes up the feather bed, and don't turn over the straw tick only about twice a year, and so it warn't in no danger of getting stole, now.

But I knowed better. I had it out of there before they was half-way down stairs. I groped along up to my cubby, and hid it there till I could get a chance to do better. I judged I better hide it outside of the house somewheres, because if they missed it they would give the house a good ransacking. I knowed that very well. Then I turned in, with my clothes all on; but I couldn't a gone to sleep, if I'd a wanted to, I was in such a sweat to get through with the business. By-and-by I heard the king and the duke come up; so I rolled off of my pallet and laid with my chin at the top of my ladder and waited to see if anything was going to happen. But nothing did.

So I held on till all the late sounds had quit and the early ones hadn't begun, yet; and then I slipped down the ladder.

Chapter XXVII

I crept to their doors and listened; they was snoring, so I tip-toed along, and got down stairs all right. There warn't a sound anywheres. I peeped through a crack of the dining-room door, and see the men that was watching the corpse all sound asleep on their chairs. The door was open into the parlor, where the corpse was laying, and there was a candle in both rooms. I passed along, and the parlor door was open; but I see there warn't nobody in there but the remainders of Peter; so I shoved on by; but the front door was locked, and the key wasn't there. Just then I heard somebody coming down the stairs, back behind me. I run in the parlor, and took a swift look around, and the only place I see to hide the bag was in the coffin. The lid was shoved along about a foot, showing the dead man's face down in there, with a wet cloth over it, and his shroud on. I tucked the money-bag in under the lid, just down beyond where his hands was crossed, which made me creep, they was so cold, and then I run back across the room and in behind the door.

The person coming was Mary Jane. She went to the coffin, very soft, and kneeled down and looked in; then she put up her handkerchief and I see she begun to cry, though I couldn't hear her, and her back was to me. I slid out, and as I passed the dining-room I thought I'd make sure them watchers hadn't seen me; so I looked through the crack and everything was all right. They hadn't stirred.

I slipped up to bed, feeling ruther blue, on accounts of the thing playing out that way after I had took so much trouble and run so much resk about it. Says I, if it could stay where it is, all right; because when we get down the river a hundred mile or two, I could write back to Mary Jane, and she could dig him up again and get it; but that ain't the thing that's going to happen; the thing that's going to happen is, the money 'll be found when they come to screw on the lid. Then the king 'll get it again, and it 'll be a long day before he gives anybody another chance to smouch it from him. Of course I *wanted* to slide down and get it out of there, but I dasn't try it. Every minute it was getting earlier, now, and pretty soon some of them watchers would begin to stir, and I might get catched — catched with six thousand dollars in my hands that nobody hadn't hired me to take care of. I don't wish to be mixed up in no such business as that, I says to myself.

When I got down stairs in the morning, the parlor was shut up, and the watchers was gone. There warn't nobody around but the family and the widow Bartley and our tribe. I watched their faces to see if anything had been happening, but I couldn't tell.

Towards the middle of the day the undertaker come, with his man, and they set the coffin in the middle of the room on a couple of chairs, and then set all our chairs in rows, and borrowed more from the neighbors till the hall and the parlor and the dining-room was full. I see the coffin lid was the way it was before, but I dasn't go to look in under it, with folks around.

Then the people begun to flock in, and the beats and the girls took seats in the front row at the head of the coffin, and for a half an hour the people filed around slow, in single rank, and looked down at the dead man's face a minute, and some dropped in a tear, and it was all very still and solemn, only the girls and the beats holding handkerchiefs to their eyes and keeping their heads bent, and sobbing a little. There warn't no other sound but the scraping of the feet on the floor, and blowing noses — because people always blows them more at a funeral than they do at other places except church.

When the place was packed full, the undertaker he slid around in his black gloves with his softy soothering ways, putting on the last touches, and getting people and things all ship-shape and comfortable, and making no more sound than a cat. He never spoke; he moved people around, he squeezed in late ones, he opened up passage-ways, and done it all with nods, and signs with his hands. Then he took his place over against the wall. He was the softest, glidingest, stealthiest man I ever see; and there warn't no more smile to him than there is to a ham.

They had borrowed a melodeum — a sick one; and when everything was ready, a young woman set down and worked it, and it was pretty skreeky and colicky, and everybody joined in and sung, and Peter was the only one that had a good thing, according to my notion. Then the Reverend Hobson opened up, slow and solemn, and begun to talk; and straight off the most outrageous row busted out in the cellar a body ever heard; it was only one dog, but he made a most powerful racket, and he kept it up, right along; the parson he had to stand there, over the coffin, and wait—you couldn't hear yourself think. It was right down awkward, and nobody didn't seem to know what to do. But pretty soon they see that long-legged undertaker make a sign to the preacher as much as to say, "Don't you worry—just depend on me." Then he stooped down and begun to glide along the wall, just his shoulders showing over the people's heads. So he glided along, and the pow-wow and racket getting more and more outrageous all the time; and at last, when he had gone around two sides of the room, he disappears down cellar. Then, in about two seconds we heard a whack, and the dog he finished up with a most amazing howl or two, and then everything was dead still, and the parson begun his solemn talk where he left off. In a minute or two here comes this undertaker's back and shoulders gliding along the wall again; and so he glided, and glided, around three sides of the room, and then rose up, and shaded his mouth with his hands, and stretched his neck out towards the preacher, over the people's heads, and says, in a kind of a coarse whisper, "*He had a rat!*" Then he drooped down and glided along the wall again to his place. You could see it was a great satisfaction to the people, because naturally they wanted to know. A little thing like that don't cost nothing, and it's just the little things that makes a man to be looked up to and liked. There warn't no more popular man in town than what that undertaker was.

Well, the funeral sermon was very good, but pison long and tiresome; and then the king he shoved in and got off some of his usual rubbage, and at last the job was through, and the undertaker begun to sneak up on the coffin with his screw-driver. I was in a sweat then, and watched him pretty keen. But he never meddled at all; just slid the lid along, as soft as mush, and screwed it down tight and fast. So there I was! I didn't know whether the money was in there, or not. So, says I, spose somebody has hogged that bag on the sly?—now how do *I* know whether to write to Mary Jane or not? 'Spose she dug him up and didn't find nothing—what would she think of me? Blame it, I says, I might get hunted up and jailed; I'd better lay low and keep dark, and not write at all; the thing's awful mixed, now; trying to better it, I've worsened it a hundred times, and I wish to goodness I'd just let it alone, dad fetch the whole business!

They buried him, and we come back home, and I went to watching faces again—I couldn't help it, and I couldn't rest easy. But nothing come of it; the faces didn't tell me nothing.

The king he visited around, in the evening, and sweetened every body up, and made himself ever so friendly; and he give out the idea that his congregation over in England would be in a sweat about him, so he must hurry and settle up the estate right away, and leave for home. He was very sorry he was so pushed, and so was everybody; they wished he could stay longer, but they said they could see it couldn't be done. And he said of course him and William would take the girls home with them; and that pleased everybody too, because then the girls would be well fixed, and amongst their own relations; and it pleased the girls, too — tickled them so they clean forgot they ever had a trouble in the world; and told him to sell out as quick as he wanted to, they would be ready. Them poor things was that glad and happy it made my heart ache to see them getting fooled and lied to so, but I didn't see no safe way for me to chip in and change the general tune.

Well, blamed if the king didn't bill the house and the niggers and all the property for auction straight off — sale two days after the funeral; but anybody could buy private beforehand if they wanted to.

So the next day after the funeral, along about noontime, the girls' joy got the first jolt; a couple of nigger traders come along, and the king sold them the niggers reasonable, for three-day drafts as they called it, and away they went, the two sons up the river to Memphis, and their mother down the river to Orleans. I thought them poor girls and them niggers would break their hearts for grief; they cried around each other, and took on so it most made me down sick to see it. The girls said they hadn't ever dreamed of seeing the family separated or sold away from the town. I can't ever get it out of my memory, the sight of them poor miserable girls and niggers hanging around each other's necks and crying; and I reckon I couldn't a stood it all but would a had to bust out and tell on our gang if I hadn't knowed the sale warn't no account and the niggers would be back home in a week or two.

The thing made a big stir in the town, too, and a good many come out flatfooted and said it was scandalous to separate the mother and the children that way. It injured the frauds some; but the old fool he bulled right along, spite of all the duke could say or do, and I tell you the duke was powerful uneasy.

Next day was auction day. About broad-day in the morning, the king and the duke come up in the garret and woke me up, and I see by their look that there was trouble. The king says:

"Was you in my room night before last?"

"No, your majesty" — which was the way I always called him when nobody but our gang warn't around.

"Was you in there yisterday er last night?"

"No, your majesty."

"Honor bright, now — no lies."

"Honor bright, your majesty, I'm telling you the truth. I hain't been anear your room since Miss Mary Jane took you and the duke and showed it to you."

The duke says:

"Have you seen anybody else go in there?"

"No, your grace, not as I remember, I believe."

"Stop and think."

I studied a while, and see my chance, then I says:

"Well, I see the niggers go in there several times."

Both of them give a little jump; and looked like they hadn't ever expected it, and then like they *had.* Then the duke says:

"What, *all* of them?"

"No — leastways not all at once. That is, I don't think I ever see them all come *out* at once but just one time."

"Hello — when was that?"

"It was the day we had the funeral. In the morning. It warn't early, because I overslept. I was just starting down the ladder, and I see them."

"Well, go on, go on — what did they do? How'd they act?"

"They didn't do nothing. And they didn't act anyway, much, as fur as I see. They tip-toed away; so I seen, easy enough, that they'd shoved in there to do up your majesty's room, or something, sposing you was up; and found you *warn't* up, and so they was hoping to slide out of the way of trouble without waking you up, if they hadn't already waked you up."

"Great guns, *this* is a go!" says the king; and both of them looked pretty sick, and tolerable silly. They stood there a thinking and scratching their heads, a minute, and then the duke he bust into a kind of little raspy chuckle, and says:

"It does beat all, how neat the niggers played their hand. They let on to be *sorry* they was going out of this region! and I believed they *was* sorry. And so did you, and so did everybody. Don't ever tell *me* any more that a nigger ain't got any histrionic talent. Why, the way they played that thing, it would fool *anybody.* In my opinion there's a fortune in 'em. If I had capital and a theatre, I wouldn't want a better lay out than that — and here we've gone and sold 'em for a song. Yes, and ain't privileged to sing the song, yet. Say, where *is* that song? — that draft."

"In the bank for to be collected. Where *would* it be?"

"Well, *that's* all right then, thank goodness."

Says I, kind of timid-like:

"Is something gone wrong?"

The king whirls on me and rips out:

"None o' your business! You keep your head shet, and mind y'r own affairs — if you got any. Long as you're in this town, don't you forget *that,* you hear?" Then he says to the duke, "We got to jest swaller it, and say noth'n: mum's the word for *us.*"

As they was starting down the ladder, the duke he chuckles again, and says:

"Quick sales *and* small profits! It's a good business — yes."

The king snarls around on him and says,

"I was trying to do for the best, in sellin' 'm out so quick. If the profits has turned out to be none, lackin' considable, and none to carry, is it my fault any more'n it's yourn?"

"Well, *they'd* be in this house yet, and we *wouldn't* if I could a got my advice listened to."

The king sassed back, as much as was safe for him, and then swapped around and lit into *me* again. He give me down the banks for not coming and *telling* him I see the niggers come out of his room acting that way — said any fool would a *knowed* something was up. And then waltzed in and cussed *himself* a while; and said it all come of him not laying late and taking his natural rest that morning; and he'd be blamed if he'd ever do it again. So they went off a jawing; and I felt dreadful glad I'd worked it all off onto the niggers and yet hadn't done the niggers no harm by it.

Chapter XXVIII

By-and-by it was getting-up time; so I come down the ladder and started for down stairs, but as I come to the girls' room, the door was open, and I see Mary Jane setting by her old hair trunk, which was open and she'd been packing things in it — getting ready to go to England. But she had stopped now, with a folded gown in her lap, and had her face in her hands, crying. I felt awful bad to see it; of course anybody would. I went in there, and says:

"Miss Mary Jane, you can't abear to see people in trouble, and *I* can't — most always. Tell me about it."

So she done it. And it was the niggers — I just expected it. She said the beautiful trip to England was most about spoiled for her; she didn't know *how* she was ever going to be happy there, knowing the mother and the children warn't ever going to see each other no more — and then busted out bitterer than ever, and flung up her hands, and says:

"Oh, dear, dear, to think they ain't *ever* going to see each other any more!"

"But they *will* — and inside of two weeks — and I *know* it!" says I.

Laws it was out before I could think! — and before I could budge, she throws her arms around my neck, and told me to say it *again*, say it *again*, say it *again*!

I see I had spoke too sudden, and said too much, and was in a close place. I asked her to let me think a minute; and she set there, very impatient and excited, and handsome, but looking kind of happy and eased-up, like a person that's had a tooth pulled out. So I went to studying it out. I says to myself, I reckon a body that ups and tells the truth when he is in a tight place, is taking considerable many resks, though I ain't had no experience, and can't say for certain; but it looks so to me, anyway; and yet here's a case where I'm blest if it don't look to me like the truth is better, and actuly *safer*, than a lie. I must lay it by in my mind, and think it over some time or other, it's so kind of strange and unregular. I never see nothing like it. Well, I says to myself at last, I'm agoing to chance it; I'll up and tell the truth this time, though it does seem most like setting down on a kag of powder and touching it off just to see where you'll go to. Then I says:

"Miss Mary Jane, is there any place out of town a little ways, where you could go and stay three or four days?"

"Yes — Mr. Lothrop's. Why?"

"Never mind why, yet. If I'll tell you how I know the niggers will see each other again — inside of two weeks — here in this house — and *prove* how I know it — will you go to Mr. Lothrop's and stay four days?"

"Four days!" she says; "I'll stay a year!"

"All right," I says, "I don't want nothing more out of *you* than just your word — I druther have it than another man's kiss-the-Bible." She smiled, and reddened up very sweet, and I says, "If you don't mind it, I'll shut the door — and bolt it."

Then I come back and set down again, and says:

"Don't you holler. Just set still, and take it like a man. I got to tell the truth, and you want to brace up, Miss Mary, because it's a bad kind, and going to be hard to take, but there ain't no help for it. These uncles of yourn ain't no uncles at all — they're a couples of frauds — regular dead-beats. There, now we're over the worst of it — you can stand the rest middling easy."

It jolted her up like everything, of course; but I was over the shoal water now, so I went right along, her eyes a blazing higher and higher all the time, and told her every blame thing, from where we first struck that young fool going up to the steamboat, clear through to where she flung herself onto the king's breast at the front door and he kissed her sixteen or seventeen times — and then up she jumps, with her face afire like sunset, and says:

"The brute! Come — don't waste a minute — not a *second* — we'll have them tarred and feathered, and flung in the river!"

Says I:

"Cert'nly. But do you mean, *before* you go to Mr. Lothrop's, or ——"

"Oh," she says, "what am I *thinking* about!" she says, and set right down again. "Don't mind what I said — please don't — you *won't*, now, *will* you?" Laying her silky hand on mine in that kind of a way that I said I would die first. "I never thought, I was so stirred up," she says; "now go on, and I won't do so any more. You tell me what to do, and whatever you say, I'll do it."

"Well," I says, "it's a rough gang, them two frauds, and I'm fixed so I got to travel with them a while longer, whether I want to or not — I druther not tell you why — and if you was to blow on them this town would get me out of their claws, and I'd be all right, but there'd be another person that you don't know about who'd be in big trouble. Well, we got to save *him*, hain't we? Of course. Well, then, we won't blow on them."

Saying them words put a good idea in my head. I see how maybe I could get me and Jim rid of the frauds; get them jailed here, and then leave. But I didn't want to run the raft in day-time, without anybody aboard to answer questions but me; so I didn't want the plan to begin working till pretty late to-night. I says:

"Miss Mary Jane, I'll tell you what we'll do — and you won't have to stay at Mr. Lothrop's so long, nuther. How fur is it?"

"A little short of four miles — right out in the country, back here."

"Well, that'll answer. Now you go along out there, and lay low till nine or half-past, to-night, and then get them to fetch you home again — tell them you've thought of something. If you get here before eleven, put a candle in this window, and if I don't turn up, wait *till* eleven, and *then* if I don't turn up it means I'm gone, and out of the way, and safe. Then you come out and spread the news around, and get these beats jailed."

"Good," she says, "I'll do it."

"And if it just happens so that I don't get away, but get took up along with them, you must up and say I told you the whole thing beforehand, and you must stand by me all you can."

"Stand by you, indeed I will. They sha'n't touch a hair of your head!" she says, and I see her nostrils spread and her eyes snap when she said it, too.

"If I get away, I sha'n't be here," I says, "to prove these rapscallions ain't your uncles, and I couldn't do it if I *was* here. I could swear they was beats and bummers, that's all; though that's worth something. Well, there's others can do that better than what I can — and they're people that ain't going to be doubted as quick as I'd be. I'll tell you how to find them. Gimme a pencil and a piece of paper. There — '*Royal Nonesuch, Bricksville.*' Put it away, and don't lose it. When the court wants to find out something about these two, let them send up to Bricksville and say they've got the men that played the Royal Nonesuch, and ask for some witnesses — why, you'll have that entire town down here before you can hardly wink, Miss Mary. And they'll come a-biling, too."

I judged we had got everything fixed about right, now. So I says:

"Just let the auction go right along, and don't worry. Nobody don't have to pay for the things they buy till a whole day after the auction, on accounts of the short notice, and they ain't going out of this till they get that money — and the way we've fixed it the sale ain't going to count, and they ain't going to *get* no money. It's just like the way it was with the niggers — it warn't no sale, and the niggers will be back before long. Why, they can't collect the money for the *niggers*, yet — they're in the worst kind of a fix, Miss Mary."

"Well," she says, "I'll run down to breakfast now, and then I'll start straight for Mr. Lothrop's."

"'Deed, *that* ain't the ticket, Miss Mary Jane," I says, "by no manner of means; go *before* breakfast."

"Why?"

"What did you reckon I wanted you to go at all for, Miss Mary?"

"Well, I never thought — and come to think, I don't know. What was it?"

"Why, it's because you ain't one of these leather-face people. I don't want no better book that what your face is. A body can set down and read it off like coarse print. Do you reckon you can go and face your uncles, when they come to kiss you good-morning, and never——"

"There, there, don't! Yes, I'll go before breakfast — I'll be glad to. And leave my sisters with them?"

"Yes — never mind about them. They've got to stand it yet a while. They might suspicion something if all of you was to go. I don't want you to see them, nor your sisters, nor nobody in this town — if a neighbor was to ask how is your uncles this morning, your face would tell something. No, you go right along, Miss Mary Jane, and I'll fix it with all of them. I'll tell Miss Susan to give your love to your uncles and say you've went away for a few hours for to get a little rest and change, or to see a friend, and you'll be back to-night or early in the morning."

"Gone to see a friend is all right, but I won't have my love given to them."

"Well, then, it sha'n't be." It was well enough to tell *her* so — no harm in it. It was only a little thing to do, and no trouble; and it's the little things that smoothes people's roads the most, down here below; it would make Mary Jane comfortable, and it wouldn't cost nothing. Then I says: "There's one more thing — that bag of money."

"Well, they've got that; and it makes me feel pretty silly to think *how* they got it."

"No, you're out, there. They hain't got it."

"Why, who's got it?"

"I wish I knowed, but I don't. I *had* it, because I stole it from them: and I stole it to give to you; and I know where I hid it, but I'm afraid it ain't there no more. I'm awful sorry, Miss Mary Jane, I'm just as sorry as I can be; but I done the best I could; I did, honest. I come nigh getting caught, and I had to shove it into the first place I come to, and run — and it warn't a good place."

"Oh, stop blaming yourself — it's too bad to do it, and I won't allow it — you couldn't help it; it wasn't your fault. Where did you hide it?"

I didn't want to set her to thinking about her troubles again; and I couldn't seem to get my mouth to tell her what would make her see that corpse laying in the coffin with that bag of money on his stomach. So for a minute I didn't say nothing — then I says:

"I'd ruther not *tell* you where I put it, Miss Mary Jane, if you don't mind letting me off; but I'll write it for you on a piece of paper, and you can read it along the road to Mr. Lothrop's, if you want to. Do you reckon that'll do?"

"Oh, yes."

So I wrote: "I put it in the coffin. It was in there when you was crying there, away in the night. I was behind the door, and I was mighty sorry for you, Miss Mary Jane."

It made my eyes water a little, to remember her crying there all by herself in the night, and them devils laying there right under her own roof, shaming her and robbing her; and when I folded it up and give it to her, I see the water come into her eyes, too; and she shook me by the hand, hard, and says:

"*Good*-bye — I'm going to do everything just as you've told me; and if I don't ever see you again, I sha'n't ever forget you, and I'll think of you a many and a many a time, and I'll *pray* for you, too!" — and she was gone.

Pray for me! I reckoned if she knowed me she'd take a job that was more nearer her size. But I bet she done it, just the same — she was just that kind. She had the grit to pray for Judus if she took the notion — there warn't no back-down to her, I judge. You may say what you want to, but in my opinion she had more sand in her than any girl I ever see; in my opinion she was just full of sand. It sounds like flattery, but it ain't no flattery. And when it comes to beauty — and goodness too — she lays over them all. I hain't ever seen her since that time that I see her go out of that door; no, I hain't ever seen her since, but I reckon I've thought of her a many and a many a million times, and of her saying she would pray for me; and if ever I'd a thought it would do any good for me to pray for *her*, blamed if I wouldn't a done it or bust.

Well, Mary Jane she lit out the back way, I reckon; because nobody see her go. When I struck Susan and the hare-lip, I says:

"What's the name of them people over on t'other side of the river that you-all goes to see sometimes?"

They says:

"There's several; but it's the Proctors, mainly."

"That's the name," I says; "I most forgot it. Well, Miss Mary Jane she told me to tell you she's gone over there in a dreadful hurry — one of them's sick."

"Which one?"

"I don't know; leastways I kinder forget; but I think it's ——"

"Sakes alive, I hope it ain't *Hanner?*"

"I'm sorry to say it," I says, "but Hanner's the very one."

"My goodness — and she so well only last week! Is she took bad?"

"It ain't no name for it. They set up with her all night, Miss Mary Jane said, and they don't think she'll last many hours."

"Only think of that, now! What's the matter with her!"

I couldn't think of anything reasonable, right off that way, so I says:

"Mumps."

"Mumps your granny! They don't set up with people that's got the mumps."

"They don't, don't they? You better bet they do with *these* mumps. These mumps is different. It's a new kind, Miss Mary Jane said."

"How's it a new kind?"

"Because it's mixed up with other things."

"What other things?"

"Well, measles, and whooping-cough, and erysiplas, and consumption, and yaller janders, and brain fever, and I don't know what all."

"My land! And they call it the *mumps?*"

"That's what Miss Mary Jane said."

"Well, what in the nation do they call it the *mumps* for?"

"Why, because it *is* the mumps. That's what it starts with."

"Well, ther' ain't no sense in it. A body might stump his toe, and take pison, and fall down the well, and break his neck, and bust his brains out, and somebody come along and ask what killed him, and some numskull up and say, 'Why, he stumped his *toe.*' Would ther' be any sense in that? No. And ther' ain't no sense in *this*, nuther. Is it ketching?"

"Is it *ketching?* Why, how you talk. Is a *harrow* catching? — in the dark? If you don't hitch onto one tooth, you're bound to on another, ain't you? And you can't get away with that tooth without fetching the whole harrow along, can you? Well, these kind of mumps is a kind of a harrow, as you may say — and it ain't no slouch of a harrow, nuther, you come to get it hitched on good."

"Well, it's awful, *I* think," says the hare-lip. "I'll go to Uncle Harvey and ——"

"Oh, yes," I says, "I *would*. Of *course* I would. I wouldn't lose no time."

"Well, why wouldn't you?"

"Just look at it a minute, and maybe you can see. Hain't your uncles obleeged to get along home to England as fast as they can? And do you reckon they'd be mean enough to go off and leave you to go all that journey by yourselves? *You* know they'll wait for you. So fur, so good. Your uncle Harvey's a preacher, ain't he? Very well, then; is a *preacher* going to deceive a steamboat clerk? is he going to deceive a *ship clerk?* — so as to get them to let Miss Mary Jane go aboard? Now *you* know he ain't. What *will* he do, then? Why, he'll say, 'It's a great pity, but my church matters has got to get along the best way they can; for my niece has been exposed to the dreadful pluribus-unum mumps, and so it's my bounden duty to set down here and wait the three months it takes to show on her if she's got it.' But never mind, if you think it's best to tell your uncle Harvey ——"

"Shucks, and stay fooling around here when we could all be having good times in England whilst we was waiting to find out whether Mary Jane's got it or not? Why, you talk like a muggins."

"Well, anyway, maybe you better tell some of the neighbors."

"Listen at that, now. You do beat all, for natural stupidness. Can't you *see* that *they'd* go and tell? Ther' ain't no way but just to not tell anybody at *all*."

"Well, maybe you're right — yes, I judge you *are* right."

"But I reckon we ought to tell Uncle Harvey she's gone out a while, anyway, so he won't be uneasy about her?"

"Yes, Miss Mary Jane she wanted you to do that. She says, 'Tell them to give Uncle Harvey and William my love and a kiss, and say I've run over the river to see Mr. — Mr. — what *is* the name of that rich family your uncle Peter used to think so much of? — I mean the one that ——"

"Why, you must mean the Apthorps, ain't it?"

"Of course; bother them kind of names, a body can't ever seem to remember them, half the time, somehow. Yes, she said, say she has run over for to ask the Apthorps to be sure and come to the auction and buy this house, because she allowed her uncle Peter would ruther they had it than anybody else; and she's going to stick to them till they say they'll come, and then, if she ain't too tired, she's coming home; and if she is, she'll be home in the morning anyway. She said, don't say nothing about the Proctors, but only about the Apthorps — which'll be perfectly true, because she *is* going there to speak about their buying the house; I know it, because she told me so, herself."

"All right," they said, and cleared out to lay for their uncles, and give them the love and the kisses, and tell them the message.

Everything was all right now. The girls wouldn't say nothing because they wanted to go to England; and the king and the duke would ruther Mary Jane was off working for the auction than around in reach of Doctor Robinson. I felt very good; I judged I had done it pretty neat — I reckoned Tom Sawyer couldn't a done it no neater himself. Of course he would a throwed more style into it, but I can't do that very handy, not being brung up to it.

Well, they held the auction in the public square, along towards the end of the afternoon, and it strung along, and strung along, and the old man he was on hand and looking his level pisonest, up there longside of the auctioneer, and chipping in a little Scripture, now and then, or a little goody-goody saying, of some kind, and the duke he was around goo-gooing for sympathy all he knowed how, and just spreading himself generly.

But by-and-by the thing dragged through, and everything was sold. Everything but a little old trifling lot in the graveyard. So they'd got to work *that* off — I never see such a giraftt as the king was for wanting to swallow *everything*. Well, whilst they was at it, a steamboat landed, and in about two minutes up comes a crowd a whooping and yelling and laughing and carrying on, and singing out:

"*Here's* your opposition line! here's your two sets o' heirs to old Peter Wilks — and you pays your money and you takes your choice!"

Chapter XXIX

They was fetching a very nice looking old gentleman along, and a nice looking younger one, with his right arm in a sling. And my souls, how the people yelled, and laughed, and kept it up. But I didn't see no joke about it, and I judged it would strain the duke and the king some to see any. I reckoned they'd turn pale. But no, nary a pale did *they* turn. The duke he never let on he suspicioned what was up, but just went a goo-gooing around, happy and satisfied, like a jug that's googling out butter-milk; and as for the king, he just gazed and gazed down sorrowful on them newcomers like it give him the stomach-ache in his very heart to think there could be such frauds and rascals in the world. Oh, he done it admirable. Lots of the principal people gethered around the king, to let him see they was on his side. That old gentleman that had just come looked all puzzled to death. Pretty soon he begun to speak, and I see, straight off, he pronounced *like* an Englishman, not the king's way, though the king's *was* pretty good, for an imitation. I can't give the old gent's words, nor I can't imitate him; but he turned around to the crowd, and says, about like this:

"This is a surprise to me which I wasn't looking for; and I'll acknowledge, candid and frank, I ain't very well fixed to meet it and answer it; for my brother and me has had misfortunes, he's broke his arm, and our baggage got put off at a town above here, last night in the night by a mistake. I am Peter Wilks's brother Harvey, and this is his brother William, which can't hear nor speak — and can't even make signs to amount to much, now 't he's only got one hand to work them with. We are who we say we are; and in a day or two, when I get the baggage, I can prove it. But, up till then, I won't say nothing more, but go to the hotel and wait."

So him and the new dummy started off; and the king he laughs, and blethers out:

"Broke his arm — *very* likely *ain't* it? — and very convenient, too, for a fraud that's got to make signs, and hain't learnt how. Lost their baggage! That's *mighty* good! — and mighty ingenious — under the *circumstances!*"

So he laughed again; and so did everybody else, except three or four, or maybe half a dozen. One of these was that doctor; another one was a sharp looking gentleman, with a carpet-bag of the old-fashioned kind made out of carpet-stuff, that had just come off of the steamboat and was talking to him in a low voice, and glancing towards the king now and then and nodding their heads — it was Levi Bell, the lawyer that was gone up to Louisville; and another one was a big rough husky that come along and listened to all the old gentleman said, and was listening to the king now. And when the king got done, this husky up and says:

"Say, looky here; if you are Harvey Wilks, when'd you come to this town?"

"The day before the funeral, friend," says the king.

"But what time o' day?"

"In the evenin' — 'bout an hour er two before sundown."

"*How'd* you come?"

"I come down on the *Susan Powell*, from Cincinnati."

"Well, then, how'd you come to be up at the Pint in the *mornin'* — in a canoe?"

"I warn't up at the Pint in the mornin'."

"It's a lie."

Several of them jumped for him and begged him not to talk that way to an old man and a preacher.

"Preacher be hanged, he's a fraud and a liar. He was up at the Pint that mornin'. I live up there, don't I? Well, I was up there, and he was up there. I *see* him there. He come in a canoe, along with Tim Collins and a boy."

The doctor he up and says:

"Would you know the boy again if you was to see him, Hines?"

"I reckon I would, but I don't know. Why, yonder he is, now. I know him perfectly easy."

It was me he pointed at. The doctor says:

"Neighbors, I don't know whether the new couple is frauds or not; but if *these* two ain't frauds, I am an idiot, that's all. I think it's our duty to see that they don't get away from here till we've looked into this thing. Come along, Hines; come along, the rest of you. We'll take these fellows to the tavern and affront them with t'other couple, and I reckon we'll find out *something* before we get through."

It was nuts for the crowd, though maybe not for the king's friends; so we all started. It was about sundown. The doctor he led me along by the hand, and was plenty kind enough, but he never let *go* my hand.

We all got in a big room in the hotel, and lit up some candles, and fetched in the new couple. First, the doctor says:

"I don't wish to be too hard on these two men, but *I* think they're frauds, and they may have complices that we don't know nothing about. If they have, won't the complices get away with that bag of gold Peter Wilks left? It ain't unlikely. If these men ain't frauds, they won't object to sending for that money and letting us keep it till they prove they're all right — ain't that so?"

Everybody agreed to that. So I judged they had our gang in a pretty tight place, right at the outstart. But the king he only looked sorrowful, and says:

"Gentlemen, I wish the money was there, for I ain't got no disposition to throw anything in the way of a fair, open, out-and-out investigation o' this misable business; but alas, the money ain't there; you k'n send and see, if you want to."

"Where is it, then?"

"Well, when my niece give it to me to keep for her, I took and hid it inside o' the straw tick o' my bed, not wishin' to bank it for the few days we'd be here, and considerin' the bed a safe place, we not bein' used to niggers, and suppos'n' 'em honest, like servants in England. The niggers stole it the very next mornin' after I had went down stairs; and when I sold 'em, I hadn't missed the money yit, so they got clean away with it. My servant here k'n tell you 'bout it, gentlemen."

The doctor and several said "Shucks!" and I see nobody didn't alto-gether believe him. One man asked me if I see the niggers steal it. I said no, but I see them sneaking out of the room and hustling away, and I never thought nothing, only I reckoned they was afraid they had waked up my master and was trying to get away before he made trouble with them. That was all they asked me. Then the doctor whirls on me and says:

"Are *you* English too?"

I says yes; and him and some others laughed, and said, "Stuff!"

Well, then they sailed in on the general investigation, and there we had it, up and down, hour in, hour out, and nobody never said a word about supper, nor ever seemed to think about it — and so they kept it up, and kept it up; and it *was* the worst mixed-up thing you ever see. They made the king tell his yarn, and they made the old gentleman tell his'n; and anybody but a lot of prejudiced chuckleheads would a *seen* that the old gentleman was spinning truth and t'other one lies. And by-and-by they had me up to tell what I knowed. The king he give me a left-handed look out of the corner of his eye, and so I knowed enough to talk on the right side. I begun to tell about Sheffield, and how we lived there, and all about the English Wilkses, and so on; but I didn't get pretty fur till the doctor begun to laugh; and Levi Bell, the lawyer, says:

"Set down, my boy, I wouldn't strain myself, if I was you. I reckon you ain't used to lying, it don't seem to come handy; what you want is practice. You do it pretty awkward."

I didn't care nothing for the compliment, but I was glad to be let off, anyway.

The doctor he started to say something, and turns and says:

"If you'd been in town at first, Levi Bell ——"

The king broke in and reached out his hand, and says:

"Why, is this my poor dead brother's old friend that he's wrote so often about?"

The lawyer and him shook hands, and the lawyer smiled and looked pleased, and they talked right along a while, and then got to one side and talked low; and at last the lawyer speaks up and says:

"That'll fix it. I'll take the order and send it, along with your brother's, and then they'll know it's all right."

So they got some paper and a pen, and the king he set down and twisted his head to one side, and chawed his tongue, and scrawled off something; and then they give the pen to the duke — and then for the first time, the duke looked sick. But he took the pen and wrote. So then the lawyer turns to the new old gentleman and says:

"You and your brother please write a line or two and sign your names."

The old gentleman wrote, but nobody couldn't read it. The lawyer looked powerful astonished, and says:

"Well, it beats *me*"—and snaked a lot of old letters out of his pocket, and examined them, and then examined the old man's writing, and then *them* again; and then says: "These old letters is from Harvey Wilks; and here's *these* two's handwritings, and anybody can see *they* didn't write them" (the king and the duke looked sold and foolish, I tell you, to see how the lawyer had took them in), "and here's *this* old gentleman's handwriting, and anybody can tell, easy enough, *he* didn't write them—fact is, the scratches he makes ain't properly *writing*, at all. Now here's some letters from——"

The new old gentleman says:

"If you please, let me explain. Nobody can read my hand but my brother there—so he copies for me. It's *his* hand you've got there, not mine."

"*Well!*" says the lawyer, "this *is* a state of things. I've got some of William's letters too; so if you'll get him to write a line or so we can com——"

"He *can't* write with his left hand," says the old gentleman. "If he could use his right hand, you would see that he wrote his own letters and mine too. Look at both, please—they're by the same hand."

The lawyer done it, and says:

"I believe it's so—and if it ain't so, there's a heap stronger resemblance than I'd noticed before, anyway. Well, well, well! I thought we was right on the track of a slution, but it's gone to grass, partly. But anyway, *one* thing is proved—*these* two ain't either of 'em Wilkses"—and he wagged his head towards the king and the duke.

Well, what do you think?—that muleheaded old fool wouldn't give in *then!* Indeed he wouldn't. Said it warn't no fair test. Said his brother William was the cussedest joker in the world, and hadn't *tried* to write—*he* see William was going to play one of his jokes the minute he put the pen to paper. And so he warmed up and went warbling and warbling right along, till he was actuly beginning to believe what he was saying, *himself*—but pretty soon the new old gentleman broke in, and says:

"I've thought of something. Is there anybody here that helped to lay out my br—helped to lay out the late Peter Wilks for burying?"

"Yes," says somebody, "me and Ab Turner done it. We're both here."

Then the old man turns towards the king, and says:

"Peraps this gentleman can tell me what was tattooed on his breast?"

Blamed if the king didn't have to brace up mighty quick, or he'd a squshed down like a bluff bank that the river has cut under, it took him so sudden—and mind you, it was a thing that was calculated to make most *anybody* sqush to get fetched such a solid one as that without any notice—because how was *he* going to know what was tattooed on the man? He whitened a little; he couldn't help it; and it was mighty still in there, and everybody bending a little forwards and gazing at him. Says I to myself, *Now* he'll throw up the sponge—there ain't no more use. Well, did he? A body can't hardly believe it, but he didn't. I reckon he thought he'd keep the thing up till he tired them people out, so they'd thin out, and him and the duke could break loose and get away. Anyway, he set there, and pretty soon he begun to smile, and says:

"Mf! It's a *very* tough question, *ain't* it! *Yes*, sir, I k'n tell you what's tattooed on his breast. It's jest a small, thin, blue arrow—that's what it is; and if you don't look clost, you can't see it. *Now* what do you say—hey?"

Well, *I* never see anything like that old blister for clean out-and-out cheek.

The new old gentleman turns brisk towards Ab Turner and his pard, and his eye lights up like he judged he'd got the king *this* time, and says:

"There—you've heard what he said! Was there any such mark on Peter Wilks's breast?"

Both of them spoke up and says:

"We didn't see no such mark."

"Good!" says the old gentleman. "Now, what you *did* see on his breast was a small dim P, and a B (which is an initial he dropped when he was young), and a W, with dashes between them, so: P—B—W"—and he marked them that way on a piece of paper. "Come—ain't that what you saw?"

Both of them spoke up again, and says:

"No, we *didn't*. We never seen any marks at all."

Well, everybody *was* in a state of mind, now; and they sings out:

"The whole *bilin'* of 'm 's frauds! Le's duck 'em! le's drown 'em! le's ride 'em on a rail!" and everybody was whooping at once, and there was a rattling pow-wow. But the lawyer he jumps on the table and yells, and says:

"Gentlemen—gentle*men!* Hear me just a word—just a *single* word—if you PLEASE! There's one way yet—let's go and dig up the corpse and look."

That took them.

"Hooray!" they all shouted, and was starting right off; but the lawyer and the doctor sung out:

"Hold on, hold on! Collar all these four men and the boy, and fetch *them* along, too!"

"We'll do it!" they all shouted: "and if we don't find them marks we'll lynch the whole gang!"

I *was* scared, now, I tell you. But there warn't no getting away, you know. They gripped us all, and marched us right along, straight for the graveyard, which was a mile and a half down the river, and the whole town at our heels, for we made noise enough, and it was only nine in the evening.

As we went by our house I wished I hadn't sent Mary Jane out of town; because now if I could tip her the wink, she'd light out and save me, and blow on our dead-beats.

Well, we swarmed along down the river road, just carrying on like wild-cats; and to make it more scary, the sky was darking up, and the lightning beginning to wink and flitter, and the wind to shiver amongst the leaves. This was the most awful trouble and most dangersome I ever was in; and I was kinder stunned; everything was going so different from what I had allowed for; stead of being fixed so I could take my own time, if I wanted to, and see all the fun, and have Mary Jane at my back to save me and set me free when the close-fit come, here was nothing in the world betwixt me and sudden death but just them tattoo-marks. If they didn't find them —

I couldn't bear to think about it; and yet, somehow, I couldn't think about nothing else. It got darker and darker, and it was a beautiful time to give the crowd the slip; but that big husky had me by the wrist — Hines — and a body might as well try to give Goliar the slip. He dragged me right along, he was so excited; and I had to run to keep up.

When they got there they swarmed into the graveyard and washed over it like an overflow. And when they got to the grave, they found they had about a hundred times as many shovels as they wanted, but nobody hadn't thought to fetch a lantern. But they sailed into digging, anyway, by the flicker of the lightning, and sent a man to the nearest house a half a mile off, to borrow one.

So they dug and dug, like everything; and it got awful dark, and the rain started, and the wind swished and swushed along, and the lightning come brisker and brisker, and the thunder boomed; but them people never took no notice of it, they was so full of this business; and one minute you could see everything and every face in that big crowd, and the shovelfuls of dirt sailing up out of the grave, and the next second the dark wiped it all out, and you couldn't see nothing at all.

At last they got out the coffin, and begun to unscrew the lid, and then such another crowding, and shouldering, and shoving as there was, to scrouge in and get a sight, you never see; and in the dark, that way, it was awful. Hines he hurt my wrist dreadful, pulling and tugging so, and I reckon he clean forgot I was in the world, he was so excited and panting.

All of a sudden the lightning let go a perfect sluice of white glare, and somebody sings out:

"By the living jingo, here's the bag of gold on his breast!"

Hines let out a whoop, like everybody else, and dropped my wrist and give a big surge to bust his way in and get a look, and the way I lit out and shinned for the road in the dark, there ain't nobody can tell.

I had the road all to myself, and I fairly flew — leastways I had it all to myself except the solid dark, and the now-and-then glares, and the buzzing of the rain, and the thrashing of the wind, and the splitting of the thunder; and sure as you are born I did clip it along!

When I struck the town, I see there warn't nobody out in the storm, so I never hunted for no back streets, but humped it straight through the main one; and when I begun to get towards our house I aimed my eye and set it. No light there; the house all dark — which made me feel sorry and disappointed, I didn't know why. But at last, just as I was sailing by, *flash* comes the light in Mary Jane's window! and my heart swelled up sudden, like to bust; and the same second the house and all was behind me in the dark, and wasn't ever going to be before me no more in this world. She *was* the best girl I ever see, and had the most sand.

The minute I was far enough above the town to see I could make the tow-head, I begun to look sharp for a boat to borrow; and the first time the lightning showed me one that wasn't chained, I snatched it and shoved. It was a canoe, and warn't fastened with nothing but a rope. The tow-head was a rattling big distance off, away out there in the middle of the river, but I didn't lose no time; and when I struck the raft at last, I was so fagged I would a just laid down to blow and gasp if I could afforded it. But I didn't. As I sprung aboard I sung out:

"Out with you Jim, and set her loose! Glory be to goodness, we're shut of them!"

Jim lit out, and was a coming for me with both arms spread, he was so full of joy; but when I glimpsed him in the lightning, my heart shot up in my mouth, and I went overboard backwards; for I forgot he was old King Lear and a drownded A-rab all in one, and it most scared the livers and lights out of me. But Jim fished me out, and was going to hug me and bless me, and so on, he was so glad I was back and we was shut of the king and the duke, but I says:

"Not now — have it for breakfast, have it for breakfast! Cut loose and let her slide!"

So, in two seconds, away we went, a sliding down the river, and it *did* seem so good to be free again and all by ourselves on the big river and nobody to bother us. I had to skip around a bit, and jump up and crack my heels a few times, I couldn't help it; but about the third crack, I noticed a sound that I knowed mighty well — and held my breath and listened and waited — and sure enough, when the next flash busted out over the water, here they come! — and just a laying to their oars and making their skiff hum! It was the king and the duke.

So I wilted right down onto the planks, then, and give up; and it was all I could do to keep from crying.

Chapter XXX

When they got aboard, the king went for me, and shook me by the collar, and says:

"Tryin' to give us the slip, was ye, you pup! Tired of our company — hey?"

I says:

"No, your majesty, we warn't — *please* don't, your majesty!"

"Quick, then, and tell us what *was* your idea, or I'll shake the insides out o' you!"

"Honest, I'll tell you everything, just as it happened, your majesty. The man that had aholt of me was very good to me, and kept saying he had a boy about as big as me that died last year, and he was sorry to see a boy in such a dangerous fix; and when they was all took by surprise by finding the gold, and made a rush for the coffin, he lets go of me and whispers, 'Heel it, now, or they'll hang ye, sure!' and I lit out. It didn't seem no good for *me* to stay — *I* couldn't do nothing, and I didn't want to be hung if I could get away. So I never stopped running till I found the canoe; and when I got here I told Jim to hurry, or they'd catch me and hang me yet, and said I was afeard you and the duke wasn't alive, now, and I was awful sorry, and so was Jim, and was awful glad when we see you coming, you may ask Jim if I didn't."

Jim said it was so; and the king told him to shut up, and said, "Oh, yes, it's *mighty* likely!" and shook me up again, and said he reckoned he'd drownd me. But the duke says:

"Leggo the boy, you old idiot! Would *you* a done any different? Did you inquire around for *him*, when you got loose? *I* don't remember it."

So the king let go of me, and begun to cuss that town and everybody in it. But the duke says:

"You better a blame sight give *yourself* a good cussing, for you're the one that's entitled to it most. You hain't done a thing, from the start, that had any sense in it, except coming out so cool and cheeky with that imaginary blue-arrow mark. That *was* bright — it was right down bully; and it was the thing that saved us. For if it hadn't been for that, they'd a jailed us till them Englishmen's baggage come — and then — the penitentiary, you bet! But that trick took 'em to the graveyard, and the gold done us a still bigger kindness; for if the excited fools hadn't let go all holts and made that rush to get a look, we'd a slept in our cravats tonight — cravats warranted to *wear*, too — longer than *we'd* need 'em."

They was still a minute — thinking — then the king says, kind of absent-minded like:

"Mf! And we reckoned the *niggers* stole it!"

That made me squirm!

"Yes," says the duke, kinder slow, and deliberate, and sarcastic, "We did."

After about a half a minute, the king drawls out:

"Leastways — *I* did."

The duke says, the same way:

"On the contrary — *I* did."

The king kind of ruffles up, and says:

"Looky here, Bilgewater, what'r you referrin' to?"

The duke says, pretty brisk:

"When it comes to that, maybe you'll let me ask, what was *you* referring to?"

"Shucks!" says the king, very sarcastic; "but *I* don't know — maybe you was asleep, and didn't know what you was about."

The duke bristles right up, now, and says:

"Oh, let *up* on this cussed nonsense — do you take me for a blame' fool? Don't you reckon *I* know who hid that money in that coffin?"

"*Yes*, sir! I know you *do* know — because you done it yourself!"

"It's a lie!" — and the duke went for him. The king sings out:

"Take y'r hands off! — leggo my throat! — I take it all back!"

The duke says:

"Well, you just own up, first, that you *did* hide that money there, intending to give me the slip one of these days, and come back and dig it up, and have it all to yourself."

"Wait jest a minute, duke — answer me this one question, honest and fair; if you didn't put the money there, say it, and I'll b'lieve you, and take back everything I said."

"You old scoundrel, I didn't, and you know I didn't. There, now!"

"Well, then, I b'lieve you. But answer me only jest this one more —

now *don't* git mad; didn't you have it in your *mind* to hook the money and hide it?"

The duke never said nothing for a little bit; then he says:

"Well — I don't care if I *did*, I didn't *do* it, anyway. But you not only had it in mind to do it, but you *done* it."

"I wisht I may never die if I done it, duke, and that's honest. I won't say I warn't *goin'* to do it, because I *was*; but you — I mean somebody — got in ahead o' me."

"It's a lie! You done it, and you got to *say* you done it, or ——"

The king begun to gurgle, and then he gasps out:

"'Nough! — *I own up!*"

I was very glad to hear him say that, it made me feel much more easier than what I was feeling before. So the duke took his hands off, and says:

"If you ever deny it again, I'll drown you. It's *well* for you to set there and blubber like a baby — it's fitten for you, after the way you've acted. I never see such an old ostrich for wanting to gobble everything — and I a trusting you all the time, like you was my own father. You ought to been ashamed of yourself to stand by and hear it saddled onto a lot of poor niggers and you never say a word for 'em. It makes me feel ridiculous to think I was soft enough to *believe* that rubbage. Cuss you, I can see, now, why you was so anxious to make up the deffesit — you wanted to get what money I'd got out of the Nonesuch and one thing or another, and scoop it *all!*"

The king says, timid, and still a snuffling:

"Why, duke, it was you that said make up the deffersit, it warn't me."

"Dry up! I don't want to hear no more *out* of you!" says the duke. "And *now* you see what you *got* by it. They've got all their own money back, and all of *ourn* but a shekel or two, *besides*. G'long to bed — and don't you deffersit *me* no more deffersits, long 's *you* live!"

So the king sneaked into the wigwam, and took to his bottle for comfort; and before long the duke tackled *his* bottle; and so in about a half an hour they was as thick as thieves again, and the tighter they got, the lovinger they got; and went off a snoring in each other's arms. They both got powerful mellow, but I noticed the king didn't get mellow enough to forget to remember to not deny about hiding the money-bag again. That made me feel easy and satisfied. Of course when they got to snoring, we had a long gabble, and I told Jim everything.

Chapter XXXI

We dasn't stop again at any town, for days and days; kept right along
down the river. We was down south in the warm weather, now, and a
mighty long ways from home. We begun to come to trees with Spanish
moss on them, hanging down from the limbs like long gray beards. It
was the first I ever see it growing, and it made the woods look solemn
and dismal. So now the frauds reckoned they was out of danger, and they
begun to work the villages again.

First they done a lecture on temperance; but they didn't make
enough for them both to get drunk on. Then in another village they
started a dancing school; but they didn't know no more how to dance
than a kangaroo does; so the first prance they made, the general public
jumped in and pranced them out of town. Another time they tried a go
at yellocution; but they didn't yellocute long till the audience got up and
give them a solid good cussing and made them skip out. They tackled
missionarying, and mesmerizering, and doctoring, and telling fortunes,
and a little of everything; but they couldn't seem to have no luck. So at
last they got just about dead broke, and laid around the raft, as she
floated along, thinking, and thinking, and never saying nothing, by the
half a day at a time, and dreadful blue and desperate.

And at last they took a change, and begun to lay their heads together
in the wigwam and talk low and confidential two or three hours at a
time. Jim and me got uneasy. We didn't like the look of it. We judged
they was studying up some kind of worse deviltry than ever. We turned it
over and over, and at last we made up our minds they was going to break
into somebody's house or store, or was going into the counterfeit-money
business, or something. So then we was pretty scared, and made up an
agreement that we wouldn't have nothing in the world to do with such
actions, and if we ever got the least show we would give them the cold
shake, and clear out and leave them behind. Well, early one morning we
hid the raft in a good safe place about two mile below a little bit of a
shabby village, named Pikesville, and the king he went ashore, and told
us all to stay hid whilst he went up to town and smelt around to see if
anybody had got any wind of the Royal Nonesuch there yet. ("House to
rob, you *mean*," says I to myself; "and when you get through robbing it
you'll come back here and wonder what's become of me and Jim and
the raft — and you'll have to take it out in wondering.") And he said if he
warn't back by midday, the duke and me would know it was all right, and
we was to come along.

So we staid where we was. The duke he fretted and sweated around, and was in a mighty sour way. He scolded us for everything, and we couldn't seem to do nothing right; he found fault with every little thing. Something was a-brewing, sure. I was good and glad when midday come and no king; we could have a change, anyway — and maybe a chance for *the* change, on top of it. So me and the duke went up to the village, and hunted around there for the king, and by-and-by we found him in the back room of a little low doggery, very tight, and a lot of loafers bullyragging him for sport, and he a cussing and threatening with all his might, and so tight he couldn't walk, and couldn't do nothing to them. The duke he begun to abuse him for an old fool, and the king begun to sass back; and the minute they was fairly at it, I lit out, and shook the reefs out of my hind legs, and spun down the river road like a deer — for I see our chance; and I made up my mind that it would be a long day before they ever see me and Jim again. I got down there all out of breath but loaded up with joy, and sung out —

"Set her loose, Jim, we're all right, now!"

But there warn't no answer, and nobody come out of the wigwam. Jim was gone! I set up a shout — and then another — and then another one; and run this way and that in the woods, whooping and screeching; but it warn't no use — old Jim was gone. Then I set down and cried; I couldn't help it. But I couldn't set still long. Pretty soon I went out on the road, trying to think what I better do, and I run across a boy walking, and asked him if he'd seen a strange nigger, dressed so and so, and he says:

"Yes."

"Whereabouts?" says I.

"Down to Silas Phelps's place, two mile below here. He's a runaway nigger, and they've got him. Was you looking for him?"

"You bet I ain't! I run across him in the woods about an hour or two ago, and he said if I hollered he'd cut my livers out — and told me to lay down and stay where I was; and I done it. Been there ever since; afeard to come out."

"Well," he says, "you needn't be afeard no more, becuz they've got him. He run off f'm down South, som'ers."

"It's a good job they got him."

"Well, I *reckon!* There's two hunderd dollars reward on him. It's like picking up money out'n the road."

"Yes, it is — and *I* could a had it if I'd been big enough; I see him *first.* Who nailed him?"

"It was an old fellow — a stranger — and he sold out his chance in him for forty dollars, becuz he's got to go up the river and can't wait. Think o' that, now! You bet *I'd* wait, if it was seven year."

"That's me, every time," says I. "But maybe his chance ain't worth no more than that, if he'll sell it so cheap. Maybe there's something ain't straight about it."

"But it *is*, though — straight as a string. I see the handbill myself. It tells all about him, to a dot — paints him like a picture, and tells the plantation he's frum, below Newr*leans*. No-sirree-*bob*, they ain't no trouble 'bout *that* speculation, you bet you. Say, gimme a chaw tobacker, won't ye?"

I didn't have none, so he left. I went to the raft, and set down in the wigwam to think. But I couldn't come to nothing. I thought till I wore my head sore, but I couldn't see no way out of the trouble. After all this long journey, and after all we'd done for them scoundrels, here was it all come to nothing, everything all busted up and ruined, because they could have the heart to serve Jim such a trick as that, and make him a slave again all his life, and amongst strangers, too, for forty dirty dollars.

Once I said to myself it would be a thousand times better for Jim to be a slave at home where his family was, as long as he'd *got* to be a slave, and so I'd better write a letter to Tom Sawyer and tell him to tell Miss Watson where he was. But I soon give up that notion, for two things: she'd be mad and disgusted at his rascality and ungratefulness for leaving her, and so she'd sell him straight down the river again; and if she didn't, everybody naturally despises an ungrateful nigger, and they'd make Jim feel it all the time, and so he'd feel ornery and disgraced. And then think of *me*! It would get all around, that Huck Finn helped a nigger to get his freedom; and if I was to ever see anybody from that town again, I'd be ready to get down and lick his boots for shame. That's just the way: a person does a low-down thing, and then he don't want to take no consequences of it. Thinks as long as he can hide it, it ain't no disgrace. That was my fix exactly. The more I studied about this, the more my conscience went to grinding me, and the more wicked and low-down and ornery I got to feeling. And at last, when it hit me all of a sudden that here was the plain hand of Providence slapping me in the face and letting me know my wickedness was being watched all the time from up there in heaven, whilst I was stealing a poor old woman's nigger that hadn't ever done me no harm, and now was showing me there's One that's always on the lookout, and ain't agoing to allow no such miserable doings to go only just so fur and no further, I most dropped in my tracks I was so scared. Well, I tried the best I could to kinder soften it up somehow for myself, by saying I was brung up wicked, and so I warn't so much to blame; but something inside of me kept saying, "There was the Sunday school, you could a gone to it; and if you'd a done it they'd a learnt you, there, that people that acts as I'd been acting about that nigger goes to everlasting fire."

It made me shiver. And I about made up my mind to pray; and see if I couldn't try to quit being the kind of a boy I was, and be better. So I kneeled down. But the words wouldn't come. Why wouldn't they? It warn't no use to try and hide it from Him. Nor from *me*, neither. I knowed very well why they wouldn't come. It was because my heart warn't right; it was because I warn't square; it was because I was playing double. I was letting *on* to give up sin, but away inside of me I was holding on to the biggest one of all. I was trying to make my mouth *say* I would do the right thing and the clean thing, and go and write to that nigger's owner and tell where he was; but deep down in me I knowed it was a lie — and He knowed it. You can't pray a lie — I found that out.

So I was full of trouble, full as I could be; and didn't know what to do. At last I had an idea; and I says, I'll go and write the letter — and *then* see if I can pray. Why, it was astonishing, the way I felt as light as a feather, right straight off, and my troubles all gone. So I got a piece of paper and a pencil, all glad and excited, and set down and wrote:

Miss Watson your runaway nigger Jim is down here two mile below Pikesville and Mr. Phelps has got him and he will give him up for the reward if you send.
                                                                    HUCK FINN.

I felt good and all washed clean of sin for the first time I had ever felt so in my life, and I knowed I could pray now. But I didn't do it straight off, but laid the paper down and set there thinking — thinking how good it was all this happened so, and how near I come to being lost and going to hell. And went on thinking. And got to thinking over our trip down the river; and I see Jim before me, all the time, in the day, and in the night-time, sometimes moonlight, sometimes storms, and we a floating along, talking, and singing, and laughing. But somehow I couldn't seem to strike no places to harden me against him, but only the other kind. I'd see him standing my watch on top of his'n, stead of calling me, so I could go on sleeping; and see him how glad he was when I come back out of the fog; and when I come to him again in the swamp, up there where the feud was; and such-like times; and would always call me honey, and pet me, and do everything he could think of for me, and how good he always was; and at last I struck the time I saved him by telling the men we had small-pox aboard, and he was so grateful, and said I was the best friend old Jim every had in the world, and the *only* one he's got now; and then I happened to look around, and see that paper.

It was a close place. I took it up, and held it in my hand. I was a trembling, because I'd got to decide, forever, betwixt two things, and I knowed it. I studied a minute, sort of holding my breath, and then says to myself:

"All right, then, I'll *go* to hell" — and tore it up.

It was awful thoughts, and awful words, but they was said. And I let them stay said; and never thought no more about reforming. I shoved the whole thing out of my head; and said I would take up wickedness again, which was in my line, being brung up to it, and the other warn't. And for a starter, I would go to work and steal Jim out of slavery again; and if I could think up anything worse, I would do that, too; because as long as I was in, and in for good, I might as well go the whole hog.

Then I set to thinking over how to get at it, and turned over considerable many ways in my mind; and at last fixed up a plan that suited me. So then I took the bearings of a woody island that was down the river a piece, and as soon as it was fairly dark I crept out with my raft and went for it, and hid it there, and then turned in. I slept the night through, and got up before it was light, and had my breakfast, and put on my store clothes, and tied up some others and one thing or another in a bundle, and took the canoe and cleared for shore. I landed below where I judged was Phelps's place, and hid my bundle in the woods, and then filled up the canoe with water, and loaded rocks into her and sunk her where I could find her again when I wanted her, about a quarter of a mile below a little stream sawmill that was on the bank.

Then I struck up the road, and when I passed the mill I see a sign on it, "Phelps's Sawmill," and when I come to the farm-houses, two or three hundred yards further along, I kept my eyes peeled, but didn't see nobody around, though it was good daylight, now. But I didn't mind, because I didn't want to see nobody just yet — I only wanted to get the lay of the land. According to my plan, I was going to turn up there from the village, not from below. So I just took a look, and shoved along, straight for town. Well, the very first man I see, when I got there, was the duke. He was sticking up a bill for the Royal Nonesuch — three-night performance — like that other time. *They* had the cheek, them frauds! I was right on him, before I could shirk. He looked astonished, and says:

"Hel-*lo!* Where'd *you* come from?" Then he says, kind of glad and eager, "Where's the raft? — got her in a good place?"

I says:

"Why, that's just what I was agoing to ask your grace."

Then he didn't look so joyful — and says:

"What was your idea for asking *me?*" he says.

"Well," I says, "when I see the king in that doggery yesterday, I says to

myself, we can't get him home for hours, till he's soberer; so I went a
loafing around town to put in the time, and wait. A man up and offered
me ten cents to help him pull a skiff over the river and back to fetch a
sheep, and so I went along; but when we was dragging him to the boat,
and the man left me aholt of the rope and went behind him to shove
him along, he was too strong for me, and jerked loose and run, and we
after him. We didn't have no dog, and so we had to chase him all over
the country till we tired him out. We never got him till dark, then we
fetched him over, and I started down for the raft. When I got there and
see it was gone, I says to myself, "they've got into trouble and had to
leave; and they've took my nigger, which is the only nigger I've got in the
world, and now I'm in a strange country, and ain't got no property no
more, nor nothing, and no way to make my living;' so I set down and
cried. I slept in the woods all night. But what *did* become of the raft
then? — and Jim, poor Jim!"

"Blamed if *I* know — that is, what's become of the raft. That old fool
had made a trade and got forty dollars, and when we found him in the
doggery the loafers had matched half dollars with him and got every
cent but what he'd spent for whisky; and when I got him home late last
night and found the raft gone, we said, 'That little rascal has stole our raft
and shook us, and run off down the river.' "

"I wouldn't shake my *nigger*, would I? — the only nigger I had in the
world, and the only property."

"We never thought of that. Fact is, I reckon we'd come to consider
him *our* nigger; yes, we did consider him so — goodness knows we had
trouble enough for him. So when we see the raft was gone, and we flat
broke, there warn't anything for it but to try the Royal Nonesuch another
shake. And I've pegged along ever since, dry as a powder-horn. Where's
that ten cents? Give it here."

I had considerable money, so I give him ten cents, but begged him to
spend it for something to eat, and give me some, because it was all the
money I had, and I hadn't had nothing to eat since yesterday. He never
said nothing. The next minute he whirls on me and says:

"Do you reckon that nigger would blow on us? We'd skin him if he
done that!"

"How can he blow? Hain't he run off?"

"No! That old fool sold him, and never divided with me, and the
money's gone."

"*Sold* him?" I says, and begun to cry; "why, he was *my* nigger, and that
was my money. Where is he? — I want my nigger."

"Well, you can't *get* your nigger, that's all — so dry up your blubbering.

Looky here — do you think *you'd* venture to blow on us? Blamed if I think I'd trust you. Why, if you *was* to blow on us ——"

He stopped, but I never see the duke look so ugly out of his eyes before. I went on a-whimpering, and says:

"I don't want to blow on nobody; and I ain't got no time to blow, nohow. I got to turn out and find my nigger."

He looked kinder bothered, and stood there with his bills fluttering on his arm, thinking, and wrinkling up his forehead. At last he says:

"I'll tell you something. We got to be here three days. If you'll promise you won't blow, and won't let the nigger blow, I'll tell you where to find him."

So I promised, and he says:

"A farmer by the name of Silas Ph ——" and then he stopped. You see he started to tell me the truth; but when he stopped, that way, and begun to study and think again, I reckoned he was changing his mind. And so he was. He wouldn't trust me; he wanted to make sure of having me out of the way the whole three days. So pretty soon he says: "The man that bought him is named Abram Foster — Abram G. Foster — and he lives forty mile back here in the country, on the road to Lafayette."

"All right," I says, "I can walk it in three days. And I'll start this very afternoon."

"No, you won't, you'll start *now*; and don't you lose any time about it, neither, nor do any gabbling by the way. Just keep a tight tongue in your head and move right along, and then you won't get into trouble with *us*, d'ye hear?"

That was the order I wanted, and that was the one I played for. I wanted to be left free to work my plans.

"So clear out," he says; "and you can tell Mr. Foster whatever you want to. Maybe you can get him to believe that Jim *is* your nigger — some idiots don't require documents — leastways I've heard there's such down South here. And when you tell him the handbill and the reward's bogus, maybe he'll believe you when you explain to him what the idea was for getting 'em out. Go 'long, now, and tell him anything you want to; but mind you don't work your jaw any *between* here and there."

So I left, and struck for the back country. I didn't look around, but I kinder felt like he was watching me. But I knowed I could tire him out at that. I went straight out in the country as much as a mile, before I stopped; then I doubled back through the woods towards Phelps's. I reckoned I better start in on my plan straight off, without fooling around, because I wanted to stop Jim's mouth till these fellows could get away. I didn't want no trouble with their kind. I'd seen all I wanted to of them, and wanted to get entirely shut of them.

Chapter XXXII

When I got there it was all still and Sunday-like, and hot and sunshiny —
the hands was gone to the fields; and there was them kind of faint
dronings of bugs and flies in the air that makes it seem so lonesome and
like everybody's dead and gone; and if a breeze fans along and quivers
the leaves, it makes you feel mournful, because you feel like it's spirits
whispering — spirits that's been dead ever so many years — and you
always think they're talking about *you*. As a general thing it makes a body
wish *he* was dead, too, and done with it all.

Phelps's was one of these little one-horse cotton plantations; and they
all look alike. A rail fence round a two-acre yard; a stile, made out of logs
sawed off and up-ended, in steps, like barrels of a different length, to
climb over the fence with, and for the women to stand on when they are
going to jump onto a horse; some sickly grass-patches in the big yard, but
mostly it was bare and smooth, like an old hat with the nap rubbed off;
big double log house for the white folks — hewed logs, with the chinks
stopped up with mud or mortar, and these mud-stripes been whitewashed some time or another; round-log kitchen, with a big broad, open
but roofed passage joining it to the house; log smoke-house back of the
kitchen; three little log nigger-cabins in a row t'other side the smoke-
house; one little hut all by itself away down against the back fence, and
some out-buildings down a piece the other side; ash-hopper, and big
kettle to bile soap in, by the little hut; bench by the kitchen door, with
bucket of water and a gourd; hound asleep there, in the sun; more
hounds asleep, round about; about three shade-trees away off in a
corner; some currant bushes and gooseberry bushes in one place by the
fence; outside of the fence a garden and a water-melon patch; then the
cotton fields begins; and after the fields, the woods.

I went around and clumb over the back stile by the ash-hopper, and
started for the kitchen. When I got a little ways, I heard the dim hum of a
spinning-wheel wailing along up and sinking along down again; and
then I knowed for certain I wished I was dead — for that *is* the lone-
somest sound in the whole world.

I went right along, not fixing up any particular plan, but just trusting
to Providence to put the right words in my mouth when the time come;
for I'd noticed that Providence always did put the right words in my
mouth, if I left it alone.

When I got half-way, first one hound and then another got up and
went for me, and of course I stopped and faced them, and kept still. And
such another pow-wow as they made! In a quarter of a minute I was a

kind of a hub of a wheel, as you may say — spokes made out of dogs — circle of fifteen of them packed together around me, with their necks and noses stretched up towards me, a barking and howling; and more a coming; you could see them sailing over fences and around corners from everywheres.

A nigger woman come tearing out of the kitchen with a rolling-pin in her hand, singing out, "Begone! *you* Tige! you Spot! begone, sah!" and she fetched first one and then another of them a clip and sent him howling, and then the rest followed; and the next second, half of them come back, wagging their tails around me and making friends with me. There ain't no harm in a hound, nohow.

And behind the woman comes a little nigger girl and two little nigger boys, without anything on but tow-linen shirts, and they hung onto their mother's gown, and peeped out from behind her at me, bashful, the way they always do. And here comes the white woman running from the house, about forty-five or fifty year old, bareheaded, and her spinning-stick in her hand; and behind her comes her little white children, acting the same way the little niggers was doing. She was smiling all over so she could hardly stand — and says:

"It's *you*, at last! — *ain't* it?"

I out with a "Yes'm," before I thought.

She grabbed me and hugged me tight; and then gripped me by both hands and shook and shook; and the tears come in her eyes, and run down over; and she couldn't seem to hug and shake enough, and kept saying, "You don't look as much like your mother as I reckoned you would, but law sakes, I don't care for that, I'm *so* glad to see you! Dear, dear, it does seem like I could eat you up! Childern, it's your cousin Tom! — tell him howdy."

But they ducked their heads, and put their fingers in their mouths, and hid behind her. So she run on:

"Lize, hurry up and get him a hot breakfast, right away — or did you get your breakfast on the boat?"

I said I had got it on the boat. So then she started for the house, leading me by the hand, and the children tagging after. When we got there, she set me down in a split-bottomed chair, and set herself down on a little low stool in front of me, holding both of my hands, and says:

"Now I can have a *good* look at you; and laws-a-me, I've been hungry for it a many and a many a time, all these long years, and it's come at last! We been expecting you a couple of days and more. What's kep' you? — boat get aground?"

"Yes'm — she ——"

"Don't say yes'm — say Aunt Sally. Where'd she get aground?"

I didn't rightly know what to say, because I didn't know whether the boat would be coming up the river or down. But I go a good deal on instinct; and my instinct said she would be coming up — from down towards Orleans. That didn't help me much, though; for I didn't know the names of bars down that way. I see I'd got to invent a bar, or forget the name of the one we got aground on — or — Now I struck an idea, and fetched it out:

"It warn't the grounding — that didn't keep us back but a little. We blowed out a cylinder-head."

"Good gracious! anybody hurt?"

"No'm. Killed a nigger."

"Well, it's lucky; because sometimes people do get hurt. Two years ago last Christmas, your uncle Silas was coming up from Newrleans on the old *Lally Rook*, and she blowed out a cylinder-head and crippled a man. And I think he died afterwards. He was a Babtist. Your uncle Silas knowed a family in Baton Rouge that knowed his people very well. Yes, I remember, now, he *did* die. Mortification set in, and they had to amputate him. But it didn't save him. Yes, it was mortification — that was it. He turned blue all over, and died in the hope of a glorious resurrection. They say he was a sight to look at. Your uncle's been up to the town every day to fetch you. And he's gone again, not more'n an hour ago; he'll be back any minute, now. You must a met him on the road, didn't you? — oldish man, with a ——"

"No, I didn't see nobody, Aunt Sally. The boat landed just at daylight, and I left my baggage on the wharf-boat and went looking around the town and out a piece in the country, to put in the time and not get here too soon; and so I come down the back way."

"Who'd you give the baggage to?"

"Nobody."

"Why, child, it'll be stole!"

"Not where I hid it I reckon it won't," I says.

"How'd you get your breakfast so early on the boat?"

It was kinder thin ice, but I says:

"The captain see me standing around, and told me I better have something to eat before I went ashore; so he took me in the texas to the officers' lunch, and give me all I wanted."

I was getting so uneasy I couldn't listen good. I had my mind on the children all the time; I wanted to get them out to one side, and pump them a little, and find out who I was. But I couldn't get no show, Mrs. Phelps kept it up and run on so. Pretty soon she made the cold chills streak all down my back, because she says:

"But here we're a running on this way, and you hain't told me a word

about Sis, nor any of them. Now I'll rest my works a little, and you start
up yourn; just tell me *everything* — tell me all about 'm all — every one of
'm; and how they are, and what they're doing, and what they told you to
tell me; and every last thing you can think of."

Well, I see I was up a stump — and up it good. Providence had stood
by me this fur, all right, but I was hard and tight aground, now. I see it
warn't a bit of use to try to go ahead — I'd *got* to throw up my hand. So I
says to myself, here's another place where I got to resk the truth. I
opened my mouth to begin; but she grabbed me and hustled me in
behind the bed, and says:

"Here he comes! stick your head down lower — there, that'll do; you
can't be seen, now. Don't you let on you're here. I'll play a joke on him.
Childern, don't you say a word."

I see I was in a fix, now. But it warn't no use to worry; there warn't
nothing to do but just hold still, and try and be ready to stand from under
when the lightning struck.

I had just one little glimpse of the old gentleman when he come in,
then the bed hid him. Mrs. Phelps she jumps for him and says:

"Has he come?"

"No," says her husband.

"Good-*ness* gracious!" she says, "what in the world *can* have become
of him?"

"I can't imagine," says the old gentleman; "and I must say, it makes
me dreadful uneasy."

"Uneasy!" she says, "I'm ready to go distracted! He *must* a come; and
you've missed him along the road. I *know* it's so — something *tells* me
so."

"Why Sally, I *couldn't* miss him along the road — *you* know that."

"But oh, dear, dear, what *will* Sis say! He must a come! You must a
missed him. He ——"

"Oh, don't distress me any more'n I'm already distressed. I don't know
what in the world to make of it. I'm at my wit's end, and I don't mind
acknowledging 't I'm right down scared. But there's no hope that he's
come; for he *couldn't* come and me miss him. Sally, it's terrible — just
terrible — something's happened to the boat, sure!"

"Why, Silas! Look yonder! — up the road! — ain't that somebody coming?"

He sprung to the window at the head of the bed, and that give Mrs.
Phelps the chance she wanted. She stooped down quick, at the foot of
the bed, and give me a pull, and out I come; and when he turned back
from the window, there she stood, a-beaming and a-smiling like a house

afire, and I standing pretty meek and sweaty alongside. The old gentleman stared, and says:

"Why, who's that?"

"Who do you reckon 't is?"

"I haint no idea. Who *is* it?"

"It's *Tom Sawyer!*"

By jings, I most slumped through the floor. But there warn't no time to swap knives; the old man grabbed me by the hand and shook, and kept on shaking; and all the time, how the woman did dance around and laugh and cry; and then how they both did fire off questions about Sid, and Mary, and the rest of the tribe.

But if they was joyful, it warn't nothing to what I was; for it was like being born again, I was so glad to find out who I was. Well, they froze to me for two hours; and at last when my chin was so tired it couldn't hardly go, any more, I had told them more about my family — I mean the Sawyer family — than ever happened to any six Sawyer families. And I explained all about how we blowed out a cylinder-head at the mouth of White River and it took us three days to fix it. Which was all right, and worked first rate; because *they* didn't know but what it would take three days to fix it. If I'd a called it a bolt-head it would a done just as well.

Now I was feeling pretty comfortable all down one side, and pretty uncomfortable all up the other. Being Tom Sawyer was easy and comfortable; and it stayed easy and comfortable till by-and-by I hear a steamboat coughing along down the river — then I says to myself, spose Tom Sawyer come down on that boat? — and spose he steps in here, any minute, and sings out my name before I can throw him a wink to keep quiet? Well, I couldn't *have* it that way — it wouldn't do at all. I must go up the road and waylay him. So I told the folks I reckoned I would go up to the town and fetch down my baggage. The old gentleman was for going along with me, but I said no, I could drive the horse myself, and I druther he wouldn't take no trouble about me.

Chapter XXXIII

So I started for town, in the wagon, and when I was half-way I see a wagon coming, and sure enough it was Tom Sawyer, and I stopped and waited till he come along. I says "Hold on!" and it stopped alongside, and his mouth opened up like a trunk, and staid so; and he swallowed two or three times like a person that's got a dry throat, and then says:

"I hain't ever done you no harm. You know that. So then, what you want to come back and ha'nt *me* for?"

I says:

"I hain't come back — I hain't been *gone*."

When he heard my voice, it righted him up some, but he warn't quite satisfied yet. He says:

"Don't you play nothing on me, because I wouldn't on you. Honest injun, now, you ain't a ghost?"

"Honest injun, I ain't," I says.

"Well — I — I — well, that ought to settle it, of course; but I can't somehow seem to understand it, no way. Looky here, warn't you ever murdered *at all?*"

"No. I warn't ever murdered at all — I played it on them. You come in here and feel of me if you don't believe me."

So he done it; and it satisfied him; and he was that glad to see me again, he didn't know what to do. And he wanted to know all about it right off; because it was a grand adventure, and mysterious, and so it hit him where he lived. But I said, leave it alone till by-and-by; and told his driver to wait, and we drove off a little piece, and I told him the kind of a fix I was in, and what did he reckon we better do? He said, let him alone a minute, and don't disturb him. So he thought and thought, and pretty soon he says:

"It's all right, I've got it. Take my trunk in your wagon, and let on it's your'n; and you turn back and fool along slow, so as to get to the house about the time you ought to; and I'll go towards town a piece, and take a fresh start, and get there a quarter or a half an hour after you; and you needn't let on to know me, at first."

I says:

"All right; but wait a minute. There's one more thing — a thing that *nobody* don't know but me. And that is, there's a nigger here that I'm a trying to steal out of slavery — and his name is *Jim* — old Miss Watson's Jim."

He says:

"What! Why Jim is ——"

He stopped and went to studying. I says:

"*I* know what you'll say. You'll say it's a dirty low-down business; but what if it is? — *I'm* low down; and I'm agoing to steal him, and I want you to keep mum and not let on. Will you?"

His eye lit up, and he says:

"I'll *help* you steal him!"

Well, I let go all holts then, like I was shot. It was the most astonishing speech I ever heard — and I'm bound to say Tom Sawyer fell, considerable, in my estimation. Only I couldn't believe it. Tom Sawyer a *nigger stealer!*

"Oh, shucks," I says, "you're joking."

"I ain't joking, either."

"Well, then," I says, "joking or no joking, if you hear anything said about a runaway nigger, don't forget to remember that *you* don't know nothing about him, and *I* don't know nothing about him."

Then we took the trunk and put it in my wagon, and he drove off his way, and I drove mine. But of course I forgot all about driving slow, on accounts of being glad and full of thinking; so I got home a heap too quick for that length of a trip. The old gentleman was at the door, and he says:

"Why, this is wonderful. Who ever would a thought it was in that mare to do it. I wish we'd a timed her. And she hain't sweated a hair — not a hair. It's wonderful. Why, I wouldn't take a hunderd dollars for that horse now; I wouldn't, honest; and yet I'd a sold her for fifteen before, and thought 'twas all she was worth."

That's all he said. He was the innocentest, best old soul I ever see. But it warn't surprising; because he warn't only just a farmer, he was a preacher, too, and had a little one-horse log church down back of the plantation, which he built it himself at his own expense, for a church and school-house, and never charged nothing for his preaching, and it was worth it, too. There was plenty other farmer-preachers like that, and done the same way, down South.

In about half an hour Tom's wagon drove up to the front stile, and Aunt Sally she see it through the window because it was only about fifty yards, and says:

"Why, there's somebody come! I wonder who 'tis? Why, I do believe it's a stranger. Jimmy" (that's one of the children), "run and tell Lize to put on another plate for dinner."

Everybody made a rush for the front door, because, of course, a stranger don't come *every* year, and so he lays over the yaller fever, for interest, when he does come. Tom was over the stile and starting for the house; the wagon was spinning up the road for the village, and we was all bunched in the front door. Tom had his store clothes on, and an audience — and that was always nuts for Tom Sawyer. In them circumstances it warn't no trouble to him to throw in an amount of style that was suitable. He warn't a boy to meeky along up that yard like a sheep; no, he come ca'm and important, like the ram. When he got afront of us, he lifts his hat ever so gracious and dainty, like it was the lid of a box that had butterflies asleep in it and he didn't want to disturb them, and says:

"Mr. Archibald Nichols, I presume?"

"No, my boy," says the old gentleman, "I'm sorry to say 't your driver has deceived you; Nichols's place is down a matter of three mile more. Come in, come in."

Tom he took a look back over his shoulder, and says, "Too late — he's out of sight."

"Yes, he's gone, my son, and you must come in and eat your dinner with us; and then we'll hitch up and take you down to Nichols's."

"Oh, I *can't* make you so much trouble; I couldn't think of it. I'll walk — I don't mind the distance."

"But we won't *let* you walk — it wouldn't be Southern hospitality to do it. Come right in."

"Oh, *do*," says Aunt Sally; "it ain't a bit of trouble to us, not a bit in the world. You *must* stay. It's a long, dusty three mile, and we *can't* let you walk. And besides, I've already told 'em to put on another plate, when I see you coming; so you mustn't disappoint us. Come right in, and make yourself at home."

So Tom he thanked them very hearty and handsome, and let himself be persuaded, and come in; and when he was in, he said he was a stranger from Hicksville, Ohio, and his name was William Thompson — and he made another bow.

Well, he run on, and on, and on, making up stuff about Hicksville and everybody in it he could invent, and I getting a little nervous, and wondering how this was going to help me out of my scrape; and at last, still talking along, he reached over and kissed Aunt Sally right on the mouth, and then settled back again in his chair, comfortable, and was going on talking; but she jumped up and wiped it off with the back of her hand, and says:

"You owdacious puppy!"

He looked kind of hurt, and says:

"I'm surprised at you, m'am."

"You're s'rp — Why, what do you reckon *I* am? I've a good notion to take and — say, what do you mean by kissing me?"

He looked kind of humble, and says:

"I didn't mean nothing, m'am. I didn't mean no harm. I — I — thought you'd like it."

"Why, you born fool!" She took up the spinning-stick, and it looked like it was all she could do to keep from giving him a crack with it. "What made you think I'd like it?"

"Well, I don't know. Only, they — they — told me you would."

"*They* told you I would. Whoever told you 's *another* lunatic. I never heard the beat of it. Who's *they*?"

"Why — everybody. They all said so, m'am."

It was all she could do to hold in; and her eyes snapped, and her fingers worked like she wanted to scratch him; and she says:

"Who's 'everybody?' Out with their names — or ther'll be an idiot short."

He got up and looked distressed, and fumbled his hat, and says:

"I'm sorry, and I warn't expecting it. They told me to. They all told me to. They all said kiss her; and said she'll like it. They all said it — every one of them. But I'm sorry, m'am, and I won't do it no more — I won't, honest."

"You won't, won't you? Well, I sh'd *reckon* you won't!"

"No'm, I'm honest about it; I won't ever do it again. Till you ask me."

"Till I *ask* you! Well, I never see the beat of it in my born days! I lay you'll be the Methusalem-numskull of creation before ever *I* ask you — or the likes of you."

"Well," he says, "it does surprise me so. I can't make it out, somehow. They said you would, and I thought you would. But — " He stopped and looked around slow, like he wished he could run across a friendly eye, somewhere's; and fetched up on the old gentleman's, and says, "Didn't *you* think she'd like me to kiss her, sir?"

"Why, no, I — I — well, no, I b'lieve I didn't."

Then he looks on around, the same way, to me — and says:

"Tom, didn't *you* think Aunt Sally 'd open out her arms and say, 'Sid Sawyer —— ' "

"My land!" she says, breaking in and jumping for him, "you impudent young rascal, to fool a body so — " and was going to hug him, but he fended her off, and says:

"No, not till you've asked me, first."

So she didn't lose no time, but asked him; and hugged him and kissed him, over and over again, and then turned him over to the old man, and he took what was left. And after they got a little quiet again, she says:

"Why, dear me, I never see such a surprise. We warn't looking for *you*, at all, but only Tom. Sis never wrote to me about anybody coming but him."

"It's because it warn't *intended* for any of us to come but Tom," he says; "but I begged and begged, and at the last minute she let me come, too; so, coming down the river, me and Tom thought it would be a first-rate surprise for him to come here to the house first, and for me to by-and-by tag along and drop in and let on to be a stranger. But it was a mistake, Aunt Sally. This ain't no healthy place for a stranger to come."

"No — not impudent whelps, Sid. You ought to had your jaws boxed; I hain't been so put out since I don't know when. But I don't care, I don't mind the terms — I'd be willing to stand a thousand such jokes to have you here. Well, to think of that performance! I don't deny it, I was most putrified with astonishment when you give me that smack."

We had dinner out in that broad open passage betwixt the house and the kitchen; and there was things enough on that table for seven families — and all hot, too; none of your flabby tough meat that's laid in a cupboard in a damp cellar all night and tastes like a hunk of old cold cannibal in the morning. Uncle Silas he asked a pretty long blessing over it, but it was worth it; and it didn't cool it a bit, neither, the way I've seen them kind of interruptions do, lots of times.

There was a considerable good deal of talk, all the afternoon, and me and Tom was on the lookout all the time, but it warn't no use, they didn't happen to say nothing about any runaway nigger, and we was afraid to try to work up to it. But at supper, at night, one of the little boys says:

"Pa, mayn't Tom and Sid and me go to the show?"

"No," says the old man, "I reckon there ain't going to be any; and you couldn't go if there was; because the runaway nigger told Burton and me all about that scandalous show, and Burton said he would tell the people; so I reckon they've drove the owdacious loafers out of town before this time."

So there it was! — but *I* couldn't help it. Tom and me was to sleep in the same room and bed; so, being tired, we bid good-night and went up to bed, right after supper, and clumb out of the window and down the lightning-rod, and shoved for the town; for I didn't believe anybody was going to give the king and the duke a hint, and so, if I didn't hurry up and give them one they'd get into trouble sure.

On the road Tom he told me all about how it was reckoned I was murdered, and how pap disappeared, pretty soon, and didn't come back no more, and what a stir there was when Jim run away; and I told Tom all about our Royal Nonesuch rapscallions, and as much of the raft-voyage as I had time to; and as we struck into the town and up through the middle of it — it was as much as half-after eight, then — here comes a raging rush of people, with torches, and an awful whooping and yelling, and banging tin pans and blowing horns; and we jumped to one side to let them go by; and as they went by, I see they had the king and the duke astraddle of a rail — that is, I knowed it *was* the king and the duke, though they was all over tar and feathers, and didn't look like nothing in the world that was human — just looked like a couple of monstrous big soldier-plumes. Well, it made me sick to see it; and I was sorry for them poor pitiful rascals, it seemed like I couldn't ever feel any hardness against them any more in the world. It was a dreadful thing to see. Human beings *can* be awful cruel to one another.

We see we was too late — couldn't do no good. We asked some

stragglers about it, and they said everybody went to the show looking very innocent; and laid low and kept dark till the poor old king was in the middle of his cavortings on the stage; then somebody give a signal, and the house rose up and went for them.

So we poked along back home, and I warn't feeling so brash as I was before, but kind of ornery, and humble, and to blame, somehow — though I hadn't done nothing. But that's always the way; it don't make no difference whether you do right or wrong, a person's conscience ain't got no sense, and just goes for him *anyway*. If I had a yaller dog that didn't know no more than a person's conscience does, I would pison him. It takes up more room than all the rest of a person's insides, and yet ain't no good, nohow. Tom Sawyer he says the same.

Chapter XXXIV

We stopped talking, and got to thinking.

By-and-by Tom says:

"Looky here, Huck, what fools we are, to not think of it before! I bet I know where Jim is."

"No! Where?"

"In that hut down by the ash-hopper. Why, looky here. When we was at dinner, didn't you see a nigger man go in there with some vittles?"

"Yes."

"What did you think the vittles was for?"

"For a dog."

"So'd I. Well, it wasn't for a dog."

"Why?"

"Because part of it was watermelon."

"So it was — I noticed it. Well, it does beat all, that I never thought about a dog not eating watermelon. It shows how a body can see and don't see at the same time."

"Well, the nigger unlocked the padlock when he went in, and he locked it again when he come out. He fetched uncle a key, about the time we got up from table — same key, I bet. Watermelon shows man, lock shows prisoner; and it ain't likely there's two prisoners on such a little plantation, and where the people's all so kind and good. Jim's the prisoner. All right — I'm glad we found it out detective fashion; I wouldn't give shucks for any other way. Now you work your mind and study out a plan to steal Jim, and I will study out one, too; and we'll take the one we like the best."

What a head for just a boy to have! If I had Tom Sawyer's head, I wouldn't trade it off to be a duke, nor mate of a steamboat, nor clown in a circus, nor nothing I can think of. I went to thinking out a plan, but only just to be doing something; I knowed very well where the right plan was going to come from. Pretty soon, Tom says:

"Ready?"

"Yes," I says.

"All right—bring it out."

"My plan is this," I says. "We can easy find out if it's Jim in there. Then get up my canoe to-morrow night, and fetch my raft over from the island. Then the first dark night that comes, steal the key out of the old man's britches, after he goes to bed, and shove off down the river on the raft, with Jim, hiding daytimes and running nights, the way me and Jim used to do before. Wouldn't that plan work?"

"*Work?* Why cert'nly, it would work, like rats a fighting. But it's too blame' simple; there ain't nothing *to* it. What's the good of a plan that ain't no more trouble than that? It's as mild as goose-milk. Why, Huck, it wouldn't make no more talk than breaking into a soap factory."

I never said nothing, because I warn't expecting nothing different; but I knowed mighty well that whenever he got *his* plan ready it wouldn't have none of them objections to it.

And it didn't. He told me what it was, and I see in a minute it was worth fifteen of mine, for style, and would make Jim just as free a man as mine would, and maybe get us all killed besides. So I was satisfied, and said we would waltz in on it. I needn't tell what it was, here, because I knowed it wouldn't stay the way it was. I knowed he would be changing it around, every which way, as we went along, and heaving in new bullinesses wherever he got a chance. And that is what he done.

Well, one thing was dead sure; and that was, that Tom Sawyer was in earnest and was actuly going to help steal that nigger out of slavery. That was the thing that was too many for me. Here was a boy that was respectable, and well brung up; and had a character to lose; and folks at home that had characters; and he was bright and not leather-headed; and knowing and not ignorant; and not mean, but kind; and yet here he was, without any more pride, or rightness, or feeling, than to stoop to this business, and make himself a shame, and his family a shame, before everybody. I *couldn't* understand it, no way at all. It was outrageous, and I knowed I ought to just up and tell him so; and so be his true friend, and let him quit the thing right where he was, and save himself. And I *did* start to tell him; but he shut me up, and says:

"Don't you reckon I know what I'm about? Don't I generly know what I'm about?"

"Yes."

"Didn't I *say* I was going to help steal the nigger?"

"Yes."

"*Well* then."

That's all he said, and that's all I said. It warn't no use to say any more; because when he said he'd do a thing, he always done it. But *I* couldn't make out how he was willing to go into this thing; so I just let it go, and never bothered no more about it. If he was bound to have it so, *I* couldn't help it.

When we got home, the house was all dark and still; so we went on down to the hut by the ash-hopper, for to examine it. We went through the yard, so as to see what the hounds would do. They knowed us, and didn't make no more noise than country dogs is always doing when anything comes by in the night. When we got to the cabin, we took a look at the front and the two sides; and on the side I warn't acquainted with — which was the north side — we found a square window-hole, up tolerable high, with just one stout board nailed across it. I says:

"Here's the ticket. This hole's big enough for Jim to get through, if we wrench off the board."

Tom says:

"It's as simple as tit-tat-toe, three-in-a-row, and as easy as playing hooky. I should *hope* we can find a way that's a little more complicated than *that*, Huck Finn."

"Well then," I says, "how'll it do to saw him out, the way I done before I was murdered, that time?"

"That's more *like*," he says. "It's real mysterious, and troublesome, and good," he says; "but I bet we can find a way that's twice as long. There ain't no hurry; le's keep on looking around."

Betwixt the hut and the fence, on the back side, was a lean-to, that joined the hut at the eaves, and was made out of plank. It was as long as the hut, but narrow — only about six foot wide. The door to it was at the south end, and was padlocked. Tom he went to the soap kettle, and searched around and fetched back the iron thing they lift the lid with; so he took it and prized out one of the staples. The chain fell down, and we opened the door and went in, and shut it, and struck a match, and see the shed was only built against the cabin and hadn't no connection with it; and there warn't no floor to the shed, nor nothing in it but some old rusty played-out hoes, and spades, and picks, and a crippled plow. The match went out, and so did we, and shoved in the staple again, and the door was locked as good as ever. Tom was joyful. He says:

"Now we're all right. We'll *dig* him out. It'll take about a week!"

Then we started for the house, and I went in the back door — you only have to pull a buckskin latch-string, they don't fasten the doors — but that warn't romantical enough for Tom Sawyer: no way would do him but he must climb up the lightning-rod. But after he got up half-way about three times, and missed fire and fell every time, and the last time most busted his brains out, he thought he'd got to give it up; but after he was rested, he allowed he would give her one more turn for luck, and this time he made the trip.

In the morning we was up at break of day, and down to the nigger cabins to pet the dogs and make friends with the nigger that fed Jim — if it *was* Jim that was being fed. The niggers was just getting through breakfast and starting for the fields; and Jim's nigger was piling up a tin pan with bread and meat and things; and whilst the others was leaving, the key come from the house.

This nigger had a good-natured, chuckle-headed face, and his wool was all tied up in little bunches with thread. That was to keep witches off. He said the witches was pestering him awful, these nights, and making him see all kinds of strange things, and hear all kinds of strange words and noises, and he didn't believe he was ever witched so long, before, in his life. He got so worked up, and got to running on so about his troubles, he forgot all about what he'd been agoing to do. So Tom says:

"What's the vittles for? Going to feed the dogs?"

The nigger kind of smiled around graduly over his face, like when you heave a brickbat in a mud puddle, and he says:

"Yes, Mars Sid, *a* dog. Cur'us dog, too. Does you want to go en look at 'im?"

"Yes."

I hunched Tom, and whispers:

"You going, right here in the day-break? *That* warn't the plan."

"No, it warn't — but it's the plan *now*."

So, drat him, we went along, but I didn't like it much. When we got in, we couldn't hardly see anything, it was so dark; but Jim was there, sure enough, and could see us; and he sings out:

"Why, *Huck!* En good *lan'*! ain't dat Misto Tom?"

I just knowed how it would be; I just expected it. *I* didn't know nothing to do; and if I had, I couldn't a done it; because that nigger busted in and says:

"Why, de gracious sakes! do he know you genlmen?"

We could see pretty well, now. Tom he looked at the nigger, steady and kind of wondering, and says:

"Does *who* know us?"

"Why, dish-yer runaway nigger."

"I don't reckon he does; but what put that into your head?"

"What *put* it dar? Didn' he jis' dis minute sing out like he knowed you?"

Tom says, in a puzzled-up kind of way:

"Well, that's mighty curious. *Who* sung out? *When* did he sing out? *What* did he sing out?" And turns to me, perfectly c'am, and says, "Did *you* hear anybody sing out?"

Of course there warn't nothing to be said but the one thing; so I says:

"No; *I* ain't heard nobody say nothing."

Then he turns to Jim, and looks him over like he never see him before; and says:

"Did you sing out?"

"No, sah," says Jim; "*I* hain't said nothing, sah."

"Not a word?"

"No, sah, I hain't said a word."

"Did you ever see us before?"

"No, sah; not as *I* knows on."

So Tom turns to the nigger, which was looking wild and distressed, and says, kind of severe:

"What do you reckon's the matter with you, anyway? What made you think somebody sung out?"

"Oh, it's de dad-blame' witches, sah, en I wisht I was dead, I do. Dey's awluz at it, sah, en dey do mos' kill me, dey sk'yers me so. Please to don't tell nobody 'bout it sah, er ole Mars Silas he'll scole me; 'kase he say dey *ain't* no witches. I jis' wish to goodness he was heah now — *den* what would he say! I jis' bet he couldn' fine no way to git aroun' it *dis* time. But it's awluz jis' so; people dat's *sot*, stays sot; dey won't look into nothn' en fine it out f'r deyselves, en when *you* fine it out en tell um 'bout it, dey doan' b'lieve you."

Tom give him a dime, and said we wouldn't tell nobody; and told him to buy some more thread to tie up his wool with; and then looks at Jim, and says:

"I wonder if Uncle Silas is going to hang this nigger. If I was to catch a nigger that was ungrateful enough to run away, *I* wouldn't give him up, I'd hang him." And whilst the nigger stepped to the door to look at the dime and bite it to see if it was good, he whispers to Jim, and says:

"Don't ever let on to know us. And if you hear any digging going on nights, it's us: we're going to set you free."

Jim only had time to grab us by the hand and squeeze it, then the nigger come back, and we said we'd come again some time if the nigger wanted us to; and he said he would, more particular if it was dark, because the witches went for him mostly in the dark, and it was good to have folks around then.

Chapter XXXV

It would be most an hour, yet, till breakfast, so we left, and struck down into the woods; because Tom said we got to have *some* light to see how to dig by, and a lantern makes too much, and might get us into trouble; what we must have was a lot of them rotten chunks that's called fox-fire and just makes a soft kind of a glow when you lay them in a dark place. We fetched an armful and hid it in the weeds, and set down to rest, and Tom says, kind of dissatisfied:

"Blame it, this whole thing is just as easy and awkard as it can be. And so it makes it so rotten difficult to get up a difficult plan. There ain't no watchman to be drugged — now there *ought* to be a watchman. There ain't even a dog to give a sleeping-mixture to. And there's Jim chained by one leg, with a ten-foot chain, to the leg of his bed: why, all you got to do is to lift up the bedstead and slip off the chain. And Uncle Silas he trusts everybody; sends the key to the punkinheaded nigger, and don't send nobody to watch the nigger. Jim could a got out of that window hole before this, only there wouldn't be no use trying to travel with a ten-foot chain on his leg. Why, drat it, Huck, it's the stupidest arrangement I ever see. You got to invent *all* the difficulties. Well, we can't help it, we got to do the best we can with the materials we've got. Anyhow, there's one thing — there's more honor in getting him out through a lot of difficulties and dangers, where there warn't one of them furnished to you by the people who it was their duty to furnish them, and you had to contrive them all out of your own head. Now look at just that one thing of the lantern. When you come down to the cold facts, we simply got to *let on* that a lantern's resky. Why, we could work with a torchlight procession if we wanted to, *I* believe. Now, whilst I think of it, we got to hunt up something to make a saw out of, the first chance we get."

"What do we want of a saw?"

"What do we *want* of it? Hain't we got to saw the leg of Jim's bed off, so as to get the chain loose?"

"Why, you just said a body could lift up the bedstead and slip the chain off."

"Well, if that ain't just like you, Huck Finn. You *can* get up the infant-schooliest ways of going at a thing. Why, hain't you ever read any books at all? — Baron Trenck, nor Casanova, nor Benvenuto Chelleeny, nor Henri IV., nor none of them heroes? Whoever heard of getting a prisoner loose in such an old-maidy way as that? No; the way all the best authorities does, is to saw the bed-leg in two, and leave it just so, and swallow the sawdust, so it can't be found, and put some dirt and grease around the sawed place so the very keenest seneskal can't see no sign of its being sawed, and thinks the bed-leg is perfectly sound. Then, the night you're ready, fetch the leg a kick, down she goes; slip off your chain, and there you are. Nothing to do but hitch your rope-ladder to the battlements, shin down it, break your leg in the moat — because a rope-ladder is nineteen foot too short, you know — and there's your horses and your trusty vassles, and they scoop you up and fling you across a saddle and away you go, to your native Langudoc, or Navarre, or wherever it is. It's gaudy, Huck. I wish there was a moat to this cabin. If we get time, the night of the escape, we'll dig one."

I says:

"What do we want of a moat, when we're going to snake him out from under the cabin?"

But he never heard me. He had forgot me and everything else. He had his chin in his hand, thinking. Pretty soon, he sighs, and shakes his head; then sighs again, and says:

"No, it wouldn't do — there ain't necessity enough for it."

"For what?" I says.

"Why, to saw Jim's leg off," he says.

"Good land!" I says, "why, there ain't *no* necessity for it. And what would you want to saw his leg off for, anyway?"

"Well, some of the best authorities has done it. They couldn't get the chain off, so they just cut their hand off, and shoved. And a leg would be better still. But we got to let that go. There ain't necessity enough in this case; and besides, Jim's a nigger and wouldn't understand the reasons for it, and how it's the custom in Europe; so we'll let it go. But there's one thing — he can have a rope-ladder; we can tear up our sheets and make him a rope-ladder easy enough. And we can send it to him in a pie; it's mostly done that way. And I've et worse pies."

"Why, Tom Sawyer, how you talk," I says; "Jim ain't got no use for a rope-ladder."

"He *has* got use for it. How *you* talk, you better say; you don't know nothing about it. He's *got* to have a rope-ladder; they all do."

"What in the nation can he *do* with it?"

"*Do* with it? He can hide it in his bed, can't he? That's what they all do; and *he's* got to, too. Huck, you don't ever seem to want to do anything that's regular; you want to be starting something fresh all the time. Spose he *don't* do nothing with it? ain't it there in his bed, for a clew, after he's gone? and don't you reckon they'll want clews? Of course they will. And you wouldn't leave them any? That would be a *pretty* howdy-do, *wouldn't* it! I never heard of such a thing."

"Well," I says, "if it's in the regulations, and he's got to have it, all right, let him have it; because I don't wish to go back on no regulations; but there's one thing, Tom Sawyer — if we go to tearing up our sheets to make Jim a rope-ladder, we're going to get into trouble with Aunt Sally, just as sure as you're born. Now, the way I look at it, a hickry-bark ladder don't cost nothing, and don't waste nothing, and is just as good to load up a pie with, and hide in a straw tick, as any rag ladder you can start; and as for Jim, he ain't had no experience, and so *he* don't care what kind of a ——"

"Oh, shucks, Huck Finn, if I was as ignorant as you, I'd keep still — that's what *I'd* do. Who ever heard of a state prisoner escaping by a hickry-bark ladder? Why, it's perfectly ridiculous."

"Well, all right, Tom, fix it your own way; but if you'll take my advice, you'll let me borrow a sheet off the clothes-line."

He said that would do. And that give him another idea, and he says:

"Borrow a shirt, too."

"What do we want of a shirt, Tom?"

"Want it for Jim to keep a journal on."

"Journal your granny — *Jim* can't write."

"Spose he *can't* write — he can make marks on the shirt, can't he, if we make him a pen out of an old pewter spoon or a piece of an old iron barrel-hoop?"

"Why, Tom, we can pull a feather out of a goose and make him a better one; and quicker, too."

"*Prisoners* don't have geese running around the donjon-keep to pull pens out of, you muggins. They *always* make their pens out of the hardest, toughest, troublesomest piece of old brass candlestick or something like that they can get their hands on; and it takes them weeks and weeks, and months and months to file it out, too, because they've got to do it by rubbing it on the wall. *They* wouldn't use a goose-quill if they had it. It ain't regular."

"Well, then, what'll we make him the ink out of?"

"Many makes it out of iron-rust and tears; but that's the common sort and women; the best authorities uses their own blood. Jim can do that; and when he wants to send any little common ordinary mysterious message to let the world know where he's captivated, he can write it on the bottom of a tin plate with a fork and throw it out of the window. The Iron Mask always done that, and it's a blame' good way, too."

"Jim ain't got no tin plates. They feed him in a pan."

"That ain't anything; we can get him some."

"Can't nobody *read* his plates."

"That ain't got nothing to *do* with it, Huck Finn. All *he's* got to do is to write on the plate and throw it out. You don't *have* to be able to read it. Why, half the time you can't read anything a prisoner writes on a tin plate, or anywhere else."

"Well, then, what's the sense in wasting the plates?"

"Why, blame it all, it ain't the *prisoner's* plates."

"But it's *somebody's* plates, ain't it?"

"Well, spos'n it is? What does the *prisoner* care whose ———"

He broke off there, because we heard the breakfast-horn blowing. So we cleared out for the house.

Along during that morning I borrowed a sheet and a white shirt off of the clothes-line; and I found an old sack and put them in it, and we went down and got the fox-fire, and put that in too. I called it borrowing, because that was what pap always called it; but Tom said it warn't borrowing, it was stealing. He said we was representing prisoners; and prisoners don't care how they get a thing so they get it, and nobody don't blame them for it, either. It ain't no crime in a prisoner to steal the thing he needs to get away with, Tom said; it's his right; and so, as long as we was representing a prisoner, we had a perfect right to steal anything on this place we had the least use for, to get ourselves out of prison with. He said if we warn't prisoners it would be a very different thing, and nobody but a mean ornery person would steal when he warn't a prisoner. So we allowed we would steal everything there was that come handy. And yet he made a mighty fuss, one day, after that, when I stole a watermelon out of the nigger patch and eat it; and he made me go and give the niggers a dime, without telling them what it was for. Tom said that what he meant was, we could steal anything we *needed*. Well, I says, I needed the watermelon. But he said I didn't need it to get out of prison with, there's where the difference was. He said if I'd a wanted it to hide a knife in, and smuggle it to Jim to kill the seneskal with, it would a been all right. So I let it go at that, though I couldn't see no advantage in my representing a prisoner, if I got to set down and chaw over a lot of gold-leaf distinctions like that, every time I see a chance to hog a watermelon.

Well, as I was saying, we waited that morning till everybody was settled down to business, and nobody in sight around the yard; then Tom he carried the sack into the lean-to whilst I stood off a piece to keep watch. By-and-by he come out, and we went and set down on the wood-pile, to talk. He says:

"Everything's all right, now, except tools; and that's easy fixed."

"Tools?" I says.

"Yes."

"Tools for what?"

"Why, to dig with. We ain't agoing to *gnaw* him out, are we?"

"Ain't them old crippled picks and things in there good enough to dig a nigger out with?" I says.

He turns on me looking pitying enough to make a body cry, and says:

"Huck Finn, did you *ever* hear of a prisoner having picks and shovels, and all the modern conveniences in his wardrobe to dig himself out with? Now I want to ask you — if you got any reasonableness in you at all — what kind of a show would *that* give him to be a hero? Why, they might as well lend him the key, and done with it. Picks and shovels — why they wouldn't furnish 'em to a king."

"Well, then," I says, "if we don't want the picks and shovels, what do we want?"

"A couple of case-knives."

"To dig the foundations out from under that cabin with?"

"Yes."

"Confound it, it's foolish, Tom."

"It don't make no difference how foolish it is, it's the *right* way — and it's the regular way. And there ain't no *other* way, that ever *I* heard of, and I've read all the books that gives any information about these things. They always dig out with a case-knife — and not through dirt, mind you; generly it's through solid rock. And it takes them weeks and weeks and weeks, and for ever and ever. Why, look at one of them prisoners in the bottom dungeon of the Castle Deef, in the harbor of Marseilles, that dug himself out that way; how long was *he* at it, you reckon?"

"I don't know."

"Well, guess."

"I don't know. A month and a half?"

"*Thirty-seven year* — and he come out in China. *That's* the kind. I wish the bottom of *this* fortress was solid rock."

"*Jim* don't know nobody in China."

"What's *that* got to do with it? Neither did that other fellow. But you're always a-wandering off on a side issue. Why can't you stick to the main point?"

"All right — *I* don't care where he comes out, so he *comes* out; and Jim don't, either, I reckon. But there's one thing, anyway — Jim's too old to be dug out with a case-knife. He won't last."

"Yes he will *last*, too. You don't reckon it's going to take thirty-seven years to dig out through a *dirt* foundation, do you?"

"How long will it take, Tom?"

"Well, we can't resk being as long as we ought to, because it mayn't take very long for Uncle Silas to hear from down there by New Orleans. He'll hear Jim ain't from there. Then his next move will be to advertise

Jim, or something like that. So we can't resk being as long digging him out as we ought to. By rights I reckon we ought to be a couple of years; but we can't. Things being so uncertain, what I recommend is this: that we really dig right in, as quick as we can; and after that, we can *let on*, to ourselves, that we was at it thirty-seven years. Then we can snatch him out and rush him away the first time there's an alarm. Yes, I reckon that'll be the best way."

"Now, there's *sense* in that," I says. "Letting on don't cost nothing; letting on ain't no trouble; and if it's any object, I don't mind letting on we was at it a hundred and fifty year. It wouldn't strain me none, after I got my hand in. So I'll mosey along now, and smouch a couple of case-knives."

"Smouch three," he says; "we want one to make a saw out of."

"Tom, if it ain't unregular and irreligious to sejest it," I says, "there's an old rusty saw-blade around yonder sticking under the weatherboarding behind the smoke-house."

He looked kind of weary and discouraged-like, and says:

"It ain't no use to try to learn you nothing, Huck. Run along and smouch the knives — three of them." So I done it.

Chapter XXXVI

As soon as we reckoned everybody was asleep, that night, we went down the lightning-rod, and shut ourselves up in the lean-to, and got out our pile of fox-fire, and went to work. We cleared everything out of the way, about four or five foot along the middle of the bottom log. Tom said he was right behind Jim's bed now, and we'd dig in under it, and when we got through there couldn't nobody in the cabin ever know there was any hole there, because Jim's counterpin hung down most to the ground, and you'd have to raise it up and look under to see the hole. So we dug and dug, with the case-knives, till most midnight; and then we was dog-tired, and our hands was blistered, and yet you couldn't see we'd done anything, hardly. At last I says:

"This ain't no thirty-seven year job, this is a thirty-eight year job, Tom Sawyer."

He never said nothing. But he sighed, and pretty soon he stopped digging, and then for a good little while I knowed he was thinking. Then he says:

"It ain't no use, Huck, it ain't agoing to work. If we was prisoners it would, because then we'd have as many years as we wanted, and no hurry; and we wouldn't get but a few minutes to dig, every day, while they was changing watches, and so our hands wouldn't get blistered, and we could keep it up right along, year in and year out, and do it right, and the way it ought to be done. But *we* can't fool along, we got to rush; we ain't got no time to spare. If we was to put in another night this way, we'd have to knock off for a week to let our hands get well — couldn't touch a case-knife with them sooner."

"Well, then, what we going to do, Tom?"

"I'll tell you. It ain't right, and it ain't moral, and I wouldn't like it to get out — but there ain't only just the one way; we got to dig him out with the picks, and *let on* it's case-knives."

"*Now* you're *talking!*" I says; "your head gets leveler and leveler all the time, Tom Sawyer," I says. "Picks is the thing, moral or no moral; and as for me, I don't care shucks for the morality of it, nohow. When I start in to steal a nigger, or a watermelon, or a Sunday-school book, I ain't no ways particular how it's done so it's done. What I want is my nigger; or what I want is my watermelon; or what I want is my Sunday-school book; and if a pick's the handiest thing, that's the thing I'm agoing to dig that nigger or that watermelon or that Sunday-school book out with; and I don't give a dead rat what the authorities thinks about it nuther."

"Well," he says, "there's excuse for picks and letting-on in a case like this; if it warn't so, I wouldn't approve of it, nor I wouldn't stand by and see the rules broke — because right is right, and wrong is wrong, and a body ain't got no business doing wrong when he ain't ignorant and knows better. It might answer for *you* to dig Jim out with a pick, *without* any letting-on, because you don't know no better; but it wouldn't for me, because I do know better. Gimme a case-knife."

He had his own by him, but I handed him mine. He flung it down, and says:

"Gimme a *case-knife.*"

I didn't know just what to do — but then I thought. I scratched around amongst the old tools, and got a pick-ax and give it to him, and he took it and went to work, and never said a word.

He was always just that particular. Full of principle.

So then I got a shovel, and then we picked and shoveled, turn about, and made the fur fly. We stuck to it about a half an hour, which was as long as we could stand up; but we had a good deal of a hole to show for it. When I got up stairs, I looked out at the window and see Tom doing his level best with the lightning-rod, but he couldn't come it, his hands was so sore. At last he says:

"It ain't no use, it can't be done. What you reckon I better do? Can't you think up no way?"

"Yes," I says, "but I reckon it ain't regular. Come up the stairs, and let on it's a lightning-rod."

So he done it.

Next day Tom stole a pewter spoon and a brass candlestick in the house, for to make some pens for Jim out of, and six tallow candles; and I hung around the nigger cabins, and laid for a chance, and stole three tin plates. Tom said it wasn't enough; but I said nobody wouldn't ever see the plates that Jim throwed out, because they'd fall in the dog-fennel and jimpson weeds under the window-hole — then we could tote them back and he could use them over again. So Tom was satisfied. Then he says:

"Now, the thing to study out is, how to get the things to Jim."

"Take them in through the hole," I says, "when we get it done."

He only just looked scornful, and said something about nobody ever heard of such an idiotic idea, and then he went to studying. By-and-by he said he had ciphered out two or three ways, but there warn't no need to decide on any of them yet. Said we'd got to post Jim first.

That night we went down the lightning-rod a little after ten, and took one of the candles along, and listened under the window-hole, and heard Jim snoring; so we pitched it in, and it didn't wake him. Then we whirled in with the pick and shovel, and in about two hours and a half the job was done. We crept in under Jim's bed and into the cabin, and pawed around and found the candle and lit it, and stood over Jim a while, and found him looking hearty and healthy, and then we woke him up gentle and gradual. He was so glad to see us he most cried; and called us honey, and all the pet names he could think of; and was for having us hunt up a cold chisel to cut the chain off of his leg with, right away, and clearing out without losing any time. But Tom he showed him how unregular it would be, and set down and told him all about our plans, and how we could alter them in a minute any time there was an alarm; and not to be the least afraid, because we would see he got away, *sure*. So Jim he said it was all right, and we set there and talked over old times a while, and then Tom asked a lot of questions, and when Jim told him Uncle Silas come in every day or two to pray with him, and Aunt Sally come in to see if he was comfortable and had plenty to eat, and both of them was kind as they could be, Tom says:

"*Now* I know how to fix it. We'll send you some things by them."

I said, "Don't do nothing of the kind; it's one of the most jackass ideas I ever struck;" but he never paid no attention to me; went right on. It was his way when he'd got his plans set.

So he told Jim how we'd have to smuggle in the rope-ladder pie, and other large things, by Nat, the nigger that fed him, and he must be on the lookout, and not be surprised, and not let Nat see him open them; and we would put small things in uncle's coat pockets and he must steal them out; and we would tie things to aunt's apron strings or put them in her apron pocket, if we got a chance; and told him what they would be and what they was for. And told him how to keep a journal on the shirt with his blood, and all that. He told him everything. Jim he couldn't see no sense in the most of it, but he allowed we was white folks and knowed better than him; so he was satisfied, and said he would do it all just as Tom said.

Jim had plenty corn-cob pipes and tobacco; so we had a right down good sociable time; then we crawled out through the hole, and so home to bed, with hands that looked like they'd been chawed. Tom was in high spirits. He said it was the best fun he ever had in his life, and the most intellectural; and said if he only could see his way to it we would keep it up all the rest of our lives and leave Jim to our children to get out; for he believed Jim would come to like it better and better the more he got used to it. He said that in that way it could be strung out to as much as eighty year, and would be the best time on record. And he said it would make us all celebrated that had a hand in it.

In the morning we went out to the wood-pile and chopped up the brass candlestick into handy sizes, and Tom put them and the pewter spoon in his pocket. Then we went to the nigger cabins, and while I got Nat's notice off, Tom shoved a piece of candlestick into the middle of a corn-pone that was in Jim's pan, and we went along with Nat to see how it would work, and it just worked noble; when Jim bit into it it most mashed all his teeth out; and there warn't ever anything could a worked better. Tom said so himself. Jim he never let on but what it was only just a piece of rock or something like that that's always getting into bread, you know; but after that he never bit into nothing but what he jabbed his fork into it in three or four places, first.

And whilst we was a standing there in the dimmish light, here comes a couple of the hounds bulging in, from under Jim's bed; and they kept on piling in till there was eleven of them, and there warn't hardly room in there to get your breath. By jings, we forgot to fasten that lean-to door. The nigger Nat he only just hollered "witches!" once, and keeled over onto the floor amongst the dogs, and begun to groan like he was dying. Tom jerked the door open and flung out a slab of Jim's meat, and the dogs went for it, and in two seconds he was out himself and back again and shut the door, and I knowed he'd fixed the other door too. Then he went to work on the nigger, coaxing him and petting him, and asking him if he'd been imagining he saw something again. He raised up, and blinked his eyes around, and says:

"Mars Sid, you'll say I's a fool, but if I didn't b'lieve I see most a million dogs, er devils, er some'n, I wisht I may die right heah in dese tracks. I did, mos' sholy. Mars Sid, I *felt* um — I *felt* um, sah; dey was all over me. Dad fetch it, I jis' wisht I could git my han's on one er dem witches jis' wunst — on'y jis' wunst — it's all *I'd* ast. But mos'ly I wisht dey'd lemme 'lone, I does."

Tom says:

"Well, I tell you what *I* think. What makes them come here just at this runaway nigger's breakfast-time? It's because they're hungry; that's the reason. You make them a witch pie; that's the thing for *you* to do."

"But my lan', Mars Sid, how's *I* gwyne to make 'm a witch pie? I doan' know how to make it. I hain't ever hearn er sich a thing b'fo.' "

"Well, then, I'll have to make it myself."

"Will you do it, honey? — will you? I'll wusshup de groun' und' yo' foot, I will!"

"All right, I'll do it, seeing it's you, and you've been good to us and showed us the runaway nigger. But you got to be mighty careful. When we come around, you turn your back; and then whatever we've put in the pan, don't you let on you see it at all. And don't you look, when Jim unloads the pan — something might happen, I don't know what. And above all, don't you *handle* the witch-things."

"*Hannel* 'm Mars Sid? What *is* you a talkin' 'bout? I wouldn' lay de weight er my finger on um, not f'r ten hund'd thous'n' billion dollars, I wouldn't."

Chapter XXXVII

That was all fixed. So then we went away and went to the rubbage-pile in the back yard where they keep the old boots, and rags, and pieces of bottles, and wore-out tin things, and all such truck, and scratched around and found an old tin washpan and stopped up the holes as well as we could, to bake the pie in, and took it down cellar and stole it full of flour, and started for breakfast and found a couple of shingle-nails that Tom said would be handy for a prisoner to scrabble his name and sorrows on the dungeon walls with, and dropped one of them in Aunt Sally's apron pocket which was hanging on a chair, and t'other we stuck in the band of Uncle Silas's hat, which was on the bureau, because we heard the children say their pa and ma was going to the runaway nigger's house this morning, and then went to breakfast, and Tom dropped the pewter spoon in Uncle Silas's coat pocket, and Aunt Sally wasn't come yet, so we had to wait a little while.

And when she come she was hot, and red, and cross, and couldn't hardly wait for the blessing; and then she went to sluicing out coffee with one hand and cracking the handiest child's head with her thimble with the other, and says:

"I've hunted high, and I've hunted low, and it does beat all, what *has* become of your other shirt."

My heart fell down amongst my lungs and livers and things, and a hard piece of corn-crust started down my throat after it and got met on the road with a cough and was shot across the table and took one of the children in the eye and curled him up like a fishing-worm, and let a cry out of him the size of a war-whoop, and Tom he turned kinder blue around the gills, and it all amounted to a considerable state of things for about a quarter of a minute or as much as that, and I would a sold out for half price if there was a bidder. But after that we was all right again — it was the sudden surprise of it that knocked us so kind of cold. Uncle Silas he says:

"It's most uncommon curious, I can't understand it. I know perfectly well I took it *off*, because ———"

"Because you hain't got but one *on*. Just *listen* at the man! *I* know you took it off, and know it by a better way than your wool-gethering memory, too, because it was on the clo'es-line yesterday — I see it there myself. But it's gone — that's the long and the short of it, and you'll just have to change to a red flann'l one till I can get time to make a new one. And it'll be the third I've made in two years; it just keeps a body on the jump to keep you in shirts; and whatever you do manage to *do* with 'm all, is more'n *I* can make out. A body'd think you *would* learn to take some sort of care of 'em, at your time of life."

"I know it, Sally, and I do try all I can. But it oughtn't to be altogether my fault, because you know I don't see them nor have nothing to do with them except when they're on me; and I don't believe I've ever lost one of them *off* of me."

"Well, it ain't *your* fault if you haven't, Silas — you'd a done it if you could, I reckon. And the shirt ain't all that's gone, nuther. Ther's a spoon gone; and *that* ain't all. There was ten, and now ther's only nine. The calf got the shirt I reckon, but the calf never took the spoon, *that's* certain."

"Why, what else is gone, Sally?"

"Ther's six *candles* gone — that's what. The rats could a got the candles, and I reckon they did; I wonder they don't walk off with the whole place, the way you're always going to stop their holes and don't do it; and if they warn't fools they'd sleep in your hair, Silas — *you'd* never find it out; but you can't lay the *spoon* on the rats, and that I *know*."

"Well, Sally, I'm in fault, and I acknowledge it; I've been remiss; but I won't let to-morrow go by without stopping up them holes."

"Oh, I wouldn't hurry, next year'll do. Matilda Angelina Araminta *Phelps!*"

Whack comes the thimble, and the child snatches her claws out of the sugar-bowl without fooling around any. Just then, the nigger woman steps onto the passage, and says:

"Missus, dey's a sheet gone."

"A *sheet* gone! Well, for the land's sake!"

"I'll stop up them holes *to-day*," says Uncle Silas, looking sorrowful.

"Oh, *do* shet up! — spose the rats took the *sheet?* *Where's* it gone, Lize?"

"Clah to goodness I hain't no notion, Miss Sally. She wuz on de clo's-line yistiddy, but she done gone; she ain' dah no mo,' now."

"I reckon the world *is* coming to an end. I *never* see the beat of it, in all my born days. A shirt, and a sheet, and a spoon, and six can ——"

"Missus," comes a young yaller wench, "dey's a brass cannelstick miss'n."

"Cler out from here, you hussy, er I'll take a skillet to ye!"

Well, she was just a biling. I begun to lay for a chance; I reckoned I would sneak out and go for the woods till the weather moderated. She kept a raging right along, running her insurrection all by herself, and everybody else mighty meek and quiet; and at last Uncle Silas, looking kind of foolish, fishes up that spoon out of his pocket. She stopped, with her mouth open and her hands up; and as for me, I wished I was in Jeruslem or somewheres. But not long; because she says:

"It's *just* as I expected. So you had it in your pocket all the time; and like as not you've got the other things there, too. How'd it get there?"

"I reely don't know, Sally," he says, kind of apologizing, "or you know I would tell. I was a-studying over my text in Acts Seventeen, before breakfast, and I reckon I put it in there, not noticing, meaning to put my Testament in, and it must be so, because my Testament ain't in, but I'll go and see, and if the Testament is where I had it, I'll know I didn't put it in, and that will show that I laid the Testament down and took up the spoon, and ——"

"Oh, for the land's sake! Give a body a rest! Go 'long now, the whole kit and biling of ye; and don't come nigh me again till I've got back my peace of mind."

I'd a heard her, if she'd a said it to herself, let alone speaking it out; and I'd a got up and obeyed her, if I'd a been dead. As we was passing through the setting-room, the old man he took up his hat, and the shingle-nail fell out on the floor, and he just merely picked it up and laid it on the mantel-shelf, and never said nothing, and went out. Tom see him do it, and remembered about the spoon, and says:

"Well, it ain't no use to send things by *him* no more, he ain't reliable." Then he says: "But he done us a good turn with the spoon, anyway, without knowing it, and so we'll go and do him one without *him* knowing it — stop up his rat-holes."

There was a noble good lot of them, down cellar, and it took us a whole hour, but we done the job tight and good, and ship-shape. Then we heard steps on the stairs, and blowed out our light, and hid; and here comes the old man, with a candle in one hand and a bundle of stuff in t'other, looking as absent-minded as year before last. He went a mooning around, first to one rat-hole and then another, till he'd been to them all. Then he stood about five minutes, picking tallow-drip off of his candle and thinking. Then he turns off slow and dreamy towards the stairs, saying:

"Well, for the life of me I can't remember when I done it. I could show her now that I warn't to blame on account of the rats. But never mind — let it go. I reckon it wouldn't do no good."

And so he went on a mumbling up stairs, and then we left. He was a mighty nice old man. And always is.

Tom was a good deal bothered about what to do for a spoon, but he said we'd got to have it; so he took a think. When he had ciphered it out, he told me how we was to do; then we went and waited around the spoon-basket till we see Aunt Sally coming, and then Tom went to counting the spoons and laying them out to one side, and I slid one of them up my sleeve, and Tom says:

"Why, Aunt Sally, there ain't but nine spoons, *yet*."

She says:

"Go 'long to your play, and don't bother me. I know better, I counted 'm myself."

"Well, I've counted them twice, Aunty, and *I* can't make but nine." She looked out of all patience, but of course she come to count — anybody would.

"I declare to gracious ther' *ain't* but nine!" she says. "Why, what in the world — plague *take* the things, I'll count 'm again."

So I slipped back the one I had, and when she got done counting, she says:

"Hang the troublesome rubbage, ther's *ten*, now!" and she looked huffy and bothered both. But Tom says:

"Why, Aunty, I don't think there's ten."

"You numskull, didn't you see me *count* 'm?"

"I know, but ——"

"Well, I'll count 'm *again*."

So I smouched one, and they come out nine same as the other time. Well, she *was* in a tearing way — just a trembling all over, she was so mad. But she counted and counted, till she got that addled she'd start to count-in the *basket* for a spoon, sometimes; and so, three times they come out right, and three times they come out wrong. Then she grabbed up the basket and slammed it across the house and knocked the cat galley-west; and she said clȅr out and let her have some peace, and if we come bothering around her again betwixt that and dinner, she'd skin us. So we had the odd spoon; and dropped it in her apron pocket whilst she was a giving us our sailing-orders, and Jim got it all right, along with her shingle-nail, before noon. We was very well satisfied with this business, and Tom allowed it was worth twice the trouble it took, because he said *now* she couldn't ever count them spoons twice alike again to save her life; and wouldn't believe she'd counted them right, if she *did*; and said that after she'd about counted her head off, for the next three days, he judged she'd give it up and offer to kill anybody that wanted her to ever count them any more.

So we put the sheet back on the line, that night, and stole one out of her closet; and kept on putting it back and stealing it again, for a couple of days, till she didn't know how many sheets she had, any more, and said she didn't *care*, and warn't agoing to bullyrag the rest of her soul out about it, and wouldn't count them again not to save her life, she druther die first.

So we was all right now, as to the shirt and the sheet and the spoon and the candles, by the help of the calf and the rats and the mixed-up counting; and as to the candlestick, it warn't no consequence, it would blow over by-and-by.

But that pie was a job; we had no end of trouble with that pie. We fixed it up away down in the woods, and cooked it there; and we got it done at last, and very satisfactory, too; but not all in one day; and we had to use up three washpans full of flour, before we got through, and we got burnt pretty much all over, in places, and eyes put out with the smoke; because, you see, we didn't want nothing but a crust, and we couldn't prop it up right, and she would always cave in. But of course we thought of the right way at last; which was to cook the ladder, too, in the pie. So then we laid in with Jim, the second night, and tore up the sheet all in little strings, and twisted them together, and long before daylight we had a lovely rope, that you could a hung a person with. We let on it took nine months to make it.

And in the forenoon we took it down to the woods, but it wouldn't go in the pie. Being made of a whole sheet, that way, there was rope enough for forty pies, if we'd a wanted them, and plenty left over for soup, or sausage, or anything you choose. We could a had a whole dinner.

But we didn't need it. All we needed was just enough for the pie, and so we throwed the rest away. We didn't cook none of the pies in the washpan, afraid the solder would melt; but Uncle Silas he had a noble brass warming-pan which he thought considerable of, because it belonged to one of his ancestors with a long wooden handle that come over from England with William the Conqueror in the *Mayflower* or one of them early ships and was hid away up garret with a lot of other old pots and things that was valuable, not on account of being any account because they warn't, but on account of them being relicts, you know, and we snaked her out, private, and took her down there, but she failed on the first pies, because we didn't know how, but she come up smiling on the last one. We took and lined her with dough, and set her in the coals, and loaded her up with rag-rope, and put on a dough roof, and shut down the lid, and put hot embers on top, and stood off five foot, with the long handle, cool and comfortable, and in fifteen minutes she turned out a pie that was a satisfaction to look at. But the person that et it would want to fetch a couple of kags of toothpicks along, for if that rope-ladder wouldn't cramp him down to business, I don't know nothing what I'm talking about, and lay him in enough stomach-ache to last him till next time, too.

Nat didn't look, when we put the witch-pie in Jim's pan; and we put the three tin plates in the bottom of the pan under the vittles; and so Jim got everything all right, and as soon as he was by himself he busted into the pie and hid the rope-ladder inside of his straw tick, and scratched some marks on a tin plate and throwed it out of the window-hole.

Chapter XXXVIII

Making them pens was a distressid-tough job, and so was the saw; and Jim allowed the inscription was going to be the toughest of all. That's the one which the prisoner has to scrabble on the wall. But we had to have it; Tom said we'd *got* to; there warn't no case of a state prisoner not scrabbling his inscription to leave behind, and his coat of arms.

"Look at Lady Jane Grey," he says; "look at Gilford Dudley; look at old Northumberland! Why, Huck, spose it *is* considerble trouble? — what you going to do? — how you going to get around it? Jim's *got* to do his inscription and coat of arms. They all do."

Jim says:

"Why, Mars Tom, I hain't got no coat o' arms; I hain't got nuffn but dish-yer ole shirt, en you knows I got to keep de journal on dat."

"Oh, you don't understand, Jim; a coat of arms is very different."

"Well," I says, "Jim's right, anyway, when he says he hain't got no coat of arms, because he hain't."

"I reckon *I* knowed that," Tom says, "but you bet he'll have one before he goes out of this — because he's going out *right*, and there ain't going to be no flaws in his record."

So whilst me and Jim filed away at the pens on a brickbat apiece, Jim a making his'n out of the brass and I making mine out of the spoon, Tom set to work to think out the coat of arms. By-and-by he said he'd struck so many good ones he didn't hardly know which to take, but there was one which he reckoned he'd decide on. He says:

"On the scutcheon we'll have a bend *or* in the dexter base, a saltire *murrey* in the fess, with a dog, couchant, for common charge, and under his foot a chain embattled, for slavery, with a chevron *vert* in a chief engrailed, and three invected lines on a field *azure*, with the nombril points rampant on a dancette indented; crest, a runaway nigger, *sable*, with his bundle over his shoulder on a bar sinister: and a couple of gules for supporters, which is you and me; motto, *Maggiore fretta, minore atto*. Got it out of a book — means, the more haste, the less speed."

"Geewhillikins," I says, "but what does the rest of it mean?"

"We ain't got no time to bother over that," he says, "we got to dig in like all git-out."

"Well, anyway," I says, "what's *some* of it? What's a fess?"

"A fess — a fess is — *you* don't need to know what a fess is. I'll show him how to make it when he gets to it."

"Shucks, Tom," I says, "I think you might tell a person. What's a bar sinister?"

"Oh, *I* don't know. But he's got to have it. All the nobility does."

That was just his way. If it didn't suit him to explain a thing to you, he wouldn't do it. You might pump at him a week, it wouldn't make no difference.

He'd got all that coat of arms business fixed, so now he started in to finish up the rest of that part of the work, which was to plan out a mournful inscription — said Jim got to have one, like they all done. He made up a lot, and wrote them out on a paper, and read them off, so:

1. *Here a captive heart busted.*

2. *Here a poor prisoner, forsook by the world and friends, fretted out his sorrowful life.*

3. *Here a lonely heart broke, and a worn spirit went to its rest, after thirty-seven years of solitary captivity.*

4. *Here, homeless and friendless, after thirty-seven years of bitter captivity, perished a noble stranger, natural son of Louis XIV.*

Tom's voice trembled, whilst he was reading them, and he most broke down. When he got done, he couldn't no way make up his mind which one for Jim to scrabble onto the wall, they was all so good; but at last he allowed he would let him scrabble them all on. Jim said it would take him a year to scrabble such a lot of truck onto the logs with a nail, and he didn't know how to make letters, besides; but Tom said he would block them out for him, and then he wouldn't have nothing to do but just follow the lines. Then pretty soon he says:

"Come to think, the logs ain't agoing to do; they don't have log walls in a dungeon: we got to dig the inscriptions into a rock. We'll fetch a rock."

Jim said the rock was worse than the logs; he said it would take him such a pison long time to dig them into a rock, he wouldn't ever get out. But Tom said he would let me help him do it. Then he took a look to see how me and Jim was getting along with the pens. It was most pesky tedious hard work and slow, and didn't give my hands no show to get well of the sores, and we didn't seem to make no headway, hardly. So Tom says:

"I know how to fix it. We got to have a rock for the coat of arms and mournful inscriptions, and we can kill two birds with that same rock. There's a gaudy big grindstone down at the mill, and we'll smouch it, and carve the things on it, and file out the pens and the saw on it, too."

It warn't no slouch of an idea; and it warn't no slouch of a grindstone nuther; but we allowed we'd tackle it. It warn't quite midnight, yet, so we cleared out for the mill, leaving Jim at work. We smouched the grindstone, and set out to roll her home, but it was a most nation tough job. Sometimes, do what we could, we couldn't keep her from falling over, and she come mighty near mashing us, every time. Tom said she was going to get one of us, sure, before we got through. We got her half way; and then we was plumb played out, and most drownded with sweat. We see it warn't no use, we got to go and fetch Jim. So he raised up his bed and slid the chain off of the bed-leg, and wrapt it round and round his neck, and we crawled out through our hole and down there, and Jim and me laid into that grindstone and walked her along like nothing; and Tom superintended. He could out-superintend any boy I ever see. He knowed how to do everything.

Our hole was pretty big, but it warn't big enough to get the grindstone through; but Jim he took the pick and soon made it big enough. Then Tom marked out them things on it with the nail, and set Jim to work on them, with the nail for a chisel and an iron bolt from the rubbage in the lean-to for a hammer, and told him to work till the rest of his candle quit on him, and then he could go to bed, and hide the grindstone under his straw tick and sleep on it. Then we helped him fix his chain back on the bed-leg, and was ready for bed ourselves. But Tom thought of something, and says:

"You got any spiders in here, Jim?"

"No, sah, thanks to goodness I hain't, Mars Tom."

"All right, we'll get you some."

"But bless you, honey, I doan' *want* none. I's afeard un um. I jis' 's soon have rattlesnakes aroun'."

Tom thought a minute or two, and says:

"It's a good idea. And I reckon it's been done. It *must* a been done; it stands to reason. Yes, it's a prime good idea. Where could you keep it?"

"Keep what, Mars Tom?"

"Why, a rattlesnake."

"De goodness gracious alive, Mars Tom! Why, if dey was a rattlesnake to come in heah, I'd take en bust right out thoo dat log wall, I would, wid my head."

"Why, Jim, you wouldn't be afraid of it, after a little. You could tame it."

"*Tame* it!"

"Yes—easy enough. Every animal is grateful for kindness and petting, and they wouldn't *think* of hurting a person that pets them. Any book will tell you that. You try—that's all I ask; just try for two or three days. Why, you can get him so, in a little while, that he'll love you; and sleep with you; and won't stay away from you a minute; and will let you wrap him round your neck and put his head in your mouth."

"*Please*, Mars Tom—*doan'* talk so! I can't *stan'* it! He'd *let* me shove his head in my mouf—fer a favor, hain't it? I lay he'd wait a pow'ful long time 'fo' I *ast* him. En mo' en dat, I doan' *want* him to sleep wid me."

"Jim, don't act so foolish. A prisoner's *got* to have some kind of a dumb pet, and if a rattlesnake hain't ever been tried, why, there's more glory to be gained in your being the first to ever try it than any other way you could ever think of to save your life."

"Why, Mars Tom, I doan' *want* no sich glory. Snake take 'n bite Jim's chin off, den *whah* is de glory? No, sah, I doan' want no sich doin's."

"Blame it, can't you *try*? I only *want* you to try—you needn't keep it up if it don't work."

"But de trouble all *done*, ef de snake bite me while I's a tryin' him.

Mars Tom, I's willin' to tackle mos' anything 'at ain't onreasonable, but ef you en Huck fetches a rattlesnake in heah for me to tame, I's gwyne to *leave*, dat's *shore*."

"Well, then, let it go, let it go, if you're so bullheaded about it. We can get you some garter-snakes and you can tie some buttons on their tails, and let on they're rattlesnakes, and I reckon that'll have to do."

"I k'n stan' *dem*, Mars Tom, but blame' 'f I couldn' get along widout um, I tell you dat. I never knowed b'fo', 't was so much bother and trouble to be a prisoner."

"Well, it *always* is, when it's done right. You got any rats around here?"

"No, sah, I hain't seed none."

"Well, we'll get you some rats."

"Why, Mars Tom, I doan' *want* no rats. Dey's de dad-blamedest creturs to sturb a body, en rustle roun' over 'im, en bite his feet, when he's tryin' to sleep, I ever see. No, sah, gimme g'yarter-snakes, 'f I's got to have 'm, but doan' gimme no rats, I ain' got no use f'r um, skasely."

"But Jim, you *got* to have 'em — they all do. So don't make no more fuss about it. Prisoners ain't ever without rats. There ain't no instance of it. And they train them, and pet them, and learn them tricks, and they get to be as sociable as flies. But you got to play music to them. You got anything to play music on?"

"I ain' got nuffn but a coase comb en a piece o' paper, en a juice-harp; but I reck'n dey wouldn' take no stock in a juice-harp."

"Yes they would. *They* don't care what kind of music 'tis. A jews-harp's plenty good enough for a rat. All animals likes music — in a prison they dote on it. Specially, painful music; and you can't get no other kind out of a jews-harp. It always interests them; they come out to see what's the matter with you. Yes, you're all right; you're fixed very well. You want to set on your bed, nights, before you go to sleep, and early in the mornings, and play your jews-harp; play The Last Link is Broken — that's the thing that'll scoop a rat, quicker'n anything else: and when you've played about two minutes, you'll see all the rats, and the snakes, and spiders, and things begin to feel worried about you, and come. And they'll just fairly swarm over you, and have a noble good time."

"Yes, *dey* will, I reck'n, Mars Tom, but what kine er time is *Jim* havin'? Blest if I kin see de pint. But I'll do it ef I got to. I reck'n I better keep de animals satisfied, en not have no trouble in de house."

Tom waited to think over, and see if there wasn't nothing else; and pretty soon he says:

"Oh — there's one thing I forgot. Could you raise a flower here, do you reckon?"

"I doan' know but maybe I could, Mars Tom; but it's tolable dark in heah, en I ain' got no use f'r no flower, nohow, en she'd be a pow'ful sight o' trouble."

"Well, you try it, anyway. Some other prisoners has done it."

"One er dem big cat-tail-lookin' mullen-stalks would grow in heah, Mars Tom, I reck'n, but she wouldn' be wuth half de trouble she'd coss."

"Don't you believe it. We'll fetch you a little one, and you plant it in the corner, over there, and raise it. And don't call it mullen, call it Pitchiola—that's its right name, when it's in a prison. And you want to water it with your tears."

"Why, I got plenty spring water, Mars Tom."

"You don't *want* spring water; you want to water it with your tears. It's the way they always do."

"Why, Mars Tom, I lay I kin raise one er dem mullen-stalks twyste wid spring water whiles another man's a *start'n* one wid tears."

"That ain't the idea. You *got* to do it with tears."

"She'll die on my han's, Mars Tom, she sholy will; kase I doan' skasely ever cry."

So Tom was stumped. But he studied it over, and then said Jim would have to worry along the best he could with an onion. He promised he would go to the nigger cabins and drop one, private, in Jim's coffee-pot, in the morning. Jim said he would "jis' 's soon have tobacker in his coffee;" and found so much fault with it, and with the work and bother of raising the mullen, and jews-harping the rats, and petting and flattering up the snakes and spiders and things, on top of all the other work he had to do on pens, and inscriptions, and journals, and things, which made it more trouble and worry and responsibility to be a prisoner than anything he ever undertook, that Tom most lost all patience with him; and said he was just loadened down with more gaudier chances than a prisoner ever had in the world to make a name for himself, and yet he didn't know enough to appreciate them, and they was just about wasted on him. So Jim he was sorry, and said he wouldn't behave so no more, and then me and Tom shoved for bed.

Chapter XXXIX

In the morning we went up to the village and bought a wire rat trap and fetched it down, and unstopped the best rat hole, and in about an hour we had fifteen of the bulliest kind of ones; and then we took it and put it in a safe place under Aunt Sally's bed. But while we was gone for spiders, little Thomas Franklin Benjamin Jefferson Elexander Phelps found it

there, and opened the door of it to see if the rats would come out, and
they did; and Aunt Sally she come in, and when we got back she was a
standing on top of the bed raising Cain, and the rats was doing what they
could to keep off the dull times for her. So she took and dusted us both
with the hickry, and we was as much as two hours catching another
fifteen or sixteen, drat that meddlesome cub, and they warn't the like-
liest, nuther, because the first haul was the pick of the flock. I never see a
likelier lot of rats than what that first haul was.

We got a splendid stock of sorted spiders, and bugs, and frogs, and
caterpillars, and one thing or another; and we like-to got a hornet's nest,
but we didn't. The family was at home. We didn't give it right up, but
staid with them as long as we could; because we allowed we'd tire them
out or they'd got to tire us out, and they done it. Then we got allycum-
pain and rubbed on the places, and was pretty near all right again, but
couldn't set down convenient. And so we went for the snakes, and
grabbed a couple of dozen garters and house-snakes, and put them in a
bag, and put it in our room, and by that time it was supper time, and a
rattling good honest day's work; and hungry? — oh, no, I reckon not! And
there warn't a blessed snake up there, when we went back — we didn't
half tie the sack, and they worked out, somehow, and left. But it didn't
matter much, because they was still on the premises somewheres. So we
judged we could get some of them again. No, there warn't no real
scarcity of snakes about the house for a considerble spell. You'd see them
dripping from the rafters and places, every now and then; and they
generly landed in your plate, or down the back of your neck, and most of
the time where you didn't want them. Well, they was handsome, and
striped, and there warn't no harm in a million of them; but that never
made no difference to Aunt Sally, she despised snakes, be the breed what
they might, and she couldn't stand them no way you could fix it; and
every time one of them flopped down on her, it didn't make no difference what she was doing, she would just lay that work down and light
out. I never see such a woman. And you could hear her whoop to
Jericho. You couldn't get her to take aholt of one of them with the tongs.
And if she turned over and found one in bed, she would scramble out
and lift a howl that you would think the house was afire. She disturbed
the old man so, that he said he could most wish there hadn't ever been
no snakes created. Why, after every last snake had been gone clear out of
the house for as much as a week, Aunt Sally warn't over it yet; she warn't
near over it; when she was setting thinking about something, you could
touch her on the back of her neck with a feather and she would jump
right out of her stockings. It was very curious. But Tom said all women
was just so. He said they was made that way; for some reason or other.

We got a licking every time one of our snakes come in her way; and she allowed these lickings warn't nothing to what she would do if we ever loaded up the place again with them. I didn't mind the lickings, because they didn't amount to nothing; but I minded the trouble we had, to lay in another lot. But we got them laid in, and all the other things; and you never see a cabin as blithesome as Jim's was when they'd all swarm out for music and go for him. Jim didn't like the spiders, and the spiders didn't like Jim; and so they'd lay for him and make it mighty warm for him. And he said that between the rats, and the snakes, and the grindstone, there warn't no room in bed for him, skasely; and when there was, a body couldn't sleep, it was so lively, and it was always lively, he said, because *they* never all slept at one time, but took turn about, so when the snakes was asleep the rats was on deck, and when the rats turned in the snakes come on watch, so he always had one gang under him, in his way, and t'other gang having a circus over him, and if he got up to hunt a new place, the spiders would take a chance at him as he crossed over. He said if he ever got out, this time, he wouldn't ever be a prisoner again, not for a salary.

Well, by the end of three weeks, everything was in pretty good shape. The shirt was sent in early, in a pie, and every time a rat bit Jim he would get up and write a little in his journal whilst the ink was fresh; the pens was made, the inscriptions and so on was all carved on the grindstone; the bed-leg was sawed in two, and we had et up the sawdust, and it give us a most amazing stomach-ache. We reckoned we was all going to die, but didn't. It was the most undigestible sawdust I ever see; and Tom said the same. But as I was saying, we'd got all the work done, now, at last; and we was all pretty much fagged out, too, but mainly Jim. The old man had wrote a couple of times to the plantation below Orleans to come and get their runaway nigger, but hadn't got no answer, because there warn't no such plantation; so he allowed he would advertise Jim in the St. Louis and New Orleans papers; and when he mentioned the St. Louis ones, it give me the cold shivers, and I see we hadn't no time to lose. So Tom said, now for the nonnamous letters.

"What's them?" I says.

"Warnings to the people that something is up. Sometimes it's done one way, sometimes another. But there's always somebody spying around, that gives notice to the governor of the castle. When Louis XVI. was going to light out of the Tooleries, a servant girl done it. It's a very good way, and so is the nonnamous letters. We'll use them both. And it's usual for the prisoner's mother to change clothes with him, and she stays in, and he slides out in her clothes. We'll do that too."

"But looky here, Tom, what do we want to *warn* anybody for, that something's up? Let them find it out for themselves — it's their look-out."

"Yes, I know; but you can't depend on them. It's the way they've acted from the very start — left us to do *everything*. They're so confiding and mullet-headed they don't take notice of nothing at all. So if we don't *give* them notice, there won't be nobody nor nothing to interfere with us, and so after all our hard work and trouble this escape 'll go off perfectly flat: won't amount to nothing — won't be nothing *to* it."

"Well, as for me, Tom, that's the way I'd like."

"Shucks," he says, and looked disgusted. So I says:

"But I ain't going to make no complaint. Anyway that suits you suits me. What you going to do about the servant-girl?"

"You'll be her. You slide in, in the middle of the night, and hook that yaller girl's frock."

"Why, Tom, that'll make trouble next morning; because of course she prob'bly hain't got any but that one."

"I know; but you don't want it but fifteen minutes, to carry the nonnamous letter and shove it under the front door."

"All right, then, I'll do it; but I could carry it just as handy in my own togs."

"You wouldn't look like a servant-girl *then*, would you?"

"No, but there won't be nobody to see what I look like, *anyway*."

"That ain't got nothing to do with it. The thing for us to do, is just to do our *duty*, and not worry about whether anybody *sees* us do it or not. Hain't you got no principle at all?"

"All right, I ain't saying nothing; I'm the servant-girl. Who's Jim's mother?"

"I'm his mother. I'll hook a gown from Aunt Sally."

"Well, then, you'll have to stay in the cabin when me and Jim leaves."

"Not much. I'll stuff Jim's clothes full of straw and lay it on his bed to represent his mother in disguise, and Jim 'll take the nigger woman's gown off of me and wear it, and we'll all evade together. When a prisoner of style escapes, it's called an evasion. It's always called so when a king escapes, f'rinstance. And the same with a king's son; it don't make no difference whether he's a natural one or an unnatural one."

So Tom he wrote the nonnamous letter, and I smouched the yaller wench's frock, that night, and put it on, and shoved it under the front door, the way Tom told me to. It said:

> Beware. Trouble is brewing. Keep a sharp lookout.
>   UNKNOWN FRIEND.

Next night we stuck a picture which Tom drawed in blood, of a skull and crossbones, on the front door; and next night another one of a coffin, on the back door. I never see a family in such a sweat. They couldn't a been worse scared if the place had a been full of ghosts laying for them behind everything and under the beds and shivering through the air. If a door banged, Aunt Sally she jumped, and said "ouch!" if anything fell, she jumped and said "ouch!" if you happened to touch her, when she warn't noticing, she done the same; she couldn't face noway and be satisfied, because she allowed there was something be-hind her every time — so she was always a whirling around, sudden, and saying "ouch," and before she'd get two-thirds around, she'd whirl back again, and say it again; and she was afraid to go to bed, but she dasn't set up. So the thing was working very well, Tom said; he said he never see a thing work more satisfactory. He said it showed it was done right.

So he said, now for the grand bulge! So the very next morning at the streak of dawn we got another letter ready, and was wondering what we better do with it, because we heard them say at supper they was going to have a nigger on watch at both doors all night. Tom he went down the lightning-rod to spy around; and the nigger at the back door was asleep, and he stuck it in the back of his neck and come back. This letter said:

> *Don't betray me, I wish to be your friend. There is a desprate gang of cutthroats from over in the Ingean Territory going to steal your runaway nigger to-night, and they have been trying to scare you so as you will stay in the house and not bother them. I am one of the gang, but have got religgion and wish to quit it and lead a honest life again, and will betray the helish design. They will sneak down from northards, along the fence, at midnight exact, with a false key, and go in the nigger's cabin to get him. I am to be off a piece and blow a tin horn if I see any danger; but stead of that, I will BA like a sheep as soon as they get in and not blow at all; then whilst they are getting his chains loose, you slip there and lock them in, and can kill them at your leasure. Don't do anything but just the way I am telling you, if you do they will suspicion something and raise whoopjamboreehoo. I do not wish any reward but to know I have done the right thing.*
> UNKNOWN FRIEND.

Chapter XL

We was feeling pretty good, after breakfast, and took my canoe and went over the river a fishing, with a lunch, and had a good time, and took a look at the raft and found her all right, and got home late to supper, and found them in such a sweat and worry they didn't know which end they was standing on, and made us go right off to bed the minute we was done supper, and wouldn't tell us what the trouble was, and never let on a word about the new letter, but didn't need to, because we knowed as much about it as anybody did, and as soon as we was half up stairs and her back was turned, we slid for the cellar cubboard and loaded up a good lunch and took it up to our room and went to bed, and got up about half-past eleven, and Tom put on Aunt Sally's dress that he stole and was going to start with the lunch, but says:

"Where's the butter?"

"I laid out a hunk of it," I says, "on a piece of a corn-pone."

"Well, you *left* it laid out, then — it ain't here."

"We can get along without it," I says.

"We can get along *with* it, too," he says; "just you slide down cellar and fetch it. And then mosey right down the lightning-rod and come along. I'll go and stuff the straw into Jim's clothes to represent his mother in disguise, and be ready to *ba* like a sheep and shove soon as you get there."

So out he went, and down cellar went I. The hunk of butter, big as a person's fist, was where I had left it, so I took up the slab of corn-pone with it on, and blowed out my light, and started up stairs, very stealthy, and got up to the main floor all right, but here comes Aunt Sally with a candle, and I clapped the truck in my hat, and clapped my hat on my head, and the next second she see me; and she says:

"You been down cellar?"

"Yes'm."

"What you been doing down there?"

"Noth'n."

"*Noth'n!*"

"No'm."

"Well, then, what possessed you to go down there, this time of night?"

"I don't know'm."

"You don't *know*? Don't answer me that way, Tom, I want to know what you been *doing* down there?"

"I hain't been doing a single thing, Aunt Sally, I hope to gracious if I have."

I reckoned she'd let me go, now, and as a generl thing she would; but I spose there was so many strange things going on she was just in a sweat about every little thing that warn't yard-stick straight; so she says, very decided:

"You just march into that setting-room and stay there till I come. You been up to something you no business to, and I lay I'll find out what it is before *I'm* done with you."

So she went away as I opened the door and walked into the setting-room. My, but there was a crowd there! Fifteen farmers, and every one of them had a gun. I was most powerful sick, and slunk to a chair and set down. They was setting around, some of them talking a little, in a low voice, and all of them fidgety and uneasy, but trying to look like they warn't; but I knowed they was, because they was always taking off their hats, and putting them on, and scratching their heads, and changing their seats, and fumbling with their buttons. I warn't easy myself, but I didn't take my hat off, all the same.

I did wish Aunt Sally would come, and get done with me, and lick me, if she wanted to, and let me get away and tell Tom how we'd overdone this thing, and what a thundering hornet's nest we'd got ourselves into, so we could stop fooling around, straight off, and clear out with Jim before these rips got out of patience and come for us.

At last she come, and begun to ask me questions, but I *couldn't* answer them straight, I didn't know which end of me was up; because these men was in such a fidget now, that some was wanting to start right *now* and lay for them desperadoes, and saying it warn't but a few minutes to mid-night; and others was trying to get them to hold on and wait for the sheep-signal; and here was aunty pegging away at the questions, and me a shaking all over and ready to sink down in my tracks I was that scared; and the place getting hotter and hotter, and the butter beginning to melt and run down my neck and behind my ears; and pretty soon, when one of them says, "*I'm* for going and getting in the cabin *first*, and right *now*, and catching them when they come," I most dropped; and a streak of butter come a trickling down my forehead, and Aunt Sally she see it, and turns white as a sheet, and says:

"For the land's sake what *is* the matter with the child! — he's got the brain fever as shore as you're born, and they're oozing out!"

And everybody runs to see, and she snatches off my hat, and out comes the bread, and what was left of the butter, and she grabbed me, and hugged me, and says:

"Oh, what a turn you did give me! and how glad and grateful I am it ain't no worse; for luck's against us, and it never rains but it pours, and when I see that truck I thought we'd lost you, for I knowed by the color and all, it was just like your brains would be if — Dear, dear, whyd'nt you *tell* me that was what you'd been down there for, *I* wouldn't a cared. Now cler out to bed, and don't lemme see no more of you till morning!"

I was up stairs in a second, and down the lightning-rod in another one, and shinning through the dark for the lean-to. I couldn't hardly get my words out, I was so anxious; but I told Tom as quick as I could, we must jump for it, now, and not a minute to lose — the house full of men, yonder, with guns!

His eyes just blazed; and he says:

"No! — is that so? *Ain't* it bully! Why, Huck, if it was to do over again, I bet I could fetch two hundred! If we could put it off till ——"

"Hurry! *hurry!*" I says. "Where's Jim?"

"Right at your elbow; if you reach out your arm you can touch him. He's dressed, and everything's ready. Now we'll slide out and give the sheep-signal."

But then we heard the tramp of men, coming to the door, and heard them begin to fumble with the padlock; and heard a man say:

"I *told* you we'd be too soon; they haven't come — the door is locked. Here, I'll lock some of you into the cabin and you lay for 'em in the dark and kill 'em when they come; and the rest scatter around a piece, and listen if you can hear 'em coming."

So in they come, but couldn't see us in the dark, and most trod on us whilst we was hustling to get under the bed. But we got under all right, and out through the hole, swift but soft — Jim first, me next, and Tom last, which was according to Tom's orders. Now we was in the lean-to, and heard trampings close by outside. So we crept to the door, and Tom stopped us there and put his eye to the crack, but couldn't make out nothing, it was so dark; and whispered and said he would listen for the steps to get further, and when he nudged us Jim must glide out first, and him last. So he set his ear to the crack and listened, and listened, and listened, and the steps a scraping around, out there, all the time; and at last he nudged us, and we slid out, and stooped down, not breathing, and not making the least noise, and slipped stealthy towards the fence, in Injun file, and got to it, all right, and me and Jim over it; but Tom's britches catched fast on a splinter on the top rail, and then he hear the steps coming, so he had to pull loose, which snapped the splinter and made a noise; and as he dropped in our tracks and started, somebody sings out:

"Who's that? Answer, or I'll shoot!"

But we didn't answer; we just unfurled our heels and shoved. Then there was a rush, and a *bang, bang, bang!* and the bullets fairly whizzed around us! We heard them sing out:

"Here they are! They've broke for the river! after 'em, boys! And turn loose the dogs!"

So here they come, full tilt. We could hear them, because they wore boots, and yelled, but we didn't wear no boots, and didn't yell. We was in the path to the mill; and when they got pretty close onto us, we dodged into the bush and let them go by, and then dropped in behind them. They'd had all the dogs shut up, so they wouldn't scare off the robbers; but by this time somebody had let them loose, and here they come, making pow-wow enough for a million; but they was our dogs; so we stopped in our tracks till they catched up; and when they see it warn't nobody but us, and no excitement to offer them, they only just said howdy, and tore right ahead towards the shouting and clattering; and then we up steam again and whizzed along after them till we was nearly to the mill, and then struck up through the bush to where my canoe was tied, and hopped in and pulled for dear life towards the middle of the river, but didn't make no more noise than we was obleeged to. Then we struck out, easy and comfortable, for the island where, my raft was; and we could hear them yelling and barking at each other all up and down the bank, till we was so far away the sounds got dim and died out. And when we stepped onto the raft, I says:

"*Now*, old Jim, you're a free man *again*, and I bet you won't ever be a slave no more."

"En a mighty good job it wuz, too, Huck. It 'uz planned beautiful, en it 'uz *done* beautiful; en dey ain't *nobody* kin git up a plan dat's mo' mixed-up en splendid den what dat one wuz."

We was all as glad as we could be, but Tom was the gladdest of all, because he had a bullet in the calf of his leg.

When me and Jim heard that, we didn't feel so brash as what we did before. It was hurting him considerble, and bleeding; so we laid him in the wigwam and tore up one of the duke's shirts for to bandage him, but he says:

"Gimme the rags, I can do it myself. Don't stop, now; don't fool around here, and the evasion booming along so handsome; man the sweeps, and set her loose! Boys, we done it elegant!—'deed we did. I wish *we'd* a had the handling of Louis XVI., there wouldn't a been no 'Son of Saint Louis, ascend to heaven!' wrote down in *his* biography: no, sir, we'd a whooped him over the *border*—that's what we'd a done with *him*—and done it just as slick as nothing at all, too. Man the sweeps— man the sweeps!"

But me and Jim was consulting—and thinking. And after we'd thought a minute, I says:

"Say it, Jim."

So he says:

"Well, den, dis is de way it look to me, Huck. Ef it wuz *him* dat 'uz bein' sot free, en one er de boys wuz to git shot, would he say, 'Go on en save me, nemmine 'bout a doctor f'r to save dis one? Is dat like Mars Tom Sawyer? Would he say dat? You *bet* he wouldn't't! *Well*, den, is *Jim* gwyne to say it? No, sah—I doan' budge a step out'n dis place, 'dout a *doctor*; not if it's forty year!"

I knowed he was white inside, and I reckoned he'd say what he did say—so it was all right, now, and I told Tom I was agoing for a doctor. He raised considerble row about it, but me and Jim stuck to it and wouldn't budge; so he was for crawling out and setting the raft loose himself; but we wouldn't let him. Then he give us a piece of his mind — but it didn't do no good.

So when he see me getting the canoe ready, he says:

"Well, then, if you're bound to go, I'll tell you the way to do, when you get to the village. Shut the door, and blindfold the doctor tight and fast, and make him swear to be silent as the grave, and put a purse full of gold in his hand, and then take and lead him all around the back alleys and everywheres, in the dark, and then fetch him here in the canoe, in a roundabout way amongst the islands, and search him and take his chalk away from him, and don't give it back to him till you get him back to the village, or else he will chalk this raft so he can find it again. It's the way they all do."

So I said I would, and left, and Jim was to hide in the woods when he see the doctor coming, till he was gone again.

Chapter XLI

The doctor was an old man; a very nice, kind-looking old man, when I got him up. I told him me and my brother was over on Spanish Island hunting, yesterday afternoon, and camped on a piece of a raft we found, and about midnight he must a kicked his gun in his dreams, for it went off and shot him in the leg, and we wanted him to go over there and fix it and not say nothing about it, nor let anybody know, because we wanted to come home this evening, and surprise the folks.

"Who is your folks?" he says.

"The Phelpses, down yonder."

"Oh," he says. And after a minute, he says: "How'd you say he got shot?"

"He had a dream," I says, "and it shot him."

"Singular dream," he says.

So he lit up his lantern, and got his saddle-bags, and we started. But when he see the canoe, he didn't like the look of her — said she was big enough for one, but didn't look pretty safe for two. I says:

"Oh, you needn't be afeard, sir, she carried the three of us, easy enough."

"What three?"

"Why, me and Sid, and — and — and *the guns*; that's what I mean."

"Oh," he says.

But he put his foot on the gunnel, and rocked her; and shook his head, and said he reckoned he'd look around for a bigger one. But they was all locked and chained; so he took my canoe, and said for me to wait till he come back, or I could hunt around further, or maybe I better go down home and get them ready for the surprise, if I wanted to. But I said I didn't; so I told him just how to find the raft, and then he started.

I struck an idea, pretty soon. I says to myself, spos'n he can't fix that leg just in three shakes of a sheep's tail, as the saying is? spos'n it takes him three or four days? What are we going to do? — lay around there till he lets the cat out of the bag? No, sir, I know what *I'll* do. I'll wait, and when he comes back, if he says he's got to go any more, I'll get down there, too, if I swim; and we'll take and tie him, and keep him, and shove out down the river; and when Tom's done with him, we'll give him what it's worth, or all we got, and then let him get shore.

So then I crept into a lumber pile to get some sleep; and next time I waked up the sun was away up over my head! I shot out and went for the doctor's house, but they told me he'd gone away in the night, some time or other, and warn't back yet. Well, thinks I, that looks powerful bad for Tom, and I'll dig out for the island, right off. So away I shoved, and turned the corner, and nearly rammed my head into Uncle Silas's stomach! He says:

"Why, *Tom!* Where you been, all this time, you rascal?"

"*I* hain't been nowheres," I says, "only just hunting for the runaway nigger — me and Sid."

"Why, where ever did you go?" he says. "Your aunt's been mighty uneasy."

"She needn't," I says, "because we was all right. We followed the men and the dogs, but they out-run us, and we lost them; but we thought we heard them on the water, so we got a canoe and took out after them, and crossed over but couldn't find nothing of them; so we cruised along up-shore till we got kind of tired and beat out; and tied up the canoe and went to sleep, and never waked up till about an hour ago, then we paddled over here to hear the news, and Sid's at the post-office to see what he can hear, and I'm a branching out to get something to eat for us, and then we're going home."

So then we went to the post-office to get "Sid"; but just as I suspicioned, he warn't there; so the old man he got a letter out of the office, and we waited a while longer but Sid didn't come; so the old man said come along, let Sid foot it home, or canoe-it, when he got done fooling around — but we would ride. I couldn't get him to let me stay and wait for Sid; and he said there warn't no use in it, and I must come along, and let Aunt Sally see we was all right.

When we got home, Aunt Sally was that glad to see me she laughed and cried both, and hugged me, and give me one of them lickings of hern that don't amount to shucks, and said she'd serve Sid the same when he come.

And the place was plumb full of farmers and farmers' wives, to dinner; and such another clack a body never heard. Old Mrs. Hotchkiss was the worst; her tongue was agoing all the time. She says:

"Well, Sister Phelps, I've ransacked that-air cabin over an' I b'lieve the nigger was crazy. I says so to Sister Damrell — didn't I, Sister Damrell? — s'I, he's crazy, s'I — them's the very words I said. You all hearn me: he's crazy, s'I; everything shows it, s'I. Look at that-air grindstone, s'I; want to tell *me* 't any cretur 'ts in his right mind 's agoin' to scrabble all them crazy things onto a grindstone, s'I? Here sich 'n' sich a person busted his heart; 'n' here so 'n' so pegged along for thirty-seven year, 'n' all that — natcherl son o' Louis somebody, 'n' sich everlast'n rubbage. He's plumb crazy, s'I; it's what I says in the fust place, it's what I says in the middle, 'n' it's what I says last 'n' all the time — the nigger's crazy — crazy 's Nebokoodneezer, s'I."

"An' look at that-air ladder made out'n rags, Sister Hotchkiss," says old Mrs. Damrell, "what in the name o' goodness *could* he ever want of ——"

"The very words I was a-sayin' no longer ago th'n this minute to Sister Utterback, 'n' she'll tell you so herself. Sh-she, look at that-air rag ladder, sh-she; 'n' s'I, yes, *look* at it, s'I — what *could* he a wanted of it, s'I. Sh-she, Sister Hotchkiss, sh-she ——"

"But how in the nation'd they ever *git* that grindstone *in* there, *any*way? 'n' who dug that-air *hole*? 'n' who ——"

"My very *words*, Brer Penrod! I was a-sayin' — pass that-air sasser o' m'lasses, won't ye? — I was a-sayin' to Sister Dunlap, jist this minute, how *did* they git that grindstone in there, s'I. Without *help*, mind you — 'thout *help*! *Thar's* wher' 'tis. Don't tell *me*, s'I; there *wuz* help, s'I; 'n' ther' wuz a *plenty* help, too, s'I; ther's ben a *dozen* a-helpin' that nigger, 'n' I lay I'd skin every last nigger on this place, but *I'd* find out who done it, s'I; 'n' moreover, s'I ——"

"A *dozen* says you! — *forty* couldn't a done everything that's been done. Look at them case-knife saws and things, how tedious they've been made; look at that bed-leg sawed off with 'm, a week's work for six men; look at that nigger made out'n straw on the bed; and look at ——"

"You may *well* say it, Brer Hightower! It's jist as I was a-sayin' to Brer Phelps, his own self. S'e, what do *you* think of it, Sister Hotchkiss, s'e? think o' what, Brer Phelps, s'I? think o' that bed-leg sawed off that a way, s'e? *think* of it, s'I? I lay it never sawed *itself* off, s'I — somebody *sawed* it, s'I; that's my opinion, take it or leave it, it mayn't be no 'count, s'I, but sich as 't is, it's my opinion, s'I, 'n' if anybody k'n start a better one, s'I, let him *do* it, s'I, that's all. I says to Sister Dunlap, s'I ——"

"Why, dog my cats, they must a ben a house-full o' niggers in there every night for four weeks, to a done all that work, Sister Phelps. Look at that shirt — every last inch of it kivered over with secret African writ'n done with blood! Must a ben a raft uv 'm at it right along, all the time, amost. Why, I'd give two dollars to have it read to me; 'n' as for the niggers that wrote it, I 'low I'd take 'n' lash 'm t'll ——"

"People to *help* him, Brother Marples! Well, I reckon you'd *think* so, if you'd a been in this house for a while back. Why, they've stole everything they could lay their hands on — and we a watching, all the time, mind you. They stole that shirt right off o' the line! and as for that sheet they made the rag ladder out of ther' ain't no telling how many times they *didn't* steal that; and flour, and candles, and candlesticks, and spoons, and the old warming-pan, and most a thousand things that I disremember, now, and my new calico dress; and me, and Silas, and my Sid and Tom on the constant watch day *and* night, as I was a telling you, and not a one of us could catch hide nor hair, nor sight nor sound of them; and here at the last minute, lo and behold you, they slides right in under our noses, and fools us, and not only fools *us* but the Injun Territory robbers too, and actuly gets *away* with that nigger, safe and sound, and that with sixteen men and twenty-two dogs right on their very heels at that very time! I tell you, it just bangs anything I ever *heard* of. Why, *sperits* couldn't a done better, and been no smarter. And I reckon they must a *been* sperits — because, *you* know our dogs, and ther' ain't no better; well, them dogs never even got on the *track* of 'm, once! You explain *that* to me, if you can! — *any* of you!"

"Well, it does beat ——"

"Laws alive, I never ——"

"So help me, I wouldn't a be ——"

"*House* thieves as well as ——"

"Goodnessgracioussakes, I'd a ben afeard to *live* in sich a ——"

" 'Fraid to *live!* — why, I was that scared I das'nt hardly go to bed, or get up, or lay down, or *set* down, Sister Ridgeway. Why, they'd steal the very — why, goodness sakes, you can guess what kind of a fluster *I* was in by the time midnight come, last night. I hope to gracious if I warn't afraid they'd steal some o' the family! I was just to that pass, I didn't have no reasoning faculties no more. It looks foolish enough, *now*, in the daytime; but I says to myself, there's my two poor boys asleep, 'way up stairs in that lonesome room, and I declare to goodness I was that uneasy 't I crep' up there and locked 'em in! I *did*. And anybody would. Because, you know, when you get scared, that way, and it keeps running on, and getting worse and worse, all the time, and your wits gets to addling, and you get to doing all sorts o' wild things, and by-and-by you think to yourself, spos'n *I* was a boy, and was away up there, and the door ain't locked, and you ——" She stopped, looking kind of wondering, and then she turned her head around slow, and when her eye lit on me — I got up and took a walk.

Says I to myself, I can explain better how we come to not be in that room this morning, if I go out to one side and study over it a little. So I done it. But I dasn't go fur, or she'd a sent for me. And when it was late in the day, the people all went, and then I come in and told her the noise and shooting waked up me and "Sid," and the door was locked, and we wanted to see the fun, so we went down the lightning-rod, and both of us got hurt a little, and we didn't never want to try *that* no more. And then I went on and told her all what I told Uncle Silas before; and then she said she'd forgive us, and maybe it was all right enough anyway, and about what a body might expect of boys, for all boys was a pretty harum-scarum lot, as fur as she could see; and so, as long as no harm hadn't come of it, she judged she better put in her time being grateful we was alive and well and she had us still, stead of fretting over what was past and done. So then she kissed me, and patted me on the head, and dropped into a kind of a brown study; and pretty soon jumps up, and says:

"Why, lawsamercy, it's most night, and Sid not come yet! What *has* become of that boy?"

I see my chance; so I skips up and says:

"I'll run right up to town and get him," I says.

"No you won't," she says. "You'll stay right wher' you are; *one's* enough to be lost at a time. If he ain't here to supper, your uncle 'll go."

Well, he warn't there to supper; so right after supper uncle went.

He come back about ten, a little bit uneasy; hadn't run across Tom's track. Aunt Sally was a good *deal* uneasy; but Uncle Silas he said there warn't no occasion to be — boys will be boys, he said, and you'll see this one turn up in the morning, all sound and right. So she had to be satisfied. But she said she'd set up for him a while, anyway, and keep a light burning, so he could see it.

And then when I went up to bed she come up with me and fetched her candle, and tucked me in, and mothered me so good I felt mean, and like I couldn't look her in the face; and she set down on the bed and talked with me a long time, and said what a splendid boy Sid was, and didn't seem to want to ever stop talking about him; and kept asking me every now and then, if I reckoned he could a got lost, or hurt, or maybe drownded, and might be laying at this minute, somewheres, suffering or dead, and she not by him to help him, and so the tears would drip down, silent, and I would tell her that Sid was all right, and would be home in the morning, sure; and she would squeeze my hand, or maybe kiss me, and tell me to say it again, and keep on saying it, because it done her good, and she was in so much trouble. And when she was going away, she looked down in my eyes, so steady and gentle, and says:

"The door ain't going to be locked, Tom; and there's the window and the rod; but you'll be good, *won't* you? And you won't go? For *my* sake."

Laws knows I *wanted* to go, bad enough, to see about Tom, and was all intending to go; but after that, I wouldn't a went, not for kingdoms.

But she was on my mind, and Tom was on my mind; so I slept very restless. And twice I went down the rod, away in the night, and slipped around front, and see her setting there by her candle in the window with her eyes towards the road and the tears in them; and I wished I could do something for her, but I couldn't, only to swear that I wouldn't never do nothing to grieve her any more. And the third time, I waked up at dawn, and slid down, and she was there yet, and her candle was most out, and her old gray head was resting on her hand, and she was asleep.

Chapter XLII

The old man was up town again, before breakfast, but couldn't get no track of Tom; and both of them set at the table, thinking, and not saying nothing, and looking mournful, and their coffee getting cold, and not eating anything. And by-and-by the old man says:

"Did I give you the letter?"

"What letter?"

"The one I got yesterday out of the post-office."

"No, you didn't give me no letter."

"Well, I must a forgot it."

So he rummaged his pockets, and then went off somewheres where he had laid it down, and fetched it, and give it to her. She says:

"Why, it's from St. Petersburg — it's from Sis."

I allowed another walk would do me good; but I couldn't stir. But before she could break it open, she dropped it and run — for she see something. And so did I. It was Tom Sawyer on a mattress; and that old doctor; and Jim, in *her* calico dress, with his hands tied behind him; and a lot of people. I hid the letter behind the first thing that come handy, and rushed. She flung herself at Tom, crying, and says:

"Oh, he's dead, he's dead, I know he's dead!"

And Tom he turned his head a little, and muttered something or other, which showed he warn't in his right mind; then she flung up her hands, and says:

"He's alive, thank God! And that's enough!" and she snatched a kiss of him, and flew for the house to get the bed ready, and scattering orders right and left at the niggers and everybody else, as fast as her tongue could go, every jump of the way.

I followed the men to see what they was going to do with Jim; and the old doctor and Uncle Silas followed after Tom into the house. The men was very huffy, and some of them wanted to hang Jim, for an example to all the other niggers around there, so they wouldn't be trying to run away, like Jim done, and making such a raft of trouble, and keeping a whole family scared most to death for days and nights. But the others said, don't do it, it wouldn't answer at all, he ain't our nigger, and his owner would turn up and make us pay for him, sure. So that cooled them down a little, because the people that's always the most anxious for to hang a nigger that hain't done just right, is always the very ones that ain't the most anxious to pay for him when they've got their satisfaction out of him.

They cussed Jim considerble, though, and give him a cuff or two, side the head, once in a while, but Jim never said nothing, and he never let on to know me, and they took him to the same cabin, and put his own clothes on him, and chained him again, and not to no bed-leg, this time, but to a big staple drove into the bottom log, and chained his hands, too, and both legs, and said he warn't to have nothing but bread and water to eat, after this, till his owner come or he was sold at auction, because he didn't come in a certain length of time, and filled up our hole, and said a couple of farmers with guns must stand watch around about the cabin every night, and a bull-dog tied to the door in the day-time; and about this time they was through with the job and was tapering off with a kind of generl good-bye cussing, and then the old doctor comes and takes a look, and says:

"Don't be no rougher on him than you're obleeged to, because he ain't a bad nigger. When I got to where I found the boy, I see I couldn't cut the bullet out without some help, and he warn't in no condition for me to leave, to go and get help; and he got a little worse and a little worse, and after a long time he went out of his head, and wouldn't let me come anigh him, any more, and said if I chalked his raft he'd kill me, and no end of wild foolishness like that, and I see I couldn't do anything at all with him; so I says, I got to have *help*, somehow; and the minute I says it, out crawls this nigger from somewheres, and says he'll help, and he done it, too, and done it very well. Of course I judged he must be a runaway nigger, and there I *was*! and there I had to stick, right straight along all the rest of the day, and all night. It was a fix, I tell you! I had a couple of patients with the chills, and of course I'd of liked to run up to town and see them, but I dasn't, because the nigger might get away, and then I'd be to blame; and yet never a skiff come close enough for me to hail. So there I had to stick, plumb till daylight this morning; and I never see a nigger that was a better nuss or faithfuller, and yet he was resking his freedom to do it, and was all tired out, too, and I see plain enough he'd been worked main hard, lately. I liked the nigger for that; I tell you, gentlemen, a nigger like that is worth a thousand dollars — and kind treatment, too. I had everything I needed, and the boy was doing as well there as he would a done at home — better, maybe, because it was so quiet; but there I *was*, with both of 'm on my hands; and there I had to stick, till about dawn this morning; then some men in a skiff come by, and as good luck would have it, the nigger was setting by the pallet with his head propped on his knees, sound asleep; so I motioned them in, quiet, and they slipped up on him and grabbed him and tied him before he knowed what he was about, and we never had no trouble. And the boy being in a kind of a flighty sleep, too, we muffled the oars and hitched the raft on, and towed her over very nice and quiet, and the nigger never made the least row nor said a word, from the start. He ain't no bad nigger, gentlemen; that's what I think about him."

Somebody says:

"Well, it sounds very good, doctor, I'm obleeged to say."

Then the others softened up a little, too, and I was mighty thankful to that old doctor for doing Jim that good turn; and I was glad it was according to my judgment of him, too; because I thought he had a good heart in him and was a good man, the first time I see him. Then they all agreed that Jim had acted very well, and was deserving to have some notice took of it, and reward. So every one of them promised, right out and hearty, that they wouldn't cuss him no more.

Then they come out and locked him up. I hoped they was going to say he could have one or two of the chains took off, because they was rotten heavy, or could have meat and greens with his bread and water, but they didn't think of it, and I reckoned it warn't best for me to mix in, but I judged I'd get the doctor's yarn to Aunt Sally, somehow or other, as soon as I'd got through the breakers that was laying just ahead of me. Explanations, I mean, of how I forgot to mention about Sid being shot, when I was telling how him and me put in that dratted night paddling around hunting the runaway nigger.

But I had plenty time. Aunt Sally she stuck to the sick-room all day and all night; and every time I see Uncle Silas mooning around, I dodged him.

Next morning I heard Tom was a good deal better, and they said Aunt Sally was gone to get a nap. So I slips to the sick-room, and if I found him awake I reckoned we could put up a yarn for the family that would wash. But he was sleeping, and sleeping very peaceful, too; and pale, not fire-faced the way he was when he come. So I set down and laid for him to wake. In about a half an hour, Aunt Sally comes gliding in, and there I was, up a stump again! She motioned me to be still, and set down by me, and begun to whisper, and said we could all be joyful now, because all the symptoms was first rate, and he'd been sleeping like that for ever so long, and looking better and peacefuller all the time, and ten to one he'd wake up in his right mind.

So we set there watching, and by-and-by he stirs a bit, and opened his eyes very natural, and takes a look, and says:

"Hello, why I'm at *home*! How's that? Where's the raft?"

"It's all right," I says.

"And *Jim?*"

"The same," I says, but couldn't say it pretty brash. But he never noticed, but says:

"Good! Splendid! *Now* we're all right and safe! Did you tell Aunty?"

I was going to say yes; but she chipped in and says:

"About what, Sid?"

"Why, about the way the whole thing was done."

"What whole thing?"

"Why, *the* whole thing. There ain't but one; how we set the runaway nigger free — me and Tom."

"Good land! Set the run — What *is* the child talking about! Dear, dear, out of his head again!"

"No, I ain't out of my HEAD; I know all what I'm talking about. We *did* set him free — me and Tom. We laid out to do it, and we *done* it. And we done it elegant, too." He'd got a start, and she never checked him up, just set and stared and stared, and let him clip along, and I see it warn't no use for *me* to put in. "Why, Aunty, it cost us a power of work — weeks of it — hours and hours, every night, whilst you was all asleep. And we had to steal candles, and the sheet, and the shirt, and your dress, and spoons, and tin plates, and case-knives, and the warming-pan, and the grindstone, and flour, and just no end of things, and you can't think what work it was to make the saws, and pens, and inscriptions, and one thing or another, and you can't think *half* the fun it was. And we had to make up the pictures of coffins and things, and nonnamous letters from the robbers, and get up and down the lightning-rod, and dig the hole into the cabin, and make the rope-ladder and send it in cooked up in a pie, and send in spoons and things to work with, in your apron pocket——"

"Mercy sakes!"

——"and load up the cabin with rats and snakes and so on, for company for Jim; and then you kept Tom here so long with the butter in his hat that you come near spiling the whole business, because the men come before we was out of the cabin, and we had to rush, and they heard us and let drive at us, and I got my share, and we dodged out of the path and let them go by, and when the dogs come they warn't interested in us, but went for the most noise, and we got our canoe, and made for the raft, and was all safe, and Jim was a free man, and we done it all by ourselves, and *wasn't* it bully, Aunty!"

"Well, I never heard the likes of it in all my born days! So it was *you*, you little rapscallions, that's been making all this trouble, and turned everybody's wits clean inside out and scared us all most to death. I've as good a notion as ever I had in my life, to take it out o' you this very minute. To think, here I've been, night after night, a — *you* just get well once, you young scamp, and I lay I'll tan the Old Harry out o' both o' ye!"

But Tom, he *was* so proud and joyful, he just *couldn't* hold in, and his tongue just *went* it.— she a-chipping in, and spitting fire all along, and both of them going it at once, like a cat-convention; and she says:

"*Well*, you get all the enjoyment you can out of it *now*, for mind I tell you if I catch you meddling with him again ——"

"Meddling with *who?*" Tom says, dropping his smile and looking surprised.

"With *who?* Why, the runaway nigger, of course. Who'd you reckon?"

Tom looks at me very grave, and says:

"Tom, didn't you just tell me he was all right? Hasn't he got away?"

"*Him?*" says Aunt Sally; "the runaway nigger? 'Deed he hasn't. They've got him back, safe and sound, and he's in that cabin again, on bread and water, and loaded down with chains, till he's claimed or sold!"

Tom rose square up in bed, with his eye hot, and his nostrils opening and shutting like gills, and sings out to me:

"They hain't no *right* to shut him up! *Shove!* — and don't you lose a minute. Turn him loose! he ain't no slave; he's as free as any cretur that walks this earth!"

"What *does* the child mean?"

"I mean every word I *say*, Aunt Sally, and if somebody don't go, *I'll* go. I've knowed him all his life, and so has Tom, there. Old Miss Watson died two months ago, and she was ashamed she ever was going to sell him down the river, and *said* so; and she set him free in her will."

"Then what on earth did *you* want to set him free for, seeing he was already free?"

"Well, that *is* a question, I must say; and *just* like women! Why, I wanted the *adventure* of it; and I'd a waded neck-deep in blood to — goodness alive, AUNT POLLY!"

If she warn't standing right there, just inside the door, looking as sweet and contented as an angel half-full of pie, I wish I may never!

Aunt Sally jumped for her, and most hugged the head off of her, and cried over her, and I found a good enough place for me under the bed, for it was getting pretty sultry for *us*, seemed to me. And I peeped out, and in a little while Tom's Aunt Polly shook herself loose and stood there looking across at Tom over her spectacles — kind of grinding him into the earth, you know. And then she says:

"Yes, you *better* turn y'r head away — I would if I was you, Tom."

"Oh, deary me!" says Aunt Sally; "*is* he changed so? Why, that ain't *Tom*, it's Sid; Tom's — Tom's — why, where is Tom? He was here a minute ago."

"You mean where's Huck *Finn* — that's what you mean! I reckon I hain't raised such a scamp as my Tom all these years, not to know him when I *see* him. That *would* be a pretty howdy-do. Come out from under that bed, Huck Finn."

So I done it. But not feeling brash.

Aunt Sally she was one of the mixed-upest looking persons I ever see; except one, and that was Uncle Silas, when he come in, and they told it all to him. It kind of made him drunk, as you may say, and he didn't know nothing at all the rest of the day, and preached a prayer-meeting sermon that night that give him a rattling ruputation, because the oldest man in the world couldn't a understood it. So Tom's Aunt Polly, she told all about who I was, and what; and I had to up and tell how I was in such a tight place that when Mrs. Phelps took me for Tom Sawyer — she chipped in and says, "Oh, go on and call me Aunt Sally, I'm used to it, now, and 'tain't no need to change" — that when Aunt Sally took me for Tom Sawyer, I had to stand it — there warn't no other way, and I knowed he wouldn't mind, because it would be nuts for him, being a mystery, and he'd make an adventure out of it and be perfectly satisfied. And so it turned out, and he let on to be Sid, and made things as soft as he could for me.

And his Aunt Polly she said Tom was right about old Miss Watson setting Jim free in her will; and so, sure enough, Tom Sawyer had gone and took all that trouble and bother to set a free nigger free! and I couldn't ever understand, before, until that minute and that talk, how he *could* help a body set a nigger free, with his bringing-up.

Well, Aunt Polly she said that when Aunt Sally wrote to her that Tom and *Sid* had come, all right and safe, she says to herself:

"Look at that, now! I might have expected it, letting him go off that way without anybody to watch him. So now I got to go and trapse all the way down the river, eleven hundred mile, and find out what that creetur's up to, *this* time; as long as I couldn't seem to get any answer out of you about it."

"Why, I never heard nothing from you," says Aunt Sally.

"Well, I wonder! Why, I wrote to you twice, to ask you what you could mean by Sid being here."

"Well, I never got 'em, Sis."

Aunt Polly, she turns around slow and severe, and says:

"You, Tom!"

"Well—*what?*" he says, kind of pettish.

"Don't you what *me*, you impudent thing—hand out them letters."

"What letters?"

"*Them* letters. I be bound, if I have to take aholt of you I'll ——"

"They're in the trunk. There, now. And they're just the same as they was when I got them out of the office. I hain't looked into them, I hain't touched them. But I knowed they'd make trouble, and I thought if you warn't in no hurry, I'd ——"

"Well, you *do* need skinning, there ain't no mistake about it. And I wrote another one to tell you I was coming; and I spose he ——"

"No, it come yesterday; I hain't read it yet, but *it's* all right, I've got that one."

I wanted to offer to bet two dollars she hadn't, but I reckoned maybe it was just as safe to not to. So I never said nothing.

Chapter the last

The first time I catched Tom, private, I asked him what was his idea, time of the evasion?—what it was he'd planned to do if the evasion worked all right and he managed to set a nigger free that was already free before? And he said, what he had planned in his head, from the start, if we got Jim out all safe, was for us to run him down the river, on the raft, and have adventures plumb to the mouth of the river, and then tell him about his being free, and take him back up home on a steamboat, in style, and pay him for his lost time, and write word ahead and get out all the niggers around, and have them waltz him into town with a torchlight procession and a brass band, and then he would be a hero, and so would we. But I reckoned it was about as well the way it was.

We had Jim out of the chains in no time, and when Aunt Polly and Uncle Silas and Aunt Sally found out how good he helped the doctor nurse Tom, they made a heap of fuss over him, and fixed him up prime, and give him all he wanted to eat, and a good time, and nothing to do. And we had him up to the sick-room; and had a high talk; and Tom give Jim forty dollars for being prisoner for us so patient, and doing it up so good, and Jim was pleased most to death, and busted out, and says:

"*Dah*, now, Huck, what I tell you? — what I tell you up dah on Jackson islan'? I *tole* you I got a hairy breas', en what's de sign un it; en I *tole* you I ben rich wunst, en gwineter to be rich *agin*; en it's come true; en heah she *is!* *Dah*, now! doan' talk to *me* — signs is *signs*, mine I tell you; en I knowed jis' 's well 'at I 'uz gwineter be rich agin as I's a stannin' heah dis minute!"

And then Tom he talked along, and talked along, and says, le's all three slide out of here, one of these nights, and get an outfit, and go for howling adventures amongst the Injuns, over in the Territory, for a couple of weeks or two; and I says, all right, that suits me, but I ain't got no money for to buy the outfit, and I reckon I couldn't get none from home, because it's likely pap's been back before now, and got it all away from Judge Thatcher and drunk it up.

"No he hain't," Tom says; "it's all there, yet — six thousand dollars and more; and your pap hain't ever been back since. Hadn't when I come away, anyhow."

Jim says, kind of solemn:

"He ain't a comin' back no mo', Huck."

I says:

"Why, Jim?"

"Nemmine why, Huck — but he ain't comin' back no mo'."

But I kept at him; so at last he says:

"Doan' you 'member de house dat was float'n down de river, en dey wuz a man in dah, kivered up, en I went in en unkivered him and didn' let you come in? Well, den, you k'n git yo' money when you wants it; kase dat wuz him."

Tom's most well, now, and got his bullet around his neck on a watch-guard for a watch, and is always seeing what time it is, and so there ain't nothing more to write about, and I am rotten glad of it, because if I'd a knowed what a trouble it was to make a book I wouldn't a tackled it and ain't agoing to no more. But I reckon I got to light out for the Territory ahead of the rest, because Aunt Sally she's going to adopt me and sivilize me and I can't stand it. I been there before.

THE END. YOURS TRULY, HUCK FINN

Study Guide

Text by
Corinna Siebert Ruth
(M.A., California State University–Fresno)

Department of English
Reedley High School
Reedley, California

Contents

> **Each chapter includes List of Characters,**
> **Summary, Analysis, Study Questions and**
> **Answers, and Suggested Essay Topics.**

SECTION ONE

Introduction

The Life and Work of Mark Twain

Mark Twain, the pen name of Samuel Langhorne Clemens, was born in Florida, Missouri, on November 30, 1835. When he was four years old, his family moved to the Mississippi River town of Hannibal, Missouri. It was here he learned the folkways of the people who would later become the characters in his novel, The Adventures of Huckleberry Finn.

The steamboats on the Mississippi River were a familiar sight for Twain during his childhood. From Hannibal he could see the island where Huck and Jim hide in the novel and the forest where Pap takes Huck when he kidnaps him. In Huckleberry Finn, Twain draws heavily from his childhood experiences and observations.

When Twain was 11, his father died, and he left school to work as an apprentice to a printer. When he was 21, he decided to fulfill his childhood dream and become a riverboat pilot. It was during this time that he became familiar with the towns along the Mississippi River that Huck and Jim pass on their journey.

It was also his riverboat experience that influenced his pen name, "Mark Twain." In measuring the depth of the river, the cry "Mark Twain" meant that the river was two fathoms deep—safe water for a steamboat.

Twain died in 1910. Two daughters, an infant son, and his wife preceded him in death. Halley's Comet, which appears approximately every 75 years, appeared the year that he was born, and just as Twain himself predicted, it returned again the week he died.

Humor has become synonymous with Mark Twain's personality as an American writer. His wide use of exaggeration and local dialects in his writing, accompanied by the narrator's serious tone, produces a humorous effect. In this way his writing captures the provincial flavor of the American West.

Master List of Characters

Huckleberry Finn—Narrator of the novel. Son of the town drunkard. The Widow Douglas, his guardian, tries to "sivilize" him.

Jim—Miss Watson's black slave. Huckleberry Finn's traveling companion on the raft.

Widow Douglas—Huck's guardian while his pap is gone. She is determined to civilize Huck.

Miss Watson—The widow's sister who tries to improve Huck's manners.

Tom Sawyer—Huck's best friend who conjures up intriguing plans derived from his imagination and the books he reads.

Pap—Huck's drunken father who kidnaps Huck and locks him in a cabin.

Aunt Polly—Tom Sawyer's aunt and guardian.

Judge Thatcher—The good-hearted judge who invests Huck's money.

Tommy Barnes, Jo Harper, and Ben Rogers—Members of Tom and Huck's gang.

Mrs. Judith Loftus—A lady whom Huck visits while he is disguised as a girl.

Bill and Jim Turner, Jake Packard—Men whom Huck discovers arguing on a sinking ship.

The Grangerfords and the Shepherdsons—Two feuding families. The Grangerfords adopt Huck for a time.

The duke and the king—Two conmen who pretend to be royalty. They join Huck and Jim on the raft. They also appear as impostors at the funeral of Peter Wilks.

Buck Harkness—He tries to turn the people against Colonel Sherburn.

Boggs—Drunkard in Arkansas who is shot by Colonel Sherburn.

Colonel Sherburn—The man who shoots Boggs.

Peter Wilks—A wealthy man who has died. The family is waiting for his brothers from England to attend the funeral.

Mary Jane, Joanna, and Susan—The three nieces of the dead Peter Wilks.

William and Harvey Wilks—Peter Wilks' two brothers from England whom the duke and the king impersonate.

Levi Bell and Dr. Robinson—A lawyer and a doctor who suspect that the king and the duke are frauds.

Silas Phelps—Aunt Sally's husband who buys Jim.

Aunt Sally Phelps—Silas Phelps' wife. Tom Sawyer's Aunt Sally.

Summary of the Novel

Mark Twain blends many comic elements into the story of Huck Finn, a boy about 13 years old, living in pre-Civil War Missouri. Huck, the novel's narrator, has been living with the Widow Douglas and her sister, Miss Watson, in the town of St. Petersburg. They have been trying to "sivilize" him with proper dress, manners, and religious piety. He finds this life constraining and false and would rather live free and wild. When his father hears that Huck has come into a large amount of money, he kidnaps him and locks him in an old cabin across the river. To avoid his father's cruel beatings, Huck elaborately stages his own death and then escapes to Jackson's Island. He finds Jim, Miss Watson's runaway slave, on the island, and the two decide to hide out together. To avoid danger of discovery, they decide to float down the river on a raft they had found earlier. Sleeping during the day and traveling at night, they plan to connect with the Ohio River at Cairo, Illinois, which would lead them north into the free states, where slavery is outlawed. They miss Cairo in the fog one night and find themselves floating deeper into slave territory. While they are searching for a canoe, a steamship hits the raft and damages it. Huck and Jim are separated.

Huck swims ashore where he meets the feuding Grangerfords and Shepherdsons. He claims to be George Jackson, a passenger who fell from a steamboat and swam to shore. After witnessing a violent eruption of the feud in which many people are killed, he finds Jim, and they return to the raft.

They continue down the river. Two conmen, calling themselves a king and a duke, find their way to the raft. In one of the towns the king and the duke impersonate the two brothers of Peter Wilks, who has just died and left a small fortune. Huck thwarts their plan to swindle Wilks' family out of their inheritance. The king and the duke escape, but further down the river the two decide to sell Jim to Silas Phelps, who turns out to be Tom Sawyer's uncle.

Visiting his aunt and uncle, Tom persuades Huck to join him in an elaborate, ridiculous plan to free Jim. Huck prefers a quicker escape for Jim but caves in to Tom's wishes. Only after Tom's plan has been played out, and Jim recaptured, does Tom reveal that Miss Watson had actually freed Jim two months earlier, just before she died. Huck decides to "light out for the Territory," to head west toward the frontier before anyone can attempt to "sivilize" him again.

Estimated Reading Time

The reading of the novel is slowed somewhat by an unfamiliarity with Twain's use of regional dialects and nonstandard English. After the first few chapters, a familiarity with the unique speech of each of the characters should, however, speed the reading process. The reader should be able to finish the novel in approximately 12 hours.

Twain's Seven Dialects in the "Explanatory"

Twain's "Explanatory" in The Adventures of Huckleberry Finn was written to clarify the different dialects used in the novel. Ironically, his explanation has been the subject of confusion and controversy among critics ever since it was published. The varying dialects have often been difficult to differentiate, and some inconsistencies are apparent in the speech patterns of the characters. It is easy to see why critics could view the "Explanatory" as just another one of Twain's comic witticisms they had come to associate with his writings. The consistencies of the characters' nonstandard speech patterns far outweigh the inconsistencies, however, and this leads us to believe Twain was serious about the seven dialects used in the novel.

David Carkeet, who has done extensive research in Twain's use of literary dialects, believes "Clemens's recall was imperfect; his attempt at consistency, at least in Huck's dialect, falls short." Carkeet attributes this "imperfect recollection" to the fact that Twain wrote three-fifths of the novel after he had put the book aside for two years. This led to several pronunciation changes, particularly in the speech of Huck, in the last three-fifths of the novel.

Carkeet concludes that the seven dialects were assigned to the following characters:

Missouri Negro: Jim (and four other minor characters)

Southwestern: Arkansas Gossips (Sister Hotchkiss et al.)

Ordinary "Pike County": Huck, Tom, Aunt Polly, Ben Rogers, Pap, Judith Loftus

Modified "Pike County": Thieves on the Sir Walter Scott

Modified "Pike County": King

Modified "Pike County": Bricksville Loafers

Modified "Pike County": Aunt Sally and Uncle Silas Phelps

Representing the living speech of Twain's day, the following examples of the seven dialects typify a uniqueness of language found in the areas along the Mississippi River.

Missouri Negro: Jim

"Goodness gracious, is dat you, Huck? En you ain' dead-you ain't drownded-you's back ag'in? It's too good for true, honey, it's too good for true. Lemme look at you chile, lemme feel o' you. No, you ain' dead! you's back ag'in, 'live en soun', jis de same ole Huck-de same ole Huck, thanks to goodness!"

Extremist form of the backwoods Southwestern dialect: Arkansas Gossips (Sister Hotchkiss)

"Look at that-air grindstone, s'I; want to tell me't any cretur 't's in his right mind's a-goin' to scrabble all them crazy things onto a grindstone? s'I."

Ordinary "Pike County": Huck

"My folks was living in Pike County, in Missouri, where I was born, and they all died off but me and pa and my brother Ike."

Modified "Pike County": Thief on the Sir Walter Scott, Jake Packard

"I'm unfavorable to killin' a man as long as you can git aroun' it, it ain't good sense, it ain't good morals. Ain't I right?"

Modified "Pike County": King

"Well, I'd ben a-runnin' a little temperence revival thar 'bout a week...and business a-growin' all the time, when somehow or another a little report got around last night that I had a way of puttin' in my time with a private jug on the sly."

Modified "Pike County": Bricksville Loafers

"Gimme a chaw 'v tobacker, Hank."

"Cain't; I hain't got but one chaw left. Ask Bill."

Modified "Pike County": Aunt Sally and Uncle Silas Phelps

"Good-ness gracious!" she says, "what in the world can have become of him?"

"I can't imagine," says the old gentleman; "and I must say it makes me dreadful uneasy."

"Uneasy!" she says: "I'm ready to go distracted! He must 'a' come; and you've missed him along the road. I know it's so—something tells me so...Why Silas! Look yonder-up the road!—ain't that somebody coming?"

Twain wrote in the late nineteenth century when literary dialects were the fashion of the times. Although he helped to create the dialectal mode of writing in American literature, he, at the same time, drew from his contemporaries who were following the same tradition. It is impossible to imagine Huckleberry Finn written in standard English. Twain's writings were not made up of the dead language of the European past, but exuded the living colloquial speech of his day. This is what has made The Adventures of Huckleberry Finn a truly American novel.

SECTION TWO

Huckleberry Finn

Chapter I (page 1)

New Characters:

Huckleberry Finn: the protagonist and narrator

Widow Douglas: Huck's guardian

Miss Watson: the widow's sister

Tom Sawyer: Huck's best friend

Summary

Huck Finn introduces himself as a character who has already appeared in Mark Twain's earlier novel, The Adventures of Tom Sawyer. He briefly reviews the end of Tom Sawyer's story, reminding the reader how he and Tom found money that robbers had hidden in a cave. Judge Thatcher has invested the money for them, six thousand dollars apiece in gold, and the interest alone is now worth a dollar a day, a large amount of money at that time.

The Widow Douglas has taken Huck in as her son, and is trying to civilize him by teaching him proper dress and proper manners. To make matters worse, the Widow's sister, Miss Watson, lives with her and relentlessly nags Huck about his behavior.

Huck is lonely and discouraged despite the Widow Douglas' efforts to give him a good home. He accidentally kills a spider and is sure it will bring him bad luck. Soon after the clock strikes midnight, Huck sneaks out of his upstairs bedroom window to answer Tom Sawyer's mysterious call.

Analysis

   Twain's choice of a 13-year-old narrator supplies much of the humor in the novel. The narrator, Huck Finn, reports the events and ideas through his own eyes, and often his innocence and truthfulness contrast sharply with the Widow Douglas' sense of propriety. In the first chapter, Miss Watson holds herself up to Huck as the epitome of a virtuous woman. Although Huck does not see the contradiction between her intolerance of him and her belief that she was going to the "good place" (heaven), he naively replies, "Well, I couldn't see no advantage in going where she was going, so I made up my mind I wouldn't try for it." It is this kind of frankness that allows Twain to comment on the hypocrisy of society through the eyes of a young and innocent narrator.

   Through Huck's encounters with Miss Watson and the Widow Douglas, Twain satirizes the religious sensibility of the day. Huck finds the widow's story of Moses boring and unrelated to everyday life. Miss Watson's concept of the "good place," where one would go around playing a harp and singing all day, does not appeal to him at all. Besides, they required their slaves to come in for prayers before they went to bed at night, a flagrant contradiction to the principles of Christianity in which they professed to believe. In this novel, Twain satirizes the pious Christians who professed kindness and civility, but who bought and sold slaves as property before the Civil War.

   The theme of individual freedom is brought out in Huck's aversion to the Widow Douglas and her attempts to change him. Later in the novel, the journey down the river will be an escape from the hypocrisy of society's corrupt institutions and a search for freedom from that society for both Huck and Jim.

Study Questions

1. Give a brief summary of the end of the novel, The Adventures of Tom Sawyer.

2. Why did Twain choose a young boy as the narrator for the novel?

3. Name one of the major themes of the novel.

4. Give an example of superstition in Chapter I.

CH. I

5. Compare the character of the Widow Douglas to her sister, Miss Watson.

6. At what period in history does the story take place?

7. Give an example of satire (a device in literature that blends criticism of society with humor) in Chapter I.

8. What do the Widow Douglas and Miss Watson try to teach Huck in order to civilize him?

9. What did the slaves do before they went to bed at night?

10. Who gave the catcall after midnight?

Answers

1. Tom and Huck found the six thousand dollars in gold that the robbers had hidden in the cave. Judge Thatcher invested it for them.

2. Twain uses Huck's comments as an innocent and truthful criticism of society.

3. One major theme of the novel is individual freedom. Huck searches for freedom from the constraints of a corrupt society, and Jim searches for freedom from slavery.

4. Huck accidentally flips a spider into a candle and is sure it will bring him bad luck.

5. The Widow Douglas seems less demanding of Huck than does Miss Watson. She asks her sister to "ease up" on Huck during the spelling lesson.

6. The story takes place before the Civil War, when slavery was still legal in the southern United States.

7. One example of satire is Huck's decision not to go to the "good place" if Miss Watson would be there.

8. They teach him proper dress, proper manners, and regular Bible reading.

9. They came into the house for prayers.

10. Tom Sawyer was calling for Huck.

CH. I

Suggested Essay Topics

1. The Widow Douglas and her sister, Miss Watson, are both trying to "sivilize" Huck. Compare and contrast their attitudes toward Huck. What method does each one use in her efforts to turn him into a "respectable" citizen? How do those methods differ? How are they the same? Cite examples from the novel to support your argument.

2. Analyze the scene where Huck flips the spider into the candle. Why does he feel that this would bring him bad luck? How does this scene foreshadow superstition in the novel? Support your answer with examples from the novel.

3. Twain chooses a 13-year-old boy as narrator for his novel. In what way does this help to accomplish Twain's purpose? Discuss the ways in which a young, innocent narrator can make a profound statement about the hypocrisy of his society. Explain your answer.

Chapters II–III (pages 3–11)

New Characters:

Jim: Miss Watson's black slave

Jo Harper and **Ben Rogers:** two members of Tom and Huck's gang

Tommy Barnes: the youngest member of the gang

Summary

As Huck and Tom Sawyer tiptoe through the garden, Huck stumbles over a root, which gets the attention of Jim, Miss Watson's slave. He calls out, but the boys, afraid of being caught sneaking out at night, become extremely quiet. Jim sits down between them but falls asleep before he is aware that they are near enough to touch. Tom cannot resist the temptation to play a trick on Jim. He hangs Jim's hat in the tree, knowing that Jim will wonder how it got there. The next day, seeing his hat in the tree, Jim conjures up stories about witches and how they rode him around the world. He is proud of this and consequently the envy of all the other slaves in the neighborhood.

Having sneaked out, Huck and Tom meet Joe Harper, Ben Rogers, and the other members of Tom's "band of robbers." Tom Sawyer's gang is patterned after the "pirate books," and "robber books" that he has read. They take a skiff down the Mississippi River for several miles to explore the cave that Tom has found earlier. As they organize their gang, the boys take an oath to keep the gang a secret, signing their names in blood. If anyone tells the secret, that boy and his family must be killed. Tom sets the rules. They will become masked highwaymen, stopping stages and carriages, killing the people on board and robbing them of their possessions. Tom wants to kidnap people for ransom, but neither he nor the other boys know what "ransom" means.

When Huck returns early in the morning, his clothes are very dirty, and he receives a scolding from Miss Watson. There is news in town about a drowned body found up the river. Most people think it is Huck's father, but Huck is sure that it is not.

The boys play robbers for a month but soon tire of it, since they haven't killed anyone. Furthermore, Tom's "Spaniards" and "A-rabs" with hundreds of elephants, camels, and mules, loaded down with diamonds, turn out to be only a Sunday school picnic. Tom blames the incident on magicians who have, with the help of genies, changed the Spaniard and A-rab scene into a Sunday school picnic, but Huck feels it is only "one of Tom Sawyer's lies."

Analysis

In these chapters we meet Jim, a prominent character in the novel. His superstitious beliefs are a recurrent thematic element throughout the novel. In this case, it has been his bad luck to have ridden around the world with witches. Twain's satire of the institution of slavery will reach its greatest height through the character of Jim, and his warm human relationship with Huck, in subsequent chapters.

Tom Sawyer is introduced in this chapter as a foil to Huck. Tom's imaginative but impractical romantic notions, taken from the books he reads, are challenged by Huck when he goes to the woods to rub the old tin lamp. When the genie does not appear, he decides that the whole thing is just another one of "Tom Sawyer's lies." Twain is satirizing Tom's romantic adventure stories. Tom must do everything by the book, and the height of absurdity is his insistence upon kidnapping people for ransom when he doesn't even know what the word means.

The Mississippi River is introduced as a symbolic image. Twain contrasts the freedom and peacefulness of life on the river with the corruption of society on the shore. In one short line we sense the river's power: "...the river, a whole mile broad, and awful still and grand." Life on the river will ultimately become an idyllic escape for Huck and Jim.

Study Questions

1. Where does Tom take Huck and the gang?

2. What does Jim think has happened when he finds his hat hanging in the tree?

3. When Tom's gang tries to rob the rich "Spaniards" and "A-rabs," who do they actually rob?

4. Where does Tom get his ideas for robbing and killing people?

5. If anyone reveals the secrets of the gang, the boy and his family must be killed. Whom does Huck offer as his family to be killed?

6. Contrast the personalities of Huck and Tom.

7. Whose slave is Jim?

8. Who are Joe Harper and Ben Rogers?

9. What purpose does the Mississippi River serve in the novel?

10. How wide is the river in this chapter?

Answers

1. Tom takes Huck and the gang to the cave through the hole that he had discovered earlier.

2. Jim thinks that he has been ridden around the world by witches.

3. The gang tries to rob a Sunday school picnic. To their humiliation, it is a primer class filled with very young children.

4. He gets them from the books he reads. One of those books is Don Quixote.

5. Huck offers Miss Watson because he would rather give her up than anyone else.

6. Huck is literal-minded, realistic, and practical, but Tom is romantic and imaginative.

7. Jim is Miss Watson's slave. This is another criticism of Miss Watson as an unfavorable character in the novel.

8. Joe Harper and Ben Rogers are boys in Tom Sawyer's gang.

9. The Mississippi River acts as a symbolic setting in the novel, representing an idyllic escape from the corruption of society.

10. The river is a mile wide, which gives it a majestic power.

Suggested Essay Topics

1. Although Huck Finn and Tom Sawyer are presented as contrasting characters in the novel, they are alike in many ways. Compare and contrast the characters of Huck and Tom, giving examples from the novel to support your argument.

2. Analyze Jim's idea that he has been ridden around the world by witches. Why was he proud? Were the slaves the only ones who believed Jim's story? Does Huck believe it? Explain your answer.

3. Analyze the role of respectability in Tom Sawyer's supposedly lawless gang. Why is it mandatory for each member to have a respectable family? Examine the idea that Huck, who has had more experience with breaking the law than any of the others, comes close to being excluded from the gang.

Chapters IV–V (pages 11–17)

New Characters:

Judge Thatcher: former judge who invests Huck's money for him

Pap: Huck's father

The new judge: tries to reform Pap

The new judge's wife: takes Pap into her house

Summary

Huck has been going to school for about three or four months and has learned to read and write. Although he plays "hooky" occasionally, he is learning to tolerate school. He is also becoming more comfortable living with the widow.

Huck has almost forgotten his father until one day he sees his footprints in the snow. Pap's bootheel has left the imprint of a cross made of nails, used to ward off the devil. Afraid his father has come for his money, Huck wastes no time getting to Judge Thatcher's whom he begs to take the six thousand dollars and one hundred fifty dollars interest. The judge, surprised and puzzled, finally buys the "property" from him for a dollar.

Huck then consults Jim, who relies on his hairball from the stomach of an ox to tell Huck's fortune. Jim listens while the hairball talks to him, but he does not get a straight answer. Huck's fears are not unfounded, however; when he goes up to his room, he finds Pap waiting for him. Huck is startled and afraid, but Pap's dirty, sickly image soon calms his fears, and he speaks right up when his father starts harassing him about his fine clothes and his education. Pap, however, threatens to "take it out of him" for trying to be better than his own father. He grabs the dollar the judge had given Huck, so he can go downtown for some whiskey. He tries to get the rest of Huck's money from Judge Thatcher, but the judge ignores his request. Later Judge Thatcher and the Widow Douglas go to court to try to win custody of Huck, but the new judge grants custody to Pap. Pap promises to "turn over a new leaf." The new judge and his wife give him dinner, a new coat, and a clean bed, but he sneaks out in the middle of the night and trades his new coat for a jug of whiskey. He gets drunk, falls off the porch, and breaks his arm.

Analysis

Huck is slowly becoming accustomed to the proper dress and manners he had such an aversion to earlier in the novel. Huck's changed attitude toward school and living in a civilized manner makes his father's sudden appearance seem even more untimely.

Huck's fear that his father is back in town drives him to see Judge Thatcher. Huck realizes that his pap has come for his six thousand dollars. If he gets rid of the money, Huck is sure his father will leave him alone. His vivid memories of his father's beatings prompt him to give the money to Judge Thatcher. At first the judge seems confused by the immediacy of Huck's secret request, but when the judge arranges to buy his "property" for one dollar he seems to understand Huck's dilemma. He is afraid his pap will be after him for the money.

Superstition is a recurrent theme in these chapters. After Huck spills the salt, he is certain that bad luck will be the result. His fears are justified when he sees Pap's footprints in the snow. In desperation he goes to Jim for help. Jim's hairball, taken from the stomach of an ox, speaks to him, but the spirit inside the hairball keeps wavering from one answer to another. The hairball tells him that perhaps Pap will stay or perhaps he'll leave. Twain's subtle mockery of superstition is reflected in the tone of this scene.

Pap's attitude, contrary to that of a normal, loving parent, is one of jealousy and anger because of his son's accomplishments. He scolds Huck for his ability to read and write only because he does not want him to be better than his father.

Study Questions

1. How does Huck feel about school in these chapters?

2. How does Huck know his pap is back in town?

3. Why is Huck in a big hurry to give Judge Thatcher his money?

4. What does Judge Thatcher give Huck in exchange for the six thousand dollars?

5. Huck consults Jim about his father. What does he want to know?

6. How does Pap feel about Huck's ability to read and write?

7. Who goes to court to gain custody of Huck?

8. Who takes Pap into their house in an attempt to reform him?

9. Does Pap turn over a new leaf as he says he will? Explain your answer.

10. What is Twain's commentary on superstition in Chapter IV?

Answers

1. At first he hated school, but as time went on it became easier and he actually began to like it.

2. He sees his footprints in the snow. Pap has a unique cross in his left bootheel to ward off the devil.

3. He feels that if he gets rid of his six thousand dollars, Pap will leave him alone.

4. He gives him one dollar. In this way Huck has sold it rather than given it away.

5. Jim relies on his hairball to work magic. Huck wants to know about his father, but the hairball wavers back and forth giving him opposing answers.

6. Pap is jealous of his son. He does not want his son to be better than he is, nor to put on "airs."

7. Judge Thatcher and the Widow Douglas want the court to take Huck away from his father. They want to save Huck from his father's abuse.

8. The new judge and his wife give him their spare room, food to eat, and new clothes to wear.

9. No. He sneaks out in the middle of the night, exchanges his coat for whiskey, gets drunk, and breaks his arm.

10. Twain is subtly satirizing superstition in this chapter, particularly in the hairball incident. It is obvious neither the hairball's spirit nor Jim are sure of anything since one answer is consistently juxtaposed with the opposite answer following it.

Suggested Essay Topics

1. Superstition is a recurring theme in the novel. Analyze Twain's satiric treatment of the hairball scene. Examine the answers Huck receives about his life. How does Jim keep the hairball's comments believable?

2. Analyze the relationship of Huck and his father. In what ways was he different from the ideal? How did this influence Huck's feelings about society as a whole? Explain your reasoning.

3. Analyze Judge Thatcher's reactions to Huck's request to take his money. Why did the judge exchange one dollar for six-thousand dollars? Was he cheating Huck? Explain your answer.

Chapters VI–VII (pages 17–27)

Summary

Huck continues to go to school despite the thrashings from his father. With a firm resoluteness he is determined to continue his education, more to spite his father than for any other reason. Pap is waiting around for the court to decide about Huck's money, but it is a slow process. He hangs around the Widow Douglas' house too much, and she threatens to make trouble for him. Angered by her attempts to intimidate him, he decides to kidnap Huck and head for the Illinois side of the river in a skiff. They settle in an old abandoned cabin where he keeps Huck locked up when he goes into town for supplies. In spite of all this, living in the woods is relaxing and easy for Huck, and he wonders why he had ever liked the civilized life at the widow's.

Pap sometimes locks him in the cabin for days at a time, however, and beats him habitually. One night he gets drunk and chases Huck around the cabin with a knife. When his father threatens to hide him in an even more desolate area, so the widow will never be able to find him, he begins to plan an elaborate scheme of escape by faking his own death.

The "June rise" of the river brings with it a canoe loosened from its moorings somewhere upstream. Thinking it might come in handy, Huck quickly hides it in the bushes along the bank. Later Pap finds a log raft floating down the river. He locks Huck in the cabin and promptly goes back into town to sell the logs. Huck then begins his plan of escape. Before Pap has crossed the river, Huck has sawed his way out of the cabin. He loads his canoe with the necessary supplies, then shoots a wild pig, smashes the door with an ax, and scatters the pig's blood around. He covers the ax with hair and blood to make it look as if he had been murdered. He then hides in the canoe until dark. Just as he is leaving, he hears his pap coming back unexpectedly. Staying in the shade of the riverbank, he escapes unnoticed and heads toward Jackson's Island in the middle of the river. He arrives just before breakfast.

Analysis

Twain's characterization of Pap in these chapters is a sad commentary on a society that would grant custody of a child to such a father. After his father's drunken harangue in the middle of the night, and his earlier threat to hide him in an even more remote area, Huck decides he must escape to save his life.

He prefers the freedom of the woods to living in the civilized manner of the Widow Douglas. His freedom is, however, tainted by his father's frightening behavior. He wants to leave, but he is sure he does not want to go back to the widow. Consequently, his plan of escape must convince them both that he is dead. He plans each step with intricate detail. He wishes Tom Sawyer were there to throw in the "fancy touches," but Tom's romantic plan, based on the books he had read, would probably have failed, as it did in the raid on the Sunday school picnic. Here again, Twain is satirizing Tom's false romantic notions. Huck is practical and down-to-earth, and Twain endorses his actions by portraying him as a survivor.

Study Questions

1. Pap kidnaps Huck. Where does he take him?

2. Why does Huck want people to think that he is dead?

3. Does Pap get Huck's six thousand dollars?

4. What does Pap do with Huck when he goes to town for supplies?

5. What tool does Huck use to escape from the cabin?

6. Why does Huck kill the pig?

7. What does the "June rise" of the river bring with it for Huck?

8. Why does Huck wish Tom Sawyer were with him?

9. Why does Huck suddenly enjoy school?

10. Huck sleeps in the canoe just before he escapes to Jackson's Island. What is he waiting for?

Answers

1. Pap takes Huck to a deserted cabin in the woods on the Illinois side of the Mississippi River.

2. He does not want his pap nor the Widow Douglas to search for him.

3. No. He does not have the patience to wait around for the court's decision.

4. He locks Huck in the cabin so he will not run away.

5. He uses a rusty old saw. His pap is careful not to leave any knives around while he is gone, but Huck finds the saw between the rafter and clapboards of the roof.

6. He killed the pig so he could smear the blood around to make it look as if he had been murdered with an ax.

7. The "June rise" causes a canoe to wash up on shore that Huck hides for his escape.

8. Huck wishes Tom Sawyer was there to help him stage his own death. He feels Tom would give it that "fancy touch."

9. He goes to school to spite his father. His father forbids him to go near the school.

10. Huck is waiting for it to get dark so he will not be seen on the river.

Suggested Essay Topics

1. Huck seems to adapt to almost any situation. He has become accustomed to civilized life with the Widow Douglas. Later he finds life in the woods carefree and easy. Analyze the character of Huck. Discuss possible reasons for his adaptability to different situations. Use examples from the novel to support your argument.

2. In the novel Pap does not appear to be a civilized man. Discuss ways in which he does, however, fit into the larger society. Does he compare to the Widow Douglas in any way? Explain your answer.

3. Huck wishes Tom Sawyer were with him to add some "fancy touches" to his plan of escape. Discuss the difference between Huck's scheme of faking his death and the attack on the "A-rabs" and "Spaniards" in Chapter III. Cite examples from the novel to support your ideas.

Chapters VIII–IX (pages 27–39)

Summary

    Huck has a comfortable feeling as he wakes up on Jackson's Island the next morning. Too lazy to get up and cook breakfast, he watches the sun filter through the tall trees, spotting the ground with "freckled places." His peace is soon interrupted, however, with the loud "boom" of the cannon being fired from a ferryboat loaded with prominent townspeople who are looking for his murdered body. The cannon is fired over the water periodically to make Huck's supposed dead body come to the surface. Since he has had no breakfast, he is getting hungry, but he does not dare risk starting a fire because he is afraid they will see the smoke. He suddenly remembers that loaves of bread, filled with quicksilver, are also used to locate drowned bodies. Snagging one of the loaves with a stick, he removes the quicksilver and eats the bread for breakfast. The ferryboat skirts the shore of the island, sounding the cannon occasionally, while its passengers look for Huck's washed-up body. After an uneventful search, the boat finally leaves.

Three days pass and Huck gets lonely. He decides to explore the three-mile-long island. He feels satisfied that the different types of berries and green summer grapes that he finds will come in handy, but he is suddenly startled by the ashes of a campfire that is still smoking. Terrified, he runs back to his camp, hides his possessions in his canoe, and climbs a tree. After two hours he decides to come down and paddle to the Illinois side of the river, but after arriving he soon hears the voices of other campers. Afraid they will spot him, he goes back to the island. After a fearful, sleepless night, he resolves to find out who is on the island with him. When he discovers the spot where he had seen the ashes, he notices a tall man wrapped in a blanket still sleeping. Hiding in the bushes, Huck waits and soon realizes it is Miss Watson's slave, Jim. Relieved and happy, Huck jumps out, startling Jim, who thinks that he is seeing Huck's ghost. Huck convinces him that he is, indeed, very much alive; he tells Jim the story of his escape. Jim, in turn, also confesses that he has "run off." Huck promises not to tell, in spite of the fact that people will call him a "low-down Abolitionist." Jim explains that he had seen slave traders in the area and overheard Miss Watson say she was tempted to sell him down the river for eight hundred dollars.

Huck and Jim move their belongings into a cave in a high bluff that Huck had found earlier while he was exploring the island. Here they are sheltered from thunderstorms and hidden from people who might happen to come to the island. The move seems to come just in time, for it begins to rain and the river continues to rise for ten or twelve days, flooding the low spot where Huck's camp had been before. They explore the island in their canoe, and one night they find a large raft that has floated down in the rising waters.

Another night a two-story frame house floats by. They climb into the top story and find many useful items. As they are rummaging around, they run into a dead man who has been shot in the back. Jim covers him with old rags and asks Huck not to look at his ghastly face. They load their new-found possessions into the canoe and head back to the island.

Analysis

The playful, relaxed tone at the beginning of Chapter VIII is set in juxtaposition to the preceding chapter where Huck frantically escapes from the clutches of his abusive father. It is noteworthy that he does not, however, run into the waiting arms of the Widow Douglas. Twain's theme of individual freedom is apparent in the contrast of the natural life on the island where Huck is "comfortable and satisfied," to the respectable, hypocritical life on the shore where he faces the tyranny of his father and the Widow Douglas. Although the island offers peace and freedom, by the same token it is also the agent of loneliness and fear. This is true when Huck cannot sleep for fear of the dangers that might be connected to the smoking campfire he has discovered. He has left behind all of society, but now he is lonely. The island and the river, symbolic of freedom, are also subjected to dangerous river currents and treacherous storms, but it is at those times that Huck's language is at its most artistic level.

"And here would come a blast of wind...and then a perfect ripper of a gust would follow along and set the branches to tossing their arms as if they was just wild; and next, when it was just about the bluest and blackest—fst! it was as bright as glory...and then go rumbling, grumbling, tumbling, down the sky towards the under side of the world, like rolling empty barrels down-stairs."

This poetic description of a frightening thunderstorm is followed by his words to Jim. "I wouldn't want to be nowhere else but here." To Huck the constraints of society are missing on the island and that is all that matters.

Huck quickly makes his decision to help Jim escape from slavery even though people would call him a "low-down Abolitionist." Throughout the novel, Huck encounters this moral dilemma several times. The choice between the hypocritical values of society and Huck's friendship with Jim is the central conflict of the novel. This is also where Twain employs his most biting satire. One example is the comment Jim makes about being poor. He decides that he is not poor now because he owns himself, and he is worth eight hundred dollars.

Superstition is shown as pervading the society of Huck's day. Shooting cannons to bring a dead body to the surface seems the ultimate satiric treatment of the theme of superstition, particularly since the participants are the educated townspeople. Ironically, the floating bread on the water finds Huck as it was meant to do. Similarly, the house that floated down with the floodwaters of the river supplied Huck and Jim with many items for their survival on the island.

Study Questions

1. What interrupts Huck's comfortable and relaxed feeling the first morning on the island?

2. Why are the townspeople on the river that morning?

3. What is found in the bread that is floating on the water?

4. Whose campfire does Huck find?

5. What will people say if they discover that Huck is harboring a slave?

6. What is Miss Watson tempted to do with her slave, Jim?

7. What happens to the island when it rains?

8. What do Huck and Jim find on the island that has been washed down by the flood?

9. A large two-story house floats down the river past the island. What do Huck and Jim find in the house?

10. Where do Huck and Jim make their home on the island?

Answers

1. The interruption is the loud "boom" of the cannon coming from the ferryboat.

2. They are on the river to try and locate Huck's dead body.

3. Quicksilver is put in the bread because they feel that it will locate a dead body in the river.

4. Huck finds Jim's campfire, but he does not know whose it is at the time.

5. People will call Huck a low-down Abolitionist.

6. Miss Watson is tempted to sell him down the river for eight hundred dollars.

7. It becomes flooded with three or four feet of water at the lower end of the island.

8. They find a large raft.

9. Huck and Jim find a dead man in the house. In the last chapter of the novel Huck will learn that it was the body of his father.

10. They make their home in a cave on a high bluff. This provides shelter when it rains and protection from people who might be looking for Jim.

Suggested Essay Topics

1. Huck's most poetic language is prompted by a severe thunderstorm on the island. Discuss the reasons for this. In what way does the storm inspire him? Why is he not afraid of the storm? Use examples from the novel to support your argument.

2. If Huck keeps Jim's secret of his escape, people will call him a "low-down Abolitionist." In what way are those words more effective when spoken by a young narrator? Explain the irony in Huck's statement. What is Twain's message about the hypocritical values of his society? Explain your answer with examples from the novel.

3. Miss Watson could sell Jim for eight hundred dollars. He, therefore, feels rich because he owns himself. Explain Twain's use of satire in Jim's statement . What was Twain's attitude toward slavery in this passage? Explain your answer.

Chapters X–XI (pages 39–47)

New Character:

Mrs. Judith Loftus: a lady whom Huck visits in town

Summary

The next morning Huck wants to discuss the dead man he and Jim had seen in the two-story frame house, but Jim says talking about it will bring bad luck. Huck argues that touching a snakeskin with his hands was supposed to have brought bad luck too, but to the contrary they have found all those useful items in the floating house and eight dollars besides. They have, in his opinion, had nothing but good luck. Jim's predictions come true, however, when a rattlesnake bites him that evening. Huck plays a joke on Jim by putting a dead rattlesnake in his blanket. When Jim goes to bed, the snake's mate is curling around the dead snake and bites Jim in the heel. Jim's leg is swollen for four days, and Pap's whiskey comes in handy for the pain.

Huck is getting bored on the island and decides to go into town to see what is happening. Jim likes the idea but cautions him to go at night so he will not be seen. He suggests that Huck disguise himself as a girl. Thinking it is a good idea, Huck dresses in the calico gown and sunbonnet they had found earlier in the floating house.

Trying hard to concentrate on being a girl, Huck paddles to town in his canoe and finds the house of a woman who has been in town only two weeks. Passing as Sarah Williams, he tells her his mother is ill, and he is looking for his uncle's house. She insists it is too dark for a girl to be out alone, and she wants Huck/Sarah to wait so her husband can escort him to his uncle's house.

Huck learns the latest gossip as he waits. Although Mrs. Loftus is new in town, she has already heard of Huck's supposed murder and Jim's escape. She tells him that at first people thought it was Pap who murdered Huck, but later, after Jim ran away, he became the murder suspect and there is a three hundred dollar reward offered for Jim. She has seen smoke on Jackson's Island, and her husband is going over after midnight to check out her suspicions that Jim might be hiding on the island.

When Huck hears this, he tries to stay calm but suddenly forgets his name is Sarah Williams. When she throws him a ball of lead, he claps his legs together to catch it in his lap. Since girls would spread their legs to catch a ball in their skirt, Mrs. Loftus realizes Huck is a boy. He finally admits it but tells another story about being an orphan who was being abused by his stepfather, so he ran away and decided to live with his uncle. She finally lets him go, telling him to be sure to contact her, Mrs. Judith Loftus, if he needs any help.

He quickly heads back to the island, makes a fire in his old campsite, and goes back to the cave. Jim is already asleep. He warns him to get going because "They're after us." Without a word, Jim hurriedly gets to work packing the raft and the canoe. Huck checks to see whether there is a strange boat on the river. When he sees that all is clear they slip away in dead silence.

Analysis

In Chapter X the theme of superstition is again brought out when the rattlesnake bites Jim. Jim thinks his bad luck is attributed to the fact that Huck has touched a snakeskin with his bare hands a few days ago, but Huck knows the real reason. He is aware that he acted irresponsibly when he put the dead rattlesnake in Jim's blanket for a joke. Although it is too late, he remembers that the mate of a dead snake will come later and curl around it. Sorry for what he has done, Huck calls himself a fool and does not tell Jim it is his fault because he knows it would hurt him. In these chapters we begin to see Huck's growing concern for Jim's welfare. When Mrs. Loftus tells Huck that people in town think Jim is Huck's murderer, Huck is shocked. One can almost see his hand clasp over his mouth after his short retort, "Why he—." He hopes Mrs. Loftus has not noticed because he feels he should keep quiet to protect Jim. By contrast, Huck responds with little emotion to the suggestion that "Some think old Finn done it himself." In light of Huck's relationship with his father, the idea does not surprise him.

Huck's hurried return to the island and his warning to Jim that "they're after us," shows the close relationship that has already formed between them. In reality they are after Jim but in Huck's close identity with Jim, it never occurs to Huck that he and Jim are not in this together.

Study Questions

1. What does a rattlesnake do when its mate dies?

2. Jim thinks there is a reason why the rattlesnake bit him. What is the reason?

3. Why does Huck dress like a girl?

4. How long does it take for Jim's swelling on his leg to go down?

5. What is the name of the forty-year-old woman whom Huck talks to in town?

6. What crime is Jim accused of?

7. Why does Huck build a fire at his old campsite?

8. How does Mrs. Loftus know that Huck is not a girl?

9. What reward is offered for Huck's father?

10. How does Huck react when Mrs. Loftus says that people think Jim murdered Huck?

Answers

1. The rattlesnake finds its mate and coils around it.

2. Jim thinks the snake bit him because Huck touched a snake-skin with his bare hands.

3. Huck dresses to disguise himself so nobody will recognize him in town.

4. It takes four days and four nights.

5. Her name is Mrs. Judith Loftus. Her husband wants to find Jim for the three hundred dollar reward.

6. Jim is accused of murdering Huck.

7. He builds a fire to distract the people who are hunting for Jim until they can get off the island.

8. Mrs. Loftus observes the way Huck catches the lump of lead

by clapping his legs together. She can also tell by the way he threads a needle.

9. The reward is two hundred dollars because he is a murder suspect.

10. Huck is completely surprised, but he tries to stay calm so she will not suspect his connection with Jim.

Suggested Essay Topics

1. Huck's growing concern for Jim's welfare is evident in many ways. Discuss the events where this concern is reflected in Huck's behavior. In what ways does he protect Jim from danger? Cite examples from the novel to support your argument.

2. Huck's ability to tell a story in order to get himself out of a "tight" situation is one of his greatest strengths. How does this apply to his encounter with Mrs. Judith Loftus? What does he do when she realizes he is a boy? Explain your answer.

3. When Huck curls up the snake at the foot of Jim's blanket, he does not tell Jim that he has done it. What is his reason for keeping his little joke a secret? What lesson does Huck learn from it? How would Jim have felt if Huck would have told the truth? Discuss your answer.

Chapters XII–XIII (pages 47–57)

New Characters:

Jim Turner: robber and potential informer on the Walter Scott

Bill and Jake Packard: robbers conspiring to kill Jim Turner

Captain: watchman of the ferryboat

Summary

After traveling all night, Huck and Jim tie up to a towhead on the Illinois side of the river. The towhead, a sandbar thick with cottonwood trees, is an ideal spot to hide during the day and watch the steamboats go up and down the river. Killing time until dark, Huck tells Jim all about his conversation with the woman on the shore.

He explains that he had built the campfire to throw the woman's husband off track, but Jim maintains that if her husband was as smart as she obviously was, he would have used dogs to track a runaway slave.

When they are sure it is dark, Jim builds a wigwam in the middle of the raft for protection from the hot sun and the rain. In the middle he builds a firebox in order to keep warm on cool nights. They also build an extra steering oar and a stick to hang a signal lantern for the steamboats coming downstream. Since the river is still in flood stage, the boats traveling upstream against the current are no problem to them. They are taking the easy water on the sides.

They travel for five nights, drifting with a strong four-mile-an-hour current before they come upon the brilliant lights of St. Louis. Huck goes ashore every night for supplies and buys staples such as bacon but he "lifts a chicken" and "borrows a watermelon." They also shoot wildlife with their gun. All in all, they eat very well.

Five nights below St. Louis they run into a fierce thunderstorm. From their wigwam shelter they spot a wrecked steamboat in the glare of the lightning. Despite Jim's warning to leave it alone, Huck has an itching desire to go aboard to see what he can find. Jim finally gives in, however, and soon they are groping in the dark toward the "texas" containing the pilothouse and officers' quarters. When they see a light and hear voices, Jim is ready to go back, but Huck's curiosity gets the best of him when he hears a loud voice cry out: "Oh, please don't, boys; I swear I won't ever tell!" A loud argument ensues, and, although Jim has already gone back to the raft, Huck reasons that Tom Sawyer wouldn't go back now and neither will he. Huck creeps closer and sees two looters who are ready to kill their partner in crime, Jim Turner, because he has threatened to inform the authorities.

Seeing the seriousness of the situation, Huck backs away into a stateroom, but Bill and Jake Packard unknowingly follow him into the same room to discuss the matter. They decide to wait the two hours or so for the steamboat to break up and drown Jim Turner, saving them the trouble. As soon as Huck can get away he finds Jim to inform him that a "gang of murderers" is operating, and they need to cut their boat loose so that the murderers cannot get away. Jim then tells him the raft has broken loose during the storm.

They realize they need to find the robbers' boat for themselves. Happily they find the "skiff," but just as they are ready to climb in, Packard beats them to it. Luckily Huck and Jim escape detection. Packard and Bill are in the boat ready to take off when they get into an argument about the money left in Jim Turner's pockets. They go back, and while they are gone, Huck and Jim move into the boat. They cut the rope, and the current takes them downstream.

A little while later Huck's conscience begins to bother him, and he decides to get somebody to rescue the robbers. Huck and Jim catch up with their raft a few miles downstream. Jim boards the raft, and Huck stays in the skiff. He instructs Jim to take the raft two miles downstream while he finds someone who might help with the rescue. He finds a watchman on a ferryboat who is impressed with his sob story about his family, stuck on the wrecked Walter Scott, who will drown unless someone rescues them. Following a lead from the watchman, Huck convinces him that the niece of Hornback, a very wealthy man in town, is on board the Walter Scott, and that the reward will surely be a sizable one.

In a little while the steamboat comes floating downstream deep in the water. Huck sees the ferryboat moving around the wreck in an effort to locate the bodies, but it soon heads for shore. Although he does not expect to find anyone alive, Huck paddles around it and shouts, but there is no response, so he joins Jim two miles downstream. They head for shore and get some much-needed sleep.

Analysis

Chapter XII is the beginning of the adventurous odyssey down the Mississippi. In contrast to life on the shore, the journey on the river is presented as a solemn experience where "we didn't ever feel like talking loud, and it warn't often that we laughed." It would almost seem disrespectful to the "big, still river" to disturb its peacefulness. In the journey down the river we see Huck's movement away from civilization, with its corrupt institutions, and toward the natural world of the river. Here Huck's feeling for the natural beauty of the river gives the novel a mythological characteristic. When Huck "lifts a chicken," or "borrows a watermelon," Twain is satirizing the human need to rationalize our wrongdoings. It is another attack on Pap, who brought Huck up to believe it is all right to "borrow" things if one intends to bring them back someday.

Exploring the wrecked steamboat, the Walter Scott, is an irresistible adventure for Huck. Here again, he wishes Tom Sawyer were with him. He speaks admiringly of Tom's ability to enjoy an adventure with "style." The reason for going on board the steamboat is to see whether they could confiscate anything of value to Huck and Jim. This time Huck has bit off more than he can chew, and he almost gets trapped on the boat when his raft floats away. He is saved only by chance when the thieves go back to get the money.

As Huck and Jim escape from the steamboat leaving the robbers to die, Huck's conscience begins to bother him, and he decides to find help for them. As his relationship with Jim deepens, Huck shows a growing concern for other human beings as well.

As in the earlier situation with Mrs. Loftus, Huck fabricates another one of his stories to convince the captain of the ferryboat to rescue the people on the wrecked Walter Scott. Following a lead from the captain himself about Hornback's wealth, Huck creates a story about Hornback's niece who is supposedly trapped on the wrecked steamboat. The captain of the ferryboat immediately takes action to save her.

Study Questions

1. What is a towhead?

2. After it gets dark Jim builds a protection from the rain. What does he build?

3. What is the "texas" part of a steamboat?

4. Why does Huck want to rescue the robbers on the wrecked steamboat?

5. Why does Huck wish Tom Sawyer could be with him to explore the wrecked steamboat?

6. What does Huck finally say to get action from the captain of the ferryboat?

7. What does Huck mean when he says "I lifted a chicken" and "borrowed a watermelon"?

8. What happens to the raft while Huck and Jim explore the wrecked steamboat?

9. Do they find the raft again?

10. What happened to the skiff at the end of Chapter XIII?

Answers

1. A towhead is a sandbar that has a thick growth of cotton-woods on it.

2. Jim builds a wigwam in the center of the raft. He adds a place to build a fire in cool weather.

3. The "texas" on a steamboat contains the pilothouse and officers' quarters.

4. Huck's conscience bothers him after he takes their boat and leaves them to die.

5. Huck knows that Tom would add excitement and "style" to his adventure.

6. He tells him that the niece of the richest man in town is trapped on the wrecked steamboat.

7. Huck means that he stole them both, but rationalizes his actions by saying that it is not stealing if you intend to pay the owner back someday.

8. The raft has floated away in the storm and Huck and Jim are left stranded.

9. Yes. They catch up with the raft a few miles downstream.

10. Huck and Jim sank the skiff so there could be no incriminating evidence in connection with the robbers.

Suggested Essay Topics

1. Huck's journey on the river is filled with adventures, but it is also a symbolic journey. What does his journey symbolize? How does his relationship with Jim tie in to the symbolism? Compare the symbolism of the shore to that of the river. Use examples from the novel to support your view.

2. The Adventures of Huckleberry Finn is often referred to as the embodiment of mythological characteristics. In what way does the journey down the river represent these characteristics? How is Huck's escape from society and his love for the natural world of the river incorporated into this idea? Explain your answer.

3. Twain uses satire to expose people's ability to rationalize their wrongdoings. In what way does Twain employ that device in the incident where Huck "lifts chickens" and "borrows watermelons"? What do the words "lifts" and "borrows" connote? Give examples from the novel to support your argument.

Chapters XIV–XV (page 57–65)

Summary

Jim and Huck take a breather after their narrow escape from the wrecked steamboat and the gang of robbers. They spend time looking over their "truck," or goods, that the robber gang had stolen and loaded into the skiff. They find interesting articles of clothing, books, blankets, and boots, but the most valuable find is the boxes of cigars. They spend all afternoon talking, and Huck reads the newly-acquired books about kings, dukes, and earls. They get into a lengthy discussion about how royalty wears fancy clothes and everyone addresses them with "your majesty, your lordship, or your grace." King Solomon from the Bible is the only king Jim has ever heard of, and he is not impressed with him. He does not think a wise king would suggest cutting his child in half and giving each wife one-half just to settle a dispute.

Huck changes the subject by telling Jim about Louis XVI of France who was beheaded. His son, the Dauphin, supposedly died in prison. There were rumors, however, that he had escaped and had come to America. Jim does not seem to understand the idea that the Dauphin would speak French.

Huck also explains to Jim that their experience in the steamboat was called an adventure, but Jim wants nothing more to do with Huck's adventures. He does not relish the thought of coming so close to death again.

In three more nights Huck and Jim intend to reach Cairo, Illinois where they will pick up the Ohio River and travel north into the free states. They run into some trouble, however, when the raft, tied to a sapling, is pulled by the strong current and tears the tree out by the roots. Jim and the raft are immediately swallowed up in the fog, and he and Huck are separated for several hours. The fog finally clears and Huck finds the raft. When he sees that Jim is asleep, he quietly sneaks on board. He plays a trick on Jim, pretending he had been there all along, and that Jim had dreamt the whole experience of being lost in the fog. Jim is finally convinced.

In an effort to get Jim back to reality, however, he points to the "leaves" and "rubbish" left on the raft. When Jim realizes Huck's trick has made a fool of him, he is deeply hurt. Huck apologizes and promises there will be no more "mean tricks."

Analysis

In Chapter XIV Huck and Jim are relaxing after their big scare on the Walter Scott. Their new reading material stimulates discussion about kings and dukes. Their easy bantering back and forth illustrates their human characteristics. Twain's satiric treatment of royalty is evident in this scene. Huck's exasperation with Jim's lack of understanding of King Solomon leads him to change the subject. Talk of Louis XVI and his son the "Dolphin" (Dauphin) is a foreshadowing of the conmen's appearance as the king and the duke in Chapter XIX.

There is imminent danger that Jim and Huck will be permanently separated when they lose sight of each other in the fog one night. Huck is immediately "dismal and lonesome." Later Jim is elated when he realizes Huck is, indeed, alive and well. The threat of possible separation has brought their relationship into painful focus, especially in the last scene when Jim is hurt by Huck's trick which is designed to make a fool of Jim. Through it all, they discover how they feel about each other. Jim's heart was broken when he thought Huck was lost, and Jim learns that Huck would not have played a trick on him "if I'd 'a' knowed it would make him feel that way."

Jim's interpretation of his supposed dream carries with it ominous predictions of trouble ahead. If they minded their own business, however, and didn't talk back to the "quarrelsome people," he thinks they would get to the free states and out of trouble.

Study Questions

1. How did Jim feel about Huck's "adventure" on the Walter Scott?

2. Which king was familiar to Jim?

3. Who was the French king who was beheaded?

4. Who was his son?

5. Why are Huck and Jim separated in the fog?

6. What kind of trick does Huck play on Jim?

7. How does Jim feel about the trick?

8. How many nights will it take to get to Cairo?

9. Where has Huck learned about kings?

10. Which river will Huck and Jim travel to get to the free states?

Answers

1. Jim said he did not want any more adventures because he did not want to risk getting caught, nor did he want to risk his life.

2. King Solomon was the biblical king who had many wives.

3. His name was Louis XVI. He was the king during the French Revolution.

4. His son was the Dauphin, Louis Charles, who was imprisoned and was thought to have died there. Rumors had it that he might have escaped, however, and fled to America.

5. The raft has broken away from the young tree (sapling) it was tied to, and Huck's canoe follows one side of an island while Jim's raft follows the other side.

6. Huck tricks Jim into believing that he has been on the raft all along and that they were never separated in the fog.

7. Jim feels that Huck has been making a fool of him and he is hurt.

8. It will be three nights of good traveling, but the fog changes their plans.

9. Huck has probably learned about kings from books he has read and is continuing to read on the raft.

10. The Ohio River will lead them into Illinois and to the free states. Illinois was, in fact, a free state in the antebellum South.

Suggested Essay Topics

1. The relationship between Huck and Jim is brought into focus in these chapters. How does their frightening separation in the fog draw them closer together? How do they feel about each other at this point in the novel? Give examples from the novel to support your viewpoint.

2. Huck and Jim carry on a lengthy conversation about royalty. In what way does Twain satirize royalty in these chapters? What is Jim's opinion of King Solomon? Why does he feel that way? Give examples from the novel to support your argument.

Chapters XVI–XVII (page 65–79)

New Characters:

Two men on a skiff: men looking for runaway slaves

Buck Grangerford: a boy Huck's age

Bob and Tom: members of the Grangerford family

Betsy: Grangerford's slave

Summary

Huck and Jim rest all day and start for Cairo at dark. When he thinks about Cairo and gaining his freedom, Jim's excitement mounts, but Huck becomes increasingly uneasy. Painfully aware that he is helping a slave escape to freedom, his conscience suddenly bothers him. This time he cannot seem to rationalize his actions as he has done before. He does not think Miss Watson, Jim's owner, deserves such treatment. When Jim incessantly chatters on about buying his wife and children or getting an Abolitionist to help steal them, Huck reaches the breaking point. He decides that he must paddle ashore in the canoe at the first sign of a light and turn Jim in. Unaware of Huck's intentions, Jim helps prepare the canoe, padding the seat with his coat. He tells Huck that he is the best friend he has ever had. At this, Huck falters a bit, but he still feels he must turn Jim in. When two men in a skiff come along, he weakens, however. He tells them one of his stories about his sick family on board, leading the men to believe they all have smallpox. Out of guilt for not helping a young boy with a sick family, they each give him twenty dollars and hurriedly leave. He feels bad for having "done wrong" but reasons that he would have felt just as bad if he had turned Jim in and done the right thing. Next time, Huck decides, he will just do what is the "handiest."

The next town they come to is on high ground. Since there is no high ground around Cairo, they begin to suspect that perhaps they had passed Cairo in the fog that night. Jim immediately blames the rattlesnake skin for his bad luck. At daylight their suspicions are confirmed when they see the clear Ohio River water flowing into the muddy Mississippi. Since they cannot take the raft upstream, they will try to paddle the canoe back to Cairo. When they get back to the raft after dark, however, the canoe is missing. Their only choice is to continue downriver until they can purchase another canoe. But their streak of bad luck is not over yet. That night a steamboat runs straight into their raft. Huck and Jim dive off into the water, and Huck swims to shore, but he sees no sign of Jim.

On land Huck runs into a pack of vicious dogs who will not let him pass. The owners of the dogs come out fully armed, demanding to know his name and his possible association with the Shepherdsons. Seeing that he is harmless, they cordially invite him to stay as long as he likes. He befriends their 13-year-old son Buck, who is Huck's age.

Huck gives his name as George Jackson but forgets it by morning. He tricks Buck into spelling his name, and then he remembers. Huck goes into a long description of the house. He naively admires the furnishings in the Grangerford parlor and takes an interest in the morbid crayon drawings and sentimental poetry having been created by their dead daughter Emmeline Grangerford.

Analysis

For the second time, Huck faces a moral decision forcing him to come to grips with the idea that he is helping a slave escape to freedom. On Jackson's Island his decision was made without thinking. His only concern then was that people would call him a "low-down Abolitionist." Twain's biting satire reaches its greatest height when Huck censures Jim for wanting to steal his own wife and children. Huck, a product of the society of his day, believes that Jim's rights to his own children are superseded by those of the slaveowner. He accuses Jim of trying to steal "children that belonged to a man I didn't even know; a man that hadn't ever done me no harm." Huck does eventually make a choice not to turn Jim in, but in doing so he also believes he has done the wrong thing. Ironically, he sees his choice as a weakness, when in reality it is his greatest strength.

After the raft has drifted south of Cairo, their journey down the Mississippi, deeper into slave territory, is necessarily thwarted. The raft is then destroyed by the steamboat and Huck and Jim are separated. It is at this point, critics believe, Twain's difficulty with the plot caused him to set the book aside for two years. In the meantime Twain was publishing other works.

In Chapter XVII, as was true in earlier chapters, Huck's character remains consistent in his ability to conjure up a story when he needs it to get himself out of a difficult situation. The slave hunters are vulnerable to his subtle suggestion that there might be smallpox aboard the raft, and the spontaneity and ease with which he pulls up a believable story to tell the Grangerfords characterizes Huck as a young boy with an amazing understanding of the foibles of human nature.

Huck's lengthy description of the Grangerford house, decorated with gaudy furnishings and the pen and crayon drawings of Emmeline Grangerford, is a satire against morbid art and poor taste in decorating. Twain's satire is punctuated at the end of the chapter with an example of Emmeline's repulsive, sentimental poetry. Buck does not need to convince us that Emmeline seldom thought about her verse but would, instead, just "slap down a line," then scratch it if it didn't rhyme and "slap down another one."

Study Questions

1. Why does Huck's conscience bother him as they approach what they think is Cairo?

2. What does Huck tell the slave hunters about his predicament?

3. What do the men in the skiff do for Huck?

4. Does Huck feel better after he has protected Jim from the slave hunters?

5. What destroys the raft?

6. How can Huck and Jim tell that they have missed Cairo in the fog?

7. Why does Jim think they have had such bad luck?

8. Why does Huck go into long descriptions of the furnishings and pictures in the Grangerford's house?

9. Who do the Grangerfords think Huck might be when the dogs bark at him?

10. What has happened to Jim in these chapters?

Answers

1. He feels he is responsible for helping Jim, a runaway slave, gain his freedom.

2. He tells them that his pap, his mam, and Mary Ann are sick on the raft. He leads them to believe they have smallpox.

3. Out of guilt they each give him $20.

4. He does not feel better at first. He feels as if he has done the wrong thing.

5. A steamboat navigating on a semi-foggy river runs into them.

6. They can tell that they are below the Ohio River because clear water from the Ohio is drifting into the muddy Mississippi.

7. He feels it all comes from handling the snakeskin.

8. Twain is using satire to attack sentimentalism and bad taste in art and in home furnishings.

9. They think Huck could be a Shepherdson, their enemy.

10. Jim dives off the raft when the steamboat wrecks it, and Huck calls his name repeatedly but cannot find him.

Suggested Essay Topics

1. Huck makes a moral decision concerning Jim's freedom in Chapter XVI. How does this decision affect Huck as a character in the novel? Discuss the first time in the novel that he made a decision to help Jim escape to freedom. How did the decision affect him then? Cite examples from the novel to support your view.

2. There is irony in the statement Jim makes about stealing his children. In what way is it ironic that Jim's children belong to someone else? Why did Huck feel it was morally wrong for Jim to claim his children as his own? Give examples from the novel to support your argument.

3. Critics believe Twain stopped writing the novel for a few years after he finished Chapter XVI. Why would this have been a difficult place for Twain to continue? How does the setting of the novel change at this point? Explain your answer.

Chapters XVIII–XIX (pages 79–95)

New Characters:

Colonel Grangerford: father of the Grangerford family

Mrs. Grangerford: mother of the family

Miss Charlotte: member of the family (twenty-five years old)

Miss Sophia: her twenty-year-old sister

Harney Sheperdson: the man Miss Sophia marries

Jack: Huck's personal servant

Duke of Bridgewater: an imposter

The Dauphin: an imposter, supposed son of the late Louis XVI, King of France

Summary

Huck's description of Colonel Grangerford, from his white linen suit to his gentlemanly ways, paints a picture of a typical aristocratic landowner of the day. He is a wealthy man who supplies each member of his family with a private servant.

The Shepherdsons are another aristocratic clan in the area. According to Huck they are as "well-born, and rich, and grand" as the Grangerfords. While Huck and Buck Grangerford are out hunting one day, Buck hears a horse and suddenly takes cover in the bushes. When Harney Shepherdson gallops by, Buck opens fire with his gun and knocks Harney's hat off of his head. Harney, gun in hand, heads straight for the boys, but they run all the way home where they must face the colonel. He feels Buck should have stepped into the middle of the road to face his enemy with bravery.

Huck questions Buck about the feud and he naively explains that it is a quarrel one man has with another man. He kills him, and the brothers retaliate with more killing until "everybody's killed off, and there ain't no more feud." The feud started 30 years ago, but nobody knows why.

On Sunday the Grangerfords and Shepherdsons sit in church together with their guns held "between their knees" while they listen to the minister's sermon on brotherly love. In the afternoon Miss Sophia secretly asks Huck to get the Testament she has forgotten at church. He sees no one at church except a few hogs who have wandered in through the open door. Pulling a note from the Testament, Miss Sophia makes Huck promise not to tell anyone.

Jack, Huck's servant at the Grangerfords, has been following Huck around and when they are out of range of any people he beckons him to the swamp to show him some water moccasins. When Jack leaves, Huck is suddenly startled as he runs into Jim's hiding place. Jim is not surprised to see him. He tells Huck that he heard him yelling on the river the night the raft was hit by the steamboat but was afraid if he answered he might be caught and sold into slavery again. He has not contacted Huck for fear the dogs at the Grangerfords would track him down. He has been repairing the damaged raft that had been found snagged in some willow trees.

The next day Miss Sophia runs off to marry Harney Shepherdson, and the feud breaks out into a full-blown shooting match. Many people from both sides are killed. After Huck sees Buck's dead body, he takes off into the woods to find Jim and the raft. He vows never to go back, and he and Jim lose no time getting the raft onto the river again.

For several days Huck and Jim enjoy the peacefulness of the river as they again navigate the raft at night and go into hiding during the day. Early one morning Huck finds a canoe and decides to paddle up a creek for some berries. Before long he sees two men running toward him. He immediately thinks they must be after him but soon finds they are fugitives themselves, being chased by people and dogs. Relieved, he eagerly shows them a way to keep the dogs from following their scent.

The dogs are chasing a 30-year-old man who has been selling a product that takes the tartar off the teeth, but also takes the enamel along with it. The seventy-year-old man with him has been holding a temperance revival but is caught drinking on the side. He is expecting the townspeople to tar and feather him. Huck takes them to the raft. The two have not met before but share the commonality of defrauding small town people and then moving on. The 30-year-old soon claims to be the rightful Duke of Bridgewater. Not to be outdone, the older one says he is the "disappeared Dauphin," son of Louis XVI of France. It doesn't take Huck long to realize that the men are not kings nor dukes but "low-down humbugs, and frauds" instead.

Analysis

In Huck's description of Colonel Grangerford, Twain satirizes aristocratic gentlemen for being well-born, and "that's worth as much in a man as it is in a horse." The 30-year-old feud between the Grangerfords and the Shepherdsons is further criticism of aristocratic pretensions of respectability. This is particularly true when the feuding families sit in church together, their guns "between their knees," listening to a sermon on brotherly love and agreeing later that it was, indeed, a good sermon. Ironically, there is a controlled sense of respectability in Colonel Grangerford's gentle reprimand to Buck for "shooting from behind a bush," rather than bravely stepping out into the road to defend the family honor. The colonel's expectations for a 13-year-old boy make his values seem even more incongruous. Twain also brings out the ridiculousness of the feud when he has Buck describe it in the clear, straightforward language of a 13-year-old boy who doesn't even know why they are feuding.

Huck's disappointment in the Grangerford family mounts when the feud reaches a full-scale shoot-out. "It made me so sick, I most fell out of the tree." Ironically, the only redeeming feature in the whole episode is Harney and Miss Sophia's successful escape across the river.

The scene on the raft is appropriately set in juxtaposition to the bloody feud between the Shepherdsons and the Grangerfords. It brings to light the corruption and hypocrisy on the shore in opposition to the idyllic life on the raft where peace and harmony prevail. Huck's words reflect his gratitude to be back on the raft. Ironically, the raft is small, but Huck feels that "Other places do seem so cramped up and smothery, but a raft don't."

The foreshadowing of the appearance of the duke and dauphin was set in Chapter 14 when Huck read about kings, dukes, and earls in the books from the Walter Scott steamboat. Huck finds a canoe, but he does not use it to paddle upstream to the Ohio River as they had originally planned. This gives us a clue that the novel's setting will continue to focus on the journey down the Mississippi. The king and the duke are conmen who make a living presenting themselves with false identities. They do not fool people for long, however. Even Huck soon realizes that "these liars warn't no kings nor dukes at all, but just low-down humbugs and frauds."

Study Questions

1. Why are the Grangerfords and Shepherdsons feuding?

2. Name the couple who run off and get married?

3. What happens to the young couple after the shooting starts?

4. What secret does Miss Sophia ask Huck to keep?

5. Why does Huck think the duke and the king are after him when they first meet?

6. Do Huck and Jim expect to paddle their newly-found canoe up the Ohio River?

7. When Huck pulls the men out of the river, what has happened to them?

8. How does Jim feel when he sees Huck again? What does he think has happened to him?

9. Where is Huck while the shooting is going on?

10. Who leads Huck to Jim?

Answers

1. Nobody really knows except that years ago somebody shot a man who won a lawsuit.

2. Miss Sophia, a Grangerford, and Harney Shepherdson run off and get married.

3. The young couple make it safely across the river.

4. She asks Huck not to tell about the note left in her Testament.

5. He is still on guard because he is a runaway who is traveling with a runaway slave.

6. Their plans for traveling up the Ohio River have changed.

7. One of the men is Buck. He has died in a gun battle between the feuding families.

8. Jim is happy to see Huck. He was afraid Huck had been killed in the gun battle.

9. Huck has crawled up in a tree.

10. Jack helps Huck find Jim by telling him that he wants him to see a "whole stack o' water moccasins." He is actually leading him to Jim, but does not want to get mixed up in any trouble.

Suggested Essay Topics

1. Harney Shepherdson and Miss Sophia are victims of the feud between the Grangerfords and the Shepherdsons. Compare and contrast their conflict with that of Shakespeare's Romeo and Juliet. In what way was their situation the same? How was it different? Was Huck sympathetic with the young couple? Give examples from the novel to support your argument.

2. Twain employs satire throughout the novel to speak out against the hypocrisy and corruption in his society. In what way is the church service, attended by the Grangerfords and the Shepherdsons, an attack on the religion of Twain's day? How does the hog incident add to the satire? Explain your answer.

3. In these chapters life on the raft is contrasted sharply with the violence and bloodshed Huck has recently encountered on the shore. How does this contrast bring out the theme of freedom in the novel? How does Huck feel about life on the raft? How does Jim feel? Use examples from the novel to support your viewpoint.

Chapters XX–XXI (page 95–109)

New Characters:

Boggs: drunkard shot by Colonel Sherburn

Colonel Sherburn: the man who shoots Boggs

Summary

The king and the duke question the idea of traveling by night and hiding by day. Huck responds with common sense to their suspicions that Jim might be a runaway slave. He assures them that a runaway would not be traveling south. In order to be more convincing, however, he produces another imaginary story about his whole family dying and leaving him, after the debts are paid, with only sixteen dollars and the family slave Jim. His pa and four-year-old brother had fallen off the raft and drowned, so he and Jim are the only ones left. He explains that they travel at night because people are always assuming Jim is a runaway slave, and this is their way of avoiding trouble.

Satisfied with Huck's story, the king and the duke begin to settle down on the raft, making themselves at home. One night they instruct Huck and Jim to act as watchmen until a storm blows over. Without any apparent twinge of conscience they both crawl into the wigwam occupying the only beds on the raft. To make matters worse, there is a big thunderstorm that night, but Huck does not mind. He says he wouldn't have wanted to miss it "because a body don't see such a storm as that every day in the week, not by a long sight." When he is finally overcome with exhaustion, however, Jim offers to take Huck's watch. The wigwam is too full, however, so he decides to sleep out in the rain anyway.

The next day the king and the duke begin planning another "campaign," as they call it. They decide to make some money in the next town performing the balcony scene in Shakespeare's Romeo and Juliet and the swordfight in Richard III. The king will play the part of Juliet. That night they stop in town for supplies and the king decides to "work the camp meeting" for a few extra dollars. He introduces himself as a pirate from the Indian Ocean who has just become a changed man as a result of the camp meeting. He cons the people at the meeting into taking up a collection by telling them he is planning to go back to reform other pirates. In this way he collects eighty-seven dollars and seventy-five cents. In the meantime the duke has managed to swindle the owner of a printing office out of $9.50 while he also prints a handbill about Jim's escape from a plantation south of New Orleans. This gives them an alibi in case they are questioned about Jim while traveling in the daytime. They are simply going down to claim their reward for Jim's capture.

The king and the duke begin rehearsing for the Shakespearean performance that will take place in one of the next towns. When they reach a little "one-horse" town in Arkansas, the circus has already come to town, drawing the people they need for their show. The duke enthusiastically rents the courthouse and distributes the playbills around town.

While they wait for the circus to leave town, a man named Boggs rides into town for his "monthly drunk." He shouts around, threatening to kill Colonel Sherburn. People laugh and do not take him seriously until the colonel himself steps out with a gun, threatening to kill Boggs if he doesn't stop by one o'clock. In spite of the warning, Boggs continues his ceaseless tirade against Colonel Sherburn. Heeding the seriousness of the situation, the townspeople send for Boggs' daughter, but she is too late. He is dying from Colonel Sherburn's gunshot wound just as she arrives.

Analysis

Huck must necessarily produce another story at this point in the novel to protect Jim and settle the minds of the duke and the king. Throughout the novel Twain engages our sympathies for Huck when he fabricates his wildly imaginative stories. It is understood that Huck's stories are, ironically, a necessary ploy for the survival of an innately moral young man caught up in a pretentious, hypocritical society. Huck's stories are, in any case, more credible than those of the king and the duke.

Since the duke must teach Hamlet's soliloquy to the king, we sense that he is probably the one who is better educated. He has no copy of Hamlet on the raft, however, so he draws from "recollections vaults." The result is words and lines taken from several of Shakespeare's plays and thrown together in a nonsensical way. Judging from the shiftless ne'er-do-wells who hang around the muddy streets of the little river town, the people will most likely not notice mistakes in Shakespeare's text.

The thunderstorm in these chapters is reminiscent of the one observed earlier by Huck and Jim on Jackson's Island. In Huck's description of the storm he holds the natural forces in awe with no fear of the thunder and lightning. Huck's appreciation for the natural world around him is again brought out in his artistic description of the storm. Jim's tender feeling for his friend Huck is apparent when he serves half of Huck's watch for him because Huck is sleepy.

The camp meeting with all its sensationalism is a perfect opportunity for the king to make a few dollars. In this scene Twain is satirizing the gullibility of the people who hang on the king's every word. Having played these fraudulent games before, he demonstrates his skill in manipulating the crowd to take up a collection for him which amounts to $87.25. The duke has not fared as well, managing to cheat the owner of the printing office out of $9.50.

Study Questions

1. How does Huck explain the fact that they travel at night and sleep during the day?

2. What do the people at the camp meeting expect the king to do with the money they collect for him?

3. How does Jim treat Huck during the storm at night?

4. How do the duke and the king plan to make it safe for Jim to travel during the day?

5. What does the duke mean when he says he will call back Hamlet's soliloquy from "recollection's vaults"?

6. Why is the duke's version of Hamlet's soliloquy confusing?

7. Who is assigned the role of Juliet in the "Shakespearean Revival"?

8. Why does Colonel Sherburn murder Boggs?

9. What is Colonel Sherburn's ultimatum in regard to Boggs?

10. Who is called for to quiet Boggs down?

Answers

1. He tells them a story about Jim being the family slave. Since his family is all dead, Jim is all he has left. They travel at night because people suspect Jim of being a runaway when they see him.

2. They expect him to use it when he goes back to change the lives of his fellow pirates.

3. When Huck gets tired, Jim takes half of his watch so Huck can get some sleep.

4. The duke prints a playbill that advertises Jim as a runaway slave. When people see them they will tie Jim's hands and feet, show them the playbill, and tell people they are turning Jim in for the reward.

5. The duke has no copy of Hamlet aboard the raft. He says he will need to recall it from memory.

6. The duke's version is confusing because it is not Hamlet's soliloquy. It contains jumbled lines from several of Shakespeare's plays, and it makes no sense.

7. The 70-year-old king with a bald head is assigned the role of Juliet.

8. Colonel Sherburn is tired of being harassed and threatened by the drunken Boggs.

9. He gives Boggs until one o'clock to quiet down. If he doesn't, he will kill him.

10. The townspeople call for Boggs' daughter, but she arrives after he has been shot by Sherburn.

Suggested Essay Topics

1. In the novel Huck continually tells stories to get himself out of tight situations. Why doesn't this bother Huck's conscience? In what way is Huck forced to tell a lie? Is Huck morally wrong in doing so? Defend your argument with examples from the novel.

2. It is during a natural phenomenon such as a thunderstorm that Huck uses his most artistic language. Discuss Huck's feeling about the thunderstorm. Why is he not afraid of the storm? How does this symbolize his life on the river as opposed to life on the shore? Explain your answer.

3. There are many examples of gullibility in the novel. In what way does Twain satirize the gullibility of the people at the camp meeting? How does the king trick them into taking up a collection? Why do they believe him? Support your argument.

Chapters XXII–XXIII (pages 109–118)

New Character:

Buck Harkness: man who leads the lynch mob

Summary

After the shooting, someone in town suggests that Colonel Sherburn should be lynched, and the people, led by Buck Harkness, suddenly go wild. The crowd turns into an angry mob, stopping at nothing in pursuit of revenge against Sherburn. Even children run for their lives to get out of the way of the raging mob. In a frenzy they tear down Colonel Sherburn's picket fence and pour into his yard, ready for action.

The crowd suddenly calms down, however, when Sherburn steps out onto the roof of his porch flashing a double-barrel gun. At first he simply stares at them, saying nothing, but then he laughs scornfully, and stages a long diatribe criticizing the mob for its cowardice. He accuses them of hanging on to the coattail of Buck Harkness who is only "half a man." Sherburn orders them to leave, and the crowd breaks up with Buck Harkness on their heels.

After the excitement Huck decides to go to the circus. To avoid paying, he slips under the tent on the back side. With wide-eyed amazement, he watches the beautiful women on horses with their million-dollar outfits, the men showing their acrobatic skills, and the clowns cracking the funniest jokes Huck has ever heard. A supposed drunk comes along and insists upon riding the horses. The ringmaster finally gives in. At first the crowd laughs at him, but he turns out to be an accomplished rider and a part of the act.

The king and the duke stage their Shakespearean show, but they only attract twelve people who laugh inappropriately throughout the performance. Since these "lunkheads couldn't come up to Shakespeare," the duke decides to change to low comedy. He advertises their next show as the tragedy of The King's Cameleopard, or The Royal Nonesuch with a caption at the bottom that reads, "ladies and children not admitted." He thinks this would surely draw a crowd. The first night the house is packed, but the show is a fraud, consisting of the king displaying his painted body and demonstrating a few of his ludicrous antics on stage. Too embarrassed to admit they had been taken in, the townspeople speak favorably about the show in town the next day. The second night the house is again full, but the third night the king and duke hustle down to the raft and take off down the river to avoid the anger of the crowd. They have successfully conned the townspeople out of four hundred and sixty-five dollars.

Analysis

Colonel Sherburn's speech to the would-be lynch mob is a harsh invective against mob action of any kind. Twain speaks out against lynch mobs who do not fight with courage but come like cowards in the middle of the night wearing masks. As Sherburn demonstrates, the mob crumbles with cowardice when they come face to face with one strong individual.

We see the aggressive action in Twain's use of extended metaphor presenting the mob as "the front wall of the crowd" rolling "in like a wave." But when Sherburn steps out "the wave sucks back" in calm passivity. The metaphor is sustained until the end when the "crowd washed back sudden, and then broke all apart." We get the picture that the mob is as ephemeral as the ocean waves.

The king and the duke again expose the gullibility of the townspeople in the presentation of their play, The Royal Nonesuch. They pack the house with the fetching caption "ladies and children not admitted," knowing full well man's obsession with off-color and suggestive humor. Since their Shakespearean presentation, though poorly done, was not a success, the king and duke have no scruples against giving people what they want as long as it brings in money. The Royal Nonesuch, an obscene play, caters to the lowest common denominator, which is Twain's way of saying that it draws a crowd because people are morally corrupt.

Jim's reference to the king and duke as "regular rapscallions" is Twain's way of satirizing royalty. Huck responds with "all kings is mostly rapscallions." He then goes on to characterize different kings, but he is confused and historically inaccurate. He makes his point just the same. "Take them all around, they're a mighty ornery lot."

The sensitive personality of Jim is held in juxtaposition to the lynching mobs and the swindling king and duke in these chapters.

Huck speaks warmly about the many times Jim has taken his night watch for him just so he could sleep. He is also portrayed as a family man who misses his wife and children. He is nearly overcome with guilt for slapping his daughter because she was not listening to him when, in fact, she had become deaf after a bout with scarlet fever.

Study Questions

1. Who faces the mob single-handed?
2. Who is Twain satirizing in this situation?
3. What attracts the crowd at the showing of The Royal Nonesuch?
4. Why do the king and the duke leave during the third performance?
5. Approximately how many people attend the Shakespearean performance?
6. Why do the king and duke change to another show?
7. What does Huck mean when he says that all kings are "rapscallions"?
8. What does Jim do for Huck that shows he cares about him?
9. Who is Jim homesick for in these chapters?
10. What disease caused Jim's daughter's deafness?

Answers

1. Sherburn steps onto his porch and criticizes them for being cowards. He then orders them to leave.
2. Twain is satirizing the lynch mobs who come like cowards after dark wearing masks. He thinks mob activity is cowardly.
3. The caption at the bottom of the handbill that reads "ladies and children not admitted."

4. The king stays on the raft, and the duke escapes after he has collected the money. They leave to avoid the anger of the townspeople who have been swindled out of their money.

5. Twelve people attend the performance. They laugh inappropriately and leave before it is over.

6. Since their primary purpose is to make money they decide to do a show that will attract more people.

7. He does not have much respect for royalty. He sees them as insensitive men who generally get their own way.

8. Jim often serves his watch for him at night so Huck can get some sleep.

9. Jim is homesick for his wife and children and is afraid he will never see them again.

10. Scarlet fever left her with a hearing impediment.

Suggested Essay Topics

1. Twain is satirizing the lynch mob in these chapters. In what way can the individuals in a mob be seen as cowards? Discuss the psychology of a lynch mob. Why is Sherburn successful in breaking up the mob? Cite examples from the novel to support your argument.

2. Through the characters of the duke and the king, Twain is satirizing royalty. What qualities in a king would make him a "rapscallion?" How does Huck's reference to kings throughout history prove his point? Explain your answer.

3. The relationship between Huck and Jim is growing deeper as the novel progresses. How is Jim's humanity expressed through the eyes of Huck? How does Jim feel about Huck? How can Huck tell? Explain your answer.

Chapters XXIV–XXV (page 118–128)

New Characters:

Mary Jane Wilks: nineteen-year-old daughter of Peter Wilks

Susan Wilks: her sister, age 15

Joanna Wilks: the youngest sister, age 14

Dr. Robinson: Peter Wilks' friend before Wilks died

Summary

The king and the duke waste no time making plans to "work the towns" again for more money as soon as an opportunity arises. Their escapades into town have been difficult for Jim, however. He has been posing as a runaway slave who needs to be tied up while they are gone. To avoid any further discomfort for Jim, the duke devises an ingenious disguise so that people will think he is a sick Arab instead of a runaway slave. He dresses Jim in a King Lear outfit with a white wig and whiskers and paints his face, hands, neck, and ears a dull blue to make him look sick. The idea is to scare people away with his sickly, offensive appearance, but if that doesn't help, the duke advises him to step out of the wigwam and howl "like a wild beast."

They had all bought new clothes in the last town, and the king and Huck dress up and head for the steamboat in the canoe. The duke wants to try his luck in a village on the other side of the river, however. On their way to the steamboat, Huck and the king pick up a local young man who is taking a trip to South America. He leads the king into a conversation about Mr. Peter Wilks who has just died and left a small fortune. They are expecting his two brothers, Harvey and William, from England any day now. The king subtly prods him for more information until he not only knows the details surrounding Peter Wilks' death, but also the names of most of his family and close friends.

When they drop the young man at the steamboat dock, the king decides to stay in the canoe. As soon as they are alone, he instructs Huck to drop him off in a town a mile upstream and bring the duke back promptly. When he arrives, the king tells the duke the whole story and asks him to pose as the deaf and dumb brother of Peter Wilks while he acts as the other brother.

They flag a steamboat to the next town, and when they arrive people flock to the shore to meet them. The king asks directions to the place where Mr. Peter Wilks lives. One of the townspeople gently breaks the news that Mr. Wilks has died, and the king begins to moan and cry, making signs to the duke, his supposed deaf brother. The behavior of the two frauds convinces the townspeople that they are, indeed, the true brothers of Peter Wilks.

The news of their arrival spreads like wildfire and people come on the run to join them on their way to the Peter Wilks' house. When they arrive at the house, Mary Jane, Susan, and Joanna, Wilks' daughters, hug them and cry for joy. When the king and duke spot the coffin in the house, they see further opportunity to put on a convincing act with their sobbing, causing everyone in the room to break down and cry.

Calling them by name, the king invites Peter Wilks' closest friends to have supper with the family that evening. Remembering the names given to him earlier by the young informant, he calls out an impressively accurate list of names.

Mary Jane, the oldest daughter, produces her father's letter that specifies the terms of the inheritance. His daughters would receive the house and three thousand dollars in gold. Six thousand dollars in property and gold, along with the tanyard, was designated to go to Harvey and William, his brothers. The letter also reveals the hiding place of the six thousand dollars, which provides the king and duke an opportunity to get their hands on the cash. There is four hundred and fifteen dollars missing, however. To avoid suspicion they add their own money to make up the difference. They hand all the money to the girls, planning to steal it back later.

They manage to deceive all the townspeople until Dr. Robinson, one of the late Peter Wilks' closest friends, speaks up calling the king a fraud. He criticizes his fake English accent and accuses him of being an imposter. Mary Jane responds defiantly to the accusation by handing the king all of the six thousand dollars. She asks him to invest it for them, demonstrating her complete trust in the king.

Analysis

In the Wilks episode, Twain attacks the gullibility of human beings with the most biting satire demonstrated in the novel thus far. In spite of the fact that the king only "tried to talk like an Englishman" the townspeople never question his true identity.

Ironically, when Dr. Robinson, a respected member of the town, does speak up with the truth, nobody believes him. Swayed by the king's sentimentality, the townspeople hold the word of the king, a person whom they have just met, above that of Dr. Robinson whom they have known all their lives. Twain has artfully placed this scene in the atmosphere of a funeral setting when people are most vulnerable, and, therefore, most gullible. Mary Jane's determination to avoid any more pain at a time like this prompts her to reject the doctor's advice completely.

So far in the novel, Huck has been a silent spectator in the ludicrous antics of the king and the duke, but in the Wilks episode he becomes highly critical and judgmental. When the king and duke first arrive, the gullibility of the townspeople, who swallow their deceitful charades, fills him with shame. "It was enough to make a body ashamed of the human race." The depraved attitude of the frauds in the coffin scene is simply too much for Huck. "I never see anything so disgusting." Huck's moral position at this point in the novel is a foreshadowing of the ultimate moral decision he must make regarding Jim's freedom later on in the novel.

The humor in the king's repeated use of the word "orgies" in reference to the funeral ceremonies is a satire on the excessive indulgences in sentimentality exhibited in the funerals of Twain's day. Embarrassed by the king's use of the wrong word, the duke passes him a note telling him to correct it to "obseqious." The king explains that although orgies is not the commonly used term for funerals, it is the right term. "Orgies is better, because it means the thing you're after more exact." Though the king goes on with an inaccurate definition of the word, he has unknowingly made his point.

Study Questions

1. What does the duke do so that Jim does not need to be tied up in the wigwam all day?

2. Who gives the king the information about the Wilks family?

3. What are the names of the three Wilks sisters?

4. Who meets the king, the duke, and Huck when they reach the shore in the yawl?

5. How do the Wilks girls react when they see the king and the duke?

6. How does the crowd react when the king names several of Peter Wilks' closest friends and invites them for supper?

7. Does the duke say anything to the townspeople?

8. Why do the king and duke give the Wilks sisters $415 of their own money?

9. Who is Dr. Robinson? How does he feel about the king and the duke?

10. What does Dr. Robinson think about the king's English accent?

Answers

1. The duke paints his face and other parts of his body blue so he will look like a sick Arab rather than a runaway slave.

2. The king gets all his information from a "young country jake" who is taking a trip to South America. They pick him up and take him to the steamboat.

3. The three Wilks sisters are Mary Jane (19 years old), Susan (15), and Joanna (14).

4. About two dozen people meet them at the boat dock, but the news travels fast and soon the streets are flooded with curiosity seekers.

5. They welcome their long-lost uncles with open arms, since they have never seen their real uncles and don't know what they look like.

6. The crowd is impressed. The fact that he knows them by name gives him credibility as the true brother of Peter Wilks.

7. No, he does not say anything because he is supposedly the deaf brother of Peter Wilks.

8. They find that the money hidden in the basement is short $415. They want to make sure they will not be suspected of stealing.

9. Dr. Robinson is a well-respected citizen in town. He thinks the king and the duke are frauds and imposters who should be driven out of town.

10. Dr. Robinson thinks the king's imitation of an Englishman is the worst he has ever heard.

Suggested Essay Topics

1. In these chapters Twain satirizes the gullibility of the towns-people who believe an imposter like the king, but, ironically, do not believe Dr. Robinson. Write an essay comparing the gullibility of the townspeople to people in today's world. In what ways are people gullible? What makes them gullible? Explain your answer.

2. Huck has become more critical of the duke and the king than he was in preceding chapters. Why has this change taken place in his character? Explain Huck's moral development as it relates to previous chapters in the novel. Cite examples from the novel to support your argument.

3. The ultimate sacrifice in the eyes of the townspeople is when the king and the duke give the Wilks girls the whole six thousand dollars. Why do they give it away? What is their motive? What do they hope to gain? Support your argument with examples from the novel.

Chapters XXVI–XXVII (page 129–140)

Summary

After Dr. Robinson leaves, Mary Jane takes the visitors up to their rooms. The duke is assigned the spare room, Huck will sleep in the garret or attic, and the king is given Mary Jane's room.

At supper that night, Huck is obligated to stand behind the king and the duke and wait on them since he is posing as their servant. The women make degrading comments about their own cooking in order to draw compliments from their guests. Huck and Joanna eat later in the kitchen. The charade is nearly exposed as she questions him about England. His information is sketchy at best, and he often contradicts himself. While Joanna is accusing him of lying, Mary Jane and Susan step into the room and immediately jump to his defense. Mary Jane reprimands Joanna for making Huck feel ashamed and forces her to apologize. Huck is so impressed with her kindness that he asks himself, "this is a girl that I'm letting that old reptile rob her of her money?" He feels "ornery" and "low down" for not telling them about the king's fraudulent intent. Finally he can stand it no longer, so he makes up his mind to get their money back from the king and the duke, no matter what. He thinks of several ways to get the money, but for the sake of the girls and for his own safety as well as Jim's, he does not dare take chances. He finally realizes that he will need to steal the money in such a way that they will not suspect him.

He hides among Mary Jane's gowns in the king's room. After the king and duke enter the room he eavesdrops while they are discussing their plans. Nervous about Dr. Robinson's suspicions, the duke wants to take the money and run, but the king has other ideas. He plans to stay long enough to sell the property. The duke finally agrees to stay. He inadvertently reveals the hiding place of the bag of gold. To keep it safe from the servants they decide to move it from the closet to the featherbed. Huck grabs it immediately after they leave the room and takes it up to his garret. That night, after everyone is in bed, he tries to sneak outside to hide the money in the yard but finds the front door locked. When he hears someone coming, he quickly hides the money under the lid of the coffin, hoping to retrieve it later. Desperately, he tries to see whether the money is still in the coffin the next day, but someone is always around. Uncertainty about the money plagues him as they bury Mr. Wilks.

The king and the duke promise that they will take the girls to England to live with them. They are in a hurry to return so they convince them to sell the property immediately. The day after the funeral the king sells the slaves and splits the family in two. Both the Wilks girls and their servants are grief-stricken, not realizing that the whole thing is a sham. Since the sale is not legal the slaves will soon be back.

On the day of the auction the king and duke suddenly discover that the bag of gold, worth six thousand dollars, is missing. Huck pushes the blame onto the servants since he knows they are already gone and will not be harmed by the accusation.

Analysis

In these chapters Huck's humanitarian effort to help the Wilks girls is significant in his human development. He is extremely fond of Mary Jane and her sisters and feels morally obligated to recover their money since they will need it later on for their livelihood. As we have seen in his relationship to Jim, Huck's morality is based on his natural instincts and shows a responsiveness to human need rather than an adherance to the rules of society. It is when he feels "ornery and low down and mean" for allowing the king to defraud the Wilks girls that he makes his moral decision to help them. Since his decision could bring danger to himself and to the girls, he weighs his strategy carefully before he decides that stealing the money would, in fact, be the safest course to take.

In his rush to accumulate as much money as possible before they are found out, the king overrides the duke's fears about selling the slaves to a slaveholder. Later, when Huck convinces them that the slaves have stolen the six thousand dollars, the king and the duke feel tricked. Ironically, the slaves have supposedly beat them at their own game by pretending to be sorry they were leaving, then snatching the bag of money as they left. It was, of course, Huck who had taken the money, but the duke wishes he would have kept the slaves around for their "histrionic talent." He feels he could have used them in his con games but regrets that the king had "sold 'em for a song."

In this episode of the novel, Twain repeats the theme of the separation of families through the buying and selling of slaves. This is reminiscent of Miss Watson's intention of selling Jim down the river and separating him from his family. This incident reveals not only the pain of separation of mother and sons, demonstrating the humanity of the slaves, but also the caring response of the Wilks girls. It is at this point that Huck almost breaks down and exposes the king and the duke, but he knows the sales are fake, and the slaves will be home soon. His human sympathy for the injustice in this incident foreshadows his ultimate committment to Jim as Huck struggles with his conscience in subsequent chapters.

Study Questions

1. Why do the women insult their own food?

2. What incident in the novel convinces Huck that he must get the money back to the Wilks girls?

3. In what way will Huck get the money from the king and the duke?

4. Where does Huck hurriedly hide the money? Why does he choose this particular spot?

5. How do the king and the duke justify selling the property so soon after the funeral?

6. Where do the slaves go when they are sold?

7. Why does the king sell the slaves the day after the funeral? How does the duke feel about this?

8. Why does the duke wish he had kept the slaves?

9. How do the Wilks girls react when the slaves are sold?

10. Why doesn't Huck tell on the king and the duke when they allow the slaves to be separated from their families?

Answers

1. The women make degrading comments about their food so that they can elicit compliments from their guests.

2. The kindness of Mary Jane and Susan, and Joanna's apology for her accusations while they are eating in the kitchen convinces Huck that these girls do not deserve to be defrauded by the king and the duke.

3. Huck decides that stealing the money would be the safest course of action.

4. Huck hides the money in Peter Wilks' coffin. His plan to take the money outside is thwarted when the door is locked. When he hears Mary Jane's footsteps, he quickly slips the bag of gold under the coffin lid and disappears.

5. The king and duke promise to take the Wilks girls home to England to live with them. The king is in a hurry to get back because his congregation needs him back in the pulpit.

6. The two sons were sold up the river to Memphis and their mother was sold down the river to New Orleans.

7. The king meets a slaveholder and makes a quick sale. The duke feels that it was "quick sales and small profits." He is proven right when they later assume that the slaves took their six thousand dollars with them.

8. The duke admires the con game that he thinks they have played when they pretended to be sorry to leave but took the money with them. He feels he could have made a fortune with their acting talents.

9. The girls' hearts are broken to see them sold away from the town and separated from their families.

10. Huck comes close to telling on the king and the duke when he sees the reaction of the girls, but he knows they will soon be back since the sales are illegal.

Suggested Essay Topics

1. The king and the duke have been involved in several fraudulent schemes along the river. Compare and contrast the Wilks episode to The Royal Nonesuch in the last town. Why does Huck take action against the frauds in the Wilks episode? Why was he merely an observer in The Royal Nonesuch? How do

they compare? How are they different? Use examples from the novel to support your argument.

2. The two frauds have supposedly been duped through their sale of the slaves. In what way do the king and the duke judge the slaves by their own standards? In what way do they think the slaves have played a game in order to get away with the money? Defend your argument with examples from the novel.

3. The separation of families through the selling of slaves is a recurrent theme in the novel. What is Twain's attitude about this controversial issue? Cite at least two examples from the novel that deal with the separation of families and point out the way in which Twain satirizes the issue.

Chapters XXVIII–XXIX (pages 140–155)

New Characters:

Harvey Wilks: Peter Wilks' true brother

William Wilks: deaf brother of Peter Wilks

Levi Bell: Peter Wilks' lawyer friend

Hines: a husky man who believes the king is an imposter

Summary

In the morning, Huck passes Mary Jane's room and sees her crying through the open door. Heartbroken about the separation of the slaves' families, she tells Huck that her beautiful trip to England is spoiled. Uneasy about her crying, Huck quickly replies that the slaves will be back in less than two weeks. He has spoken too soon, but since he is in a "tight place," he decides to tell the truth even though it is risky. He asks Mary Jane to promise to leave town for four days if he tells her why the slaves will soon be back. If she leaves she will not be tempted to reveal to the king and the duke that she knows the truth. She gives her word, and Huck blurts out the whole story about the two rogues who have posed as her uncles and duped her out of her inheritance. Shocked, she immediately wants to tar and feather them and throw them in the river, but

Huck gently reminds her of her promise. She calms down, telling him she will do whatever he asks.

After some deliberation he thinks he can get the two frauds jailed in town so he and Jim can be rid of them. He shortens Mary Jane's stay to one day, asking her to place a candle in the window by eleven as a signal to Huck that she is at home. If he does not respond, she will know he is gone, and she can have the king and duke arrested and jailed. Huck advises her to check with the Bricksville townspeople where The Royal Nonesuch was played if she needs evidence of their fraudulent activities. She agrees to stand by Huck and attest to the fact that he is not involved with them in case he gets caught. Since he will not be seeing her again, he writes her a note telling her where the bag of money is hidden and asks her not to read it until he is gone. After she leaves, Huck explains to her sisters that Mary Jane has gone to see a sick friend. He asks them to tell their uncles it is a rich friend, however, who is interested in buying the house. The sick friend has a communicable disease, and it will delay their trip to England. Neither story is true, of course, but Huck wants to allay the suspicions the king and the duke might have about Mary Jane's absence by telling them that she is working for the auction. Since the girls are eager to start on their trip, Huck knows they will cover for Mary Jane. During the auction two more men arrive on the steamboat claiming to be Wilks' brothers, Harvey and William.

Surprised by their rude reception, Harvey Wilks is not prepared for the other claimants of Peter Wilks' inheritance. William and Harvey have been down on their luck lately. William has broken his arm, and their baggage has been misplaced in another town. William speaks only sign language, and the arm he normally uses for signing is broken. Besides, he usually writes for both brothers, but now he cannot sign his name for proof of identification. All other identification is with their lost luggage. Huck is convinced of Harvey Wilks' identity from the beginning because of his true English accent. "I see straight off he pronounced like an Englishman—not the king's way."

The majority of the townspeople still rally around the king and the duke, but a few people begin to question the king. Hines, a man in the crowd, claims to have seen him in a canoe the day before the funeral. After a long debate about identities, the new Harvey Wilks suggests that the true brother would know what was tattooed on Peter Wilks' chest. To settle the argument they must exhume the body. When they open the coffin, they are shocked to find the bag of gold. In the excitement Huck escapes in the dark and runs until he finds a boat to take to the raft. He sees Mary Jane's candle in the window but has no time to stop. He and Jim escape down the river thinking they are free of the king and the duke at last. Their happiness is short-lived, however, for soon they hear them coming over the water in a skiff.

Analysis

Throughout the novel Huck has been telling lies or concocting stories to get himself out of tight situations. It has, in fact, been necessary for his survival on the river and particularly in the towns along the river. In Chapter XXVIII, however, we finally hear him telling Mary Jane the truth. After thinking it over, he decides that "the truth is better and actuly safer than a lie." He has, in fact, already blurted out part of the truth about the slaves who will be back in two weeks. In a sense he has reached a point of no return and must tell her the whole story. He undoubtedly respects Mary Jane enough to trust her with the truth. "She was the best girl I ever see, and had the most sand." He feels a moral obligation to expose the king and the duke and keep them from exploiting her. When she leaves town, however, he must tell another one of his stories to protect her from the two frauds.

Ironically, when the men question Huck about being English, he cannot convince them. Levi Bell, the lawyer, tells him to quit trying. "I reckon you ain't used to lying, it don't seem to come handy...You do it pretty awkward." Perhaps he is awkward because the story is not his own creation. He is lying for the king and the duke and simply does not have his heart in it.

Twain's plot falls into place when the body of Peter Wilks is exhumed to solve the identification problem. The whereabouts of the bag of gold has not been ascertianed. Twain uses a believable chain of events as an angry crowd rushes to the cemetery on a dark, blustery night. Not only do they find the money, but it also affords an opportunity for yet another escape for the king and the duke, and, in this case, for Huck.

Study Questions

1. Why does Huck tell Mary Jane the truth?

2. Why does Hines think that the king is an imposter?

3. Why does Huck ask Mary Jane to leave town?

4. How does Huck tell Mary Jane that he put the bag of money in the coffin?

5. How does Levi Bell propose to find who the true Wilks brothers are?

6. What were the misfortunes of the Wilks brothers?

7. How do they finally solve the problem of identification?

8. Why don't they believe Huck when he says he's English?

9. On his way to the raft what does Huck see in the middle of town?

10. Why did Hines let go of Huck's hand allowing him to get away?

Answers

1. He sees how sad she is about the separation of the slave families and tells her they will soon be back.

2. He saw the king in a canoe the day before the funeral.

3. Huck asks Mary Jane to leave so her face will not reveal the truth about the king and the duke after Huck has told her the whole story.

4. He does not have the heart to tell her in person so he writes her a note and asks her not to read it until he has gone.

5. He tries to compare their handwriting to letters Peter Wilks has received from his brothers, but it does not work because William Wilks has broken his arm and cannot write.

6. Their baggage has been dropped off in the wrong town, and one of the brothers has broken his arm.

7. By exhuming the body of Peter Wilks to find out who is right about the tattoo on his chest.

8. Huck does not have an English accent.

9. Huck sees the candle burning in Mary Jane's window.

10. Hines was so surprised to see the bag of gold in the coffin that he forgot himself and let go of Huck's hand.

Suggested Essay Topics

1. The novel is filled with examples of stories Huck tells when he is in a tight situation. In Chapter XXVIII he decides that truth is better than lies, however. Why does he have a change of heart in this chapter? How does Huck feel about Mary Jane? Does he trust her with the truth? Does he ever lie to her? Why does he depend on lies to get through difficult situations? Cite examples from the novel to support your argument.

2. Throughout the course of the novel, Twain uses descriptions of thunderstorms. Compare and contrast the description of the thunderstorm in Chapter XXIX with descriptions in other parts of the novel. How are they the same? How is this one different? Cite examples from the novel to support your argument.

3. Mary Jane is one of Huck's favorite people in the novel. What qualities does she possess that makes Huck fond of her? How is she different from her sisters? Explain your answer.

Chapters XXX-XXXI (pages 155–164)

Summary

The king, angry at Huck for trying to give them "the slip," grabs him by the collar when they catch up with the raft. Afraid for his life, Huck tries to appease him with a story about the nice man who had held his hand on the way to the cemetery. Because he reminded him of his dead son, the man let him go, telling him to run for his life. Jim verifies Huck's story, and finally the duke comes to Huck's defense, reminding the king that he had not been concerned about Huck's whereabouts when they had run from the scene.

The king and duke begin to argue and blame each other for hiding the money in the coffin. They both acknowledge the fact that they were tempted to keep the money for themselves, but neither one admits actually hiding it. Impatient and angry, the duke catches the king by the throat, forcing him to admit he had done it. That settles the argument and before long they are "thick as thieves" again. Later, when they are asleep, Huck tells Jim the whole story.

For fear of being recognized they do not dare stop at any of the towns along the river for several days. They are approaching the warm southern climate where Spanish moss hangs from the trees. The king and duke feel it is finally safe to "work the villages" again, but they have little success. Their usual jobs of "mission-arying," "doctoring," and "mesmerizing" do not work out, and they are soon broke and desperate. They begin to talk in whispers for several hours at a time, and Huck and Jim feel uneasy. They decide to get rid of the two frauds when the next opportunity arises.

One morning they stop the raft in the village of Pikesville where the king wants to look around to make sure they have not heard of The Royal Nonesuch. Huck suspects that he wants to try something terrible like robbing a house. The king instructs the duke, Huck, and Jim to wait for him at the raft. If he does not come back by noon they will know it is all right to come into town. When the king doesn't show up, Huck and the duke go into town to look for him. When the duke finds the king in a miserable state of drunkenness, he gets angry and they begin to argue. Huck sees his chance to slip away and head for the raft, but when he gets there, Jim is gone. Out on the road he meets a young boy who has seen a man fitting Jim's description. He tells Huck that Jim is a runaway from a southern plantation who was sold by an old fellow for $40. He is now on the Phelps Plantation a few miles away.

Huck goes back to the raft to think. He cannot believe that the king could sell Jim back into slavery for "forty dirty dollars." Desperately he tries to think of what he should do. The more he thinks the more his conscience bothers him. He begins to feel "wicked and low-down and ornery" for having stolen Jim, another person's property. He tries to pray, but the words will not come. He finally decides to write a letter to Miss Watson, telling her that Jim is on the Phelps Plantation. When he finishes the letter his conscience is relieved, and he feels good and "all washed clean of sin." He begins to think of all Jim has meant to him, however, and how good he has always been to him. He tears up the letter and decides that he will "go to hell" rather than allow Jim to be sold as a slave. He makes plans to "steal Jim out of slavery again."

He hides his raft on a wooded island, and after a good night's sleep he takes the canoe to shore where he accidentally meets the duke. Surprised to see Huck, he asks about the raft, and Huck tells him the raft and Jim have been stolen. The duke begins to tell Huck that Jim is on the Silas Phelps Plantation but changes his mind and tells him he is 40 miles away instead. He wants Huck out of town for the next three days so Huck will not tell the townspeople that he and the king are frauds.

Analysis

In Chapter XXX the duke is seen in a better light than we have seen him so far in the novel. He jumps to Huck's defense, reminding the king that he would not have done any different than Huck did in order to escape. "Did you inquire around for him (Huck) when you got loose?" The duke is able to identify with Huck as another human being running from an angry mob to save his own life. Until now the duke has been portrayed as a deceitful rogue symbolizing evil and demanding to be addressed as "your grace."

In these climactic chapters Huck faces his ultimate moral decision to help Jim escape from slavery. It is the central crisis in Huck's development. In three different incidents, he struggles with this choice.

The first time, in Chapter VIII, Huck has just met Jim on Jackson's Island. His easy decision not to tell that Jim is a runaway slave comes in the wake of his determination to leave Pap and his resolution never to go back to live with the Widow Douglas. It matters little to Huck that people would call him "a low-down Abolitionist...that don't make no difference...I ain't a-going back there, anyways." His recent abandonment of society and its laws helps him to make a moral decision on human terms rather than on societal ones.

The second time is in Chapter XVI when Huck and Jim are nearing Cairo where they plan to take a steamboat up the Ohio River to the free states. In this incident the intensity of his decision has deepened. As he struggles with his conscience about allowing a slave, worth $800, to go free, the irony is clear—it never occurs to him that society might be wrong, and that he could be right. He simply realizes it is impossible for him to turn Jim in.

Although his second decision centers around the economic worth of slaves, Huck's ultimate moral choice focuses on religion. "There was the Sunday school, you could 'a' gone to it...they'd 'a' learnt you there that people that acts as I'd been acting...goes to everlasting fire." He tries to pray, but he "can't pray a lie." Ironically, when he writes the letter to Miss Watson telling her where Jim is, he is relieved to know he is no longer lost and going to hell. But he cannot leave it at that. His mind instinctively drifts to Jim's friendship and the good times they have had on the raft. Jim is undoubtedly the most devoted friend he has ever had. Huck's ultimate moral decision in the novel is, ironically, to "go to hell" for freeing Jim. He does not justify his choice. He simply makes the decision to take up wickedness again. Twain's bitter satire in this passage is a harsh invective against a society that would live by such false standards.

Study Questions

1. What do Huck and Jim do as soon as Huck gets back to the raft?

2. Who do the king and the duke blame for stealing the money?

3. Who captured Jim and sold him?

4. Where did Jim go after he was sold?

5. What does Huck tell the duke about the raft when he meets him in town?

6. Why can't Huck pray when he tries?

7. Why does Huck tear up his letter to Miss Watson?

8. Why is Chapter XXXI a climactic chapter in the novel?

9. How does Huck feel about his decision to "buy Jim out of slavery"?

10. Why doesn't Huck tell on the king and duke when he has a chance?

Answers

1. Huck and Jim hurriedly take off down the river in the raft to try to get away from the king and the duke.

2. They blame each other for stealing the money.

3. Jim was captured by the king. He sold him for $40.

4. Jim was sold to the owner of the Phelps Plantation.

5. He tells him the raft and Jim have both been stolen.

6. He can't pray because his heart isn't right. He says, you "can't pray a lie."

7. He wants to turn Jim in, but he can't go through with it.

8. It is the ultimate moral decision for Huck to help Jim to freedom.

9. Huck feels that he is wicked for doing so, but he values Jim's friendship above everything else.

10. He wants to be rid of them and have nothing more to do with them.

Suggested Essay Topics

1. Huck makes his ultimate moral decision in Chapter XXXI of the novel. What is Twain satirizing in this episode? Explain Huck's natural morality as opposed to society's morality. Use examples from the novel to support your answer.

2. Twain sheds a slightly different light on the duke in these chapters. What is different about the actions of the duke? How does this make us feel about him? Is the duke less evil than the king? Explain your answer.

3. Huck faces a moral decision to help Jim escape in three different epiodes of the novel. Explain each dilemma and describe how it affects Huck's development as a character. Cite examples from the novel to support your argument.

Chapters XXXII–XXXIII (pages 165–175)

New Characters:

Mr. Silas Phelps: Tom Sawyer's uncle

Mrs. Sally Phelps: Tom's aunt

Summary

Huck arrives at the Phelps Plantation, noticing that things are rather "still and Sunday-like." Everyone seems to be out in the fields, and Huck paints a rather bleak picture of the depressing surroundings. As he approaches the kitchen, he hears the hum of a spinning wheel. He walks up to the house, trying to decide what to say but finally leaving it to Providence. He has aroused fifteen of the sleeping dogs that quickly surround him with their barking and howling. With her rolling pin raised, a servant steps out and silences them. Hearing the commotion, Mrs. Phelps runs out to greet Huck with her spinning stick still in her hand and her children hanging around her skirts. Thinking he is Tom Sawyer, her nephew, she welcomes him with open arms.

Perplexed by her display of affection, he tries to guess who she thinks he is. She questions him about his family, but not knowing who his family is, he cannot answer and finally decides that this might be one of those times when he should risk telling the truth. It isn't until Mr. Phelps comes home, and she introduces Huck as Tom Sawyer, that he breathes easy again. They have been expecting Tom to arrive on the steamboat for the past few days and are relieved and happy that he is finally here. Comfortable with his new identity, Huck can easily invent believable stories about Tom Sawyer's family.

The noise of the steamboat on the river, however, suddenly reminds him Tom could be arriving any minute. He must ward off Tom's appearance until he can explain the misunderstanding to him. He tells Tom's aunt and uncle that he needs to go into town to pick up his baggage. Convincing them to let him go alone, he heads for town in the wagon and meets Tom Sawyer along the way. Tom thinks he is seeing a ghost, but Huck tells him that he was not murdered. Huck explains the case of mistaken identity at the Phelps Plantation to Tom. Coming up with a plan, Tom assures him all will be well. He puts his trunks in the wagon and tells him he will follow later. Huck also confides in Tom about his intent to steal Jim. To his surprise, Tom agrees to help him. Shocked that Tom would do such a thing, Huck's high opinion of him falls considerably.

In a little while Aunt Sally and Uncle Silas Phelps see a stranger coming up the driveway. The stranger is Tom Sawyer. They quickly set another plate for dinner to welcome him. He pretends to be on the wrong plantation, but they invite him to stay for dinner just the same. During the course of the conversation the so-called stranger suddenly reaches over and kisses Aunt Sally on the mouth. Shocked and insulted she calls him an "owdacious puppy." He apologizes and tells her he thought she would like it. He finally ends the practical joke by identifying himself as Sid Sawyer, Tom's brother. They laugh at his joke, showering him with hugs and kisses.

During supper one of the children begs to see the show in town that night. His dad tells him the show has been cancelled because the runaway slave informed on the actors. Huck knows immediately that it was Jim who was trying to expose the king and the duke. That night he and Tom sneak out to try to warn the pair about the danger they are in, but it is too late. They have been tarred and feathered and are being driven out of town. Huck feels responsible somehow even though he was not to blame. He denounces his conscience that "takes up more room than all the rest of a person's insides" but is of no value to him. Tom Sawyer agrees.

Analysis

Twain's depressing description of the Phelps Plantation is set in contrast to previous descriptions of the peace and tranquillity of life on the river. It is a "one-horse cotton plantation" with "sickly grass patches" and a yard that is "bare and smooth." Even the sound of the spinning wheel makes Huck feel lonesome. Huck's depiction of the plantation, symbolic of loneliness and death, reflects his mood after the loss of Jim and their idyllic life on the raft. Here, as in earlier chapters, the theme of freedom on the river stands in oppostition to the constraints of life on the shore. Jim has, after all, been sold back into slavery again, and in Huck's view, life on the shore carries with it a dismal outlook.

The appearance of Tom Sawyer lightens the tone of these chapters. We see Tom merely as a light-hearted practical joker whose morality is aligned with the society he is a part of. Huck respects his opinion, however, and holds him up as his ideal. He is astonished when Tom agrees to help him steal Jim, and because of this, his estimation of Tom is lowered. Ironically, Huck still believes his natural morality is wrong and Tom's morality, based on the mores of society, is right. What he is not aware of is that Tom knows Jim has already been given his freedom by Miss Watson. This will not be divulged until the end of the novel. Tom is, therefore, only playing the game of stealing Jim out of slavery.

Thus far in the novel Jim has been patiently bearing the inconveniences the king and duke have caused him and Huck on the raft. The "rapscallions" go too far, however, when they sell him as a slave. The king and duke underestimate Jim's intentions to get even. Although the duke mentions his suspicions to Huck, it is doubtful that he credits Jim with the ability to be instrumental in having them tarred and feathered and run out of town. Jim's action in this episode reflects a deep sense of justice.

When Huck watches the king and duke being run out of town it makes him "sick to see it." His feeling is reminiscent of his reaction to the Grangerford and Shepherdson feud in Chapter XVIII. During their last battle when most of the men are killed, Huck is repulsed as he watches the carnage from the tree. "It made me so sick I most fell out of the tree." In spite of all the king and duke have done to him, Huck's humanity is again revealed when he not only sympathizes with the pair, but tries to warn them of trouble ahead.

Study Questions

1. Why does Huck go to the Phelps Plantation?

2. Who is Huck mistaken for at the Phelps Plantation?

3. How does Huck feel when he learns that Aunt Sally thinks he is Tom Sawyer?

4. How does Tom react when Huck tells him he is going to steal Jim from the Phelps Plantation?

5. Who is the stranger that arrives at the Phelps Plantation after Huck? What does the stranger call himself?

6. Who informs Mr. Phelps about the king and the duke and their Royal Nonesuch show?

7. What happens to the king and the duke as a result?

8. What do Huck and Tom do to try to warn the king and the duke about possible trouble ahead?

9. How does Huck feel when he sees what the townspeople have done to the two frauds?

10. Why does Huck's conscience bother him concerning the incident with the king and duke?

Answers

1. Huck goes to the Phelps Plantation to try to find Jim.

2. Huck is mistaken for Tom Sawyer.

3. Huck feels relieved because he knows he can easily impersonate Tom. He can also give information about Tom's family.

4. Tom agrees to help Huck with his plan to steal Jim, but Tom already knows that Jim has been freed by Miss Watson.

5. The stranger who arrives at the Phelps Plantation is Tom Sawyer who is disguised as Sid Sawyer, Tom's brother. Since Huck is Tom and Tom is Sid, they are supposedly brothers.

6. Jim informs Mr. Phelps and Burton of the scandalous Royal Nonesuch show. Burton tells the townspeople.

7. The king and duke are tarred and feathered and run out of town.

8. Huck and Tom sneak out of the house to try to warn the fraudulent pair about their impending danger, but it is too late. They watch the tarred and feathered couple being ridden out of town on a rail.

9. It makes him feel sick to see what the townspeople have done to them. He says "human beings can be awful cruel to one another."

10. It is central to Huck's character to feel that he is to blame even though he hasn't done anything wrong. He makes a harsh statement against the wisdom of trusting one's conscience.

Suggested Essay Topics

1. Twain paints a bleak, depressing picture of the Phelps Plantation. Compare and contrast Huck's view of life on the plantation to life on the raft. In what way is his view affected by his recent loss of Jim? Cite examples from the novel to support your argument.

2. Huck is shocked when Tom Sawyer tells him he will help steal Jim out of slavery. What does Tom know about Jim and how does that affect his decision? How does Huck view Tom as a member of society? How does he view himself? Support your answer with examples from the novel.

3. Jim acts as an informant in the case of the king and duke's Royal Nonesuch show. In what way is justice being done? Why do you think Jim is seen in a different light in this section of the novel? Do his actions seem believable? Defend your argument with examples from the novel.

Chapters XXXIV–XXXV (pages 175–185)

New Character:

Nat: a slave who brings food to Jim

Summary

Tom uncovers the secret of Jim's whereabouts on the Phelps Plantation by observing one of the slaves bringing watermelon, along with other food, to a nearby hut. Since he would not be feeding watermelon to dogs, it follows that someone must be in the hut. The door to the hut is locked, and Uncle Silas holds the key. Sure that the prisoner must be Jim, Huck and Tom begin immediately to make plans to rescue him. Huck's plan is easy. He suggests they steal the key out of Uncle Silas's pants pocket, release Jim, and take off down the river on Huck's raft. Tom criticizes the plan for being "mild as goosemilk." Knowing they will do it Tom's way no matter what Huck proposes, he gives in to Tom's elaborate plans.

Huck is still wondering why a respectable, kind, and intelligent boy like Tom would stoop so low as to steal Jim out of slavery. He tries to stop him, but Tom says he knows what he is doing.

After dark they examine the hut and plan the rescue. Huck suggests several simple and practical methods such as having Jim climb out of a high window or sawing a hole in the cabin the way he had done when he escaped from Pap. Tom, however, holds out for some complicated method that would take twice as long. They finally decide to spend a week digging him out.

When they arrive at the house, Huck simply pulls the latchstring and walks in through the door. This is not romantic enough for Tom, however, who enters by climbing the lightning rods. He finally makes it after three tries and several painful falls.

In the morning they go down to the slave cabins to befriend the dogs so that they will not bark at them while they are digging Jim out. They meet the man who brings food to Jim. He naively invites them to come and see his prisoner. Jim, surprised and happy to see them, blurts out the boys' names. The man asks Huck and Tom whether Jim knows them, but they flatly deny it. They convince him that the witches are causing him to hear things. When they get a chance they whisper the plan of escape to Jim. He squeezes their hands in gratitude and promises to pretend they are strangers from now on.

Tom, disgusted that the plan of escape is too easy, is constantly trying to "invent all the difficulties." He wishes for a watchman to drug, or a dog to give a sleeping mixture to. Though one could easily slip the chain off the bedpost, Tom wants to saw the leg off Jim's bed to remove the chain. He goes so far as to consider amputating Jim's leg to get the chain off.

Instead of picks and shovels, Tom insists on digging him out with case knives because he has read about this in books. He also insists that the escape should take thirty-seven years. They need to hurry though, for when Mr. Phelps hears Jim is not from New Orleans, he will probably advertise him. They decide to "let on" or pretend that they had been at it for thirty-seven years. Huck tries to bring Tom back to practical reality, but Tom accuses him of never "having read any books at all."

Huck borrows a bedsheet from the clothesline for a rope ladder that will be put in a pie and smuggled in for the escape. He also takes a white shirt so Jim can keep a journal on it. He takes three case knives, and Tom suggests making a saw out of one of them. When Huck gingerly suggests borrowing a saw from the smokehouse, Tom is discouraged and gives up on Huck, afraid he will never be able to teach him anything about the way it should really be done. Huck finally obeys his order to get the knives.

Analysis

Huck's practical, down-to-earth solutions to problems are set in juxtaposition to Tom's romantic, unrealistic solutions in the plan to free Jim. Twain is satirizing the romantic notions inherent in the adventurous and courageous escapes that were made popular through the romance literature of his day. The contrasting personalities of Huck and Tom and their constant attempts to counter each other, lends much of the satiric humor to these chapters. On a deeper level the humor is lost, however, when we consider that Tom already knows Jim is free. He is simply playing the game for the sake of adventure. In the meantime he keeps Jim imprisoned with little regard for his suffering.

Huck admires Tom's ability to solve the mystery of Jim's hiding place. Tom's observations about dogs and their dislike for watermelons clearly puts him on an intellectually superior level, and Huck is sure he would not trade Tom's head for that of a "duke, nor mate of a steamboat, nor clown in a circus." Huck knows his plan to free Jim cannot equal Tom's, but he thinks about it just to be doing something. He is right. When he proposes his simple plan of stealing the key from Mr. Phelps' pants pocket and unlocking Jim's door, Tom does not go for it. Ironically, Huck's plan is superior to Tom's, because it is quick and efficient, and safe for Jim. Tom's plan is more bookish and has more style, but, ironically, does not accomplish what Huck's plan would. It is also a potentially dangerous plan. As Huck says, it could "get us all killed besides."

When Huck borrows the bedsheets from the clothesline, Tom sets him straight by saying it is called stealing. Huck tells him his father taught him to call it borrowing. As long as he represents a prisoner, Tom thinks it is not wrong to steal, but when Huck steals a watermelon, Tom forces him to pay the owners a dime. Ironically, Tom makes the distinction between the real world and the world of romance, but Huck cannot see any advantage in representing a prisoner if he needs to "chaw over a lot of gold-leaf distinctions." Tom feels it is all right to steal as long as they are enacting the romance story, but Huck goes beyond the story to real life. Tom's respectable upbringing tells him that is morally wrong, but Huck in his natural morality cannot see the distinction.

Study Questions

1. How does Tom finally guess Jim's whereabouts?

2. Why is Huck in awe of Tom's intelligence?

3. Why does Huck think Tom's plan for freeing Jim is better than his?

4. What is Huck's first and most practical plan of escape?

5. What are some of Huck's other plans of escape for Jim?

6. Why does Tom want to saw the bedpost leg in half?

7. Why does Huck think Tom's plan is foolish?

8. Where does Huck get the bedsheets for the rope ladder?

9. What plan do they finally adopt to free Jim?

10. How long does Tom think it should take to dig Jim out?

Answers

1. Tom sees a slave bringing a plate of food with watermelon on it to a hut on the Phelps Plantation.

2. Huck thinks Tom is exceptionally intelligent because he thought of the fact that dogs do not eat watermelons. Tom reasoned that there must, therefore, be a person in the hut.

3. Tom's plan is more romantic and has more style.

4. Huck suggests stealing the key from Mr. Phelps, unlocking the door to the hut, and escaping down the river on his raft.

5. Huck suggests that Jim crawl out of the high window. He also suggests sawing out as he had done earlier in the novel.

6. He wants to saw it in half so he can slip the chain through it and release Jim.

7. Huck thinks it is foolish because one could simply slip the chain off the bedpost without sawing it in half.

8. He takes them from the clothesline.

9. They decide to dig him out with case knives.

10. Tom thinks it should take thirty-seven years. They decide they will only imagine it took them thirty-seven years.

Suggested Essay Topics

1. The contrasting personalities of Huck and Tom provide the reader with the satiric humor in these chapters. In what way do their personalities contrast? How are Tom's romantic notions brought out in the plan to free Jim? How does Huck disagree? Cite examples from the novel to support your argument.

2. Tom and Huck disagree on the idea of stealing and borrowing. What does Huck call borrowing? What does Tom consider stealing? When does Tom consider stealing all right? When is it wrong? Support your argument with quotes from the novel.

3. In this section of the novel Tom already knows that Jim has been freed by Miss Watson. In view of this fact, how do you interpret his actions in the plan of escape? Is Tom unusually cruel to Jim by making him wait unnecessarily? Why doesn't he tell Huck and Jim? Explain your answer.

Huckleberry Finn

Chapters XXXVI–XXXVII (pages 185–194)

Summary

Tom and Huck get right to work digging a tunnel into Jim's cabin with their case knives. After several hours their hands are sore in spite of the fact that they have made little progress. Tom finally admits that his plan will not work, so they change to picks pretending they are case knives. Happy that Tom is finally becoming level-headed, Huck wholeheartedly agrees with the change of plan. They dig a sizable hole and decide to continue the next day. As usual Tom tries to climb up the lightning rod to the second floor. Dead tired and sore, he finally agrees to "let on" that the stairs are lightning rods after a bit of coaxing from Huck.

Between them the boys manage to pilfer a pewter spoon, a brass candlestick, six candles, and three tin plates. The next night when everyone is in bed they finally dig their way into Jim's cabin in two and one-half hours. Happy to see them, Jim wants to cut the chain and clear out immediately, but Tom shows him that it would be highly "unregular." He explains the plan to Jim, telling him that in case of danger the plan could be quickly altered. Tom assures Jim they will, indeed, see that he gets away. They talk about old times, and Jim informs them about the prayers Uncle Silas has with him every day or two. Aunt Sally also stops by often to make sure he is comfortable. This gives Tom the idea of smuggling things to Jim through his aunt and uncle's pockets. Jim must then sneak them out. Despite Huck's objections Tom goes right ahead with his plan.

Aunt Sally begins to notice that things are missing around the house. A big argument ensues between her and Uncle Silas. She rails at him for losing his shirt but finally concedes that the calf probably got the shirt off the line. She is sure the rats got the candles, but the pewter spoon is still a mystery. In the middle of her long diatribe on the need for Uncle Silas to stop up the rat holes, a servant announces a bedsheet is also missing. This is almost more than she can take. In the middle of it all, Uncle Silas reaches into his coat pocket and timidly pulls out the pewter spoon secretly put there by Tom. Eventually she orders all of them out of the house. Later, Tom conjures up a plan to confuse Aunt Sally about the count of the sheets and spoons by alternately taking one out and then sneaking it back so her count is inconsistent. She finally becomes thoroughly confused about the true number of her sheets and spoons.

Tom and Huck decide to bake the rope ladder into a witch pie to satisfy the hunger of the witches who are constantly aggravating Nat, giving him no peace. Nat is, of course, grateful and cooperative. The boys take the rope ladder, made with a torn-up sheet, to the woods. They have enough rope for forty pies, however, so they finally throw most of the rope ladder away. They bring the witch pie to Jim's cabin, and Nat turns his back to ward off the witches. Following directions explicitly, Jim quickly breaks open the pie, hides the rope ladder inside his mattress, and throws out the tin plates after scratching some marks on them.

Analysis

Twain's ironic use of the word "moral" in this section of the novel is reminiscent of the earlier incident on the Walter Scott. When the gang of murderers on board contemplate killing Jim Turner, they decide "it ain't good sense, it ain't good morals." Ironically, the Walter Scott would break up and kill him regardless. The moral thing to do would be to untie him and thereby save his life. In this section of the novel Tom's statement is almost identical. "It ain't right, and it ain't moral." In both cases the means to an end is all-important. In Tom's case, the moral thing to do would be to free Jim as quickly as possible instead of prolonging his agony. Huck's reply "I don't care shucks for the morality of it, nohow," shows that his morality is on human, practical terms where the end result is all-important. Besides, he does not care "what the authorities think" as long as it satisfies his own moral sensibilities.

The theme of superstition is brought out in Nat's belief that witches are haunting him. When the dogs appear in Jim's cabin, Tom leads him to believe he has seen witches. He exploits his fear of witches in order to carry out his plan.

Twain is satirizing religious people like Uncle Silas and Aunt Sally who pray with Jim and make sure he has enough to eat but are waiting eagerly for the reward offered for his capture. If no one claims him they will, of course, sell him. It is doubly ironic that even Jim, being a product of society himself, does not see through this double standard. He simply comments that "both of them was kind as they could be."

Tom explains his elaborate plan of escape to Jim all the way from smuggling the rope ladder pie into his cabin to tying things to Aunt Sally's apron strings. Jim cannot see the sense in most of the plan, "but he allowed we was white folks and knowed better than him." Jim is, of course, the sensible one who questions Tom's preposterous plan, and, ironically, the "white folks" are obviously lacking in common sense.

Study Questions

1. When the case knives are too slow for digging, what do Huck and Tom decide to use instead?

2. When Tom goes upstairs to bed what does he pretend the stairs are?

3. According to Tom why do the witches come to visit Nat at breakfast?

4. How many new shirts has Aunt Sally made in the last two years?

5. Why does Uncle Silas find the missing spoon in his pocket?

6. What two missing items have been stolen off of the clothesline?

7. What do Huck and Tom bake into the witch's pie?

8. What do Huck and Tom do to confuse Aunt Sally about her silverware?

9. Why do they need a bedsheet?

10. Why do Tom and Huck want to confuse Aunt Sally?

Answers

1. They decide to change to pick and shovel because it will be faster.

2. Tom pretends the stairs are a lightning rod.

3. Tom says the witches are hungry, and he will bake them a witch pie to satisfy their appetite at breakfast.

4. Aunt Sally has made two shirts in the last two years. If she makes a new one for Uncle Silas it will be her third shirt in the last two years.

5. Because Tom puts it there earlier. Jim is supposed to take it from Uncle Silas on one of his visits.

6. The bedsheet and the shirt are taken from the clothesline.

7. They bake a rope ladder into the witch's pie.

8. They add and remove the spoons alternately to confuse the count.

9. They need a bedsheet to make a rope later.

10. The boys want to confuse Aunt Sally so she will not keep such close watch over her belongings. They want to use some of the items for their plan of escape. They are hoping she will not notice the missing items.

Suggested Essay Topics

1. Two different types of morality are demonstrated in the novel. Contrast Huck's morality with Tom's. How are they different? Explain the origins of each of the boys' sense of morality? Cite examples from the novel to support your argument.

2. Twain often satirizes the religious sensibilities of his day through the characters in the novel. In what way is he satirizing Uncle Silas's prayers with Jim? Do you feel Uncle Silas is being kind to Jim? Why does Jim feel his kindness? Explain your answer.

Chapters XXXVIII–XXXIX (pages 194–203)

Summary

While Jim and Huck file pens out of candlesticks and a saw out of a case knife, Tom is busy working on the coat of arms for Jim. He comes up with one that is unintelligible, but it does not seem to matter as long as it comes from a book. Huck questions the meaning of such terms as "fess" and "bar sinister," but Tom refuses to answer. Since dungeon walls were always made of stone, Tom suddenly strikes upon the idea that they could chisel both the coat of arms and the mournful inscriptions on one rock. He suggests they use the grindstone down at the mill. Huck and Tom find it too heavy to move to the cabin, however, so they decide to ask Jim to help them. He willingly takes the chain off the bedpost, wraps it around his neck, and slips out through the tunnel the boys have dug. He and Huck easily role the grindstone back to the cabin as Tom "superintends" the whole thing. With a nail for a chisel and an old iron bolt for a hammer, Jim starts to work on the grindstone.

Tom decides every authentic prisoner should have to contend with spiders, snakes, rats, and a flower to water with his tears. Although Tom feels a rattlesnake would mean more "glory" for Jim, he finally decides to "let it go" after Jim threatens to leave if he forces the issue. Reluctantly Jim agrees to garter snakes instead but complains about the "bother" and "trouble" it is to be a prisoner. Tom instructs him to play music to the rats and provides him with an onion to make tears to water his Pitchiola flower. When Jim complains, Tom loses his patience and reprimands him for not appreciating the fact that he had "more gaudier chances than a prisoner ever had in the world to make a name for himself." Promising to behave, Jim finally apologizes.

The boys catch fifteen rats and decide to hide them under Aunt Sally's bed, but a little Phelps boy unknowingly releases them from the cage. The boys find Aunt Sally on top of the bed screaming in fear. Busily catching spiders, bugs, frogs, and caterpillars, Huck and Tom even try for a hornet's nest but decide to give it up. They catch several dozen garter snakes and hide them in a bag in their bedroom. When they go back upstairs all the snakes have mysteriously disappeared, only to show up later all over the house. Aunt

Sally, incensed by the whole ordeal, gives Huck and Tom their just reward by spanking them each time she sees another snake.

Unable to get any rest, Jim complains that the rats and snakes do not all sleep at the same time, keeping him on guard day and night. Each time a rat bites Jim, he writes on his shirt or journal with the fresh blood.

Since there has been no news from the plantation below New Orleans, Uncle Silas thinks he will advertise Jim in the New Orleans and St. Louis papers. The mention of St. Louis hits home to Huck, who realizes that Miss Watson will probably see the ad. Tom, however, must continue to do things by the book. The next item on his agenda is the distribution of anonymous letters warning people about Jim's escape. Huck dresses up like a servant girl and shoves the first warning under the front door. The next night skull and crossbones are placed on the door, but the third night the note warns that "a desperate gang of cutthroats" will invade the property and steal Jim.

Analysis

It is ironic that in Tom's exaggerated plan to free Jim, he must call him out of prison to help role the heavy, oversized grindstone, and, thereby, carry out the plans for his own escape. Jim could, in fact, walk away anytime, but he obviously loves the boys and would not think of betraying their trust in him. This ludicrous incident is one of the most humorous in the novel.

Twain is ridiculing the romantic mind of Tom who "superintended" the whole project. In the eyes of Huck "he knowed how to do everything." He does, of course, choose a grindstone that is too heavy for the boys to handle, and when the entrance into the cabin is not big enough for the stone, it is Jim, not Tom who quickly solves the problem. Jim also endures the tortures inflicted upon him by Tom because that is supposedly his role as a prisoner. Only in the case of the rattlesnakes does Jim refuse to cooperate with Tom's fantastic schemes. Jim's practical nature comes to the foreground when Tom, in wild abandonment, is willing to risk Jim's life just for the sake of the glory. Tom puts Jim through an ordeal that leaves him with adverse feelings about the entire prisoner experience. "He said if he ever got out this time he wouldn't ever be a prisoner again, not for a salary." Since a salary is totally foreign to Jim, the last phrase might be interpreted to mean not for a million dollars.

Tom subjects Aunt Sally, as well as Jim, to undue cruelties in this section of the novel. She must endure his antics involving rats and snakes in the house, and anonymous notes designed to terrify her and other members of the household. The suffering of others is secondary to Tom's passion to dramatize the romantic notions he has only read about in books. The incongruity of Tom's treatment of Aunt Sally and Jim is especially apparent when we consider how kind and loving both of them have been toward Tom.

Tom's knowledge of the terminology of the coat of arms is limited at best. The language is confused to the point of being unintelligible. When Tom refuses to explain the meaning of "fess" and "bar sinister" it is evident he does not know. It is obvious that Tom often covers his lack of understanding in this way. Huck, however, attributes Tom's refusal to his personalilty. "If it didn't suit him to explain a thing to you, he wouldn't do it." Tom is covering his ignorance and, thereby, saving face with Huck who looks up to him.

Study Questions

1. How were pens and saws made by Jim and Huck?

2. What does Tom decide to use for the coat of arms and the mournful inscriptions?

3. What does Jim threaten to do if Tom forces him to live with rattlesnakes?

4. What does Tom substitute for the rattlesnakes?

5. What animal bites him? What does he do with the blood?

6. How is Jim supposed to water his flower?

7. What happens to the rats under Aunt Sally's bed? How does Aunt Sally feel about them?

8. Where do the garter snakes go after they crawl out of the bag in the boys' bedroom?

9. Why does Jim have trouble sleeping at night?

10. What does Tom's last anonymous letter reveal?

Answers

1. Pens were filed out of candlesticks, and the saw was made out of a case knife.

2. Tom decides to use the grindstone at the mill.

3. Jim threatens to leave rather than risk his life with rattlesnakes.

4. Tom substitutes garter snakes for rattlesnakes. Jim agrees even though he is not happy about that either.

5. Whenever a rat bites Jim, he uses the blood to write on his shirt that is used as a journal.

6. Jim is given an onion to water his flower with his own tears.

7. The little Phelps child opens the cage door and lets the rats out. They run all over the bedroom and frighten Aunt Sally.

8. The garter snakes are spread all over the house. They hang from the rafters and drop into plates and on people's necks.

9. Jim cannot sleep because the rats, snakes, and spiders are bothering him all day and all night.

10. The letter says that a "desperate gang of cutthroats" will come to steal Jim exactly at midnight.

Suggested Essay Topics

1. Jim is taken out of his prison to help Huck and Tom with the grindstone. In what way is this humorous incident ironic? Why does Jim go back to his prison? Why doesn't he leave while he has the chance? Why don't the boys help him to escape? Explain your answer.

2. Tom often prescribes cruel treatment for Jim in order to carry out his elaborate plan of escape. How does one account for his lack of sensitivity to Jim's feelings? Is Tom a cruel person? How does Tom treat other people in the novel? Cite examples from the novel to support your argument.

3. Tom works on a coat of arms for Jim. Does he have sufficient knowledge of this subject? Is his knowledge limited? Why doesn't he give Huck the definitions of "fess" and "bar sinister"? Support your answer with examples from the novel.

Chapters XL–XLI (pages 203–213)

New Characters:

The Doctor: removes the bullet from Tom's leg

Old Mrs. Hotchkiss: a neighbor of the Phelps

Summary

After the last warning note has been sent, Huck and Tom take a picnic lunch and go fishing in the river. They check out the raft to make sure everything is in order. When they arrive home for supper that night, everyone in the house is in a state of frenzy. Worried about the threatening letter, Aunt Sally hustles them up to bed after supper without a word.

At half past eleven the boys get up and begin eating the lunch they had stolen from the cellar cupboard. Noticing the butter is missing, Tom sends Huck back to the cellar to get it while he goes to Jim's cabin to prepare the scene for the escape. Huck finds the butter and stealthily climbs up the stairs, when suddenly he runs into Aunt Sally. He quickly shoves the bread and butter under his hat. Aunt Sally questions him about his mysterious activities in the cellar, but getting nowhere she sends him into the "setting-room" until she has time to get to the bottom of it. In the room he sees fifteen farmers with guns ready to attack the cutthroats who are coming to steal Jim. The room is hot, and the butter under his hat melts and trickles down his forehead. He lifts his hat, revealing the stolen bread and butter. Relieved that his brain is not "oozing out" from brain fever, Aunt Sally hugs him and lets him go.

He runs to Jim's cabin and frantically tries to explain that the men are coming, and there is no time to lose. The men fill the dark cabin just as Huck, Tom, and Jim slip out the hole and into the lean-to. Tom finally gives the all clear signal, and the three make a run for it. Tom's britches catch on a splinter on the top rail of the fence, however, and when he pulls loose, the splinter snaps and makes a noise. Soon gunfire is heard, dogs are released, and the chase is on. The dogs are friendly, however, and the runaways make it to the raft safely. Everyone is happy, but Huck and Jim suddenly notice Tom has been shot in the leg. Tom insists they go on, but Jim refuses to leave before they get a doctor for Tom. Huck goes for the doctor, instructing Jim to hide in the woods when the doctor arrives.

Huck gets the doctor out of bed and tells him a story about Tom kicking his gun in his dreams and shooting himself in the leg. The doctor is a kind old man who agrees to help, but insists on going alone because he feels the canoe is safe for one person only. He becomes suspicious when Huck blurts out that it easily held three. Waiting for the doctor's return, Huck sleeps on a lumber pile all night. The doctor has not returned by morning, and Huck runs into Uncle Silas in town. Under pressure to explain their absence, he tells Uncle Silas that he and Sid (Tom) were all over the river last night looking for the runaway slave. Huck claims Sid is at the post office so they wait awhile, but when he does not show up, they go home to Aunt Sally who is overjoyed to see Huck.

The house is still full of people who are eager to overstate the truth about what happened the night before. Mrs. Hotchkiss is worse than the others, claiming the runaway was not in his right mind.

That night Aunt Sally tucks Huck in and asks him not to leave. Seeing her caring nature, he finds it impossible to sneak out this time, but his mind is on Tom and he sleeps restlessly. He slides down the lightning rod several times during the night, but when he sees Aunt Sally waiting up for Tom, he goes back upstairs.

Analysis

Tom's plan of escape takes on an air of sensationalism as the three runaways battle the suspense of gunfire, tracking dogs, screaming voices, pounding footsteps, and a breathtaking slide through the tunnel with the gunmen breathing down their necks. What tops off the whole romantic episode for Tom, however, is the bullet wound in his leg. They are all glad to get to the raft, "but Tom was the gladdest of all because he had a bullet in the calf of his leg." He does not want to stop now when everything is going so well. He attempts to bandage his own wound and challenges them to set the raft loose and continue the escape down the river. When Tom realizes Jim will not budge before they get a doctor for him, he instructs Huck to blindfold the doctor, put a purse full of gold in his hand, and make him swear to silence. Tom is, of course, continuing his escape plan in style according to the book. The next step is to confuse the doctor by taking him to the raft in a round-about way so he will not chalk the raft and find it again. Ironically, if Huck had followed Tom's instructions, it would probably have caused Tom's death.

When Huck is on his own, he ignores Tom's fanciful instructions and does what Huck does best—invents a story. His fantastic story is not as believable, however, as the ones he has conjured up in the past. When he tells the doctor Tom kicked his gun in his dreams, the doctor replies, "Singular dream." Interpreted to mean "peculiar dream," we sense a hint of the doctor's suspicion about the whole story. To ease his concern about what he might find there, the doctor decides to go to the raft alone, using the excuse that the canoe will not safely hold two people. Huck's slight slip of the tongue adds to further suspicion when he tells the doctor the canoe carried "the three of us easy enough." The doctor leaves Huck on the shore with instructions to go home and prepare the Phelps family for the surprise that Huck had talked about.

When Tom insists on continuing down the river with the bullet still lodged in his leg, Jim's response is an expected one for it is consistent with his character throughout the novel. Jim's unselfishness in giving up his freedom for the sake of Tom is no surprise to Huck. "I reckoned he'd say what he did say." When we consider the fact that Jim could have executed his own escape from the Phelps Plantation at any time, we realize his love for Huck and Tom, his friends, was worth more to him than his long-sought freedom. He could not seek his own freedom at the expense of his friend's life. Ironically, he feels Tom would do the same for him, but Tom is more concerned with completing his escape with style.

Study Questions

1. Where has Huck forgotten the butter for the boys' lunch?

2. Who does Huck find in the "setting-room?"

3. What happens to Tom's britches when the three are escaping to the river and the raft?

4. Why don't the dogs pay any attention to Huck, Jim, and Tom?

5. What has happened to Tom during the escape?

6. What does Huck tell the doctor about Tom's bullet wound?

7. Why does the doctor leave Huck on the shore when he goes to take care of Tom?

8. Where does Huck sleep all night?

9. What is going on at the Phelps Plantation when Huck gets there?

10. Why doesn't Huck leave the house at night to check on Tom at the raft?

Answers

1. Huck has left the butter in the cellar.

2. Huck finds fifteen farmers in the "setting room." Each of them is carrying a gun for protection.

3. Huck's britches are caught on a splinter on the top rail of the fence. When he pulls loose, the splinter snaps back and makes a noise.

4. The dogs know them and are friendly.

5. Tom was shot and has a bullet lodged in his leg.

6. Huck tells the doctor Tom was dreaming and kicked his gun, and it shot him in the leg.

7. The doctor tells Huck the canoe is not safe for two people.

8. Huck sleeps on a lumber pile.

9.   The house is still full of people telling exaggerated stories about what happened the night before.

10. Huck swears that "he wouldn't do nothing to grieve her anymore."

Suggested Essay Topics

1.   Jim unselfishly gives up his freedom so they can get a doctor for Tom. Does this act seem consistent with Jim's character? Why does he do it? Describe one other instance in the novel where Jim is unselfish. Cite examples from the novel to support your argument.

2.   Tom is happy when they reach the raft in spite of the fact that he has a bullet in his leg. Why is he happy? Why doesn't he want to see a doctor? What instructions does Tom give Huck about the doctor? How is this a part of Tom's plan of escape? Explain your answer with examples from the novel.

3.   Huck invents stories throughout the novel to get himself out of tight situations. Is Huck's story to the doctor as believable as his stories have been in the past? Does the doctor doubt Huck? Are there any flaws in his story. Use examples from the novel to support your argument.

Chapters XLII–Chapter the last
(pages 213–220)

Summary

The next morning Uncle Silas looks for Tom in town but comes back discouraged. He hands Aunt Sally a letter from her sister that he had picked up at the post office the day before. She starts to open the letter, but glances out of the window and drops it as she sees Tom being brought in on a mattress. He is followed by the doctor and Jim, who has his hands tied behind his back. Thinking Tom is dead, Aunt Sally runs up to him, but he is delirious and can only mutter something unintelligible. Aunt Sally is happy just to see him alive.

While the others go into the house with Tom, Huck follows the men who take Jim back to his cabin. He hears them cursing Jim and giving him an occasional blow on the head for running away. They threaten to hang him as an example to other runaway slaves. They chain both his legs and hands to a big staple driven into the bottom log of the cabin. He is put on a diet of bread and water, and farmers with guns plan to guard his door at night while bulldogs will be on the watch during the day. In a little while the doctor comes to check on Jim. When he sees his deplorable situation, he asks them not to punish him too severely since Jim demonstrated exemplary behavior while he was with the doctor. He explains that Jim stepped out of hiding when Tom became seriously ill and incoherent, threatening to kill the doctor. Jim offered to help and he did it well. He tells them Jim is worth one thousand dollars and kind treatment too. At this the men soften their approach slightly. Huck hopes they will remove some of the chains and alter his diet but doesn't dare suggest it.

The first chance Huck gets, he slips into the sick room. Bewildered and a bit confused, Tom soon wakes up, asking about the raft and Jim. Huck tells him all is well. Aunt Sally listens in shock as he suddenly blurts out the whole story about their fantastic scheme to free Jim, the runaway slave. Aunt Sally calls him a rapscallion, threatening to punish him if she catches him meddling with Jim again. Surprised to learn Jim did not escape, Tom orders them to release him immediately because he is not a slave. He tells them that Miss Watson, who died two months ago, "set him free in her will." Puzzled, Huck asks Tom about his motives for planning the escape. Tom tells him he did it for the adventure.

Aunt Polly appears in the doorway and the game of mistaken identities is over. She has come eleven hundred miles to see why Aunt Sally has not answered her letters. Knowing the letters would spell trouble for him, Tom admits intercepting them.

Aunt Polly confirms Jim's freedom and Jim is released. Uncle Silas, Aunt Sally, and Aunt Polly make a fuss over Jim for helping the doctor nurse Tom. Tom gives him forty dollars for being a patient prisoner. Pleased and excited, Jim tells Huck it is his hairy breast that has made him rich again just as he had predicted on Jackson's Island.

Tom suggests that the three of them go for "howling adventures" in Indian territory. When Huck complains that he has no money for such adventures, Tom tells him the six thousand dollars is still there since his father has never been back for it. Jim then reveals the secret about Huck's pap. Hesitantly, he tells him Pap was the dead man in the floating house they were exploring on the river. With no show of emotion, Huck announces his plan to "light out for the territory ahead of the rest." Aunt Sally wants to adopt him and "sivilize" him and "he can't stand it." He has been through that before.

Analysis

Twain portrays Jim as a noble character when he bravely steps out of hiding to help the doctor save Tom's life, knowing full well it will cost him his freedom and possibly his life. The doctor attests to the fact that he never saw anyone who was more faithful "and yet he was risking his freedom to do it." Jim is a profoundly sensitive human being whose feeling and sacrifice for Tom comes as no surprise. We have seen him sacrifice his sleep by taking Huck's watch on the raft. We have seen his joy when Huck returns after their separation in the fog and his deep hurt when Huck plays a trick on him. We also see him as a caring family man whose dream is to, someday, buy his wife and children out of slavery. Jim's nobility lies in his sensitive nature and is consistent throughout the novel. In the case of Tom, we would not have expected Jim to behave any other way.

The men who take Jim back to his cabin in chains get "very huffy" and want to hang him as an example to the other slaves. Their scandalous values are clear when they decide not to do it since they do not own Jim, and if the owner ever showed up, he would certainly make them pay for his loss of property. When the doctor appears on the scene to tell them of Jim's actions in nursing Tom back to health, they should, ironically, be saluting him for his heroism, but they only "soften up a little."

When Huck realizes Tom knew all along that Jim had been set free, he understands why a boy with a respectable upbringing like Tom would get mixed up in the messy business of helping a slave escape. Tom tells him he did it strictly for adventure. He was planning to prolong the adventure all the way to the "mouth of the river," and then take Jim home on a steamboat in style and bring him into town as a hero with a "torchlight procession" and a "brass band."

The novel has come full circle as we see Huck "light out for the territory," afraid Aunt Sally will "sivilize" him again as the Widow Douglas tried to do in the first chapter. Taught through his many difficult decisions to follow his instinctive, natural morality, Huck has grown into a more mature, sensitive human being. He belongs in the wilds of the "territory" where he can again be free from the hypocrisy inherent in society's constraints.

Study Questions

1. When Tom finally comes home who accompanies him?
2. How do the men treat Jim as a runaway slave?
3. What do they threaten to do to Jim to teach the other slaves a lesson?
4. Why don't they do what they feel like doing to Jim?
5. What is Jim's punishment when he gets back to his cabin?
6. When Tom wakes up what does he reveal to Aunt Sally?
7. Who arrives to surprise her sister?
8. Who first reveals Jim's freedom? How is Jim freed?
9. What happened to Pap?
10. What does Huck plan to do at the novel's end?

Answers

1. The doctor, Jim, and the men attending to Jim, accompany Tom to his home.
2. They curse him and give him an occasional blow on the head.
3. They threaten to hang Jim to teach the other slaves a lesson.
4. They are afraid Jim's owner might come back to claim him, and they would be obligated to pay for the loss of property.
5. He is chained to the floor with both legs, and his arms are also chained. He is put on a diet of bread and water.

6. Tom reveals the whole plan of Jim's escape to Aunt Sally.

7. Aunt Polly arrives from St. Petersburg and surprises everyone including her sister, Aunt Sally.

8. Tom reveals Jim's freedom to Huck and Aunt Sally. Jim was freed by Miss Watson in her will.

9. Pap was found dead by Jim in the floating house earlier in the novel. Jim does not tell Huck until the end of the novel.

10. Huck plans to "light out for the territory ahead of the rest" so Aunt Sally will not try to adopt him and "sivilize" him.

Suggested Essay Topics

1. Jim is often referred to as a noble character in the novel. In what way is his nobility shown in the last few chapters. How does he show courage by helping the doctor? Why does he do it? What price does he pay? Support your answer with examples from the novel.

2. The men who are attending to Jim want to hang him as an example to other slaves who might attempt to escape. Why do they decide against it? How does this incident satirize the morality of the men? Cite examples from the novel to explain your answer.

3. At the end of the novel Huck wants to escape so Aunt Sally will not try to "sivilize" him. How has the meaning of the word "sivilize" changed for Huck? In what way has Huck grown as a character in the novel? Give examples from the novel to support your argument.

SECTION THREE

Bibliography

Carkeet, David. "The Dialects in Huckleberry Finn." *The Critical Response to Mark Twain's Huckleberry Finn.* New York: Greenwood Press, (1991), 113-25.

Suggested Readings

DeVoto, Bernard. *Mark Twain at Work.* Cambridge, Mass.: Harvard University Press, 1942.

Liljegren, S. B. The *Revolt against Romanticism in American Literature as Evidenced in the Works of S. L. Clemens.* New York: Haskell House, 1964.

Blair, Walter, and Hamlin Hill. *America's Humor from Poor Richard*

DOVER · THRIFT · EDITIONS

FICTION

ADVENTURES OF HUCKLEBERRY FINN, Mark Twain. (0-486-28061-6)

THE ADVENTURES OF TOM SAWYER, Mark Twain. (0-486-40077-8)

ALICE'S ADVENTURES IN WONDERLAND, Lewis Carroll. (0-486-27543-4)

THE AWAKENING, Kate Chopin. (0-486-27786-0)

THE CALL OF THE WILD, Jack London. (0-486-26472-6)

CANDIDE, Voltaire. Edited by Francois-Marie Arouet. (0-486-26689-3)

A CHRISTMAS CAROL, Charles Dickens. (0-486-26865-9)

CRIME AND PUNISHMENT, Fyodor Dostoyevsky. Translated by Constance Garnett. (0-486-41587-2)

DRACULA, Bram Stoker. (0-486-41109-5)

ETHAN FROME, Edith Wharton. (0-486-26690-7)

FLATLAND, Edwin A. Abbott. (0-486-27263-X)

FRANKENSTEIN, Mary Shelley. (0-486-28211-2)

THE GIFT OF THE MAGI AND OTHER SHORT STORIES, O. Henry. (0-486-27061-0)

GREAT AMERICAN SHORT STORIES, Edited by Paul Negri. (0-486-42119-8)

GREAT EXPECTATIONS, Charles Dickens. (0-486-41586-4)

GULLIVER'S TRAVELS, Jonathan Swift. (0-486-29273-8)

HEART OF DARKNESS, Joseph Conrad. (0-486-26464-5)

JANE EYRE, Charlotte Brontë. (0-486-42449-9)

THE JUNGLE, Upton Sinclair. (0-486-41923-1)

THE METAMORPHOSIS AND OTHER STORIES, Franz Kafka. (0-486-29030-1)

MOBY-DICK, Herman Melville. (0-486-43215-7)

THE ODYSSEY, Homer. (0-486-40654-7)

THE PICTURE OF DORIAN GRAY, Oscar Wilde. (0-486-27807-7)

A PORTRAIT OF THE ARTIST AS A YOUNG MAN, James Joyce. (0-486-28050-0)

PRIDE AND PREJUDICE, Jane Austen. (0-486-28473-5)

PUDD'NHEAD WILSON, Mark Twain. (0-486-40885-X)

THE SCARLET LETTER, Nathaniel Hawthorne. (0-486-28048-9)

THE SCARLET PIMPERNEL, Baroness Orczy. (0-486-42122-8)

SIDDHARTHA, Hermann Hesse. (0-486-40653-9)

THE STRANGE CASE OF DR. JEKYLL AND MR. HYDE, Robert Louis Stevenson. (0-486-26688-5)

DOVER · THRIFT · EDITIONS

FICTION

A TALE OF TWO CITIES, Charles Dickens. (0-486-40651-2)

TREASURE ISLAND, Robert Louis Stevenson. (0-486-27559-0)

THE TURN OF THE SCREW, Henry James. (0-486-26684-2)

UNCLE TOM'S CABIN, Harriet Beecher Stowe. (0-486-44028-1)

WUTHERING HEIGHTS, Emily Brontë. (0-486-29256-8)

NONFICTION

THE IMITATION OF CHRIST, Thomas à Kempis. Translated by Aloysius Croft and Harold Bolton. (0-486-43185-1)

NARRATIVE OF SOJOURNER TRUTH, Sojourner Truth. (0-486-29899-X)

WIT AND WISDOM OF THE AMERICAN PRESIDENTS, Edited by Joslyn Pine. (0-486-41427-2)

CIVIL DISOBEDIENCE AND OTHER ESSAYS, Henry David Thoreau. (0-486-27563-9)

UTOPIA, Sir Thomas More. (0-486-29583-4)

WALDEN; OR, LIFE IN THE WOODS, Henry David Thoreau. (0-486-28495-6)

UP FROM SLAVERY, Booker T. Washington. (0-486-28738-6)

ON THE ORIGIN OF SPECIES, Charles Darwin. (0-486-45006-6)

THE DECLARATION OF INDEPENDENCE AND OTHER GREAT DOCUMENTS OF AMERICAN HISTORY, Edited by John Grafton. (0-486-41124-9)

GREAT SPEECHES, Abraham Lincoln. (0-486-26872-1)

GREAT SPEECHES BY AMERICAN WOMEN, Edited by James Daley. (0-486-46141-6)

INCIDENTS IN THE LIFE OF A SLAVE GIRL, Harriet Jacobs. (0-486-41931-2)

THE SOULS OF BLACK FOLK, W.E.B. DuBois. (0-486-28041-1)

THE AUTOBIOGRAPHY OF BENJAMIN FRANKLIN, Benjamin Franklin. (0-486-29073-5)

COMMON SENSE, Thomas Paine. (0-486-29602-4)

NARRATIVE OF THE LIFE OF FREDERICK DOUGLASS, Frederick Douglass. (0-486-28499-9)

THE WIT AND WISDOM OF ABRAHAM LINCOLN, Abraham Lincoln. Edited by Bob Blaisdell. (0-486-44097-4)

GREAT SPEECHES BY AFRICAN AMERICANS, Edited by James Daley. (0-486-44761-8)

THE CONFESSIONS OF ST. AUGUSTINE, St. Augustine. (0-486-42466-9)

THE PRINCE, Niccolò Machiavelli. (0-486-27274-5)

DOVER·THRIFT·EDITIONS

PLAYS

ANTIGONE, Sophocles. (0-486-27804-2)

CYRANO DE BERGERAC, Edmond Rostand. (0-486-41119-2)

A DOLL'S HOUSE, Henrik Ibsen. (0-486-27062-9)

DR. FAUSTUS, Christopher Marlowe. (0-486-28208-2)

HAMLET, William Shakespeare. (0-486-27278-8)

THE IMPORTANCE OF BEING EARNEST, Oscar Wilde. (0-486-26478-5)

JULIUS CAESAR, William Shakespeare. (0-486-26876-4)

KING LEAR, William Shakespeare. (0-486-28058-6)

MACBETH, William Shakespeare. (0-486-27802-6)

MEDEA, Euripides. (0-486-27548-5)

THE MERCHANT OF VENICE, William Shakespeare. (0-486-28492-1)

A MIDSUMMER NIGHT'S DREAM, William Shakespeare. (0-486-27067-X)

MUCH ADO ABOUT NOTHING, William Shakespeare. (0-486-28272-4)

OEDIPUS REX, Sophocles. (0-486-26877-2)

OTHELLO, William Shakespeare. (0-486-29097-2)

PYGMALION, George Bernard Shaw. (0-486-28222-8)

ROMEO AND JULIET, William Shakespeare. (0-486-27557-4)

THE TAMING OF THE SHREW, William Shakespeare. (0-486-29765-9)

THE TEMPEST, William Shakespeare. (0-486-40658-X)

TWELFTH NIGHT; OR, WHAT YOU WILL, William Shakespeare. (0-486-29290-8)

REA's Study Guides

Review Books, Refreshers, and Comprehensive References

Problem Solvers®
Presenting an answer to the pressing need for easy-to-understand and up-to-date study guides detailing the wide world of mathematics and science.

High School Tutors®
In-depth guides that cover the length and breadth of the science and math subjects taught in high schools nationwide.

Essentials®
An insightful series of more useful, more practical, and more informative references comprehensively covering more than 150 subjects.

Super Reviews®
Don't miss a thing! Review it all thoroughly with this series of complete subject references at an affordable price.

Interactive Flashcard Books®
Flip through these essential, interactive study aids that go far beyond ordinary flashcards.

Reference
Explore dozens of clearly written, practical guides covering a wide scope of subjects from business to engineering to languages and many more.

For information about any of REA's books, visit www.rea.com

Research & Education Association
61 Ethel Road W., Piscataway, NJ 08854
Phone: (732) 819-8880